In the Land of the Ghosts

A Story from the Realm of the Blind

William Wilkin

This is a work of fiction. Names, characters, places, and incidents either are the product of the author's imagination or are used fictitiously. Any resemblance to actual events, locales, organizations or persons, living or dead is entirely coincidental and beyond the intent of either the author or publisher.

Published by Bell Street Publishing, LLC,
7360 Middlebrook Circle,
Nashvillel, TN 37221-6545

Copyright © 2018 by Bell Street Publishing, LLC

ISBN: 978-0-9903164-8-0

First Published in the United States, 2018

Contents

Acknowledgements

I owe an immense debt of gratitude to several people who have contributed substantially to this book's artistic integrity.

There are my two sons, James Wilkin and Matthew Stone.

James contributed the digital painting on the cover which captures, as I never could, my vision of the sense of the book. He also made a number of graphic design suggestions that are incorporated in the cover design and interior of the book.

He exhibited attention to detail and artistic consistency far beyond my capabiiities.

My wife, Lou, contributed in both obvious and subtle ways to the completion of the book. She is a Spanish teacher and has extensive experience editing and correcting texts – both student and professional. Any remaining grammatical and spelling errors must not be accounted to her. They proceed from my eccentric ideas about the value of deviating from standards occasionally to accurately portray a state of mind or emotional content. A subtle way that she supported the completion of this book was her endless patience with those eccentric ideas.

In addition, she was willing to endure the many, many times that I worked into the early morning hours pursued by my characters who insisted on telling their stories at the most inconvenient hours.

She has always been emotionally constant in the shifting winds of our lives throughout the long thankless years of the struggle to bring these stories to print. Bravo Lou!

Prelude

For those of you who have not read any of the preceding books, I will warn you that this preface contains spoilers. If you want to learn about the story line to the point where this book begins, you could read the stories in sequence—*In the Realm of the Blind, The Chessmaster, The Spare Wizard, The Ministry Witch and other Tales of Perfidy, Wandering With Wizards, The Boy Genius,* and so on. However, reading the first book by itself would give you a good grounding in the Realm of the Blind.

This story takes place in the universe of the Realm of the Blind where Hogwarts School for Witchcraft and Wizardry exists. It is a residential finishing school for magical youth. It is located in northern Scotland.

The main character, James Wendt, is an English Literature Professor and Muggle (non-magical). He has been hired by the Headmaster Albus Dumbledore to bring diversity to the school and the slightest touch of liberal arts education to an institution that is basically a vocational school. He is in a relationship with the Headmistress, Minerva McGonagall. His courtship of her has gone on for nearly ten years.

Other staff at Hogwarts include Rubeus Haggrid (Professor of Magical Creatures), and Professor Flitwick (Professor of Charms), the Librarian, Ms. Pinz; and the Nurse, Madame Pomfrey.

It would be to carry coals to Newcastle to attempt a more detailed review of the story line up to this point. Instead, I will provide you with a quick glossary of the characters who are referred to in the book by more than one name. Thus forewarned, you will be forearmed against the use of multiple names or nicknames for each character:

- Nicholas Brahms aka The BG, The Boy Genius, and Nicky is a computer security guru and all-round genius.
- Wainwright is the executive officer of the USS Ohio, a Trident nuclear submarine. He is frequently referred to as the XO.

You should also be warned that there are aliens whose names (unpronounceable by humans) are replaced by nicknames by the aliens so that they can be pronounced by humans.

Imperious Curse

Frederic Longbottom arrived home particularly late one evening in early spring. He'd had a hard day or he might have noticed that the lock to his front door had scratches on it that were quite fresh. But he didn't notice that. He opened the door and walked in. He shouted to his wife, who'd already gone to bed. He heard a groan that might have been, "Come to bed." He took off his coat and put it over a chair in the living room. His wife would complain about that, but it was too late, and he was too tired to care.

A knock came at the door. Longbottom grumbled to himself about neighbors who felt free to come at any hour of the night. He yawned and opened the door. What he saw immediately caused him to jump back. The light was poor on the front porch, but what he saw must have been an arachnamanchula. It was small for its species, but what the hell was it doing on his porch in Gaithersburg, Maryland. He reached into his pants pocket, fumbling for it. Meanwhile the arachnamanchula ran into the room and pounced on him. It was strong and fast. He tried to get a grip on the wand. Meanwhile the spider had thrown him on his stomach and he felt the fangs pierce his neck. He'd got his hands on the wand and was trying to bring it up. The best he could hope for was to stun both it and him and hope that his wife, who must be wide awake with all the noise would be down and deal with the thing before it came around.

Then Longbottom got the 2nd and by far the worse fright. Somehow, someone had used the imperious curse on him. At least that was what it felt like. As an Auror, he'd trained to resist that particular curse and he thought that he was pretty good at it. But this time, he felt himself slipping away. By this time he'd managed to point his wand up at himself and the spider through his body. He knew instantly that he'd never defeat this impossible imperious curse. With his last impulse of will, he silently used the *Adavra Kedavra* curse.

The "spider" felt the body of the big man slump under his weight. That had been quite a struggle, but, she'd gotten the Soul implanted. She quickly applied "heal" to the incision that she'd made to insert the Soul. It was funny, though. Normally it healed very rapidly, but this time blood was oozing out of the wound that was showing no sign of closing, let alone healing.

What was wrong? Sure, the host had put up quite a fight, but he'd gone down. She'd not had to do any serious damage to the host. Had she? But something was definitely wrong. The host was showing no signs of life. The spider picked up an arm. It was as limp as one of the eel creatures of the planet Sun-Bright II. There was something terribly wrong. she tried to find a pulse in the neck, like she'd been trained to do. There wasn't one. He was very still and had no sound of breath.

If the host were dead, she'd have to get the Soul out of it. The wound was still wide open and blood was oozing out. She reached into the wound and felt the Soul. She applied pressure to the key points that would cause it to release itself from the nervous system of the host. Then she tried to extract the Soul. It was still clinging to the host. What in all the hell-worlds of the vampires was going on? She almost panicked but she sat very still and thought. Call the medics. That was what she had to do. She pulled her communicator out of his bag and keyed in the medical emergency number.

They were very efficient on the other end of the connection. They used the GPS in the communicator to locate her and said they'd have a unit there in minutes. And, indeed, an ambulance pulled up in a few minutes. The two medics came up to the door that was still wide open, walked in and surveyed the scene.

"What happened," one asked.

"I was doing a standard insertion. But the host died almost immediately and I'm afraid. . ." She hesitated there. She really didn't want to admit that the Soul might be dead.

The other medic finished the sentence for him, "And you can't get the Soul detached. Don't worry. This sort of thing happens every now and then. Fortunately not very often." He put on plastic gloves and reached into the wound. He was motionless for a moment and then he said, "Cold-hands give me a sensor."

The other came to look over his partner's shoulder and handed him the electronic device. It only took a few seconds. But the medic sat silent for at least two minutes. Then he said, "Cold-hands, you'd better call security. This Soul is dead and I have no idea why." The medic, Cold-hands, walked outside and seemed to be whispering into the communicator. He came back in and said, "They're on their way. It shouldn't be more than 10 minutes. We're supposed to not touch anything further and keep strangers away.'

It was closer to 15 minutes but they heard the helicopter long before it touched down in the street outside the house. There were a half-dozen uniformed security forces who came in cautiously. One called, "Clear." And then an officer entered the room. He came over to the medics and the spider.

"What happened?"

The spider retold her story and turned to the medics. The one called Cold-hands said, "This is an unnatural death. I've no reason in the world for either the host or the Soul to be dead, but they are."

The officer turned to his men, "Search the house. Bring anyone you find back here and make sure we don't have any wild hosts roaming around."

The men split up. Three went into the back rooms of the house and the other three went up stairs. The spider heard calls: "Closet on left." Then, "Clear". "Bedroom on right." Then, "Clear." "Bedroom on left."

Then there was a burst of automatic gunfire, followed almost immediately by two more. They went on and on. The spider wondered what in the world they'd found. The three from the downstairs rooms ran back into the living room. The officer ordered them to stay there and stay cool. "Take cover and be prepared for whatever comes down the stairs." Then he pulled a side arm and knelt behind an overstuffed armchair.

Then there was no more gunfire and the three security men came downstairs. The officer showed his first signs of tension, practically screaming, "What the hell was that you were shooting at? Where is it? Did it get away?"

One of his men shakily replied, "I don't know. It looked like a cat. It startled me. It was suddenly there in the middle of the bedroom and I panicked. I started shooting at it."

"Great. You've undoubtedly wakened the entire neighborhood. Where's the cat?"

"It got away." The man was still shaking.

"You probably blew a dozen holes in the walls with all that firing. It's probably in the next county by now."

The man was still shaking, "No ssssir. It just disappeared."

The officer turned to one of the other men and asked, "Did you see all that?"

"By the time I got in the room, it was a real mess. I didn't see the cat."

The officer said, "Well, a couple of you go out and make sure we're not disturbed by curious neighbors. I'm going to call in some back up."

He speed-dialed a number and asked for the duty officer. When he came on, he said, "Look, I need a medical emergency unit out here a half-hour ago. What have you got available?"

The voice on the other end of the communicator said, "We'll send out the disease response unit. It should be there within a half-hour."

The wait was long and quiet. The officer had sent a couple of men upstairs to watch for the return of the cat with strict instructions to catch it alive, if it returned. They were not anxious for that duty, but went up the stairs with their weapons at the ready.

The medical emergency unit finally arrived forty minutes later. They were dressed in white haz-mat suits and were wearing masks and plastic gloves. One of them asked, "Where's the bodies?"

The major brought them in and showed them the host. One of them asked, "Is this how the body was when it died?"

The spider answered, "Yes. I haven't moved anything."

The two medical techs examined it for a small eternity without touching it. Finally one said, "I'm going to pull the hand out of its pocket. I want to see what it was so anxious to get out."

He gently pulled the limp arm out of the pocket and gasped. "What the hell is this?"

The other asked, "What does it seem to be?"

"It seems to be a carved wooden stick of some kind. It sort of reminds me of a pointer that a teacher might use. But it's too short."

The other handed a clear plastic bag over and said, "We'll take it to the lab for testing. It might have a fast-acting nerve poison on it."

The other said, "Seems unlikely that he'd be carrying around something with a deadly nerve poison in his pocket."

"You never know with this race of hosts." He stood up and turned to the major. "Your boys really made a mess of the house, I hear."

"This is pretty spooky, wouldn't you agree? Are you really surprised that someone might get a little nervous?" the spider said.

"I suppose not. But you've got to wonder." He turned to the Major and said, "You're going to have to be quarantined here until we're sure that there isn't a communicable disease involved. Use your men to enforce the quarantine until we get fresh troops here. As soon as they arrive, be sure that all your men are inside until we release you." The other medical tech was calling someone on his cell phone.

"How long will that be?"

"Not longer than three days."

"Then we'll be free."

The medical tech looked up into his eyes. "If we rule out disease by then, yes. If we haven't ruled it out by then, you'll be transferred to a medical unit equipped for long term quarantine. We'd probably do it sooner, but we really weren't set up on this planet for that sort of thing."

"I thought all first contact units had that sort of facility?"

"First contact units do. But this was declared biologically safe three weeks ago. The quarantine unit moved on immediately after that along with the rest of the first contact teams."

The Major's eyes expanded and he said, "Oh."

The security trooper who'd fired off the rounds said, "I thought we were on top of this race."

The spider said, "Sure we are. This is just a fluke. I've never heard of anything like this in dozens of colonizations."

The security trooper said, "Yeh. That's my point."

Who Goes There

The broadcast went out over the TV networks almost immediately. The Security Forces were looking for someone who'd had experience with Colonizations gone bad. Deep Diver did. He'd been working at a water treatment plant in Philadephia when he saw the bulletin on TV.

He remembered the last time he'd been involved with something like this. He'd lost three friends in that one. It was on a world where the intelligent species had been a lot like this one, but they hadn't been the real rulers of the planet. That planet was ruled by a small cadre of creatures who were unlike any of the bizzare creatures that he had met on his travels. At first, the colonization had gone quickly and easily. And then there was suddenly a pitched battle with the Souls taking a terrible beating. It had been the only planet that the Souls had given up on. And none-too-soon. He'd lost three friends and it was looking like everyone on-planet was going to be dead in days. He had been put in command of the Security forces because he'd been the only Soul to actually see one of the creatures and live to tell about it. They had over-run his base and he'd emptied a rapid fire weapon directly at one of them. But somehow, he couldn't seem to hit it. Finally he did get it. He just had time to get to the roof where a levitation platform had picked him up and taken off at full acceleration. Even at that, one of the damn things had stolen the only other floater at the base and almost caught up with them. A cruiser had come down out of orbit and managed to vaporize it with a laser. Although, at the time, he wasn't that sure that the thing wouldn't have evaded even that threat.

He shuddered again in remembrance. Then he pulled his cell phone out of his pocket and called the number on the TV screen. Someone had answered the call immediately, and he'd been instructed to report to the space port in Columbus, Ohio. He'd gone to the AMTRACK station and caught a train for Columbus. The train was fairly crowded, but he'd gotten a seat in the observation car finally. It turned out to be a pleasant ride. The scenery was pretty, and the ride had only taken three hours. There'd been a couple of stops, but the so-called "bullet" train had hit over 300 Km/hr at times. The rental "smart" car (he'd always wondered why the hosts had called them "smart") took him out to the space port quickly. He was shocked when he'd reached the outer gate. There was an armed guard at the gate. He required identification. He'd never heard of that precaution before. On the planet where he'd lost, they hadn't required ID. They just tried to shoot anyone approaching the gate. They'd set up laser controlled automated guns. That was the only way they'd been able to keep the few bases that they'd managed to hold from being over-run.

He showed his ID, and the guard seemed to be bewildered and nervous by the requirement to actually check ID's. He'd tried to reassure the lad, "Don't worry. I'm not offended. The last time I was involved with something like this, we just shot everyone who'd approached the gate."

The young man's eyes widened in what must have been horror. "But, surely you're joking."

All Deep Diver could do was shake his head in the negative. Then a real look of horror came over the young man's face. "Yea. Not many people heard about that planet. There weren't enough survivors and nobody who'd been there wanted to admit what had happened."

He drove the car on to the parking lot and walked into the Aministration Building. There was another armed guard at the entrance. Another check of ID. He was really glad that he'd thought to bring it. At the Reception Desk, there was an efficient young man in security uniform who'd recognized him and brought him a plastic card with his picture on it. "This is the ID you'll use on the base sir. You have to hold it when you want to use it. It reads your fingerprints to identify who you are and only if you match the ID in the card, will you get admittance on this base."

Diver laughed and said, "You're a lot better than I was the last time I was in the security forces."

The young man seemed not to know what to make of the laugh. He'd not seen many planets. If you didn't develop at least a minimum sense of humor, you just didn't survive very long in the security force. He was saying, "Follow me. We'll go to meet the acting commander here." They walked down the corridor and took an elevator down a couple of levels. When they got off, they were met by another guard. He actually had a weapon raised and pointed at him. Was that a Bushmaster? It was the first lethal weapon he'd seen so far. The guard demanded that they both show ID. The other man held up his picture ID and held it between thumb and forefinger. It flashed green as long as the man was holding it. He held his own up, imitating the other security man, and he was relieved to see it flashing green. He wondered what would have happened if it had flashed red or something.

Diver didn't move but asked the guard, "Let's see yours?"

"Excuse me sir?" with a puzzled look.

"I said, 'Let's see yours.'" The puzzled look remained for a moment but Diver's companion nodded. The guard lifted his badge between thumb and forefinger, and it flashed green. Diver studied the photo, which matched the guard pretty well. "Thanks."

They went on around a corner and stopped at an office. The door was locked, but his companion's badge opened it. They went in. It was a waiting room. There was a sofa and several armchairs. There was a coffee table with current magazines and a TV in a corner. It was off. They did introductions around. It seemed that the other two who were already there waiting had been involved with troubled colonizations as well. Diver suggested that they swap stories. A short stocky man went first.

"I'm Star-Gazer. I was on the vampire world. It wasn't that they resisted so well, but the trick was figuring out a way for the vampires to survive without preying on the non-vampire hosts."

The woman, Dream Keeper, asked how they managed that.

"Oh, we finally figured out that the vampires could live on synthetic blood. But we practically had to exterminate the race before we figured that out. Once a vampire host was under a Soul's control, the Soul wouldn't allow it to suck blood from another Soul. That killed most of the vampires."

Star Gazer asked her what world she was on.

"Oh, I was on the world of the Sirens. We almost had a revolt of Souls there. The Sirens could sing with such beauty that it literally made Souls cry and forget everything else. No Soul could make the Siren host bodies sing those haunting songs that tore your heart apart. Once the Souls realized that, they couldn't bring themselves to destroy the creature that could sing those songs. It was a long hard fight on that planet. We had to exclusively use hosts from other planets to implant Souls in the Sirens. It was the longest colonization by far."

She asked Diver where he'd been.

He burst through the doorframe to the roof. He was almost blinded by the flare of unfiltered sunlight. The door wasn't there. The only evidence that there ever had been a door was a single metal hinge that had been twisted inward by the force of the impact that had removed the door.

There was a guard who signaled them to get down and shouted something, probably "Get Down." Neither he nor Jester could hear over the sound of battle. Jester was right behind him and was still carrying the assault rifle, clutched tightly in his hand that was black from the pressure that he was squeezing the rifle butt with.

The guard's shout was heard this time. He was holding a hand up with two digits extended. "Two minutes to transport pickup."

Just then, four ground support aircraft screamed by overhead, canons firing continuously at unseen targets. Seconds later there was an explosion that sent a fusillade of shrapnel over their heads. He chanced a glance over the parapet of the rooftop and saw that there were only three GSA's left flying.

The roof guard held up one digit—one minute to pick up.

He scanned the sky looking for the transport but couldn't see a sign of it. He felt it before he saw it. The shock wave of the VTOL troop carrier decelerating from faster than sound to landing speed seconds before shook him to his innermost viscera.

It hovered over the roof and about a foot above it. The dust and debris kicked up by the engines clogged his nose and gagged his throat.

The hatch popped open, and several airborne troops jumped out, hunched over. The first ran as best he could to Diver and shouted, "In, now!" He, Jester and the roof guard struggled to the ship. The troops followed immediately.

Diver felt something hit his back. He turned and saw that the middle soldier's arm must have been blown off. He fell to the roof. Diver stared, the image of the soldier writhing in agony burned into his retina forever. But the other soldier behind him grabbed Diver's right arm and dragged him into the ship. The door closed and the troops strapped them into seats.

Immediately, the troop carrier leaped upward, acceleration pinning them to their seats. Through the portholes on his side of the ship he saw the Soul's base fall away and a couple of the GSA's take up a convoy formation with them as they accelerated up.

He was beginning to feel safe when the GSA on his side dissolved in a gout of flame. The shock wave would have knocked him to the other side of the troop carrier if he'd not been strapped in. Then there was a deafening roar on the other side of the troop carrier.

He looked over to the other side of the troop carrier and didn't understand what he saw. Then, he realized what it was just before the blinding flash occurred. It was an interstellar ship that had been in orbit. They must have sent it down into the atmosphere to rescue them from the attack. The flash, no, flashes were the ten terajoule lasers of the interstellar ship firing. They would have blinded him if the portholes hadn't turned opaque.

Stunned, all he could do was wonder what had happened to the interstellar ship.

Later, they reached orbit.

Star Gazer stared at him and asked, "Are you still with us?"

He answered, "Yeh, I just remembered that I'd left the oven on."

He suggested that I could call a neighbor and ask him or her to go into my apartment and turn off the oven.

I nodded mutely.

Someone entered the room from the inner door. The man who entered said, "Please come in. We'll have your interviews now."

There was another man who introduced himself as Jester, already seated. He introduced himself and told them how the interview would work. "This will be a co-operative interview. Everyone will give his or her background and we'll decide who will be the commander of the Security Force by joint agreement."

Everyone nodded. It was a fairly common practice. Usually Souls just volunteered for jobs, and everyone knew that they wouldn't volunteer for a job that they couldn't do. But Diver knew that for really important jobs interviews were required, and they were usually these co-operative interviews.

Keeper explained that they'd just been telling their backgrounds and that Diver hadn't given his yet. Diver agreed to proceed. "I was on Kelvesta IV." With that admission, there was a collective gasp around the room, "I came only because it was requested that everyone with experience submit themselves here. I really think that I'm not qualified. As far as I know, I'm the only Soul who's been in charge of Security when a planet was lost."

Dream Keeper said, "I've never heard any details about Kelvesta. What happened?"

Diver hung his head, "No one is really sure. We encountered a race that was far smarter than we are – even smarter than any race of hosts that we've conquered."

He shook his head as though to avoid an irritating fly. Then he went on, "Actually, there turned out to be two races. One was not particularly intelligent. They were easily conquered. There were lots of them. Then we discovered that there was another race. It was far, far smarter. It was also far less numerous."

Someone asked, "What were the names of the races?"

Diver chuckled mirthlessly. "We never learned the name of the race of geniuses. The other race called themselves something like an English language word. It wasn't 'herd' but it was something that means the same. It was – oh, I can't think of it."

Dream Keeper asked, "That sounds like the word that the race on this planet uses for what they call a 'pride' – like a 'pride of lions'."

"Yes." Diver thought a moment and added, "No, it was like that but different."

Jester looked Diver in the eye and said, "I think it was 'pack' wasn't it?"

"Yes, yes! That was it." He said excitedly.

He continued, "We never even managed to get a host into one of the geniuses. They came out of nowhere. It was as though they were protectors of the other race—hiding until needed—weird. I was lucky to survive the experience. We only managed to get 40% of the Souls off the planet before we left – permanently."

Keeper said, "You poor Soul. How did you survive the devastation that must have caused you?"

Diver felt bitterness well up in him, "I was working around the clock to get as many Souls off the planet as I could. I was in denial about the size of our losses and the tragedy. Then when the last survivors were off-planet, we were traveling to our next planet, and I was in stasis. When I woke up, I had just been inserted in a host on the Sunflower planet. They live very calm lives. I was sent there to recover.

"This was my next planet after that one."

Jester spoke for the first time, "You've had experience with a very bad planet. That will be valuable experience here." He winked at Diver as each realized for the first time who the other was. Diver was surprised at the twist of fate that put the two of them on the same planet when things were apparently going bad.

Amazingly, the others agreed. They all thought that having experience with the worst was good if you were on a difficult planet. It put things in proper perspective.

Jester went on, "This one is bad."

Diver objected, "But, I've not seen any sign of real trouble. There was no doubt to anyone on Kelvesta. We were almost immediately in trouble, and every Soul knew it."

Jester said, "Yes, that was obvious, but here it's in many ways more troubling. Things have happened that we have no explanation for. On Kelvesta, it was pretty obvious that the problem was that there were creatures who were so intelligent that they couldn't be fooled by Souls running around in a native Host. Here, we just don't know what's going on.

"Each of you has a binder with a report on the problem here. There haven't been many incidents, but they've all been inexplicable. The first is reported in detail. Please read it, but first, let me tell you the gist of what happened.

"On a routine insertion, both the host and the Soul died almost instantaneously. We've had a complete autopsy – and I mean complete. We've thoroughly searched for cause of death of both and there's absolutely no reason that they're dead. Neither has an injury of any sort. There was no poison of any sort present, no nerve damage, no wound, nothing down to the molecular level.

"We've even tried reactivating some areas of the Host's brain. We can get nerve impulses to travel through the brain, but we can't get it to respond to these impulses in any way. We couldn't even remove the Soul's body without doing damage to both.

There was another gasp. It was from Keeper. That was utterly unheard of.

"They're both preserved at liquid helium temperatures – just in case anyone can think of any further tests to apply."

Everyone around the table was silent. One by one they picked up the reports and began reading. Each incident was gruesome in some unique way. One Soul and its host had been trying to insert a Soul in another when they had been immobilized. They had literally fallen to the floor frozen in their tracks. They were unable to move their eyes until their body relaxed about fifteen hours later. The Soulless host had apparently just walked away. Another Soul and host in a similar situation had been wracked with seemingly unendurable pain that had stretched on seemingly forever.

Diver thought that incident was the most frightening of all. A Soul could normally suppress almost all pain in a host and NEVER experienced pain herself – even when she couldn't suppress the pain in the host. But this was completely and instantly beyond the control of the Soul. It was as if its own body – that has no pain receptors – somehow had become truly one with its host and had to experience every hideous moment that its host did. Diver had come away from that account thankful that it had been a mercifully short report. His host body shuddered with the thought of having that experience.

When they all had finished reading the report, the other two candidates had risen one at a time and simply left the room. Jester said, "It seems to be unanimous. You're the commander. This is going to be the temporary base – because you happen to be here. But, we'll want to get to the permanent headquarters as quickly as we can."

The reality of it – being in command of another supremely difficult colonization – hadn't completely sunk in yet, but it did when Jester asked for his ID. He put it in a slot in his laptop. "I've just updated your ID so that it shows you to be the commander of this colonization, and you now have authority to do anything on this planet and in the star system in which it's embedded."

He hesitated a moment and went on, "What's your pleasure?"

Diver laughed and thought to himself, "My pleasure would be to hand command back to you." But he knew that that was not possible. He'd been appointed by the unanimous decision of his peers – the only ones qualified to make such a decision. So, he was stuck with it until the end – for good or ill. Instead, he asked, "Where is the permanent Command Headquarters?"

"In old England. We've set up in a castle – Buckingham Palace. It's got lots of room and is pretty defensible."

Diver nodded and said, "Then let's not waste time."

He was surprised to find that there was a sub-orbital plane waiting on the tarmac for him. Apparently, he wouldn't have to wait for the next Columbus to London shuttle which he later learned wasn't scheduled until the next day. He and Jester boarded, and the pilot was given clearance for take-off immediately.

He strapped in, and the steward came by for drink orders just before take-off. The hybrid plane took off like a normal commercial airliner. Then when it had got above most of the atmosphere, the pilot cut in the scram jets, and they got up to 4 klicks per second pretty quickly. For idle curiosity, he timed it – just over 7 minutes – slightly more than one "G" of force. Then they coasted for most of the rest of trip. It was about half an hour in free-fall. The steward arrived with the drinks in simulation coconuts with straws. He spent most of the time re-reading the report and making notes.

Then he and Jester talked. Jes had been with him in that awful Kelvesta assignment. He hadn't mentioned that they had known each other so that no one in the interview would be prejudiced. Jes was formally the Jester. He had a nickname – Jes. That would be how he referred to him from then on. He had a nickname too – Frank.

Jes asked about it, "How did you get a nickname of 'Frank'?"

"It's new here on this planet. I'm known for reporting with great candor. Thus, 'Frank'."

Jes laughed. "Do you always pick a nickname from the language of your host?"

"Usually other Souls give me my nickname. That name just happened."

By this time they were coming down into the atmosphere, and the pilot went through a series of very wide banking turns to burn off energy. He asked, "I hope the normal commercial flights don't go through these high "G" turns. I think I've got as much pressure on me as I want.

Jes said, "We're in a hurry."

"I guess so."

They landed at a spaceport near London, "Heathcliff" or some name like that. They found a helicopter was waiting for them. They flew in to Buckingham Palace.

14

How the World Ended

Joyce was getting tired of waiting for Fred to come to bed, but she was only half-awake. She didn't have the energy to get up and give him a hard time for not getting his butt up next to her bod.

Then he must have tripped over the armchair in the living room. What was he doing? She was going to kill when he got to bed.

She drifted off to sleep and was awakened by sirens. What was going on outside? Had a neighbor's house caught on fire? It seemed to be on their street. Had old Mrs. Mcgillicutty's house caught on fire? She decided that she had to get up and see. She forced herself to get up and drag herself to the window and pull the drape back. She saw that there were two large vans in front of HER HOUSE. Just then she saw a bunch of men who were holding some sort of guns. She was stupefied as she heard the front door slam open and running feet. There were shouts and she started toward the door of her bedroom. As she reached the center of the room she had an intuition and decided to transform to her cat form. Just as she did, the door burst open and an armed man with raised gun must have caught the end of her transformation because there was an explosion of noise. She knew there had been bullets go through the spot her chest had just been. A second burst of noise accompanied the shattering of a lamp above her head. She did the hardest thing she'd ever done—disapparated away leaving Fred behind.

She looked around and realized that she was in Estes Park. She seemed to remember that it was the place where she and Fred had had their honeymoon. She got hold of herself and thought, "What would Fred do? He was an Auror." Then she realized that she had to go to the closed Auror Office and get help. She tried to remember where the local Auror Office was. Kansas City? Even if it was, she didn't know where it was. No, the only place to go was Fred's office in Washington. He got there by the floo network, but she couldn't use her house's fireplace. Her home was crawling with Muggles, and they'd probably shoot her if she went back. It would take at least a couple of disapparations to get there. Where to next? She thought of another vacation place that they'd gone to and decided to go there. She concentrated and found herself in Golden Gate Park. There was enough moonlight to see the bridge. She could make out Alcatraz as well. Was she close enough to make it to Vancouver, Washington in the next jump? She wasn't sure, but she'd try.

She tried and somehow she appeared outside the Auror Office. She'd been there before with Fred. This was the outside. They usually entered by floo but she knew that the outside was in—what did the Muggles call it—a strip mall? No. A shopping mall. There was an old phone booth that shoppers probably thought was purely decorative. But she knew that it was the Visitor Entrance. She knew that somebody was on duty inside. Fred had had a few assignments on 3rd shift, so she knew that somebody would be there, but could you get in through the Visitor Entrance after normal working hours. She knew there was only way to find out.

She opened the phone booth door, went in and it closed automatically behind her. She picked up the television. No, it was called a telephone. Immediately, she heard a bored, sleepy voice say, "Washington Auror Office. How can I help?"

"This is Mrs. Fred Longbottom. It's an emergency. I need help."

Immediately, the voice turned alert. "Mrs. Longbottom, this is Ed Reece. Listen. I need you to hang up the phone. When you do, you'll appear at the Reception Desk. You'll find a visitor badge. You've been here before. You know how those works. Pick it up and put it on. At night it's also a port key. It'll take you into our office. Do you understand?"

Joyce nodded pointlessly and said. "Right. Hurry. I think Fred's in trouble."

She hung up and she reappeared in a large room with a number of cubicles. They all had walls that you could see over if you were standing, but if you were seated, you couldn't. She knew Ed and immediately recognized him when he appeared over a cubicle wall. He said, "Come on over to my office."

She made her way there and found that there was another Auror whom she didn't know in Ed's office. Ed introduced Phil. No last name. Which was fine because Joyce wanted to do all the talking. She started off at high speed and Ed asked her to slow down and start again. It was exasperating, but she knew that she had to keep her head. She was on the verge of hysteria. She took a deep breath and forced herself to think about what she would say. Then she began.

"Tonight, Fred was late coming home – nothing unusual."

Ed said, "Sure, he was here working late."

"I didn't think much about it at the time, because I was half-asleep, but shortly after he arrived there were noises that I thought were just his clumsy bumping around in the dark down-stairs. Then there were sirens outside, and I thought it must be somebody's house on fire. But they kept getting louder. Suddenly I realized they were right outside our house. I looked outside just in time to see two large vans pull up and a bunch of men run out with some kind of guns."

Phil interrupted, "Do you know what a hand-gun is?"

"I think so."

"Were they hand-guns?"

"No, they were large."

"OK. Go ahead."

"Anyway, they ran into our house. I heard some sort of talking for a minute downstairs. By this time, I was fully awake. I decided to go down and see what was going on. I started to walk down. Then I heard shouts and men running up the stairs. That scared me, and I decided to convert to my cat form."

Ed asked, "Are you an animagus?"

"Yes."

Phil urged her, "Then what?"

"Just as I was converting, the door to my bedroom was knocked open and a man with a gun walked in. I think that he saw me converting because he started to shoot the gun right away."

Ed asked, "Was it single shots or did they seem to be bursts of shots."

'The 2nd. Yes. Bursts of shots. There were two of them, and they just missed me, so I disapparated and made my way here."

Phil asked, "You must have disapparated at least three times, right?"

"It was three. Can't we do something! I'm afraid Fred is in terrible trouble."

Ed said, "Just a couple of questions more. There weren't any shots until the men entered your room?"

"Yes."

"And do you think they were Muggles?"

"I'm sure they were Muggles."

Phil said, "OK. We need to call in a SWAT team." He picked up a medallion that was hanging on the wall in the office and touched his wand to it. "They should be here in a couple of minutes.

"Ed, I think that they should go with Mrs. Longbottom and be ready to do magic in front of Muggles. We'll get Fred back here if at all possible."

Ed just said, "Agreed."

Phil turned to Joyce, "Do you think you can take us back to your house?"

"Of course, I'm sick about leaving him there alone with those awful Muggles."

"I understand, but you did the right thing, Joyce," Ed said and put his arm around her shoulder. That contact almost set off hysterics. She had to bite her tongue and swear under her breath, but she didn't break down.

Just then, men started disapparating into the Auror Office. They were all wearing the same brown traveling cloaks with the Auror insignia on the collar. She didn't recognize any of them. There were four altogether. Phil gave them a quick rundown, summarizing in a sentence or two everything that Joyce had told them. He finished with instructions.

"Find out what's happened. Don't risk being seen if at all possible. If you can get Fred back safely, do it."

One of them said, "If Fred, who's a pretty damn good Auror, couldn't defend himself, it must be a pretty tough bunch of Muggles."

"Right. Don't get yourself in trouble. Good luck."

The leader told Joyce that they'd be using the Floo network to get close to her home. Then they'd depend on her to disapparate them to someplace about a block or so away, and they'd do surveillance before going in. They were walking to a line of oversized fireplaces. They could all enter and hold hands. The leader said, "The Drunken Familiar". He threw some floo powder, and they were in a somewhat smaller fireplace at the edge of a large hall. There was a large, burly man with tattoos and a wand in his hand. He asked to see their ID's.

The SWAT leader just tugged on his collar and said, "See that." It was the SWAT insignia. The bouncer must have seen it a number of times. He just said, "Don't want no trouble."

"Then, get the proprietor. Albert here." He indicated one of the SWAT team, "will be in charge at this fireplace. Nobody comes in. But anyone who wants to leave can. He's going to explain to your boss what's going on. Get him now. The rest of us are leaving."

"Right." And the bouncer headed off into the crowd at the disco.

The leader turned to Joyce and said, "Now, can you disapparate all of us to your neighborhood?"

Joyce was reminded of Fred by this determined, confident Auror. She said, "Of course. Take my hand."

They did, and they suddenly found themselves in a small moonlit public park. It had swings and other play equipment, several picnic benches and some decorative shrubbery. The leader turned to one of the SWAT members and said, "John. You've got this park. It's our rally point. Keep Muggles out. Be prepared to disapparate to us if we need help. Stay hard to see. Mrs. Longbottom will disapparate us on to her house."

He turned to her and said, "Do you feel up to disapparating us into your bedroom. After the Muggle used the assault rifle the way he did, I don't think anyone will be expecting visitors to show up there again. We'll go in invisible and imperturbable."

Joyce frowned, "Imperturbable?"

"Yea. It's a new charm. It makes it very hard for others to hear you. But first, we'll use the disillusionment charm to make us all invisible." He touched the head of each of them, and a wave of transparency flowed down each of the three. Then he used the imperturbable charm. He commented, "We can hear each other, but no one can hear us until I remove it.

"Are you ready?"

She nodded and realized that he couldn't see her, so she said, "I'll take your hands. Be prepared." Then everyone's guts wrenched and they were in a dimly lit room. One of the Aurors whispered, "Shit, they sure pounded this room." There was broken glass everywhere. There were holes in walls. Some of the furniture had been turned to kindling. The leader said, "Mark, shut up. I'm going to go downstairs to see what's happening. If I'm not back in ten minutes, you and Mrs. Longbottom disapparate back to the rally point. I'll probably go directly there." Then he added, "Stay sharp. I don't want to lose anyone on my watch."

Joyce said, "The stair is to your right. At the bottom, the living room is to the left. The dining room is to the right and the kitchen is behind it."

His hand released Joyce's, and she felt like she'd just been abandoned.

Paul walked cautiously out the door. Fortunately, the Muggles had left it ajar. There were a couple of Muggles with assault rifles in the hall. He gingerly walked past the one who was at the top of the stairs and walked down as slowly and as quietly as he could. He could begin to hear voices as he reached the bottom. They were coming from the left. There were several more men with assault rifles and a couple bending over someone prone on the floor. He had taken off his shoes in the bedroom so he could walk silently as a cat. He maneuvered between a couple of armed men to where he could get a look at the figure on the floor. He recognized the body. He'd seen him around the Auror Office, but he'd never been introduced. He must be Mr. Longbottom. He almost threw up when he caught a good sight of the back of Longbottom's head. There was a flap of skin pulled back, and he could see something silvery inside that he was pretty sure didn't belong to Longbottom. In that moment, he realized that Longbottom must be dead.

A hot rage flowed up from his gut, like vomit that wanted to spew out. He held it back and started to think. Strangely, it wasn't until then that he noticed the arachnamanchula in the corner. At least that was what he thought it was at first, but he quickly realized that it wasn't one. It just resembled one. One of the men kneeling on the floor announced that he would pull something out of Fred's pocket. He slowly drew something out that he immediately recognized as a wand. The fellow was commenting on it in a cold analytic fashion.

Then, Paul had an inspiration. If he could just work close enough to reach his wand over to Fred's wand tip, he could maybe do a *priori incantum* spell and find out what the last couple of things he'd done with his wand. The man with the wand didn't seem to be in a hurry to do anything with the wand, so Paul gently approached Fred from the opposite side that the kneeling man was. He knelt himself and reached out his wand across the meter separating them. He just managed to reach Fred's wand tip with his. He silently spoke the spell and could sense the flow of spell into his wand.

He realized that he was holding his breath. He slowly backed away and almost ran into the spider or whatever it was which had just gotten up and was walking toward Fred. He gingerly sidestepped to avoid the Spider's path and then started back to the bedroom. As he stepped on the 2nd step up the staircase, there was a squeak that sounded like it was loud enough to raise the dead. Then he realized that the creak had actually come from one of the men coming down the stairs. He threw himself back against the wall as the man came down holding the railing with one hand, the gun slung over the other shoulder. He passed not more than a couple of centimeters from Paul and went on completely unaware of his presence. Paul continued his slow careful climb up the stairs. He reached the hall above. The other man was still standing at the other end of the hall. He realized that he'd still been holding his breath. He kept holding it as he entered the wrecked bedroom. He reached the center of the room and whispered. "Take my hand." All three fumbled around finding other hands, and then when they were all holding on to each other, Joyce disapparated them.

They landed in the park, and Paul removed the Disillusionment charm. They could all see each other in the waning moonlight. John joined them. They all took hands and this time Paul disapparated them to the Drunken Familiar. As soon as they arrived, Paul said to Albert,

"Come on, we're all going back to the Auror Office. This is a real emergency." They all stepped into the fireplace and disappeared.

When they stepped out of the fireplace at the Auror Office, Ed approached, and Paul said, "Get the Secretary of Magic in here immediately. We're in deep shit."

Ed just stared at him, but the instant frown on Paul's face got him moving. He went to his cube and opened a drawer of his desk. He pulled out a small bell and rang it with a small bronze hammer. The sound resounded throughout the large room. In five minutes, a hastily dressed man with robe trailing behind him came through a fireplace and said, "What the hell is going on?"

Paul was completely unperturbed. He strode up to him and said, "We're in an invasion."

That stopped the Secretary in his tracks. "What are you talking about? There isn't any threat that I'm aware of. Who is it, the Koreans?"

"No, the world is being invaded – by aliens."

"If this is a practical joke. . ." the Secretary began to threaten. And then he looked around. There were quite a lot of different expressions on people's faces but nothing that made him think that this was some elaborate practical joke. So, he changed his sentence, "You'd better have damn good proof of that. How could we be invaded and not know it!"

Paul looked grim as he said, "I saw them. There were eight apparently normal Muggles and something that looked roughly like an arachnamachala—but I'm sure it wasn't. Oh, yes, there was a dead wizard – the Auror, Fred Longbottom.

The Secretary said, "Tragic, but not entirely proof of an invasion of aliens. Muggles could have killed the Auror."

"I don't think so. I think it was. . ." Here Paul hesitated and looked at the widow Longbottom. "I'm sorry Mrs. Longbottom. I think it was suicide." She gave a little gasp and broke out into sobs.

The Secretary was genuinely angry now, "It's bad enough to besmirch his name but to do it in front of his widow. You'd better have some kind of proof."

Paul said, "I do. While I was there I had access to Longbottom's wand. I did the *priori incantus* spell. I can show it to you right now. I'm sorry, Mrs. Longbottom. You should see this too and confirm that it was your husband."

She sniffed and said, "Of course."

Paul held his wand up, and out of its tip came a ghostly grey image. First it was a man. Mrs. Longbottom's swift in-draw of breath showed that she recognized him. Then there was a small, almost invisible wisp that looked like a fuzzy worm. Paul said, "Is that your husband."

Joyce nodded. He went on, "See the other thing. It is right next to his head. I saw something that looked very like that. It was in a wound that appeared to have been surgically opened. It was at the base of his neck.

"I think that was the alien. I think that Longbottom killed himself so that he could keep himself from being controlled by that thing."

The Secretary's face had gone white. Joyce had run from the room.

The Secretary's face regained some color and he said, "But this is insane. Surely, there's got to be another explanation. We need more proof."

Ed spoke up, "Look. There're some things we can do with this shadow from the *priori incantus*." He got out his wand and said, "*Engorgio.*"

The images of Longbottom and whatever the other thing was grew much larger and details became visible in the other thing. It looked like a hairy caterpillar with at least hundreds of spindly spines. Everyone gasped. It looked truly menacing blown up to ten times normal size.

The Secretary said, "This means nothing. It could be a caterpillar."

Ed said, "Now watch this." A beam of light came from his wand and illuminated the shadows. "I call this an incantation spectrogram. The colors reveal the nature of the things in the *priori incantum*. It's very useful." The image of Longbottom turned a leafy green. The other thing turned an ochre yellow.

Ed gasped. The Secretary asked, "What is it?"

"The colors indicate the nature of the object. Intelligent magical creatures are different shades of green. For, example house elves are a very dark green. Non-intelligent magical creatures are shades of red. Muggles are white. Non-magical creatures are shades of blue. Inanimate magical objects are browns and inanimate non-magical objects are invisible."

Someone asked, "Invisible?"

"Oh, they may be a color that people can't see. I've heard Muggle scientists talk about infrared. Maybe that's it."

Paul asked, "But what's that yellow color then?"

Ed looked from face to face and said, "That's it. I've never seen that color before in a spectrogram."

The Secretary's face seemed to open and he asked, "I've never heard of this. Are you sure about all this?"

"I've been using it for over a year and a couple of months ago, I published in a peer-reviewed journal, *Forensic Magic*."

The Secretary just frowned. "OK. You've got a lot of evidence. Put it together to convince me there's no other possible conclusion."

Paul said, "OK. Let's do this reduction *ad absurdum*. Tell me what your alternative theories are that would explain this."

The Secretary said, "OK. You said that the creature that you saw was like an arachnamanchula but wasn't one. How can you be sure?"

Paul laughed, "Well, that at least is easy. How many of those creatures could you put in a small room with several people and not be attacked?"

The Secretary growled, "Well, maybe it was a new species."

Paul thought for a moment. Then he had an idea. "That creature had only six legs. That would be a huge evolutionary change not to be noticed before now."

The Secretary said, "Still, not impossible."

Paul said, "OK. Forget about the creature. What about the spectrogram? Ed, have you ever seen anything like it?"

Ed just shook his head. Then he said, "We've examined spectrograms of almost a thousand different plants, animals, and inanimate objects. There's never been anything close in all of those. This spectrogram technique has recently been accepted by the magical courts here.

The Secretary gave up on that line and tried a different one. "Maybe, Longbottom went crazy. That could explain the suicide."

Paul answered, "I've know Longbottom for a long time. I can't believe that he was crazy. I'll admit that that isn't conclusive evidence, but how many Aurors have committed suicide in the last ten years?"

The Secretary took pride in running an organization that valued all of its staff and was proactive about the health of the staff. He thought a few minutes. "OK. I guess I have to agree. Longbottom wasn't that crazy. And it's not easy to kill someone with the *Adavra Kadavra* curse. You've really got to want to do that. Kill yourself? No without a damn good reason."

The Secretary looked glum, and no one else was particularly happy. At some point Joyce had returned, but no one had noticed. She said, "You're right. My husband wouldn't kill himself except to save my life."

The Secretary was silent. He finally broke the silence and said, "I suppose there's no way out of it. Shit."

He turned to Ed. "Call in everyone. It's all hands on deck. You've got to contact the wizarding radio stations and have them put announcements on every 15 minutes. Everyone should avoid Muggles until further notice. Use Muggle-repelling charms on their homes. Notify the Auror Office of any apparent strange behavior in either Muggles or *wizard*s. We've got to find a reliable way to detect people who are infected with these things." He pointed his wand at the still ochre shade.

He turned to Paul, "You and I and Ed are going to England. We've got a special Port Key that we can use to transport there at a moment's notice. We've got to talk to the English Minister of Magic and get him to do similar things and help spread the word to the rest of the wizarding world."

Paul asked, "You mean right now?"

"Of course, right now. We don't have a second to lose. It may be too late already, but we've got to act and pray for the best."

He walked over to a broom closet and pulled a mop from it. "OK. Come on. Take hold of this and then we'll go."

Ed laughed, "The Port Key is a mop?"

"Sure, why not. Security by ignorance." Both Ed and Paul came over and grasped the mop handle. He looked over at Joyce. "Mrs. Longbottom, your husband is a hero. He's the first wizard casualty in the war for our planet. We won't forget your sacrifice or your husband's. Good luck." And with that they all three disappeared.

The Ministry

The Minister's secretary was looking forward to another dull day. She had altogether too much excitement in her life to want anything except blessed boredom at work. After all there was her live-in boyfriend who was always hanging around mooching meals off her, and then there was her mother who was in St. Mongo's trying to recover from a bad case of Spatter Goit.

It was at that moment as she was thinking about how wonderfully restful her job was that suddenly out of thin air three figures holding a mop appeared. Her mouth started to drop open, but before it could, she realized that there was a reason for three men and a mop appearing. It was the American Secretary of Magic. She summoned up her best professional face and calm voice and said, "Mr. Secretary, I'm sorry the Minister of Magic is not here now. He will be arriving at 9AM. Can I offer you some tea while you wait?"

The Secretary said, "I'd prefer coffee, if you don't mind."

She got up quickly and said, "Of course, I'll get you coffee right away. For you as well?" she asked the other two men.

Ed said, "Thanks, I'll have it with a teaspoon of sugar."

Paul said, "No thanks."

While she was out conjuring up coffee, the Minister arrived. He walked out of the fireplace that was just large enough for his bulk. He looked at the three men, one at a time and finally said, "Secretary Baker, what an unexpected surprise, er pleasure. What brings you here?"

"It's not a pleasure at all, Fudge. We've got tragic news. Please bring up the heads of your Auror's office immediately. We have to plan." Just then the secretary arrived with coffee on a tray. There was also a fourth cup and a pot of tea.

The Minister led them into his inner office. As he entered he turned and said to his Secretary, "Get Weasley and Shacklebolt up here right away. They should just walk in as quickly as they get here." He turned back to enter his office and then had another thought. "Oh, see if you can get hold of the Head of Hogwarts. And that pet Muggle of hers. What's his name, Want or Wend or something like that?"

After they were all seated in the dark mahogany paneled office, Fudge looked around as if he expected something to step out of the shadows. Baker said, "We've had an attack on a *wizard* in the US – apparently by a Muggle."

Fudge perked up and asked, "Apparent?"

"Yes, apparent. I'll ask the two Aurors that have accompanied me to explain it as soon as your Aurors arrive." Just then, Weasley and Shacklebolt knocked on the door and were invited in. They too took seats.

Paul took the lead. He explained how he'd been called in on the case by the distraught wife of the wizard who'd been killed by what superficially appeared to be Muggles. However, the American Aurors were quite sure that they weren't just Muggles. Then he brought out his wand and showed the last curse performed by it. Ed showed his spectrogram of that last curse.

"What do you suggest we do?" Fudge asked the room in general. As he said that there was another knock on the door, followed almost immediately by the door slamming open. Fudge said, "Ah, McGonagall. It's good to see you again. And good. I see you've brought the Muggle."

McGonagall turned a gimlet eye on Fudge and said, "The Muggle has a name – Professor Wendt."

Wendt shrugged and said, "I don't think that I know many of you or that you know me. I'm Professor James Wendt of Hogwarts. I teach English Literature."

Fudge introduced everyone else. Then he asked Paul to repeat his story. After the second repetition, Paul asked, "What do we do next?"

Fudge said, "We've got to keep people from panicking, but we've got to keep this attack from being repeated."

As he was saying that, his secretary entered the room hesitantly. She said, "Sir, just to remind you that you've got a meeting with the CEO of Gringott's Wizarding Bank in fifteen minutes."

"Oh, bother. Ms. Smithers, you'll have to cancel all my meetings today. Apologize profusely for me, please. There's a good girl."

"Now, what are we going to do?"

Minerva stood up and walked to the window behind Fudge. It looked out on the Atrium of the Ministry of Magic. She turned and said in her best Professorial manner, "There's only one possible course of action. We've got to bring as many Muggles into wizarding communities and protect them there as we prepare for a counter-attack."

Wendt decided to stand as well. He walked to the opposite side of the room, which didn't involve moving very far—as if to emphasize the difference between him and McGonagall. He was about to speak when he was interrupted by Baker. "Why do you—a Muggle—have a seat at this conference?"

He opened his mouth to respond when he was surprised by another interruption – from Fudge. "Baker, you've got to understand that this Muggle, was very influential in the fall of Valdemort." He choked as he said the name haltingly. It was apparent that Fudge still held even the name in something like fear. "It's extremely difficult to evaluate just how influential. But he was the one who organized the attack on the prison, Azkaban. He freed many Muggle-born and provided the camp where the army that fought the battle of Hogwarts was mostly trained and provisioned. He organized the transportation from that camp to the battle."

Paul whistled. "Are you sure that you're not at least a Squibb?"

Finally, Wendt got to speak, "As far as I know, there's not a drop of magical blood flowing in my veins. What I do is observe and deduce from those observations. Anyone – even a Muggle – can do that. I am happy that you've invited me, but I don't have any good news for you. I think that Minerva is not radical enough in the actions that she proposes.

"I think that the very existence of wizards and witches must be absolutely withheld from the invaders. That means that you've got to cut off all relations of any sort with Muggles, retreat into enclaves – like Hogwarts – and wipe the memories of all Muggles who have any knowledge of real magic. Believe me, I am reluctant to suggest that. And I have to offer myself as the first Muggle to undergo that.

"However, the intelligence, power, and ability to act unnoticed makes the threat from these aliens far more dangerous than Valdemort's. If even one wizard became. . ." Here he paused searching for a word that was strong enough and repulsive enough to meet the requirements of the moment. He went on, "If even one wizard became infected, they would soon have an army of Valdemorts and the rest of wizards and witches would fall far faster than the Ministry did once it was infested by Valdemort's servants."

The room suddenly turned as silent as infinite space. Each person seemed to be thinking about the implications of that possibility. The quiet stretched on minute after minute. Finally, Baker said, "I withdraw my objection to your being in this counsel. I think you're right with the exception that we need you more than ever we did when Valdemort was in power. You have standing to both authorize these terrible impositions on Muggles and play the gadfly to urge us on to the really difficult decisions that will be necessary to win back the world."

Ed said, "You're right. We've already lost the world. If the infiltration has gone far enough that it's come to our attention, then it's lost for Muggles and it's only a matter of time before the last ones fall. Without our taking immediate desperate actions, we'll be lost too."

Fudge shook his head, looking down toward his feet, and muttered, "Why is it always me?"

Paul said, "Do you really think that we can convince wizards to turn in their Muggle friends and relatives to have their memory wiped?"

It was generally agreed that whether they could expect it or not, they had to try. The discussion turned to the question of how. The realization that it would be necessary to have a news conference before the day was over dawned on everyone slowly. It was agreed that the conference would have to happen at 11PM British Summer time and thus 6PM Eastern Daylight Time in the States. That would catch the biggest audiences in both areas as well as much of the mid-west of the States. Fudge sent for his secretary and asked her to announce an emergency press conference for 11PM. Representatives of all the major media would be invited to the small theatre of the Ministry.

Fudge asked who should be on the stage for the new conference. The consensus was that the American Secretary and Fudge should be but then there was dispute as to who else. There was a faction that insisted that only instantaneously recognized names and faces should be on the stage.

Wendt spoke up, "Look. Really everyone in this room should be. The leaders – Baker, Fudge and McGonagall – need to be there to lend credibility to everyone else. But, the person who actually was on the scene should be there to give a concise eye-witness report. Ed should be there to give the scientific evidence that there really is an alien invasion going on. The two top officers of the British Auror Office need to be there to support their American counterparts. All of them should be there."

Fudge added. "You need to be there too."

"Why?"

"Not everybody trusts the Ministry after the . . uh . . experience with Valdemort. You lend an outsider credibility to what we have to say. And you have a way of summarizing difficult arguments into short sentences when you put your mind to it. And you think pretty fast in tough situations."

Wendt thought a moment and said, "OK. But I'm only there to answer questions. I don't have a statement. There are a lot of people who know I'm a Muggle and would look at me as an intruder – maybe as much as the aliens are."

Baker agreed and then he went on. "We've got to get the press in as quickly as possible. They'll need to have warning so that they co-operate. Can we have a pre-conference with the main press people?"

Fudge agreed and summoned his secretary. "Smithers, get a *Daily Prophet* reporter and New English Wizard Telegraph reporter and pick a couple of the Wizarding radio reporters to come in ASAP for a pre-news-conference briefing

"Oh, and bring lunch in for us – you know – fish & chips, sandwiches, some desert. We're going to be working through the night. We'll need supper as well. Say 7PM. I'm going to have to ask you to remain until well after midnight."

Her eyes goggled, but she didn't say the things that she was thinking about – such as how she'd been hoping for a quiet day.

The discussion continued and was still going when Smithers interrupted again to announce that the press had arrived. Fudge told her to send them in – with their own chairs from the outer office. There were five. Smithers introduced them, "Roberts of the National Wizard Radio Network, Philby of the Scottish Broadcasting System, Fredericks of the pirate radio station WART. Then there's Dumbledore of the *New English Wizard Telegraph* (NEWT) newspaper and Skeeter of the *Daily Prophet*."

Fudge told them about the emergency news conference at 11 PM and that they'd been invited to attend with questions. "There are a few ground rules that I want to make sure you understand. First, there will be no early leaks of anything we have to tell you this afternoon. If anything does leak from this meeting, the person who did the leak will be banned from access to Ministry sources for the balance of the incident – however long that will be."

Rita Skeeter asked THE question, "How can you ban us. We're all from major news outlets. You can't keep us out of the story. Who would replace the *Prophet*?"

Minerva sniffed and said, "My dear, we would rather replace your paper with the *Quibbler* than suffer your presence if you can't keep a news blackout when necessary."

Skeeter sniffed, "Well, the *Quibbler* has a circulation of maybe two dozen. What kind of circulation do you think they can give you?"

Minerva sniffed back, " You seem not to be aware that the *Quibbler* publisher has a fairly modern printing press and has published a new edition of Advanced Potions recently. And, we'd give Lovegood access to the Ministry printing office if necessary. They could print tens of thousands of copies on short notice – and give them away for free."

Rita's mouth gaped open and she said, "You wouldn't!" She stared at Minerva for another minute and then said, "You would, wouldn't you?"

Minerva said, "I don't make idle promises."

Rita was clearly unhappy, but she didn't say anything further. Then they outlined the incidents that they were going to talk about in the evening. Everyone started asking questions almost immediately.

Baker said, "We're not answering questions. We want the newspapers to give full page one coverage to this story in the morning papers. And feature it in every section afterwards including the sports page three."

Dumbledore asked, "How do you expect us to get a story into the sports section?"

Fudge said, "You've got all afternoon to cook up a story. I've seen you fabricate sports stories on all sorts of bizarre things."

Paul asked, "Your name is the same as."

Dumbledore added swiftly, "Yes, the same as the famous Head of Hogwarts, but we're not related at all as far as I know."

They then got the same briefing, at a higher level than would be given in the evening. Rita asked if she could ask off-the-record questions.

Wendt laughed and told her that she could ask all the off-the-record questions, and on-the-record questions that she liked but they wouldn't get any answers.

There was actually some free time before supper. The reporters had gone off to communicate with their news media and request them to start writing stories based on what they'd heard for the Women's Section and the Sports Section and the Opinion Section. The Opinion Section was easy. They were used to writing articles without facts. As a matter of fact they preferred not to have facts.

The small theatre of the Ministry was set up primarily for news conferences. There wasn't much preparation for this one – except that security was tighter than normal. Consequently, it wasn't as full as it normally was for a big news conference. At 10:00, reporters started trickling in. There was a lot of speculation on what the conference was about. There were rarely any completely hush-hush stories. The few reporters who knew what it was about weren't talking either. The rest pretty quickly figured out who was in the know and who wasn't. So, the lives of the in-the-know were difficult for the half-hour before eleven.

▽

Spot-on 11PM, the Minister of Magic and the American Secretary of Magic and a couple of Aurors as well as some unknowns stepped on the stage. A few people recognized Professor Wendt of Hogwarts and shared that knowledge with those around them.

The Minister stepped to the podium and said, "At approximately 11PM yesterday local time in Gaithersberg, Maryland, USA an attack occurred by a group of Muggle security forces on a witch & wizard who will remain anonymous for the time being. The attack was totally unprovoked and resulted in the death of the wizard. We believe that a member of the security forces was also killed in the attack.

"The witch escaped unharmed and summoned help from local Aurors, who investigated and discovered that the attack was part of an invasion of the United States and probably the entire world by aliens." Such a hubbub of questions erupted at that point that the Minister stopped speaking until order could be restored. Then he continued, "We will have ample time for questions at the end of the prepared statements. But for now, let me continue. This news conference will present the facts and some of the evidence behind this rather outrageous claim. Yes, we recognize that it is outrageous and needs thorough explanation." The minister motioned with his hands for patience.

He continued, "We will present statements by one of the Aurors who arrived at the scene initially and then from an Auror who will present evidence supporting their conclusion. We will then hear from two Head Aurors of the Ministry. Finally, the Secretary and I will present our plan to deal with this menace, which will require sacrifices from everyone. We'll open the news conference to questions afterwards."

The rest of the named speakers presented for at least the 6th time that day what they had to say. It had been pruned down to a succinct plausible consistent story line.

The first step in the response was to allow wizards forty-eight hours to either bring Muggle friends or relatives in to sanctuary or obliviate their memories of magic.

Then the floor was opened for questions.

"You want everyone to abandon their homes and group together in the larger Wizarding settlements. It's a sacrifice for most people to leave their homes on short notice and move to a strange place possibly hundreds of miles away. Isn't that a bit much to ask?"

Fudge said, "You know the protocol. Please identify yourself before asking your question."

"Feltenstein, *Witch Weekly*."

Baker stepped up and asked to provide an answer, "I don't like the idea of evacuating people either, but I want my wife and children to be safe from something worse than the Imperious Curse. They'll have to leave their home and become refugees like everyone else."

Rita was practically jumping up and down to get the attention of Fudge. "Yes, go ahead, Rita.," he said with a tired resignation.

"Skeeter, *Daily Prophet*. This is a question for Professor Wendt." Fudge looked back to Wendt, who came forward to the podium.

"Go ahead."

"Are you really sure that there is an invasions of aliens from Mars going on? Now really!"

Wendt shook his head, 'Yes, Rita. I'm sure." He said nothing more. Then Rita shouted, "Followup! Why?"

"OK, Rita. The Secretary has no reasons to lie about this and some pretty good reasons to say nothing. After all, if he said nothing, he wouldn't have to face questions like yours. So, I'm sure that he's convinced that this isn't some sort of hoax. He believes his Aurors. I don't know all those Aurors, but I can't think of a reason for them to lie and fabricate evidence. If you accept that the evidence is not fabricated, then it's pretty convincing. The local Aurors are familiar with this spectrogram technique that the American Aurors use. That's good for me. The only alternative that you've got is that I'm under the *Imperious Curse* or am someone else using Polyjuice Potion. I happily submit myself to any test that you want to prove that neither of these is true."

Rita smiled broadly as if an idea had just occurred to her. Minerva McGonagall strode forward and objected. "Now, wait one minute. I'm not sure that I want Professor Wendt to submit to any procedure you cook up."

Wendt turned to her and smiled broadly. "Don't worry Minerva, I'll submit to any procedure that Rita names."

At this, Rita's smile widened by a mile. Wendt went on, "Provided that all the reporters here witness the procedure."

Rita's smile deflated faster than a pricked balloon.

Wendt continued, "Rita, we go back a long way. Do you remember the boat on the English Channel when we first really got acquainted?"

McGonagall quickly looked back from Rita to Wendt and back to Rita. She repeated that motion rapidly, as though she couldn't believe her ears.

Meanwhile, he went on, "You were a refugee like so many other refugees?"

Rita's face took on a far-away look as though she were recalling something from a different life. "Yes, I do. Let me come closer to have a better look at you." She came forward and stared into his face and then said, "Yes, I remember. You're the same Wendt from back then. No, you're not under the *Imperious* and I'd bet that you aren't being impersonated either."

"Thanks for the vote of confidence. You're right; I am the same man from then."

McGonagall said, "Well, I would say so!"

There was general laughter. Then another reporter asked, "Willie, MSNBC. Why do you allow only 48 hours for friends of Muggles to bring them in for refugee status?"

Wendt was standing at the podium and it seemed natural for him to go ahead and answer, so he did, "It isn't that we couldn't accept Muggles after that, but we don't want wizards and witches going out and

32

exposing themselves to capture for longer than that. It's extremely important that no wizard or witch fall into alien hands."

Skeeter had another question.

"Yes, Rita. What do you want now?"

"Skeeter, *Daily Prophet*. How is it that you are so confident of being able to weed out alien-dominated Muggles?"

Wendt answered again because the answer had been his suggestion originally. "I was wondering who would ask that question. Remember that everyone – either Muggle or wizard or witch – who wants asylum has to do the Unbreakable Vow that they will not reveal anything about wizards or the location of any wizard facilities to anyone outside the facility or any alien or alien agent without specific permission from the asylum administrator.

"So?"

"Well, any Muggle or wizard for that matter who has an alien in him is immediately revealing all sorts of information to an alien. Consequently, he or she would die instantaneously on taking the oath."

Rita smiled and said, "Neat. If only you could get all the aliens to take that oath."

Another wizard rose, "Philby, the SBC, you're recommending giving up all Muggles to these invaders." It wasn't exactly a question, but the real question was obvious. Fudge started to say something and hesitated.

Wendt, who was still standing near the podium said, "You are exactly right. I volunteered to join those Muggles, stripped of my memories – of wizards and witches, of magic, of the woman I love. I would have been stripped of the knowledge of the invaders that would let me attempt a defense. I did that because these desperate measures are necessary in my opinion to allow the human race to survive – certainly the magical part and maybe even the Muggle part."

The news conference seemed to go on interminably, but finally one of the news people said, "Thank you Minister Fudge and Secretary Baker." With that it was over and everyone dispersed. The people on the stage left and rode an elevator up to the Minster's Office. In the office, the work continued.

Everyone suggested places that could be made absolutely secure. Minerva, of course, suggested Hogwarts, "Hogwarts is already extremely secure from our work to secure it from Valdemort. Hogsmeade is close by and also defended well from Muggles. We could house quite a number of people in the Castle. We'd have to give up on teaching.

Hogsmeade could be expanded quickly to house many more." No one objected.

Fudge offered Diagon Alley. "It's very large. It could accommodate many more people than live there now. It's well defended."

Again no one objected. Then Fudge went on to suggest the Ministry. Wendt got up and said, "I don't think so. As a matter of fact, I think the Ministry must be abandoned. Even the Muggles discovered it before I joined them and started helping them. It may almost be too late. The Ministry must be abandoned and it must be returned to the state of a half-finished department store."

Fudge leaped up, "Surely the Ministry is safe. We've so many defenses."

Wendt remained seated and said calmly, "No. It's probably already lost. But I would suggest a place that is safe. It could accommodate the Ministry offices and even house a lot of people."

Fudge's short temper began to show through, "Where is it then? What is the wonder asylum from the invaders?"

Wendt continued unflustered, "Azkaban. It is very well defended. We attacked it but we only found it because we had help from wizards – good wizards. Which brings up another point. We've got to find the people that I worked with and wipe their memories."

Minerva gasped and said, "Surely, there's another way. Those were good men who served the cause of free wizards everywhere. Can we not bring them to asylum?"

Wendt looked her in the eye and said, "Asylum or obliviation."

There were continuing arguments about other locations that could become asylums. A couple of other wizarding communities in England were chosen.

Wendt and McGonagall left together after the meeting was over, having been given the assignment of finding and either bring to asylum or wiping the memories of all the people that they'd worked with.

Wendt took her by the hand and whispered an address to her. It was the home of the leader of the SAS group that he had worked with. Minerva squeezed his hand. They re-appeared outside a house in an upper class housing development. It was after 1AM. Wendt took his cell phone out of his pocket and dialed a number. It rang twice and a whispered voice said, "What is it?"

Wendt replied, "This is Jim Wendt, I need to meet you ASAP."

"OK. First thing in the morning."

"Actually, I was thinking of right now."

There was a hesitation, and the next time the voice spoke it was at a normal volume. "Where are you anyway?"

"On your doorstep."

"If you'd only given me a little more warning, I could have had tea."

"Just let us in."

"Who's us?" By this time there was a light on in the living room.

"Minerva."

"OK. Just a sec."

The door opened, and they entered the house. The Major was in a robe over pajamas. "What requires a meeting after midnight on zero notice?"

"You know that I frequently have unique AND reliable information?"

"Of course, that's why I let you in." He bowed to Minerva and said, "Good evening, ma'am."

She frowned and said, "No, it's not."

The major frowned as well and said, "It's that good, then?"

Wendt asked, "May we sit? I think that this is news that's best taken seated."

The major sighed and said, "Sure." They all sat. Minerva and Wendt sat on a sofa, and the major on an armchair.

"The first thing that we have to do is make you swear the unbreakable oath."

The major whistled. "Shit. I don't remember precisely how the unbreakable oath works. But, I've got a feeling that I'd be better off not remembering."

Wendt explained, "The unbreakable oath is a binding magical contract. If you take it, and then later break it, you die. No formalities, it just happens."

The major looked even glummer. "OK. What do I have to swear to?"

Minerva said, "You have to swear never to reveal what we're about to tell you to an alien until we release you from the oath."

The major's face cleared, "Well, I thought it was going to be something that I might do accidentally. This, I'm completely safe from." He hesitated and then added less surely, "Right?"

Wendt said, "Wrong. They're everywhere, and I'd be careful about casually agreeing."

"Oh shit. You're kidding, right?" He asked hopefully.

"No."

"All right. If that's the price of admission to this party, I guess I've got to pay it. But that means that I've got to give up my oath to queen and Country."

"I'm afraid so. But strictly speaking Queen and country are only going to exist for a very short period of time and may already be gone."

There was clear distaste in the sound of his voice. "What do I do?"

Minerva stood and came over to him, "First, stand. Then grasp Wendt's right hand." He stood and Wendt stood and came over to where the two of them were standing. They both clasped hands, and Minerva got out her wand. Then she poised it over the clasped hands and said, "Do you swear that you will never reveal to any alien anything that you know about wizards or witches?"

Wendt said, 'you have to repeat the words after her."

He repeated them, and as he did so, a filament of fiery light left Minerva's wand and wrapped around their clasped hands. Minerva went on, "And this oath will last until it is released by the witch who binds it."

He had been staring at his hand. Then he looked up, and Minerva said, "Repeat." He did. More fiery light wrapped around the hands. Then Minerva said, "So be it." And the light disappeared. Everyone was silent for a moment. Then both Minerva and Wendt released long-held breath. Then the major did too.

He asked, "Why were you holding your breathes? I know why I was."

Wendt said, "We both were afraid that you'd die when you finished your oath."

"What! You made me take that bloody oath thinking that I'd die if I did?"

"Well, we weren't sure, and if you had died, it would have been because you had an alien at the base of your brain. And in that case, you wouldn't have been you."

He dropped into his chair. "Wow. You're that serious aren't you?"

They both just nodded. He went on. "Well, so in that case, I suppose that you're going to tell me that I've got to leave home and never return and join your merry band that are fighting these aliens."

Wendt and Minerva sat, and he said, "That's about the size of it. But we need to find all Muggles who have knowledge of magic and give you all asylum. That includes, of course, all the people who were on the Riddle project."

"Of course. So, you want help tracking them down, right?"

Minerva said, "Yes, and no time to lose either."

"Well, you're in luck. I brought my work laptop home. I can log on and we can look up the entire unit assigned to that project and find where they are now."

He led them into the study. The laptop was open, and the screensaver was running. He sat at the desk and wiggled the mouse. The logon panel appeared, and he said, "Sorry, I'm going to have to ask you to turn your heads." Then he laughed with a kind of bark. "Well, in for a penny, in for a pound. I don't know why I'm trying to hide it from you considering what I'm about to do." He went ahead and entered the password, and the screen cleared. He brought up a webpage, entered a password, and put his left thumb on a fingerprint reader. Then a new screen appeared, and he methodically entered search criteria. The screen that resulted had a list of names. He printed it.

"OK. This is the list of people on the old team. It's depressing how many there are. We'll have to inquire about them one at a time." So, the long laborious task of finding current assignments and contact information proceeded. It went on in silence. At one point, he said, "Damn. If I only had a programmer, he could probably write a query on the spot that would bring us all these names with current assignments, etc. quicktime."

Wendt said, "I don't care, just so long as we get them all."

The work seemed interminable. Finally, the Major said, "That's it. Everyone. Except our few civilian employees." I don't think we have current records on them.

Wendt was growing impatient. "I'll do that. Give me the list and the chair." He took the chair in front of the laptop and brought up Google and searched for the civilian employees. He quickly found addresses and phone #'s. "OK. That's it. The top one on my list is my partner."

Minerva said, "Why am I not surprised?"

Wendt just grimaced and looked up. "She's the first on the list. We've got to go find her right now."

The major picked up the phone by the laptop and started to dial the number. Wendt forced his hand down onto the cradle and said, "Not from your phone. I'll use my cell."

He quickly dialed the number. The phone rang once, twice, three times. It kept ringing like the toll of some great bell working their doom. Then it stopped. A sleepy voice said, "What's so important that you have to get me up at 3:30?"

Wendt said, "This is James Wendt."

Before he'd finished saying it, she said, "Jim, what the bloody hell is going on. Why call me at this hour?"

"It's terribly important."

She said, "Oh?" with an upward lilt to her voice.

"Minerva and I have to see you right away."

She said, "Oh." With a downward inflection.

"We're coming right now."

"I'll be ready."

Wendt hung up and said to himself, "I doubt it."

To the others he said, "We're going right now." Addressing the major he said, "Forget changing. We don't have time. And you won't be seeing this house again."

He nodded and ran to the back of the house. He was back in three minutes, carrying jeans, a dark dress shirt, a ball cap, and sneakers. He grabbed the laptop and started to put it in its case.

Wendt said, "I don't think you'll need that where we're going."

He said, "Oh, you never know."

Minerva grabbed both of their hands, and they all disappeared. They arrived outside an apartment building. Wendt went up to the door, and Minerva lit her wand so they could read the apartment #'s. But it wasn't necessary. Sally opened the door, and signaled them to come in. There was a light on at the head of the stairs several stories above. They walked up to the 3rd floor, and Sally let them into her apartment. She asked them to sit and then seemed to gaze inward for a moment. Then said, "You're here in the middle of the night because you're doing a social call?"

Wendt admitted that he had something serious that they needed to talk about. He stood up and started pacing. "Here's the deal. Do you know about the Unbreakable Oath?"

She said, "You know perfectly well that I do. What's the real deal?"

Minerva said, "Let me tell you the oath and then you can decide what you want to do." Then she gave Sally the spiel.

Sally nodded and said, "Since you're not kidding, I really don't have any choice, do I? Aliens, really?"

Wendt said, "Yes."

"I guess I've really got to do it, then. I suppose that's the only way I have to be sure that I won't betray you."

Everyone was silent for a few minutes, and then Parker said, "There is one other possibility."

Sally frowned in thought and said, "Wiping my memory?"

No one said anything. Then she decided, "I'd rather be dead than lose all those memories."

So, Minerva administered the oath. Sally held Wendt's hand as it was given. The fiery cords squeezed their hands together as though they were one.

Sally asked, "Well, you all look like you've been holding your breath. What gives?"

Wendt replied, "We weren't sure that you'd be alive after taking the oath."

Sally's mouth dropped open. "You mean, you thought I'd die and gave me the oath anyway?"

"Well, if you died, it would be because you had an alien buried in the base of your brain. It seemed like you might not want to be alive in that case." Wendt said, "But when you took my hand for the oath, I knew it was you and not some free-loading alien in your body for the ride."

Then Sally brightened and said, "Well, the one good thing about this is that we're getting the old band back together."

Everyone stared at her. Wendt recovered first, "We didn't think about it, but that's a darned good idea. We do need to get the resistance started, and the old team knows about that as well as anyone."

Parker said, "Sure, I'll bet the 'Boy Genius' would love it. He went into commerce after the team broke up. I think he's been bored."

Both Sally and I stared at Parker. Sally expressed their surprise, "How do you know about that nickname, I don't think we ever used it except when we were alone."

Parker laughed, the first laugh of the night, "You didn't know that I had your office bugged and had hidden video cameras?"

"If I'd know that, I'd not have said half the things I said. You must realize that we were speaking candidly."

"Oh, I just thought you were your usual up-front self, telling people off just the way you did in all our meetings."

The Boy Genius

Sally said, "OK. We're going after the Boy Genius. What are we waiting for?"

Minerva walked over to her, took her forearm, and started to lead her out the door. "Well, first of all, 'we' are not going to pick him up, 'we' are going to drop you off at a safe location along with Parker, and 'we,' looking significantly over at Wendt, "are going to get him."

Sally shook off Minerva's hand and said, "No." Emphatically. "We", looking significantly at Wendt, "are going to get the Boy Genius and you, I suppose, will have to tag along because we need a lift from you. I'm not going to be left out of the fun. God knows I've had little enough fun in my current job."

The women's gaze remained locked on each other and finally Minerva relaxed. She said, "I suppose that we need you with some of the 'old band'. But, we don't need to be dragging Parker around. And we definitely need at least another wizard to help transport people. We're going back to Hogwarts to drop Parker off and see whom we can pick up."

They all took hands and disappeared. A moment later they appeared at the gate to Hogwarts. There were a couple of tables set up with wizards sitting at them. There were a couple of people standing in front of one of the tables. There was an unbreakable oath being administered at that table.

Alphaeus Doge was seated behind a table. He waved at them and shouted a greeting. They walked to that table and he explained that this was the welcome station for refugees. They'd set it up within an hour of the announcement on the radio, and they were processing refugees, getting them assigned to stay at a wizarding community, and arranging transportation.

They introduced the Muggles in the group and told him that they were collecting some Muggles who knew a lot about both wizards and Muggles. Such people would be very useful in the coming battle. Wendt explained, "We'll want them all billeted together, here at Hogwarts if possible."

Doge considered a moment and said, "We'll have to have a little meeting of the welcome committee to see if that's feasible." He glanced over at the other tables. "In the meantime, we need to do the Unbreakable Oath."

Minerva said, "That won't be necessary, we've already administered the oath to both of these Muggles. What we need is another wizard to help us collect the rest of the group. Who's available?"

Just then George showed up. He was accompanied by Angelina, his wife. "Hello, hello, hello. Who do we have here? Ms. Harker, Colonel Parker, it's good to see you. I was expecting you. How about staying here at Hogwarts; it will be one big happy family again!"

Wendt said, "It's exactly what we had in mind. We need some help picking up the SAS unit that we worked with. How about coming along?"

George rubbed his hands together and said, "You bet. Are we going to snatch some Muggles right from under the noses of those aliens?"

"That's the general idea."

"OK. Let's go."

Angelina hit George on the shoulder and said, "What are you doing? Didn't you get yourself in as much trouble as you could in the Great War against Riddle?"

Wendt said to her, "Angelina, everyone is going to be involved in this one. We don't have any more choice than we did against Riddle. As a matter of fact, there was more choice then. People sat that one out and it came out OK. In this one, everyone will be involved or we'll all be dead."

George said, "Yeh, Angelina, we've got our civic duty to consider."

She shook her head and said, "Get off with you then. And mind you're back at a decent hour."

George scratched his head trying to figure out what a decent hour would be since it was almost 4 am.

Wendt said to Alphaeus, "Get Parker here a place where he can get a nap, and we'll be back as soon as we can." Then, he turned to George, "We're going to get Nicholas Brahms. You know, he was . ."

George interrupted, "The Boy Genius, sure."

"Does everyone know his private nickname?"

"Don't you know about extendible ears?"

"OK. OK. We've got to assume that everyone knows his nickname." Then Wendt gave Minerva and George the address that they were going to. They agreed to disapparate to a road crossing near there and then proceed to the Boy Genius'."

Minerva and Wendt took hands as did George and Sally. Then they appeared at a country cross-roads. They walked down the road, passed a house. Then a couple of hundred meters further down they found a two story house that would be modest by American standards but was quite normal for the English. Wendt led the way up the short winding lane that lead to the house. He had just started to climb the steps to the front door when there was an explosion. At least that was what it sounded like. It was actually the first of a series of shots. Wendt dropped to the ground and shouted, "Down everyone!"

Wendt shouted out, "Brahms, what the hell is going on?"

It was the Boy Genius' voice all right. He said, "Go away. Stay and I'll kill you."

Wendt said, "What the bloody hell is all this about?"

Wendt looked back and saw George get half-way to his feet and start to sneak around the back of the house.

The Boy Genius said, "I know about you – all of you."

"What are you talking about?"

George had gotten around to the side of the house and suddenly there was another burst of gunfire and George dropped to the ground. Meanwhile Sally had gotten up to Wendt and whispered to him, "What's he got?"

"I think it's an assault rifle." He whispered back. Then he said louder to the Genius, "Just who do you think we are?"

"I know who you are. You're all these damn aliens."

Wendt slapped his head with his fist. "Look we're not aliens."

"You can't prove it."

"Look, if we were aliens, we'd sure not be having a shouting match with you."

"Why not? You're lazy. If you can get what you want without effort, you will."

Then Minerva shouted, "Do you know who I am, Brahms?"

There was silence. Then the Boy Genius said, "Yes. You're that witch friend of Wendt."

She shouted, "Right. Don't you think that if we wanted to get you, I could do it as easy as Bob's your Uncle?"

Brahms waited before answering. "OK, I'll give you a chance. One of you comes in – unarmed, no wands and you let me examine you."

Wendt shouted out, "That's me." Minerva said, "No you don't."

Sally said, "It'll be me."

Wendt said, "No it won't. I'll be there." He got up and walked erect and slowly to the door and slowly opened it. The room was absolutely dark. Brahms voice said, "Turn around and stay still." Wendt slowly turned and waited. Suddenly there was a sharp pain at the base of his neck and he dropped. He was unconscious for a short time, and when he started to come around, the light was on and he could see the Boy Genius holding a assault rifle and bent over him.

He said, "You're OK. We'll bring the old gang in and then what happens?"

Wendt said, "We give you the unbreakable curse – just to be sure that you're not an alien, and then we go start a war."

Brahms smiled and said, "What are we waiting for?"

Wendt opened the door wide and said, "You can all come in. We've got someone to give the oath to."

Minerva came in and then George and Sally. Minerva administered the oath while Wendt took his hand. When it was over, everyone breathed easier. Wendt asked, "How did you know about the aliens?"

Brahms stared at him and said, "It's obvious, right?"

"Not quite to us mere mortals."

"Sure, it is. People suddenly start acting entirely differently. People who are greedy and bad sports suddenly are the models of civility. You know something really weird is happening with personalities. I started investigating and saw one of the beasts attack and insert one of the little bastards at the base of the guy's neck.

"It was then that I pulled some strings and got an assault rifle, ammunition, and hand grenades."

Wendt whistled, "You have hand grenades?"

"Sure" he pulled one out of his pocket. "This one was just-in-case. You know. Just in case, I needed to take one of the bastards with me when I went."

"You are serious. Well, are you ready to go? You're probably never returning here."

"Let me get my laptop. It's full of codes from the old days."

Wendt shook his head and said, "OK, get it, but we've got to disapparate before any of your neighbors call the coppers and they descend on this place." Brahms ran back into one of the back rooms and came out with a case. We all took hands and re-appeared outside the gate to Hogwarts.

Brahms shook his head and asked no one in particular, "So this is what disapparition is like. I'm amazed that any of you do this."

Wendt said, "I couldn't agree with you more." Then he asked Minerva, "Who's next on our list?"

Minerva pulled a paper out of her handbag and looked down it. "Ah, yes. Major Stevens. He's currently assigned to a post near Birmingham. Let's go."

Brahms reached out his hand and said, "Right, let's go."

Wendt shook his head. "Sorry, you're too important to take any further risks. They'll be having breakfast before long. Hogwarts has great meals. We'll see you later."

Minerva took Wendt's hand and George's and they disappeared. They were suddenly standing in front of a small cottage at the edge of a subdivision. They walked up to the door and knocked. The first light of dawn was appearing over the eastern horizon. After a moment, someone was at the door mumbling. He opened the door and Wendt said, "Sorry to bother you at this hour, but it's rather important." He followed him in. Suddenly, he felt a heavy impact at his back. He fell forward and there was a scream from behind. He thought he heard someone say *"Sempra Sepsis."* The pressure relieved, and he rolled. There seemed to be several massive shapes flowing into the room from a door at the opposite end.

Wendt reached into his pocket and pulled his purse out. Why hadn't he done this before entering the house, he cursed silently. If he had been a wizard someone would have left the room in a handbasket. He heard someone shout, *"Adavra Kedavra."* One of the shapes slumped to the floor, but more poured in. By this time, he had the purse open, and his Glok was in his hand. But there was a scream that he later recognized as Stevens – or what had been Stevens – and another impact hit him. He hit the floor again and this time succeeded in rolling over. He forced the gun up and squeezed off a round that struck Stevens in the shoulder. That forced Stevens back and gave Wendt a chance to look around and evaluate the situation. There were several of the creatures on the ground but still more coming. Was this some sort of trap? He shot off several rounds at the creatures, and one of them hit the floor dully.

The explosions sounded like the thunder of doom. He'd almost always been wearing earplugs when he'd practiced with it. He didn't realize how tremendous the sound was – especially when firing shots rapid-fire.

The other that he seemed to have hit was wobbling toward the door. He fired a couple of more rounds at it and it too hit the floor. Meanwhile the other two were firing off curses at the creatures.

Wendt shouted, "None of them can escape. We've got to kill them all."

George said, "I hear that." And he used the *Adavra Kedavra* curse again.

In another minute the room was quiet. They searched the rest of the small cottage quickly, but there didn't seem to be any live aliens left. Wendt kicked one over and fired a round into the base of what he supposed was its skull.

Minerva ran to his side and put her arms around him. She said softly in his ear, "I think they're all pretty much dead."

44

Wendt shook her off and said, "I just want to be sure that the alien at the base of their brain is dead too. That's the real threat here." He changed clips and put a round or two in the backs of the head of each of the creatures. Then he remembered Stevens. He looked around and saw that Stevens was in a corner holding his wounded shoulder. He walked over to him.

Stevens seemed to notice him for the first time since he'd been wounded. "What are you going to do to me?"

George said, "You can't just shoot an unarmed man."

Wendt asked him, "How did you know that we were coming? This was a trap." The alien said nothing. He shook it and pulled it around so that he was facing Steven's back. "Tell me or so help me, I'll. . . " and he placed the gun barrel at the base of his neck. The alien still didn't say anything.

Wendt shook his head, "Just what can I do with you? You know way too much."

Minerva grabbed his hand. "Don't. We can't do this."

The thing that looked like Stevens said, "No, you can't. It would be too cruel."

"You can talk about cruel?" He grabbed the thing and shook it, "How cruel were you to Stevens? Did you give him a chance to argue for his life?"

The thing just seemed to fold in upon itself and steel itself for the inevitable.

Wendt looked at Minerva. "Do you think that you can wipe that thing's memory and be sure that it's gone?"

Minerva's eye went from Wendt to the thing and back again to Wendt. But she said nothing.

"Well," Wendt shouted, "Can you?"

She said softly, "I'm not sure."

Wendt kicked the thing, and it cried out. "Try it. And I don't care if it never remembers anything again."

George took Minerva's wand hand and said, "I'll do it." He lifted his wand and said, "*Obliviate Maxima*." The thing shuddered.

Minerva lifted her wand and said, "*Imperious*." Then she asked the thing, "Where are you from?"

A strange voice unlike anything they'd heard before said, "That's funny. I don't know."

She shook her head and said, "I don't know."

Wendt walked slowly toward the door and said, "I'm sick of this. Let's get out of here."

They walked outside and Wendt was suddenly on his knees, vomiting. Minerva was at his side. He gasped for air and said, "Let's get out of here. I'm OK." Then they all disappeared.

Just Like Old Times

They arrived at the Hogwarts gate and found that Brahms was still there. Wendt asked him, "Why haven't you gone in and had some breakfast at least?"

Brahms looked him up and down. There was some vomit left on his shirt. Wendt hadn't realized it, but there was spider blood down his trousers and the back of his shirt. There were contusions on his arms and feet from the fight with the spider. Wendt asked, "Well, what the hell are you staring at?" He looked down at himself and said, "I guess I do look like I've been in a fight that I lost."

Brahms just shook his head and said, "No. You're still walking. The other guy isn't, I bet."

"Well, the other 'guy' isn't a 'guy', and I wouldn't be here if Minerva, or was it George, hadn't taken out the other 'guy'."

George nodded and said, "It wasn't I. I wouldn't want to be the person to molest you, mate. Minerva made short work of that thing,"

Wendt continued, "Let's just say there wasn't much left standing when we left Steven's place. He's dead. Probably had been for a while before we got there. We've got to get out there and get to the rest of the team before any more of them get attacked. I sure don't want to have to do that again."

Minerva took Wendt's hand, "We've got to get some rest and something to eat. And we've got to burn those clothes of yours."

"Right. But we've got to hand the list over to other people to keep working through it."

So, they took Brahms up to the castle, and they found some Order of the Phoenix to take over for the next eight hours. They stopped off at the Great Hall for breakfast. People stared at them, but nobody objected to their having breakfast despite how awful they all looked. By late afternoon they had finished breakfast, gotten some sleep, and felt good enough to go out again looking for more of the old team.

Brahms insisted on coming but they convinced him that he was more valuable staying in the castle and doing some thinking. They had a quick supper together and Brahms already had an idea. He opened his laptop and asked where he could plug it in. Minerva and Wendt looked at each other and broke out laughing. That particular question had probably never been asked in the entire millennium long history of Hogwarts. Brahms, of course, had no idea what the joke was.

"Well, come on. What's so funny?"

Wendt was having trouble breathing, he was laughing so hard. Between gasps, he said, "It's just that there has never been electric power here and never will be."

Brahms was aghast. For a full minute he just stood, his mouth agape. Finally he said, "You're joking! How can I work without electricity?"

Minerva was bemused and asked, "You can't work without electricity?"

He looked at her as if seeing her for the first time. "Ms. McGonagall, could you work without your wand?"

She was brought short and thought for a moment searching for a retort. She eventually said, "I apologize. You're right. Everyone has their tools. I'm sorry that I disparaged your tools. But, really, there isn't a chance in the world that we could get electricity to work here. There's way too much magic in the air."

The Boy Genius said, "I'll think about it. Maybe there'll be a way yet." He opened the laptop on the table where he'd been having supper. He pushed the on/off button and nothing happened for a moment, and then there were a whole series of rattles and light flashing on the screen. He closed the top and sighed. Then he walked out the door from the Great Hall.

Minerva turned to Wendt and asked, "Do you think he's safe here by himself?"

Wendt looked after him and said, "I think that Hogwarts may be in as much danger as he is."

At that point, Sally, came up to them and sat down with them. Wendt smelled trouble in several varieties. Sally, at least, was up front when she wanted something. She asked, 'Well, what can I do?"

Minerva looked like she was ready to suggest something but Wendt beat her to it. "Did you see the Boy Genius just leave the hall?"

"I think I did. So that WAS him."

"Yes, it was. If you hurry, you can catch up with him. He's got a good idea and I'll bet you can help."

Sally smiled for the first time since he'd seen her earlier, "Yes, boss. What is it?"

"The good idea?"

"Yes,"

"I haven't the foggiest. But that won't make any difference to you."

"You bet. I'm off."

Minerva smirked, "That was clever how you got rid of her."

"It wasn't clever, it was just good self-defense."

▽

Wendt and Minerva worked their way through the list of former team members of the SAS team. They didn't find another person who had run into aliens, and they transferred everyone to Hogwarts, one by one.

After a good bit of wrangling, there was a compromise hammered out. The new team had quarters. They replaced the Slytherins in the dungeons. Professor Slughorn had objected violently, but he was over-ridden by Minerva.

There was one former team member who had retired. When they'd tracked him down, they'd found him uncooperative. He'd met them at the front door of his flat. It was on the 4th floor of the building, which didn't have an elevator. Minerva wanted to disapparate them up and Wendt insisted on walking. "It's way too dangerous. Someone might see us."

"Oh, don't be silly. Who would see us?"

"We're walking."

They were slightly out of breath when they reached his apartment. The retiree, Sam Jacobsen, had left the service after 30 years. He was around 50 and was unhappy. He didn't take the chain bolt off and spoke to them through the slit in the doorway. "What do you want?"

Wendt was surprised by his temper. "Well, it's kind of complicated. It'd be a lot easier to explain, if you'd invite us in."

"Go away." He slammed the door.

"Wait. We have a new assignment for you."

He opened the door again, "What do you mean, assignment? Don't you know I'm retired? Mandatory. No choice. And now you want to give me a new assignment."

Minerva said in her best school teacherly tones, "Let us in this minute. We'll be happy to explain to you."

The door closed. They thought that they'd have to consider using force. However, he'd just closed it so that he could remove the chain bolt. He swung the door wide and stood behind the door. They entered and found a room that was neat but Spartan. There was not much beyond plain walls, a cheap table and chair set. There was a sofa and an entertainment center that had a large TV, a DVD player, and a few DVD's and books. From behind them, he suggested they take the sofa.

As they sat, he came out from behind the door. He was sporting a straggly beard and old fatigues. He asked, "Well, it's not like I've got a full social calendar, but I do have things to do. What's the deal?"

Wendt tried to size him up. What would he believe? How much would he have to prove? He said, "Here's the deal. There's an invasion going on."

Jacobsen shook his head and said, "So what's new. There's always an invasion going on somewhere. You're not bringing me back to fight in Rwanda or Mozambique."

"You're right, but the invasion is right here."

That seemed to pique his curiosity. "What do you mean, here?"

"I mean that there are aliens here and now, attacking people and . . ."

Jacobsen interrupted, "You're talking about Muslims, right?"

"No, I'm talking about things from outer space." Minerva interposed. With that Jacobsen laughed convulsively. He bent over almost doubled up. He gasped for breath and wheezed almost silently. His beard collected some spittle on it as he continued to laugh. Finally he regained control of himself and said,

"I can't remember when I've had such a good laugh." He looked from one to the other of them, seemingly expecting one of them to share the laugh. They both looked exasperated and exchanged glances. Then he seemed to catch on, "You're not joking are you?"

"I'm afraid not."

He invited them to sit down. He remained standing and asked, "Wendt, you remember the time that we short-sheeted Fred Weasley at the operation center back when we were all together in the big war against What's-His-Face?"

That question took him by surprise. He looked at Jacobsen warily and said, "Yes, vaguely. I remember that you were the ring-leader and had a video camera in Fred's room that night. So?"

"Well, you never did have much of a sense of humor."

"Maybe." But Wendt thought that he did have a pretty good sense of humor. He just didn't go in for physical humor much.

"This really isn't a practical joke, is it?"

Wendt began getting a little tired of having to repeat himself, "I thought we covered that ground already."

"Yeh. We did. I was just really hoping that we didn't have another desperate battle ahead of us."

"Just like that? You believe me now."

"Look mate, if you come with a cock and bull story about alien invasion—a story that would get you and your lady friend laughed out of every office in Whitehall—then I think you must be serious."

Wendt cracked a smile as he thought about how preposterous it was. It was exactly because it was a crazy story that Jacobsen believed it. "So, you believe me?"

"Sure I do. Just a minute. I've got to get something." He walked out of the room and they could hear his footsteps echoing down the corridor. Then he returned. He was carrying an assault rifle and had a backpack slung over his right shoulder.

Minerva asked, "We didn't ask you to do anything yet."

Jacobsen's face fell and he said, "Well, I thought you were looking for some help. And it's just not been the same since I retired. Nobody wants to hire an old soldier, who can't write a book or fly a helicopter. You mean that you don't want me either?"

Wendt said, "Certainly we do. I just wasn't expecting to hear you volunteer. You seemed pretty negative a short while ago."

"No. Bring them on."

"OK. You've got to take an oath first."

The lines in Jacobsen's face formed and hardened, "Don't you trust me?"

Minerva said, "Oh, we trust YOU," putting a lot of emphasis on the word, you. "It's just that we don't trust the alien who might just plant himself at the base of your brain and make you do lots of things that YOU wouldn't do."

"Really – that could happen?"

Wendt just nodded and Jacobsen whistled. Jacobsen agreed to take the pledge. When it was over, he asked, "Does this make me a wizard or something?"

Minerva said, "Sorry. No. It just makes you a target."

He wasn't happy to hear that he'd have to leave his home and head for the far north of Scotland to be safe, but in the end (especially after hearing about the consequences of breaking an unbreakable oath), he agreed.

Strange Digs

It took several days to work their way through the list of the old team. Minerva, George, and Wendt did little other than eat, sleep and disapparate to various spots around the United Kingdom. They were pretty successful. They found, evacuated, and administered the oath to more than 90% of the old team. There were 17 who had died in various accidental ways. Another six had died in the service of Queen and Country. Then there was the one who had given up his memory for Queen and Country. When they returned from their last visit – successful – they fell into bed and slept the sleep of the innocent. It was the same bed. Now that Hogwarts was bursting at the seams with refugees – both Muggle and Magical, they had a very good reason for sharing a bed. Not that they had ever bothered looking for an excuse in the past.

The next morning they slept in and then lay a-bed for a good hour. When they finally got up and shuffled down to breakfast lazily, they found that it had been cleaned up. So, they'd gone down to the kitchens to impose on the house-elves. The first one they ran into was Kretur. He was happy to see them and expressed his joy at their safe return from the land of the aliens.

Wendt commented, "Not half as happy as we are, Kretur. Now, do you happen to have something breakfasty that we might impose on your good nature to rustle up for us?"

Kretur's face took a sorrowful turn, "I'm sorry Headmistress, Professor Wendt. The last of the breakfast things went into the disposal just ten minutes ago, but I can get you some fresh tea and some bagels or – even better – would you like some scrambled eggs and bacon. I could get that for you very quickly."

They agreed to the eggs and bacon and took seats around a table in the kitchen and watched Kretur scramble the eggs without touching utensils or foodstuffs. The frying pan flew through the air to them and dumped itself out on their plates.

Minerva asked Kretur to join them. He agreed but allowed that he'd already had breakfast, so he'd just stand there. Wendt insisted that he sit, and Kretur sat very gingerly on the edge of a chair that was not pulled up to the table. He was ready to leap up to serve them at their slightest whim.

They ate silently for a couple of minutes. However, Kretur cleared his throat and asked, "Kretur can ask a question?"

"Certainly, Kretur. What can we do for you?"

"Well, it's about these aliens. What are they like?"

Wendt leaned back and said, "Well, they don't look very threatening. They're like a centipede. They're about the same size, have about the same number of small limbs. They're white."

"Kretur doesn't understand how such a little thing can be so dangerous."

Wendt didn't have an answer for that. He just looked helplessly at Minerva, who returned the stare. Finally, Kretur said resignedly, "OK." And then he added, "Can I get you anything else?"

Neither wanted anything more, so Kretur left the table.

That afternoon, Minerva found Wendt and took him out to the Quidditch pitch. He looked out around the pitch and found it to be a sea of tents. Minerva had a big smile on her face and said, "What do you think?"

"There must be several hundred tents there."

"It's over a thousand and growing every day. We've already got almost 10,000 wizards, witches and children camped there."

Wendt looked on it for a few minutes and then said, "Follow me." They walked down among the tents. There were lots of minor variations in the tents but from the exterior they looked much the same – same size, same shape. Some were highly ornamented with small screened-in porches, exotic color schemes, and flags and banners. Some looked like little castles. He approached one where a wizard sat on a camp chair outside.

He said "hello" to the wizard and asked how things were going. The wizard introduced himself as Ted. He invited them into the tent. As Wendt expected, the interior was much larger than the exterior appeared. It had eight separate "rooms" and a large common room with tables and arm chairs. "Can I get you something to drink?"

Wendt asked for a tea, and Minerva did as well. Wendt then asked how things were going.

"Oh, pretty well, considering the short notice. But, do you remember the Quidditch Cup of '95?"

"Yes. I was lucky enough to attend the final game."

"Well, there were over 100,000 fans camping in an area not much larger than this. We could accommodate a whole lot more wizards here. If we had to."

Wendt asked Minerva, "How many more do you think that we'll have to accommodate?"

Her eyes flashed up as she mentally computed. I think that we'll have another thousand or so – at most. We've been working hard to get enough tents to accommodate the last stragglers coming in. We've been begging and borrowing from other countries and, of course, we've been pushing manufacturers of tents to get us basic ones – you know, a few rooms, as quickly as they can."

Wendt asked Ted, "Do you think that you could live this way for months, maybe even a year or two?"

"Well, we'd need some things that are in pretty short supply – like pubs and Quidditch pitches. You've got to have a way to blow off some steam."

Wendt smiled and agreed. Minerva said that there was a building contractor putting up some public houses and businesses in Hogsmeade. "But that will take weeks, at least."

Ted frowned, "But what we need most of all, is to get to work winning back our world. When are we going to start to attack the bastard aliens?"

Wendt agreed that was really important but added, "We have to learn a whole lot more about them. We need to learn their weaknesses. We have to figure out how to get rid of them without their deciding to destroy the Earth."

Ted turned strident, "Come on. We've got magic. We can run them right off the planet or kill them like that." He snapped his fingers.

Wendt thought a moment of trying to weigh his words carefully. Getting an idea of what the majority of wizards thought was important, but finding a way to convince the people to buy into the ideas that the Ministry had for winning back the world was even more important. So, he started off carefully, "You're right about that. But we've got two other problems that are just as important as getting them off the planet permanently."

Ted looked at him suspiciously, "And what would those be?"

"Well, first, there are billions of people who are under the control of the aliens. We want to kill as few of those as we can."

Ted chewed on that a minute and said, "But those are just Muggles."

Minerva interrupted, "Just Muggles?"

"Well, you know what I mean. They're probably goners anyway."

Wendt said, "We don't know that for sure. We need to know whether we can rescue at least some of them before we go out to kill aliens wholesale."

Ted asked, "You said there was another problem."

Wendt went on, "Yes. It's maybe even bigger."

"Bigger than a couple of billion people dead or zombies?"

"Yes. These aliens have crossed interstellar space bringing a couple of billion aliens with them. The kind of technology that they've got – heck the kind of technology that Muggles have – could destroy all the life on earth, if they decided that they wanted to do that."

Ted's jaw dropped, "You're kidding."

Minerva said, "Not at all. I've seen it. It sure scares me – what Muggles could do if they really wanted to. Who knows what these aliens could do?"

Ted became defensive, "But we can stop Muggle technology cold. There's so many wizards right here that you probably couldn't get anything that uses eceltricity to work within fifty miles of here."

Wendt shook his head, "Sure, we can make Hogwarts pretty safe from direct Muggle or alien attack. But could we do it for the entire world?"

Ted was silent. Finally he said, "Well what can we do then?"

"That's just it, we don't know and we've got to work on finding out as quickly as we can and certainly before we do anything that would reveal that we're here and a force to be reckoned with."

▽

The next day Minerva pulled Wendt aside immediately after breakfast. "Wendt, the Ministry is going to have a conference to try to decide on next steps, now that we think we have all English wizards safely placed in camps. They want both of us – and several other Hogwarts teachers – to participate. It will take a week at least. We're going to stay there until the conference is over."

He nodded and said, "I was wondering how long it would take before someone decided to do that. Good. I'll get packed. When do we leave?"

Minerva's face reddened a bit, "Actually, James, right now. I've packed for you and we'll leave immediately."

Wendt's face fell,and he held out his hand. "OK. I'm ready."

Minerva took his hand and pulled him up.

"We're not disapparating?"

"No." she said as she led him up the stairs.

"Port key?"

"No. We're going by. . ."

But Wendt anticipated her, "Floo network."

"Right."

"You know, I really don't know which I like the least. I know there's no way of going by train, but . . ."

They reached her office with its large fireplace. The bags were on the hearth. They walked up. Wendt picked up both and walked into the fireplace. Minerva grabbed a handful of floo powder with her left hand and took Wendt's wrist with her right. Then she threw the powder down as she said something that Wendt couldn't quite make out.

They appeared in a fireplace and stepped out. Two wizards stood with wands raised and pointed at them as they walked out. One of them spoke a spell which sounded like, "*Accio Alien.*" Nothing happened. The other wizard said, "Good. Please state your name, occupation and business. "

He was looking directly at Wendt, so Wendt said, "James C. Wendt. Hogwarts professor of English. I'm here for a conference." The wizard checked a list of attendees in his hand and said, "OK. And you, miss?"

Minerva said, "You know perfectly well who I am Sturdevant. I had you in my transfiguration class three years in a row. Would you like another go at your OWL in transfiguration?"

The wizard became almost repentant and said, "No, ma'am, professor McGonagall. Here's your name badges and your room # during the stay. There will be a welcome ceremony at lunch. Here's a map of the complex."

Minerva harrumphed, and the two of them walked off. Minerva walked confidently and at a quick pace while Wendt was examining the map, "Wait up, Minerva. How do you know where you're going?"

"I don't. But I want that security wizard to think I'm omniscient."

"Well, slow down. You don't have to convince me of that."

"Because you already believe that?"

"Because I already know it's not true."

She sniggered and slowed. Meanwhile Wendt was looking around and gasped, "Do you know where we are?"

"Of course, I do."

"Do you know this is Azkaban prison?"

"I told you I'm omniscient. Of course, I know. How do you think I got us here?"

"Right. But why here?"

"Well, for one thing, this is the new location of the Ministry. Being in the heart of London was a little too risky, don't you think?"

"Oh, I agree, but I thought the Ministry would never give up the idea of its omniscience."

Minerva's smile softened and she said, "The survivors of the war with Riddle came away with a healthy respect for their enemies. They don't intend to make the same mistakes they made with him."

"I suppose our room."

Minerva corrected, "Rooms."

"Whatever. Anyway, I suppose they're prison cells."

"They're supposed to be much more comfortable."

"No Dementors, I hope."

Minerva laughed. "I don't think so."

As they were talking, a commotion arose back at the fireplaces. Wendt noticed and turned to see what was going on. There was definitely something going on. He started walking back. Minerva followed, and before they got close enough to hear carefully, they saw who it was that had caused the trouble.

Wendt strode up and said, "Hello, hello, hello. If it isn't Tom Swift and the electric Boy Genius. What brings the two of you here?"

The Boy Genius said, "I've got things that this council has to hear. George here was kind enough to give me a lift."

George said, "No. no. no. I had a great idea for defeating the aliens and I brought Brahms along for laughs."

One of the security wizards said, "Well, neither of you is on the list, so just turn yourselves around, march back into the floo network, and go where you came from."

Minerva said, "Just a minute. Weasley's pretty smart and any idea that he thinks is good is at least worth listening to."

Wendt added, "And the Boy Genius is well, a boy genius. I'd definitely rather have him on my side than on the sidelines. They should both stay."

The security wizard said, "That may all be true, but they're not on the list, and they're not staying if they're not on the list."

Wendt said, "Can you give Minerva and me a few minutes with them before you send them back?"

He looked nervous, consulted with his partner in whispers and said, "I suppose that if you don't leave this area, you can consult for a little bit." The two then withdrew several paces and a whispered conversation ensued.

Minerva said, "How in the world did you get here?"

George said, "The two of you seemed to be hatching some sort of plot, so I followed the two of you up to Ms. McGonagall's office and used extendable ears to hear what you said. I caught the destination, so we just went to Azkaban too."

Wendt said, "But why did you bring Brahms?"

"He has been trying to sell this idea to me, and I've begun to think that he knows what he's talking about."

"Well Brahms, what is it?"

"Oh, I just have this idea about spying on the aliens. But, I need some materials and a place to work. I just wanted to get permission to go ahead."

Wendt said to Minerva, "I wasn't kidding when I said that he gets good ideas. Can we just give him permission to have some of the idle wizards to help him with whatever he wants to do?"

Minerva turned to the two and said, "OK. You've got carte blanche." And then she added, "I can't believe I'm saying this. George, I want you to keep an eye on him. Don't let him do anything crazy or dangerous."

Brahms said, "But, wizards can't help me with getting technical stuff!"

Wendt laughed, "Believe me, they're your best bet for getting it. You've got permission to steal anything you need from the aliens. Just be really, really careful! George, help him steal what he needs. It probably means doing lots of disapparating and stunning lots of alien guards at warehouses."

George perked up his ears. "Yes, sir. Don't you worry; whatever he needs, we'll get it no matter how many aliens we have to stun, petrify and confund."

Minerva said to them, "Well, what are you standing around for. You're burning daylight."

After they'd taken the floo network back to Hogwarts, she shook her head and said, "I hope we've not done something that we'll regret."

Wendt nodded and said, "Desperate times, " and Minerva finished, "Desperate measures."

The conference proper got started after lunch. First there were reports on the current state of wizard knowledge about aliens. They'd already seen an example of that knowledge. There was a working group that was experimenting on aliens. They'd captured several and had tried various spells on them. The *accio* spell could be used to detect aliens. Most of the time the spell was fatal to both the alien and its host. The alien was propelled forcefully by the spell. Usually collided with hard bone at high speed and was crushed. This usually killed the host as well. The aliens that weren't killed outright had so much internal damage that they couldn't be interrogated.

They had also discovered that Veritas serum worked in a strange way on aliens. It seemed that aliens spoke a foreign language when they spoke under Veritas serum. No one had figured out how to interpret it. In one case, the human had actually been able to respond. This was taken as good evidence that at least some humans retained memories and possibly might be restored if the alien could be removed safely. But so far, healers hadn't figured out a way to do that.

After the afternoon session, there was the evening meal. It was to be formal. Wendt rummaged around in the bag that Minerva had packed for him, and Wendt came across an unfamiliar set of robes. She looked over his shoulder. He asked her, "I suppose this is your doing?"

"I don't know what you're thinking of,"

"Oh, no. These new dress robes just appeared by magic." It popped out of his mouth so quickly that he didn't have time to edit it.

She smiled and said, "As a matter of fact, that's exactly how i\they appeared."

Wendt was a little irked that she'd taken the liberty of getting him new dress robes without consulting him. "You know my old robes were perfectly good."

She put her hands on her hips and a frown on her face. "I suppose that you call that rip under the left arm perfectly fine."

He said incredulously, "There's a rip under the arm?"

Minerva sneered, "Of course, there is. As if you didn't know!"

He was still miffed and grumbling as he dressed. They had done a good job of converting the cell into a small, but serviceable room. There was a small armoire, a full-size bed that folded into a small sofa. It was good for snuggling and as a matter of fact that was all it was good for if you had two normal-sized people in it. There was a small desk and chair. They finished dressing quickly and headed down to the dining hall.

On the way, they crossed path with Pam Moertl the new Minister of Magic. She apparently had been waiting for them because she showed no surprise.

She held out her hand and said, "Professor Wendt, I've long wanted to meet you. How is it that we've never met?"

Minerva immediately inserted herself into the conversation, "Professor Wendt is a very dedicated teacher and rarely leaves Hogwarts."

Moertl said, "At least, he rarely leaves Hogwarts without you. But it's really the both of you that I want to talk to."

Wendt asked a somewhat touchy question point blank. "How did Fudge leave office?"

Pam looked him eye to eye and said, "Minister Fudge was rather overwhelmed by the prospect of dealing with another crisis that was potentially even harder to solve than Tom Riddle's. It didn't require much convincing that he could serve better in an advisory role. The Wizengemot accepted his resignation and appointed me in his place. All very simple and clean." She placed a little extra emphasis on the last word.

Minerva nodded and said, "Don't stand on formality, please proceed."

"Professor Wendt, you are well-known for your efforts among Muggles during the Great War. You probably know Muggles better than anyone among wizards. I'd like to discuss several issues with you."

"Minerva and I are at your disposal." Minerva smiled at that.

The minister said, "I'll see you after the banquet."

Wendt nodded, and they parted company. The banquet was the usual—top-heavy with speeches and drink and short on good food. It went on for almost three hours, and he looked diligently for an opportunity to sneak out. The speeches finally ran out and there was lots of general discussion going on. Wendt signaled to Minerva who had been seated over near the Minister. When she saw his wink, he got up as surreptitiously as he could and headed for the men's room. He hoped that Minerva was doing likewise.

He didn't quite reach the Men's Room when, of all people, he ran into the Minister. "Professor Wendt. Let's get out of here while we can. There are several small conference rooms where we can go to discuss things." He looked around for Minerva but didn't see her. The Minister said, "I'm sure Ms McGonagall's on her way, let's go." With that she took his forearm and urged him along.

"But. . . "

"Don't worry, she'll be along soon." She led him to a small conference room that had a sofa, a couple of chairs, and table with eight chairs. He started to sit at the table, but she urged him over to the sofa.

"This is a much easier place to talk."

She sat just to one side of center and he took the extreme other end. She looked at him directly and started immediately. "Professor Wendt." She hesitated and said, Do you mind if I call you James? It's so much slower using your title."

"No. That's OK."

"Fine. Please call me Pam."

"OK."

"Jim, you know Muggles better than any other person in the wizarding community."

"That's probably true."

"How did you become a professor at Hogwarts?"

"Well, Professor Dumbledore was looking for someone to teach English Literature, and I happened to be looking for a teaching position, having recently graduated from Stanford University."

The Minister's eyes seemed to widen in surprise, "Really. You teach English literature. I thought that you probably taught Muggle Studies or something like that."

Her eyes were both wide and innocent and in some way penetrating at the same time. He explained, "Dumbledore thought that it was important for students to be exposed to the fine arts, to literature, to to . . ." He found himself drifting back to that time when he was so poor and took a chance on the strange advert in the *Times*. He could almost see Dumbledore before his eyes as he waited near the boat house on the Serpentine. He could see Minerva just as she had been those many years ago, fresh, intelligent, beautiful, blonde. Somehow Pam had almost disappeared from his view.

A storm had been brewing outside Azkaban, and a stroke of thunder sounded. Suddenly, he was aware of where he was, and he leaped up and turned away from the Minister. He shook his head to free it from the cobwebs that had seemed to grow there. Shocked, he said, "You're a legilimens!"

Pam's voice was smooth, "Why whatever do you mean?"

"I mean that you've been mucking around in my head. I ought to walk out of here right now."

Her voice came through serene and matter-of-fact, "Do you think that a politician gets to be successful without having a little of the legilimens in her?"

"I suppose not. Is there anything you want to discuss here without trolling around in my head?"

She said, "As a matter of fact, there is. But first, purely for my curiosity, you and Minerva are actually. . . uh. . . together?"

"For the record, yes we are. I've been trying to get her to marry me for some time, but so far, she's not been having any of it."

"Amazing. I got a glimpse for a second of her through your eyes. She is an amazing woman. But she's also quite a lucky woman."

"It would be nice if you could convince her of that."

"Oh, I think she knows. But now to business. I've got a problem that I'd like your perspective on."

Wendt was suspicious. "Isn't this where Minerva should show up?"

Wendt could hear her head shake – her long blonde hair rustling on her clothes. "No. I want an unbiased, non-magical view. You're the best person to give an opinion because you know the Muggle community and the magic community intimately, if you'll excuse the expression."

"I'm not sure, I'll excuse the expression," he said, still facing away from her.

"You can turn around. I'm not going to use legilimancy on you."

"Says you."

"Yes, says me. On my honor."

Wendt could hear something, the ring of truth, perhaps, in what she said. So he turned and said, "Go ahead."

Pamela looked at him and said, "I'm worried about the goblins."

"The goblins?"

"Yes, the goblins. They are mercenary and would sell wizards and all of mankind out to the aliens if they thought they could trust them."

Wendt sat again and leaned back, thinking. "I'm worried about the goblins too but not for your reason."

For the first time Wendt heard uncertainty in the Minister's voice. "What worries you?"

"I'm worried that the goblins will fall victim to the aliens."

"But the goblins are magical, and they're ruthless. They couldn't be tricked easily. No, worry about the aliens if you want to worry about someone."

Wendt shook his head but this time sought her eyes, because he wanted her to see his sincerity. He wanted her to see that he was deadly earnest. "You've not fought them. I've been in a skirmish or two with them. They're ruthless in a way that the goblins can't imagine. The goblins are honest and their word can be generally trusted. They'll do absolutely nothing more than they've contracted to, but they are scrupulously faithful in what they actually agree to.

"On the other hand, the aliens are absolutely unscrupulous. If even one goblin approaches them, we've already lost the element of surprise and secrecy that are key to our success. All it takes is one goblin who is less than perfect in being suspicious and careful, and we're lost."

The minister had been on the edge of her seat, intently staring at him and then fell back into her seat in a silent reverie. Finally, she seemed to come out of it. "Then we need to win them as enthusiastic allies as quickly as possible."

Wendt leaned forward, "Yes. They should have been present at this conference. But it may not be too late, if you act immediately."

She stood and ran the fingers of her right hand through her long hair, dis-arranging it absent-mindedly. She whirled around and said, "Yes. I'll bring it up." She hesitated a moment, "No! You must bring it up in tomorrow's session. I'll have to oppose it vigorously but allow myself to be won over.

"Can you do that? You'll be the target of catcalls and worse."

Wendt laughed, which puzzled Pamela. He explained, "Oh, yes. I'm used to that sort of thing. Do you know that when I first started working with the Muggles in the Great War, I started out in a prison cell?"

"No, I didn't know that. Well, come to think of it, you're starting out in a prison cell here." That broke the tension, and they both laughed. "Well, go to lucky Minerva. She deserves you, I suppose."

I left and found her in our room. She quizzed me about my meeting with Pam. I was completely honest about what we'd said. She said, "I wonder if the topic of the goblins was just a ploy to get to see if you were . . uh . . available."

"I don't think so. When we got down to business, she was all business. I don't think that she'd have suggested my bringing up the goblins if she'd not been serious."

Minerva stared off into the distance and seemed lost in thought. Finally she said, "We'll see."

The next morning, there was a presentation of recommendations from a working committee that had been formed only a few days ago. Everyone interrupted their report with questions and opinions. No one seemed satisfied with it. Finally, the chair of the committee, Kingsley Shacklebolt, threw up his hands and offered to resign if someone would take the office on the spot. That silenced people.

Wendt decided that the time was right to talk about Goblins. He rose and said, "Mr. Chariman, may I speak?" Shacklebolt shook his head and said, "Go ahead."

Wendt began, "I'm Professor James Wendt from Hogwarts. I think that there's been a very important group left out of this conference, and I think it's past time that they were included."

Shacklebolt sighed and asked, "We've included representatives of house elves, and we've even been talking with the Giants. The Centaurs are safe on the grounds of Hogwarts. But who did you have in min. . ." he hesitated and then asked, "Surely, you're not talking about the Goblins?"

"Yes, sir,"

With that a dozen wizards jumped to their feet and objected. Shacklebolt restored order and said, "We'll hear people one at a time. You first, in the back."

An old wizard with white hair and a pair of glasses spoke slowly but forcefully. "Goblins are treacherous characters. They keep their bargains but will always twist every agreement to their own advantage.

They do NOT enter agreements with the hope of creating mutual good. Their only goals are those that advantage Goblins." Then he sat down.

Shacklebolt turned to Wendt and said, "What do you say to that?"

"I say that the old adage that you should keep your friends close but keep your enemies closer applies here. If we have agreements with them that exclude the aliens, then we can count on the aliens being excluded. Sure, we may have to count the silver in the end, but it's better to lose a few place settings by the time its all over, than losing the house to boot.

"It seems like an age ago, but I was once on the Board of Directors of Gringotts. I've had business dealings with them, and I've found them to be ethical and trustable – for the agreements as they are written. We do have to be careful to draft them well."

Someone else was recognized, "Goblins stood on the sidelines in the Great War against He-Who-Must-Not-Be-Named. Why should we include them now?"

Wendt stood immediately and said, "They will try to deal with the aliens if we have no agreement with them. AND they weren't completely on the sidelines. They helped with galleons."

This ignited a whirlwind of shouted arguments.

Minister Moertl banged her gavel and eventually regained control. She forced the meeting to an orderly discussion. There was not a consensus but somehow she maneuvered the meeting to the point where the Goblins would be invited to be observers of the meeting as soon as representatives could be chosen.

After the afternoon session, Pam button-holed Minerva and Wendt and asked them to meet her immediately. They went to the same meeting room where Pam and Wendt had met earlier. She let them know that she'd already been in touch with the Goblins of Gringotts, and they'd agreed to come to the meeting tomorrow. "I need people that I can count on to greet them cordially and set the example for the rest of the attendees."

Minerva said that she could count on them. She said, "Anything that can be done by smiling, you can count on us to do."

Wendt said, "If that's all, then we'll just be heading off for dinner."

Pam looked from one to the other, trying to decide which would be better to ask the question on her mind. She finally picked Minerva. "There is one last thing." Minerva's smile froze on her face.

Wendt openly said what they both felt, "I've got a bad feeling about this."

Pam took a deep breath and said, "The thing is that my office has been talking to the Goblins – quietly, on the side. The negotiations have come down to this. They'll work with us. They'll even take the unbreakable oath. They'll cooperate in what the Ministry wants to do."

Minerva said, her voice full of sarcasm, "There's just one little detail."

Pam's face was dour as she said, "Well, actually two little details. One is easy. They want a voting privilege in this counsel proportionate to their numbers relative to wizards, about 30%."

Minerva said, "And?"

Pam looked Minerva straight in the eye and said, "And, they want us to give them the Sea of Merlin."

Minerva threw up her hands, "Oh, yes. Just one little thing. The Sea of Merlin. Well, why didn't they ask for Gryffindor's sword as well? Or better, maybe the deed to Hogwarts or . . or . . the Moon."

Wendt looked from one to the other of the women in puzzlement. "The Sea of Merlin. I'll bet that it isn't his own private ocean. But what is it? I've heard of Gryffindor's sword. I've not heard of this Sea."

Pam turned to him and explained as if she were a 2nd grade teacher, "The Sea of Merlin is sort of like a large pensive. It's a large flat basin made of bronze. When you fill it with water, the large flat surface forms a mirror and you can see the future in it. Even Muggles can see the future."

Minerva shook her head and frowned, "No. no. It's only a legend. Nobody has seen it in well over a thousand years. It was supposed to have belonged to Merlin, who used it to predict the future."

Wendt smiled, "Sure. But the way I heard it, Merlin lived backward in time. He came from the future and remembered the future – not the past."

Pam shook her head and said, "Typical Muggle legend. Living backward into the past, remembering the future, it's all superstitious twaddle."

Wendt sounded indignant, "No, it isn't ALL superstitious twaddle. I suppose you've never heard of time reversal invariance."

Pam asked, "Time Reversed Inverness? What's Inverness got to do with anything?"

Wendt was warming to the topic, "No. No. Invariance. Time reversal invariance. The universe works just as well backwards in time as it does forward. It's a well-established physics principle."

Minerva said, "It's theoretical, but it's not practical – like Gopolut's 3rd law."

Pam was not ready to let it go. "Give me an example of this."

Wendt answered quickly, "Well, first, it just means that anything that happens in the real world would work just as well if you played it backwards. For example, if Minerva tossed you a quaffle. . ."

Minerva interrupted under her breath, "I'd rather hit it at her."

Wendt continued as though nothing had been said, "Then you could play that backward, Pam. It would work perfectly fine if you tossed it back to Minerva."

Pam, not to be outdone, whispered, 'Batted it back."

Wendt smiled and said, "See?"

Minerva seemed to be pondering that, but Pam asked almost immediately, "But, what if I, in my kitchen where I often am cooking gourmet meals, were to break an egg, drop it into a skillet, and fry it sunny side up, hmmmm? How does that run backwards?" By the end of the question, she had a sunny smile on her face.

Wendt pondered that a moment.

Pam simply said, "Umhmm?"

Minerva seemed frustrated but didn't seem to have a way of dealing with that frustration.

However, Wendt nodded and smiled himself. "Well, that could work backwards. I've never seen it, and I suppose you haven't either, but you have seen something very like it."

In surprise, Pam and Minerva said in almost perfect union, "I have?" They then stared at each other.

Wendt had his answer prepared. "I haven't been with you when you've seen it, but I'll describe what I saw. Then I'm sure you won't dispute what I have to say.

"The second year that I was at Hogwarts, Dumbledore set a fire in his brother Abeforth's inn to have something to show to Muggle authorities who came to investigate the death of Professor Quirrel.

After the authorities had signed off on it, Dumbledore and Snape ran the fire backwards, restoring the inn to its original condition. Why they didn't make improvements, I've no idea, but I saw flames erupt in clear air. I saw smoke be absorbed by charred wood, which became uncharred. I saw beams lift up in the air and re-assemble. It was a perfect example of time-reversal Invariance." With that he nodded his head triumphantly.

Minerva said, "But that required magic!"

Wendt pretended shocked innocence. "Magic isn't part of the real world? Hmmmm?"

The two women's smug smiles disappeared, and they appeared in intense thought trying to come up with a refutation. Finally, Minerva said, "I still think it's a trick."

Pam smiled and sidled closer to Wendt. She said, "I think you might just have something there."

Wendt sidled away and said, "OK. Back to the Sea of Merlin. If no one's seen it in over a thousand years, how does anyone know if it still exists?"

Pam said, "That's the problem. How can we promise them that if we don't know how to find it?"

Wendt replied, "I don't see how we can promise it to them. We've got to just try to bargain them out of it. Offer them something else."

Pam had the frown now, "We've been bargaining hard, but they just aren't buying anything else."

Wendt slapped his forehead and exclaimed, "The Sword of Griffyndor."

Pam stared, "What?"

"The Sword of Gryffindor. The Goblins would do anything to get that back." Wendt exclaimed. His excitement was infectious. Pam reached out and put her hand on his forearm. He went on, "Potter bribed a Goblin with it to let him rob Gringotts."

Pam squeezed and gazed raptly at him. "That sounds wonderful. This is IT."

Minerva took Pam's arm by the wrist and tried to lift it from Wendt's. "It won't work."

Both Pam and Wendt's faces turned stony, "Why not?"

"It didn't work when Potter tried it, and it won't work now. The Sword has a will of its own. Shortly after it was given to the goblin, it returned itself magically to a Gryffindor, Longbottom."

"How much good would it do if something like that happened this time."

Pam expressed everyone's feelings perfectly, "Shit!" And she released Wendt's arm.

Minerva asked, "Okay, let's try again. Where do we fit in?"

Wendt made a face and said, "That was the wrong question to ask."

Pam said, "No, that's perfect. You are from the main academic center in England. You're our best hope to find it. If you just consult your library and see if you can get a reasonable lead on it, we can take it from there."

Minerva said, "If it's understood that we're just doing research and nothing else?"

Pam reassured them that that was all that was needed. She then walked out the door, turned and said, "I'll leave you to it then."

Wendt turned to Minerva and said, "Here's another fine mess that you've gotten us into."

Minerva smiled and said, "It won't be too bad, I'll send an owl to Hermione Weasley. She loves working on this sort of problem."

"I suppose it won't be too bad."

Minerva went off to the Owlery, and Wendt waited for her before entering the Dining Room.

The next day, there was a delegation of 5 Goblins who came to the conference. They were introduced before the assembly. There was Gorblatt, Snaggur, Pip, Raggesnot, and Porphiry. The first three were from Gringotts and the other two each represented companies. One made security devices and the other represented a maker of fine art pieces. Wendt and Minerva were the first to greet them in the mid-morning break. They were conspicuously alone with them. Fortunately, they just had enough time to get some pumpkin juice and have a few minutes of discussion. Unfortunately, the only thing the Goblins wanted to discuss was the Sea of Merlin.

Minerva was very diplomatic, carefully refusing to make any commitments but trying to wheedle out any information that they had about the Sea of Merlin. Finally, the apparent leader of the group, Glorblatt, asked how they intended to obtain the Sea.

Minerva looked to Wendt, who was not at all grateful for this opportunity to display his ignorance. "Well," he began, thinking frantically for some stalling tactic, "you don't really expect us to divulge our methods do you? Isn't it enough that we're going to. . . "Here he was stuck. He didn't want to promise anything that he couldn't deliver. Finally he ended with "Isn't it enough that we're going to risk life and limb to get it for you?"

Glorblatt looked at him hard, "So, you know that it will be dangerous?"

Just then, the gong sounded for the beginning of the next session and Wendt thankfully, hurried them off to their seats. They were introduced to the conference as official observers representing all Goblins. The minister had gotten someone else to make a motion that they be made official voting delegates. The motion was discussed at length.

Finally, Glorblatt rose to speak to the motion. As an official observer, he didn't have an automatic right to speak, but the Minister permitted him to speak. He turned out to be a good diplomat. He briefly reviewed the long history of wizard/Goblins relationship. He glossed over the dicey early history and presented the recent history as a slowly improving relationship so that now the Goblins were the dominant force in wizard finance. That meant that much of the economic well-being of wizards was attributable to Goblin good will and reliability.

He then finished by adding, as if an afterthought, one last point. "We Goblins will be proud and happy to take our part in the defense of the magical world and its peoples from the deprivations of the aliens who have wantonly attacked all residents of the Earth.

Then he added, "We only ask that wizards demonstrate their good will by giving Goblin-kind a small token of friendship. We think that an appropriate gift would be the Sea of Merlin."

That caused a stir among the delegates. About half of the delegates apparently had never heard of it, and the other half were outraged. There would shortly have been pandemonium except that a delegate rose to a point of information.

"Madame Minister, I rise to a point of information, which is always in order."

Pam recognized him, and he asked, "Just what is the Sea of Merlin?"

This question permitted a lengthy discussion that revealed little more than Wendt had heard the previous day. It was largely established that no one had an idea where this artifact was. This, in turn, led to a discussion of how it could even be obtained. Pam requested an ad hoc committee be formed to find it. She winked at Wendt, who took the hint and rose to volunteer to form such a committee. Minerva volunteered, and they announced that they would meet with interested volunteers after dinner that evening. Lunch time had arrived, and further discussion was tabled until the afternoon session.

In the afternoon session, with most of the delegates a little less perturbed by the proposal to include Goblins and their demand, the original motion was approved. That evening, at supper, it was announced that the ad hoc committee would meet in the Main Meeting Room. Amazingly (to no one), when the meeting was convened, the only people present were Minerva, Pam, and Wendt. They quickly elected Wendt the chair and Minerva the secretary and Pam an ex-officio member. Pam assured them that she could obtain some additional volunteers if they needed them.

The Future of Time

They had needed help finding volunteers. There had been a couple of volunteers. George Weasley was always game for adventure, although he wasn't entirely sure that he liked the idea of going treasure hunting on behalf of the Goblins. His brother Bill, who worked with and for the goblins of Gringott's, wanted to extract something more than just a promise for them to help in the fight against the aliens but couldn't get anyone to go along. Wendt had argued that they didn't have time to negotiate and they were lucky to get the agreement to co-operate with the wizards in this fight—unlike the battle against Riddle.

In addition, the Minister had recruited a few less willing volunteers—George's brother Ron and wife, Hermione (who was not opposed to volunteering); the top magical treasure hunter, Robert Grunewald, and several definitely less than happy Aurors. The first planning meeting that they had was indicative. The meeting was held at the Ministry, and the Minister sat in at the beginning until she got disgusted with the vast differences in ideas that the various "volunteers" had. She finally got up in disgust and announced, "You are all crazy. This committee requires a dictator.'" She looked around the room seeming to look for a likely candidate. Actually she'd already decided on one

"Professor Wendt, you are the dictator. You are answerable only to me. If anyone gets out of line or refuses to go along with your reasonable requests, we still have some empty cells where malcontents can go. Maybe we can even find a few Dementors to return as guards." She looked around the room and said, "Does everyone understand that?" No one said anything. "Then the committee is yours Mr. Wendt."

Wendt started off by having the group do brainstorming on the things that needed getting done. It was a little like herding cats. Only Hermione had any idea what was involved in brainstorming. With her help, Wendt succeeded in getting the team to think about the different things that they had to accomplish before they could begin the search. They finally decided on several main efforts:

There was the research team. Its objective was finding likely places where the Sea of Merlin might be hidden. It had Hermione who seemed a shoe-in for the research part of the job. Oddly, Gruenewald was interested in it as well. He seemed to be purely an adventurer. He looked to be in his mid-thirties with tanned muscular physique and good reflexes. He claimed to have qualified for the German National Quidditch team as a beater, and certainly he looked the part.

At one point, Wendt asked him why he'd volunteered for the research team. He claimed that success in treasure hunting was largely determined by the up-front research. He claimed that no treasure-hunter could be successful without excellent research. But Wendt suspected that his interest in research in this case was as much due to Hermione's presence on the team as anything else.

Another team was assigned to do reconnaissance among the aliens. They were to find out how to move and act among them without arousing suspicion. This sort of thing was pretty much in George's line, so he and the two Aurors that had been 'voluntold' to be part of the group were actually pretty happy with the assignment. They wanted to DO something that would hurt the aliens' cause. So, they were glad to be moving among them and if they got into a fight, all the better.

Then there was the team that was trying to figure out a way to detect the Sea from a distance. That consisted of Ron, Minerva and Wendt. Theirs was the hardest job. Since there was only one Sea of Merlin, it was hard to do experiments to see what kind of spells a Sea would respond to.

▽

They had agreed to meet after 7 days to compare notes. They met this time at Hogwarts. The A team (research probable locations) reported first. There were two reports:

The Majority report, as Gruenewald termed it, consisted of his conclusions. His likely locations were the site of the Arthur round table near Penrith, Cumbria. His other location was Loch Arthur where the Lady of the Lake supposedly reclaimed the great sword.

On the other hand there was the minority report (again Gruenewald's term) offered vociferously by Mrs. Weasley. She agreed with the Lady of the Lake as a source for the Sea but placed it in France where Sir Lancelot du Lac originated. The knight was also associated with the Lady of the Lake. So Hermione selected Brocéliande, France.

That sparked a debate between the two. Gruenewald claimed that the town in France wasn't the real Brocéliande—if it ever existed.

Hermione agreed that the town of that name on the maps was almost certainly not THE Brocéliande.

She insisted that the real site was in the Parc Naturel Régional du Haut-Jura. That sparked further acrimonious debate about the sources that pointed to that location for Brocéliande. Finally, Wendt dismissed the committee with thanks.

The B team reported on what they'd discovered about traveling among aliens. Their report was much more entertaining and not nearly so unpleasant to listen to.

The three of them had begun by using dis-illusionment charms to render themselves invisible, and then they'd traveled to London to observe the aliens in action. The first thing that they noted was that there was absolutely no use of money—not pounds or euros or US Dollars or even Galleons. At first they thought that it was just an elaborate system of credit but they could find no token that was used to identify who was getting or giving credit. That had been difficult to verify but they had worked hard at it, which will be seen later.

They also eliminated any form of barter. They watched lories pull up to stores and disgorge tons of merchandise with no sign of exchange of credit or trade goods or money. They spent quite a lot of time trying to figure that out. It took hours and hours of standing and watching and listening to transactions, but they finally developed a theory. It was that the aliens had developed a Marxist economic state. Store-keepers merely notified their suppliers of when they needed to replenish a given item, and the supplier set up a shipment. When a Supplier was low on inventory, it informed the manufacturer which in turn setup a line and scheduled "employees" to man shifts to make the quantities needed. When people needed food or clothes or anything, they simply went to the relevant store and loaded up a shopping cart with what they needed/wanted. They "checked out", which just consisted of letting the storekeeper maintain a perpetual inventory so that he could re-supply when necessary. There was no "shrinkage" because you could have whatever you wanted just for asking.

This report had sparked quite a lot of discussion about the system and several protests that it was preposterous on the face of it. Wendt found it fascinating. He worked hard to come up with a reason that it couldn't work, but he was stuck.

The B team continued its report by telling about the one time that they had almost been caught out as non-aliens. They decided after spending several days figuring out the economic system that they needed to try it themselves to see whether they could blend in with the aliens, who all looked indistinguishable from humans to the best of their senses. So, they decided to select one of their number to go into a pub undisguised accompanied by the other two dis-illusioned. They would see how far they could carry on the deception. They'd had quite a hard time choosing the lucky one. Finally they decided to base it on a trial of magic. The one with the best single hex would win. One Auror, Arnold, showed his back-bogey hex—on the other Auror. It was agreed to be pretty good. The next Auror, Bertrand, had a hex that prevented a person from keeping his pants up. No matter how hard you tried, you couldn't keep them up. He demonstrated that on Arnold.

When it was George's turn he used the very simple but effective "Eat Slugs" hex on Arnold AND Bertrand. They begged to be released from it and George wouldn't do it until they agreed that he'd won. They did and admitted that they couldn't believe the effectiveness of the hex.

George revealed, "I got it from my brother Ron. He invented it at Hogwarts on the spot after an extreme provocation. Unfortunately, his wand was not working correctly, and it back-fired on him. My biggest regret at school was that I didn't get to see the effects of that hex. If it weren't for the backfire, I'd have called it truly brilliant!"

George went on telling the story of their adventure.

Since I was the lucky bloak, I got to pick the pub. I chose one that looked like it was expensive. That was silly, of course, because no one was paying for anything. Anyway we went in. I walked up to the bar and ordered an ale.

The barkeep asked me what kind. I didn't know if the aliens had changed names, so I just said, 'Your Best."

The barkeep was a real twit. He insisted that they were all good and there wasn't a best. I said, "OK. Give me what you've got on tap."

The bartender perked up and enthused, "Good choice."

"Yeah, right."

I talked with him a little while standing at the bar and sipping my ale. Then, he said, "Hey, how long have you been on-planet?"

I didn't know what was a reasonable answer, so I said, "Two weeks."

The bartender said, "Hmmm. Then you must have come in on the ship from Antares."

"Sure, sure."

Then the bartender said, "I think you got a little ale on your cheek. Here, let me see." I looked up from my ale, and he nodded and said, "Yeh." Then he took his bar cloth and wiped a spot on my cheek. "That's it."

Suddenly, I got the feeling that I wasn't alone. I slowly turned around and noticed about six gents within a couple of paces and a couple more getting up from their tables. From behind me the bartender said, "Well, just take it easy and this will go fast and painless."

I realized that I'd been found out, so I said, "Just how did you know?"

"That you're a host without a Soul? Oh, I suppose it won't make any difference if I tell you, eh boys?" The "boys" nodded. "It was your eyes. Real Soul eyes have a silver patina where the color is in host eyes. The Soul sends a couple of pseudo-pods up the optic nerve and you see the reflection of light off those."

"I see." And I reached into my right pocket.

One of the "boys" said, "Just don't pull anything out of that pocket but your hands and do it nice and slow."

I shrugged and said, "OK. Whatever you say." But instead, I grasped my wand in my pocket and sub-vocalized the spell, "Petrificus Totalis." The closest of the "boys" dropped paralyzed. The rest had either of two reactions—either they jumped back two paces or they jumped to catch their fallen comrade. I repeated the spell on the ones closest to me. They dropped, and there was real consternation.

Suddenly, somebody behind me said, "Keep, if I were you, I'd put that bottle down nice and easy." I recognized Arnie's voice. Of course, I was pretty darn glad to hear it. Then all three of us felled the few remaining aliens with spells.

Arnie asked, "OK. What now?"

Bertrand said, "Easy, we obliviate." So we did. As soon as all their memories of the last hour were gone we disapparated to Hogwarts grounds. We had a real problem. How could we imitate the silver eyes of the aliens? I remembered how the Boy Genius was a, well, genius. So, we went to consult him.

He pretended to be too busy to talk with us, but we eventually convinced him to take us seriously. Bertrand reminded him that we "looove" practical jokes. Once, we had gotten his attention, he proved why he's called the Boy Genius. He grossed us all out by throwing his head back and put his finger in his eye and pulled it back. He told us to take a close look. On the tip of his finger was what looked like a little tiny glass lens. He explained that it was something called a "contract lens" or something like that. He told us that the lenses could be tinted different colors so that you could look like you had any color eye you wanted.

He asked if we could make duplicates of his contract lenses. We agreed that we could easily, so he had us make a couple of dozen and then he asked, "OK. Do you have a way to tint glass?" His were both clear.

We all looked at each other, and no one had heard of such a thing. That had us stymied, so we decided that we'd have to see if any wizard knew how to do that. We walked the castle and grounds up and down talking to wizards, witches, house elves. We even talked to Goblins. We put signs up in the common rooms. We made announcements. Finally, a wand-maker by the name of. . .

Wendt interrupted and asked, "Olivander?"

George resumed his story.

Well, yes. It was Olivander. He said that he had a spell that could put a coat of metal on the handles of wands for ornamentation. He'd done silver. So we went to work with him. The first try was perfect. The lens was completely covered with silver, and they reflected the light so much that you couldn't see the sun through those lenses. He kept experimenting. We decided that a very thin coat of silver might let some light through and reflect some light as well.

He tried various spells and finally setled on "*Minimum Argentum*". That did seem to create a reflective surface that made the wearer seem to have silver retinas and various shades of gray irises, depending on your true eye color.

With that development we were ready to go back in the field and see if we could fool the aliens. This time, we returned to London but took on a different pub. This time Arnie insisted that he should get the chance at some free beer. We agreed reluctantly, dis-illusioned ourselves, and followed him into the pub. This time things went smoother. The bartender seemed a bit suspicious, but he couldn't find anything wrong with Arnie. Arnie had an ale and they talked about football and the World Cup. The bartender kept staring him in the eyes, but didn't find anything wrong. In the end, Arnie had a second ale. As Arnie was turning to leave the bartender asked him to hold on a minute.

"You have an amazingly well-healed neck considering that you've only been on the planet a couple of weeks."

Arnie turned and shrugged. "I guess I had a good surgeon."

The bartender kept staring at him and said, "I suppose that "no-scar" stuff really has gotten good." Then he turned and said, "Look at mine. It's still visible under good light."

Arnie felt a shiver go down his back and he said, "Yeh. You ought to ask for your money back."

The bartender jerked around, "What did you say?"

Arnie was a cool character; he immediately improvised, "Oh that's a phrase that I found in the memory of my host. I've been trying to find a place to use it."

The bartender gave a good guffaw, "Yes, there are lots of strange ideas and things in their heads. How they ever thought that money was a good idea, I'll never understand."

Arnie laughed too and said, "Hosts do think the funniest things." He turned and said good-bye over his shoulder.

The barkeep asked him to come back soon.

"Oh, I think you may eventually see more of me than you want."

The next place we tried was a drugstore. Brahms had wanted us to pick up contact lens cleaner and some other things for the care of contact lenses. Bertrand got that assignment. He grumbled all the way because he thought he deserved a shot at a bar.

All three of us went in un-disillusioned to that pharmacy. Although it was full of things that nobody recognized, there were lots of descriptive names like "no-sting", "tooth cleanser", "sun-block"--all in nondescript boxes, they had no trouble finding the contact lens kits. They needed lots because there were going to be at least eight or ten people out among the aliens searching for the Sea of Merlin—probably for weeks or even months. The woman at the checkout was not the least suspicious of the large quantities. She talked about how much better the new products were than the old ones and how even the cosmetics were better.

I asked if her host had worked at the pharmacy before the "Soul" arrived. She seemed surprised and said, 'Yes! How did you know?"

"I'm psychic. At least that's what my host used to think."

"Oh, you are such a joker! Do you think you might be back here soon?"

I looked at her and decided that she looked pretty good for a Muggle. Of course, I would be in so much trouble with Anjolina if I so much as smiled at her, that I decided to say, "No, we're from the other side of London. We just wanted to visit this area on a lark."

George finished his story and declared that they were ready to take on the world of "Souls". Arnie and Bertrand were not quite so sanguine, but they agreed that they could hold their own in small groups against the aliens.

Team C had to report that their results weren't so encouraging. They'd had lots of ideas and discarded most of them. They'd finally settled on a "theoretical" spell. That is a spell that theoretically might work to find the Sea of Merlin but that they couldn't do a test with. Wendt and Ron deferred to Minerva.

She explained that it was really Wendt's idea. It had struck him that it was an example of something he called, "Simplicity". She stopped and seemed to be stuck. She said, "Oh, just explain it yourself."

Wendt said, "Well, in Physics there's this idea of Symmetry. That just says that the rules of the universe are symmetrical in several ways. Once is space symmetry. That is, you can look at something happening in an ordinary mirror, and it could have been happening that way if the mirror were a simple window.

"Now, the interesting thing is that another symmetry is time reversal . . ."

Both Minerva and Pam said dully, "Invariance. We know all about that."

Wendt went on, "As I was saying before I was rudely interrupted, Invariance. What that means is that if you could construct a mirror that would reflect along the time axis, the world would still work sensibly as seen through that mirror."

Wendt took a deep breath, "So, maybe the Sea is really a mirror that reflects through time."

Minerva sighed, "So, maybe the Sea of Merlin was basically a glorified mirror and that its function was like a mirror's in that it transformed a view of the world. Ordinary mirrors reverse front for back. The Sea of Merlin transforms a view of the present to a view in the future.

"So, I suggested the spell, *Revellio Speculum.*"

She added that the guys had been too modest. They had tried it on all sorts of mirrors in all sorts of situations, and it had revealed mirrors at a distance of at least a kilometer. It wasn't great, but it was the only thing that they had to offer, so it was probably the best that could be offered.

They then decided that there was nothing preventing them from proceeding with their hunt. McGonagall declared that before they started their hunt, they'd have to formally give their plan to the Minister at Azkaban and get her blessing and any suggestions that she or her advisers had.

George was all for proceeding blessing or no, but his buddies on the B team convinced him that they'd be in a lot of trouble if they just went off on their own.

Le Parc Naturel Regional du Haut-Jura

The B team's goal was to present the plan at an appointment that was for a week later. In the mean time they had busied themselves with preparations. They had decided that they would disguise themselves as hikers out for a camping trip. There was an immediate debate about what kind of equipment to take. Everyone had wanted a typical wizarding tent that could be as large as a six room house inside, while appearing to be a simple tent on the outside.

However, Wendt had argued that they needed to look—on the outside at least—as much like a typical camping party as they could. He had insisted that they obtain all Muggle equipment except for the tent. The packs, canteens, sleeping bags all had to look completely authentic. So, the A team had been appointed to equip the party. That included everything from camping gear to boots, rain gear, cameras, you-name-it. That kept the research people busy. It also gave them a chance to practice hiding in plain sight among the "Souls."

In the mean time the C team worked on getting maps, French-English dictionaries, tour guide information etc. They held little background sessions so that everyone knew why they'd chosen this French Park for hiking and their back-stories.

The B team had been assigned to determine how they were going to get food, water, and other supplies to re-provision the party if the search turned into an endurance test. The B team turned out to have the easiest job. They made contact with the French equivalent of Hogwarts—Beaux Batons Academie. The headmistress, Madame Maxine was more than anxious to help and promised that they could disapparate at any time onto the grounds. They would supply them with excellent food and any emergency equipment they might need. In a pinch, they would even agree to come to the rescue if they got into "ze trouble".

Madame Maxine had even volunteered to come along herself. George had assured her that it wasn't necessary and that such an imposing figure as Madame Maxine cut would work against the party's desire not to attract attention. She reluctantly understood that necessity but wished that she could come along anyway.

So, by the time that the appointment with the Minister of Magic arrived, they were really quite ready to leave on their quest. The meeting at Azkaban started at 9AM. Wendt and Minerva had explained the overall plan at a high level with very little detail. Then the various teams—A, B, and C—explained their preparations and how they were going to parcel the park up into regions to be searched using the *Revellio* spell to try to detect the Sea of Merlin. Each of the regions was assigned to one of the three teams, which would remain together to facilitate the search.

As they approached the end of their presentation, Pam, who had been quite silent throughout looked like she was preparing to speak. When Minerva called for questions, Pam said, "I've got a question."

"Of course."

"Don't you think your party is rather small for this search?"

Minerva looked around. "Well, the truth is that this party is so large that I think it would stretch the credulity of park officials if they noticed us."

"But you have so much territory to cover and one of your teams only has two people. Surely that's risky?"

Minerva was becoming exasperated, "Well, Madame Minster, just how large do you think the party should be?"

She apparently had had this speech prepared because she launched into it with no delay and a great deal of confidence, "I think that each of your teams should have at least one, better two additional members. I suggest that the additional people be Aurors from my staff."

Minerva was clearly close to losing her temper. She took a deep breath and said, "I think that would be dangerous. We've made thorough preparations to disguise our group as aliens. It would take a fair amount of time to train your Aurors and equip them to be part of the team."

Pam leaned back with the confidence of one who holds all the cards. "Oh, I think that we can afford a little extra time to insure that this effort is a success."

Wendt took his life in his hands in trying to interpose himself between these two strong-willed witches. He said, "Madame Minister, I think that both our desires could be met by a fairly easy compromise. I suggest four additional members of the party that should be mutually acceptable to everyone and whom I think that we can incorporate quickly.

"I suggest that the additional members of the party be: Bill Weasley—he has worked for the Goblins of Gringotts and understands them better than anyone other than another Goblin. He's well-known to most of the members of the party. The Auror Longbottom—he's a recent graduate of Hogwarts and is well known to us all. Bill Weasley's wife

Fleur, who is French, and of course, knows the language and local customs well. She's got the blood of the Veela in her, which could stand the party in good stead in confrontations with the local officials. She also graduated from Beaux Batons Academie from which we are getting logistics support. Finally, I suggest a Muggle, Sally Harker, who works at Hogwarts right now in opposing the aliens. She worked with the inventor of the disguise that we use to infiltrate the aliens."

"Disguise? What kind of disguise do you use?"

Wendt explained, "The aliens all have a silver tint to their retina's. Brahms invented a way to make normal wizard or Muggle eyes look like they have that silver tint."

Pam was clearly not completely happy with the suggested list, but it did include one more of her Aurors. If she could talk them into putting one of the Aurors on each team, she'd have the source of inside information that she needed in each of the three teams. So, she reluctantly agreed to the additions.

It was agreed that they would travel to Beaux Batons via floo network that had been made international in this emergency. From there, they would dis-apparate to a location on the perimeter of the park and within a couple of kilometers of the location they'd chosen for their base camp.

Before they could travel, they got the four additional team members together and began a crash training course that included a trip into alien land to run a simulated shopping trip for provisions. There were two teams of three for these excursions—two trainees and a "pro".

Bill had agreed to join the party without any urging. Like the rest of the Weasleys he was ready for a fight against the aliens in whatever form it came, even if it meant giving something of great value to the Goblins.

His wife would follow her husband into whatever hell he chose to go.

Longbottom thought it was going to be fun—a walk in the park.

Finally, though, the Boy Genius balked. He really didn't want Sally to leave the comfort (not to mention safety) of Hogwarts, but finally Wendt convinced him.

When Wendt approached Sally about going on this expedition, she was overjoyed. She wanted to see some action rather than just "hanging around the office just like with the SAS." But she had a condition. She had to be allowed to take along some serious firepower.

It turned out that what Sally meant by serious firepower was a couple of AK47 assault rifles with sniper-scopes and banana clips for extra ammunition. Wendt hadn't believed that they had such weapons.

But Sally just smiled and asked, "You've not seen the Shrieking Shack lately, have you?"

"Well, no." He replied warily. "What's happened to it?"

"Oh, the Boy Genius has done some redecorating with the help of George. It has an arms vault and electronic code that's required to open it. We've got an arsenal that includes hand grenades, a few surface-to-air missiles and even a flame-thrower."

Sally said, "Well, we need to do some practice using these. We need to find someplace remote where we won't bother anyone."

Wendt interjected, "Especially, if we blow our feet off."

Sally just frowned and said, "Be serious."

"OK. I will. Anyway, I know a good place. But it's a fairly long walk from here. We need to find someone to disapparate us there." They took a quick survey of the people they knew. Everyone was busy with something. Finally, Sally suggested drafting a house elf, "They're supposed to be anxious to help, aren't they?"

Wendt was skeptical but agreed that it was worth a try. They made their way down to the kitchens of Hogwarts and were greeted almost immediately by a house elf whom Wendt immediately recognized as Kretur. He greeted them enthusiastically and asked if he could get them a snack.

Sally asked, "Actually, what we could really use is a lift."

"Mistress, what are you meaning, 'a lift'?"

"I mean can you disapparate us somewhere?"

"Of course, Kretur can. Where do you want to go?"

Wendt explained as best he could where the cave was that he had practiced gunnery when he first came to Hogwarts. Kretur nodded as he listened and said, "Kretur can take you close. But you'll have to find the cave for your own."

"Of course." They agreed. Kretur lifted both hands and Wendt and Sally stared at each other.

Wendt asked, "Don't we have to go outside the castle to disapparate?"

Kretur looked puzzled, "Why? Kretur disapparates to Hogsmeade all the time to buy supplies for the kitchen."

Wendt stared at him, "Really? I thought that it was impossible to disapparate within Hogwarts."

Kretur shrugged and said, "Not for house elves."

Sally said, "Well, what are we waiting for."

Then he added, "Oh, yes, we need to go to the Shrieking Shack first to get some things."

They took Kretur's hands and suddenly found themselves outside the Shrieking Shack. Sally went in and brought out the assault rifles and a box of ammo. Their hands full, they then disappeared and re-appeared on a steep hillside. Wendt thanked Kretur and said, "Could you come back to get us in say, two hours." Kretur nodded and took a look around at the bleak landscape. Just before he disapparated he said, "Masters enjoy themselves."

Sally took one of the assault rifles and said, "The first thing is to learn your weapon. I did a little training on this when I was working for the SAS. First, we'll learn to field strip and clean it. When we've gotten fair at that, we'll do some target practice."

They worked at field stripping and cleaning the piece for the whole time they were there. They got Kretur to promise to bring them the next day in the morning. At that session, they brought along a couple of real targets—much better than the makeshift ones that Wendt had used when he was training on the Glok.

They didn't have any ear protection, though. Fortunately they were practicing in the open, which was plenty loud enough. Finally after they could hit the target at 50 yards, which seemed close with the sniper scopes. However, somehow they had only fair success at hitting the target.

Wendt commented at one point, "I don't know how those snipers hit anything from 300 yards." Sally just shrugged. Toward the end of the session, they tried full automatic. It was an experience that caused Sally to comment that she hoped they never had a situation that would tempt them to use full automatic. "I'd have to be so desperate that it would have to be a pretty hideous situation where I didn't care if I hit friend or foe."

They eventually gave up and just sat around for a half hour waiting for Kretur to show up.

The next day, thus armed, they assembled in the exercise yard of the castle. They were going by team and not all the teams were ready at the same time. They looked mostly like a party of serious hikers along with a couple of hard-nosed survivalists. They hoisted their gear onto their backs and marched into the castle and into the fireplace of the Great Hall where there was just room for the dozen of them. They took hands and the next moment they were walking out of the fireplace of the Grande Salle du Beaux Batons Academie.

Fleur had gone ahead to Beaux Batons and was waiting for them. The last team to arrive was the one with Sally. When they arrived and stepped out of the hearth, both Fleur and Hermione exclaimed, almost in unison, "Why is she here?", meaning Sally.

Wendt said laconically, "Well, she's smart. She's hard working. She's brave. She's good in a fight. I'd be happy to have her at my back."

Fleur sneered, "What can zeese woman do in a fight."

Sally laughed and said, "I come 'packing'." And she pulled a large clear plastic bag out of her pack, holding it up proudly as though it were a pair of Guicci shoes.

Fleur said, "And what ees it that you have in zee bag? A collection of spare parts for a telescope?"

Hermione said, "It's an assault rifle of some sort, maybe an AK-47, isn't it."

Sally said, "Right, it's a disassembled Kalashnikov, AK47. It's the weapon of choice for freedom fighters everywhere who have to be far from a supply chain. You can drop it in mud, sand, or snow; pick it up; and be firing within seconds without jams. I can assemble it within 20 seconds and fire 20 accurate rounds per minute."

The men in the group whistled. The women were dismayed.

Madame Maxine was waiting for them with a few of the staff. She had assembled enough food for a real army. They packed as much as they could manage on their backs in their packs, and they were off.

They disapparated to the outside of the park. No one was in sight, so they quickly walked the few kilometers to the base camp site. They set up three tents. Two were fairly large and were strictly for show. The third was smaller on the outside and was the real thing. They had a large camp table set up as the Command Center with a large map of the park spread out. It had already been marked with areas to be covered, the team assigned to each, and hiking routes through each region.

Having the extra personnel was actually useful. It allowed each team to have three people and still leave three people at the base camp to watch it. Each team rotated choosing one of their number to be on the base camp detail. They were also responsible for providing a cooked evening meal.

The first several days were boring or would have been boring if the natural beauties of the park were less impressive. The park contains 1850 sq. km. They had laid out the coverage and figured that one team could cover about 12 square km. per day. So by the time a week had passed, they had covered a little over 10% of the park and were having to disapparate to get to their work areas each day.

$$\triangledown$$

On the eighth day, the rotation had Fleur, Sally and Bertrand watching the camp. The day had been a typical one. They'd picked a remote part of the park for their base camp, so they almost never saw anyone at the base camp, unlike in the field, which fairly frequently included small towns.

It was late in the afternoon, so Sally had decided to fix Bertrand's favorite menu item—fish & chips—for the meal. She was in the kitchen part of the tent, near the back. Fleur was sitting in the sun on a camp chair, sunning and reading. Bertrand had left the camp to get groceries from the store at Beaux Batons—strictly not part of the protocol but understandable since no one had even come within talking distance so far.

This afternoon, there was a visitor. Fleur didn't notice him right away because she was reading intently an article in *Witch Weekly*. As a matter of fact, she didn't notice him until he cleared his throat and said, "Bonjour, Madamoiselle."

Fleur looked up suddenly and said, "Bonjour, Monsieur."

"Comment allez-vous?"

"Je vais bien, eh vous?"

"Moi aussi."

He approached and explained that he was a park ranger and wanted to make sure that all was well in this remote camp-site. Fleur explained that everything was fine. So no assistance was needed. He began to get curious about the three tents. Was their party large?

Fleur explained that there were about a dozen of them. By this time she was beginning to get worried that he would start giving way too much attention to the camp, so she stood up and smiled her best Veela smile. The effect was not quite what she had expected. He became quite friendly, of course, but also much more curious about her, where she was from. He began to make guesses about where she was from based on her accent. "I would bet you are from Provence? Eh?"

Meanwhile inside the tent, Sally was getting seriously worried. She didn't know much French, so she was imagining the worst. She pulled one of the AK47's from the cupboard at the back of the kitchen. She fitted a clip into it and advanced a round into the chamber. Unfortunately, the ranger heard the series of clicks and became more than curious. He insisted on seeing the interior of the tent. Fleur reached into the pocket of her jeans that held her wand and grasped it. She stayed firmly planted in front of the entrance to the tent.

The ranger demanded that she move, but she stood her ground and prepared a spell. The ranger put a hand on her shoulder. Just as she was going to sub-vocalize the spell, she noticed that Bill was walking up the trail. She changed her spell at the last moment to *relashio blouse*. And she screamed. It was with good reason that she did. The spell had extended beyond her blouse and she felt it over her right breast.

Bill came running at that, reaching into his pocket. She shook her head a warning not to, for another park ranger was approaching from another direction. He also ran up.

Fleur shouted, "Leave me alone you brute." She turned toward Bill and said, "He attacked me. I think he was going to rape me."

The other ranger was in earshot by now. He looked from Fleur to the other ranger. He approached Fleur and exclaimed, "Merde! You're wounded!" Blood was seeping out of the wound and turning her blouse crimson. The ranger slung his pack off his back and said, "Please allow me to dress your wound."

Bill, acting the aggrieved husband, angrily shouted, "No way. I'll take care of her. We have first aid kits too."

The new ranger turned to the first one and said, "Renard, what were you thinking? How could you have attacked her?"

The first said, "But, Chacal, I didn't do anything!"

"Silence." Then he turned to Bill and said, "I must offer my profound apologies! I assure you that you will not be troubled again by Renard or indeed by any park officials."

Bill was being hard-nosed, "Well, I should think so. I don't like to make trouble, but if there were any repeat of this unforgivable incident, I'd certainly have to complain to the park authorities and perhaps to Paris."

"Of course, I understand, parfaitment. You shall have no fear of a repeat of our troubling you."

Bill, acting the gracious guest, said, "That's fine. Let's just all forget that it ever happened. I'm sure that this was probably just a misunderstanding." By this time several others of the party were approaching the clearing where they were camped.

The rangers made a hasty retreat. When Wendt and his team arrived, he found Bill finishing dressing the wound. He was saying, "With Ditani and good dressing, there will probably not be a scar that anyone could see."

Minerva asked, "I suppose there's an interesting story behind this?"

Bill shook his head toward Fleur who said, "Oh, everything is OK, but it got kind of. . uh . . how do you say it in anglais, 'ticklish?'. I'll tell you about it over dinner when we're all here. I don't want to have to tell it more than once."

Sally left the tent, still holding the assault rifle. Fleur looked at it with disgust and said, "You nearly got us found out, playing with that silly asinine rifle thing."

Sally just looked her in the eyes and said, "If this had turned ugly, you'd be glad that I was there with the Kalyshnikov". Then she unloaded the clip and the chamber and put it down just inside the door flap of the tent. Minerva frowned at her and said, "Not in the living room, you don't." So she carried it back to the cupboard of the kitchen.

By this time, the rest of the teams had arrived, and they began setting up for dinner. The big table could accommodate eight comfortably. This night all twelve sat around the table crowded together to hear Fleur's story as they ate. When it finished, Wendt went to another topic.

"As long as we're all here together, I'd like to talk about the rest of our mission here. We've surveyed all the land near our base camp. It seems to me that we should change the priority of our search. The higher altitude areas near the Swiss border seem like more likely places to find the Sea. What do you think?"

The debate was not very lively. Most of the teams were getting disheartened by not having any signs of success so far. Most didn't really care. The view was summarized by Robert who said, "I've said all along that we won't find it here. It doesn't matter where we search next. I just want to get this finished and then move on to better fields."

So, they did change priorities, and the next day teams went off with their new assignments.

Le Lac des Rousses

Several days passed, and the search fell back into the normal round of rising, breakfast, finding the assignments for the day, and off into the park. They usually came back to the base camp for lunch, since they could disapparate quickly there. That was especially safe now that the rangers were staying well clear of their camp. Then they returned and resumed the search for the rest of the afternoon.

One day, Wendt drew camp duty along with Hermione and Longbottom. They were all working on making sandwiches for lunch when Wendt suddenly said, "Sacre bleu. Do you realize how unusual today is?" The other two looked at each other.

Hermione said, "I don't have the vaguest. What about you Neville?"

Neville shrugged and said, "It's nearly been a month since we started the search, but I don't think it's the one month anniversary or the 4 week anniversary. You've got me."

Wendt said, "Come on! Think about the three of us."

Hermione said, "Well, let's see. We're not all one sex. We're not all former Hogwarts students. We're not all . . uh . . . I don't know. What?"

"This is the first time that all three of the Camp crew have been Hogwarts people who were actually together at the same time at Hogwarts."

Hermione said, "Yes, I think you're right. Interesting coincidence. But you know, even though we were all together at Hogwarts for—how long was it 6 years?"

Wendt answered, "Yes, six years. I was there before you and Longbottom arrived."

"Well, then, six years. In all that time, I think the three of us were never together in a class."

Longbottom said, "That's for sure. I was never in a class of yours, Professor Wendt. How was that anyway? And were you ever in one of Professor Wendts's classes?"

Hermione said, "Yes, I was in one class—in 3rd year. The only reason I was in that class was that I was using a Time Turner to attend extra classes. But why didn't our year ever have any classes with you, Professor Wendt?"

'Oh, it wasn't supposed to be that way. Professor Dumbledore had a grand plan when I was hired. Everyone was going to get two years of English literature during their career at Hogwarts. I couldn't start with a full course load right away because every course was absolutely new and I had to have extra time to do the planning.

"He gave priority to the upper classes because they only had a couple of years to get their classes in, so your classes were left till later. Then, a couple of things happened, of course. One was that I was fired at the beginning of what would have been your seventh year. At the time, Snape strongly recommended it as did Professor McGonagall. He said he was pretty sure that even wizards with Muggle sympathies would have a hard time from then on at Hogwarts. It went without saying that Muggles themselves at Hogwarts would be fired, at best. So, I didn't have much choice.

"The other thing that happened was that the year before Umbrage had tremendous influence at Hogwarts. A rather little known decree, the very first, that was never published was that there would only be one year of English Literature at Hogwarts. That year I had to choose between your class and the seventh years for that one class. I chose the seventh years and intended to do your class later. Of course that year never came.

"Hermione, I always wondered why you chose to take the course that third year of yours. It was intended to be a fourth or fifth year course."

Hermione turned red and then looked from Longbottom back to Wendt. She finally said, "Well, do you promise never to tell anyone? You too, Neville."

They both did.

She went on, 'Well, you may not know it, but among the girls at Hogwarts those years, you were considered quite exotic. I mean, you were a Muggle for heavens sake. No Muggle had ever taught at Hogwarts. And it was known that your class included poetry. You were quite young. And, well," here she blushed even more, 'Everyone knew about the 'secret' affair that you were having with Professor McGonagall. Everyone wanted in your classes.

"I think some girls were offended that you had chosen such an," here she coughed and resumed, "old lover. They hoped to upstage

Professor McGonagall by. . . by making you forget Professor McGonagall."

Wendt laughed and said, "I'd no idea that any of that was going on. Were you one of the girls who hoped to turn my head?"

Hermione flushed an even brighter shade of red, "Of course not, Professor. I just wanted to see what all the excitement was about—who it was who had turned the head of an old confirmed spinster like Professor Mcgonagall." Then she added after a moment's reflection, "And, really, I was anxious to study at least one or two non-magical courses."

Longbottom guffawed and said, "Sure, Hermione. You can put that in a bottle and sell it for horse . . ."

▽

The afternoon wore on in the field. Wendt's team was assigned to the area around the Lac des Rousses. The lake was a place of special interest to McGonagall because there were stories that it was THE lake of The Lady of the Lake. Her team was scanning the lake from the shores. It was narrow enough that it was feasible to do that without actually going out on the lake.

The afternoon had almost finished. The other two had been working the East side of the lake. With the sun nearing the horizon, they disapparated over and suggested that they call it a day and come back tomorrow.

Minerva said, "Sorry, I've picked up a pebble in my boot, I think. You two go ahead, and I'll just sit here and get it out before I head back to the camp."

They agreed and disappeared. Minerva found a relatively dry rock large enough to sit on and took off her boot and began searching for the tiny pebble that had been driving her crazy. Before she found it, she noticed a flash of light out of the corner of her eye. She looked up and found that there was a bright reflection of the setting sun coming from the hills on the east side of the lake, probably from the Swiss side of the border. There were no buildings or roads there. That excited her curiosity.

Without finishing removing the pebble, she stood up and disapparated to a spot close to the light. When she got there, she couldn't see anything that could be reflecting light. So, she lifted her wand—and for the fun of it—used the spell. Almost immediately, there was a flash of light coming from fairly close. She walked there and found a small cave opening. It was mostly overgrown, and she marveled that she had been able to see the flash from the other side of the lake. The sun must have lined up that way only once or twice a year to be visible from where she was sitting working on her boot.

She cautiously worked her way into the cave mouth. Once she was in, she could see the object that had reflected light. It was a silver shield of some sort. She could sense that the main cave was much larger than it appeared from outside. She lit her wand and had to brighten it twice to see anything of the cave walls.

She noticed a slight shimmer in a corner of the vast cavern. She walked toward the shimmer and as she approached it disappeared. She stopped and lifted her wand. She silently spoke the incantation, "*Revellio speculum.*"

The shimmer reappeared and then it resolved into a large flat basin. It appeared to be made of bronze. It rested on a large stone plinth. She was amazed that the spell worked. Then she had a decision to make. Call the rest to help evaluate the find? Or not and evaluate it herself?

She was damned if she was going to raise a false alarm. She lifted her wand shakily and walked to the plynth. She looked down into the empty bowl. The Legends said that ordinary water was all that was needed.

The incantation *aguamente* filled the bowl with water. The surface quickly settled to a smooth still mirror. Minerva stepped to the very edge of the mirror. She hesitated to look directly down into the bowl. Finally, she let herself gaze into the mirror.

The image that formed before her eyes took her breathe away. Her heart rose into her throat. She was afraid that she would not be able to speak. For, before her eyes, her reflection resolved itself and revealed an event that clearly hadn't happened yet.

There was no question. She had to call the others. The coin in her purse could be used to summon all those with matching coins. She pulled out the galleon and touched it with her wand. It glowed briefly. She only had to wait for the others to come to her.

They did. The first was Bill Weasley. He asked her, "Do you think you've found it?"

"I know I have." Just then the rest showed up. Wendt walked up to her and took her hand. "What's up?"

Minerva's heart leapt for joy. She couldn't speak for a moment. She did her best to clear her throat and finally said, "I tried it. It works."

He exclaimed, "Great! What did you see?"

Minerva flushed red. "None of your business." and then she immediately added, "I almost thought I had the mirror of Arisset."

He only said, "Hmmmm."

George asked if they could disapparate it directly back to Beaux Baton without going via their base camp. After some discussion, they decided to do that. First, Minerva removed the water. So they all took the Mirror in one hand and the hand of the next person with the other. George said "On the count of three . . . ."

They appeared out of nowhere at the gates of Beaux Baton. Wendt fell on his knees and held his head. The rest staggered before regaining their equilibrium. Wendt muttered, "I hate disapparation."

Everyone helped move the mirror to the Grande Salle. It was almost too large to take into the great hearth, but it fit along with a few wizards to send it through the floo network. Again, at Hogwarts, it was only just small enough to carry through the hearth. Then they went to the Three Broomsticks to unwind.

The next day, Minerva joined Wendt at breakfast and took his hand in hers and simply said, "After this is over we will talk."

He nodded and said, "D'accorde."

They finished breakfast and then walked to the fireplace in the Great Hall. They walked into it as she threw down floo powder and said, "Azkaban."

They walked out of the fireplace, went through Security and called for the Minister. Pam showed up in a couple of minutes and, biting her lip, said "Well?"

Wendt only said, "Is the delegation from the Goblins still here?"

Pam gave a tiny scream and, covering her mouth with her hands, said, "You did it!"

"Yes, we did."

Pam said, "Yes they are! Let's go to their suite." And they did. They knocked on the door and waited as sounds of laughter drifted from the room.

Glorblatt himself answered the door. "Well?"

Wendt asked, "Where do you want it delivered?"

Glorbatt seemed confused. He shook his head and asked, "What? I didn't call for room service."

"Why, the Sea of Merlin, of course."

Glorblatt's mouth opened and closed convulsively as though he wanted to say something but couldn't. He looked back to his fellow delegates from the Goblins to see if they'd heard the conversation. They apparently hadn't. They were still laughing and joking. He turned back to the trio, a determined look on his face, and said, "Show me. I want to see it work before I do anything."

Wendt said, "Certainly! Come with us." They walked back to the great fireplace that was the main access to Azkaban now. They all walked into the fireplace, took hands, and disappeared. They walked out of the fireplace in the Great Hall. On the raised stage at the end of the hall was a makeshift plinth with the Mirror atop it. Glorblatt looked at it with a dazed gaze on his face. In the full light of day, it was easy to see the only ornamentation on the great saucer – the constellations of the zodiac laid out around the rim. He stepped toward it hesitantly.

Glorblatt looked at Wendt and asked, "How do you activate it?"

Wendt looked to Minerva and said, "Professor McGonagall is the only one to have actually used it. How did you do it?"

She blushed and said, "I just filled it with water and gazed into it. I can fill it with water and let you look." Glorblatt nodded and she filled the basin with water, being careful not to look into it.

Glorblatt looked around and requested a chair to stand on so that he could get a good look inside. Wendt brought a chair and offered to help Glorblatt up, who refused and struggled up on his own. He gazed down into the Sea and suddenly jumped off the chair. He dropped to the ground, sat against the chair and screamed, "Remove the water." He sat breathing heavily, almost in danger of hyperventilating.

He said, "All right, all right! It's the Sea. We'll do anything you want to defeat the aliens. Do whatever you want   Only, the things I see in the Sea, are they sure to happen or can you change the future?"

Minerva sighed and said, "I hope not." She seemed to come to herself and said, "Oh, I see. You mean the things you saw. Are they sure to happen?"

"Yes, yes. What about them?"

"Oh, the legends say that these are only the reflection of things that might be—if you don't do something to change them."

Glorblatt released his breath held for some time and stood. "Yes, I'm satisfied. That is the Sea. Only, only, I didn't really believe that the Sea existed – that it was only a legend. How did you find it?"

Wendt laughed and said, "I told you that we don't reveal our secrets. Now, back to my original question – where do you want it delivered?"

"I'll have to confer with the delegation."

The Minister said, "You weren't kidding that you didn't believe that it existed. You didn't think that we'd find it. What would you have done had we admitted failure?"

Glorblatt regained some of his composure. "We don't reveal our secrets either. Take me back to Azkaban, and we'll decide." The minister and Glorblatt walked to the fireplace, entered it, and disappeared.

Minerva smiled and said, "Is it time for lunch?"

As a matter of fact it was almost, so she and Wendt just stayed in the Great Hall at the head table. They discussed the next steps they had. They had been so consumed by searching for the Sea that they had lost track of what was happening at Hogwarts. Shortly, place settings, carafes of coffee, tea and water and platters of sandwiches and vegetables appeared on the tables and people started showing up for lunch.

Wendt asked Minerva, "You were saying something about wanting to talk to me about something. How about now?"

"Oh, this is not quite the right place and . . . " But she was interrupted by someone who had approached Wendt from behind.

He pulled up a chair next to him and said, "Jim, good luck running into you. I've got something I have to talk to you about."

Minerva nodded. Wendt turned to discover the Boy Genius. He dove right into his topic as he picked up a sandwich with one hand and a handful of raw vegetables with the other. "I've been trying to get hold of you for days. You've got to come see the Control Room we've put together. There's lots of stuff going on, and we need help."

"Well I think I've got time this afternoon. I'd be glad to take a look at whatever you're peddling."

"This is serious stuff. Hurry up and eat, and we can head right out to the office."

Minerva laughed and said, "We'll take up my question later. It will wait. It's waited for years already."

Wendt looked at her quizzically but said nothing. Brahms was dragging him away and urging him to more speed. They left the Great Hall, went out the Main Door, walked down the lane, apparently toward Hogsmeade. Wendt asked, "Where the heck are we going? To Hogsmeade?"

"No. Just be patient." He virtually broke into a run. They went through Hogsmeade and kept going. Then Wendt realized where they were going. They went down the lane toward the Shrieking Shack.

Wendt asked, "We're going to the shrieking shack, right?"

Brahms said nothing, but they left the lane at the shrieking shack and walked up the overgrown walk that led to the Shack. They arrived at the Shack, and Wendt knocked on the door. A voice asked, "Who goes there?"

Brahms said impatiently, "You know perfectly where who it is. You recognize Wendt. Let us in." The door opened inwardly, and they crossed the threshold. On the other side, there was a completely unexpected interior. It had shining hard-wood floors, dark wood-paneled halls. There were electric lights, for goodness sake! Behind them, the guard, whom he remembered from the Great War, touched his hand to his helmet in a non-salute that they had used with him in the old days when he'd not really had a rank. He returned it and noticed that the guard was brandishing an M-14 with telescopic sight.

He commented to Brahms about the changes to the interior. Brahms shrugged and said, "Well, you couldn't have us falling through the floors with the heavy equipment that we brought in."

Wendt exclaimed, "Heavy equipment? I've not seen any yet."

Brahms opened a heavy mahogany door and said, "Come on in." Inside, the lighting was subdued and for good reason. There were dozens of monitors on the walls, and there were thick cables that snaked away into the next room. There were at least a dozen men sitting at monitors and keyboards. The screens on the walls showed mostly boring scenes. Most were rooms that had no occupants. The rest were outside scenes in some large city. Wendt supposed it was London, although the only one that he could identify for sure was one that watched the old department store under which the Ministry of Magic used to reside. The men mostly seemed to be reviewing documents that were displayed on the smaller screens at their desks.

Wendt's first question was spoken in a voice that betrayed wonder. "How did you get all this electronics to work here, and why are you in the Shrieking Shack. Surely there're better places that you could work?"

"No, we had to be far away from magic, and we could have built a building elsewhere, I thought it would be better to use existing buildings to make it less obvious which has new functions."

"And electricity?"

"Oh, that was sweet. I went off reconnoitering with some wizards. Let me see, Mr. Weasley was one of them. We found a warehouse where the aliens have some sweet equipment – like fuels cells that run on propane gas. We lifted a couple of hundred canisters of propane, some inverters to give us alternating power, and a few other things."

Wendt laughed. "What about the data feeds and cameras?"

"Oh, the aliens believe in efficiency. They don't rebuild things that already exist and work. They have a network of security cameras that are practically everywhere." Here the Boy Genius laughed so hard that he could hardly breathe. When he finally spoke he was still gasping and wheezing.

"They still use our old network of security cameras. They didn't change any of the software – or security. We walked right in and have been monitoring their entire security cam network. Our biggest problem is just finding the interesting cameras – like the cameras in their central Administration Building for the entire planet." He broke out laughing again, and this time had a really hard time recovering. He finally did and went on. "We can show you recordings of all their critical meetings. They really do trust that once they win a planet, they completely own it.

"Our hardest problem was finding a way to connect to their network and feed it here to our Control Center. We ended up stealing a couple of dozen kilometers of fiber optics cable and using it to connect our data center to their network. We had to break into a network hub nearby and hand-connect the cable to a port on one of their super-routers. We buried the cable except for the last few feet, where we went above ground to the wall of their building. We drilled a hole in the building, disapparated in and made the connection."

Wendt was incredulous, "Surely that much fibre optic cable must have been in dozens of huge spindles?"

"No, it all came on one spindle that a single man could carry. They really have good tech. Anyway, once we got connected, we were hyper-careful for several days and just listened. We didn't try to insert any traffic ourselves. It was unnecessary. They seem to believe in security by ignorance. Since they were using our system, we already had the codes. We use their processors to crunch the billions of video feeds and select out what we're looking for. If it hadn't been for them, we couldn't possibly put enough servers in to do that work. Even at that, we've had to put in a couple of hundred of their high-powered servers in the next room.

The Boy Genius sat down at an empty console. He pulled up another chair and motioned to Wendt to join him. Wendt sat and Brahms selected a file name. One of the screens started showing a new video. There were sounds of a door opening and people walking into the room. The people began to appear on the screen. They sat and one spoke.

"This is the first meeting of the Emergency Committee to Save New Algol. We have a chair who was able to save another world. Please meet Frank."

There was polite applause, and Frank stood. He looked around the room.. He said, "I've reviewed what's happened that isn't exactly normal. Besides the incidents that you've identified there are 50 deaths that can't be explained."

Someone spoke from the end of the table, "J looked at those cases. None were under suspicious circumstances."

Frank answered, "They were all suspicious. None were explained,

"We're going to treat all deaths as suspicious until proved otherwise." There was a collective sigh of resignation. "The ones that are not proved normal we start to analyze. We look for patterns. Where are they concentrated?"

"What do you hope to find—some hidden fortress?" asked somebody else nervously.

"Exactly."

Brahms said, "What do you think?"

"They've got the right man. . . er. . . alien for this job. We've got to keep an eye on him. Do we have an *eye* in his office?"

"Not yet. We've been trying to find it. I expect to find it soon."

"Do it. Now."

Brahms punched up another video. It showed another of the aliens from the meeting. He was in his office. The video was nearly silent except for a phone call from the alien called Frank.

Wendt said, "Keep up the good work."

That night he was in his office/quarters in Hogwarts. He had gotten in bed and turned out the lights. He'd lain down in bed and was just thinking of all the events of the day when there was a "pop" and he knew someone was in the room. He reached under his pillow and pulled his Glok out silently (he hoped). Suddenly there was a blaze of light. He swung the gun toward the source of the light, ready to fire. He almost did shoot, and then he recognized the figure.

"God damn it, Minerva! Don't you ever knock? I thought no one could disapparate in Hogwarts."

"Being Headmistress, I have certain little privileges. I didn't want anyone else to know my little secret."

"What about me?"

"Oh, you're special." she walked to his bed and sat on the edge. "I'll show you how special a little later. Those were the last words spoken in the room that night.

The next day, Wendt and Minerva were summoned to a meeting at Azkaban. The meeting turned out to be only the Minister, the Head of the Auror Office, and them. Pam started the meeting, "I don't know what Glorblatt saw in the Sea, but the Goblins have become downright accommodating. Have you got an explanation?"

Minerva said, "I think that he saw something in his personal future that had to do with the aliens, and he wants to avoid it at all costs." She hesitated and added, "When I looked into it, I saw something in my future that I want to happen at all costs."

Pam said, "I wanted a look into that thing, but now I'm not so sure. One sees something that scares him to death, and another sees something that makes her blithely happy. Well, let's just take our good luck as we find it. But, now that we've got the Goblins lined up on our side, we've not really got a next step. I guess that we've been so determined to line up the Goblins that we've not been thinking. What should we be doing?"

Wendt said, "We've got to have an overall plan for where we want to get and how we'll get there. I'd suggest a three stage approach:
- Consolidate our gains: Make sure that every wizard, Goblin and other intelligent magical creature is safe.
- Convince the aliens that they'd rather be anywhere other than here.

- Offer them a deal to let them leave that returns as many people to real life as we can manage."

Pam chuckled, "That simple, eh? Just how do you propose to do the convincing?"

Minerva said, "We demonstrate our power. They can't very well defend themselves from us, can they? They don't even know what they have to defend themselves from."

Wendt stroked Minerva's leg with his left foot under the table but said, "Right. I'd suggest embarrassing them on their own TV network. We take over the main news network based in London and run the show for ten or fifteen minutes. Demand negotiations for them to leave. Set an unreasonable date and then we're "forced' to take some punitive action that can't be denied or ignored."

The Auror Shacklebolt asked, "Just what kind of punitive action do you propose?"

"Something big but that won't cause many injuries or deaths. Something like shutting down a spaceport for a day. Maybe New Heathrow."

Wendt rubbed his hands together and said, "Immobilize their control system. Electronics can be easily sabotaged by the very presence of magic."

A few days later, Minerva and Wendt were in his office "after hours" – as a matter of fact about 11PM. He was getting "comfortable" with Minerva when the door burst open. It was Brahms. He strode in to the room a smile beaming on his face. He seemed not to notice what they'd been doing. Instead he walked to the center of the room and said, "Wendt, you've got to come right away. I've got something that you really need to see RIGHT NOW."

Minerva cleared her throat, and Brahms seemed to take notice of her for the first time. He said, "Oh, Ms. McGonagall. Sorry, you're invited too, of course."

Wendt grumbled and stood up, "It's got to be right now?"

"Oh, yes. It's really important."

"OK. I'll be down," he hesitated as he saw the look on Minerva's face, "That is, we'll be down in a few minutes. It's at the Shack, I suppose."

Brahms nodded and ran out of the room.

Minerva asked, "I suppose that's the Shrieking Shack." Wendt nodded, and she went on. "I'd heard that there was a lot of activity there, but I'd always been too busy to investigate. I suppose your Mugglc pals have done something disgusting to it."

Wendt chuckled to himself, "Well, I suppose it depends on what you mean by disgusting. Let's just go down, and you can judge for yourself."

She agreed. They put on robes and hat since it was fairly cold out that night. It was a long walk down to the Shack. What with the cool night air they felt justified to walk quite close, and Wendt had his arm around Minerva's waist. A nearly full moon was out so they didn't need wand-light to get to the Shack. This time the guard recognized them both, and they walked in directly without having to give any proof of ID.

When the door opened, Minerva was surprised by how bright the interior was and especially by the conversion of the interior to a luxurious form. She said, "Well, this is not exactly what I was expecting, but it's hard to complain about the tastes of the designer."

Brahms was waiting for them and practically sprinted up to the Main Control Room. They entered, and Minerva gasped. She'd seen TV's before, but she'd not seen anything like a wall of flat-screen monitors. "What in the world is this?"

Brahms was modest. "We've got video feeds from almost every video camera in the realm. We can see what's going on in almost any alien office that you could name. For example, the center screen at the top is the office of *Frank*." The way that he said it, you'd think that it was italicized.

Minerva said, "Frank?"

Brahms apologized, "Oh, yes. You probably haven't heard who *Frank* is." Again there was the italicization. "We learned the name of the head of the alien group that's trying to put us out of business."

Wendt was properly impressed. "You actually can see and hear everything that he does, says, hears and sees every day in his office."

"Oh, yes, we can. It's pretty amazing what we've learned already."

Minerva interrupted him. "You can't tell me that the most powerful alien in the world is somebody named 'Frank'?"

"He sure is. You have to understand about their names." And he explained that the aliens lived extremely long lives and typically inhabited several "hosts" during their lives. Usually, after a host died under them, they moved on to a new world to get a new host. Rarely did aliens stay on a world and inhabit more than one host there.

Minerva interrupted again, "What's that got to do with names?"

"Aliens normally take their name from the first host that they have. For, example, there's a planet close to here that a lot of our aliens come from. This planet, believe it or not, has an intelligent life form that is a plant. So, they all have names like Sunny, Early Bloomer, and stuff like that."

Wendt asked, "Surely, he's not a first generation on this planet. They wouldn't pick someone who's less than a year old to head up this post?"

Brahms answered, "Frank's original host was known for honesty – on some other planet. So he had a nickname that means something like that in English. I think Frank chose Frank, because it represents his real name and is a human sort of name."

Wendt was feeling that he liked this guy less and less the more that he knew him. He was obviously smart and had probably done something like this before. If he liked to identify with the hosts, then he was more likely to be able to understand them and their culture – their strengths and weaknesses.

Brahms was continuing with his talk, "I'm going to show you the video from a little while ago. Pay close attention. There's lots going on."

Brahms queued up the video. It started with Frank sitting at his desk, reading some sort of report. The first sound they heard was a knock on the door. Frank had him enter. He was carrying an IPad and something that was pretty small that might have been a miniature projector. He immediately sat and started talking.

"I see that you've got my paper report. Have you finished it?"

"Yes I was reading it a second time. Why don't you give me the executive summary?"

"Right. Well, you were right. The statistics of the unexplainable deaths are pretty amazing. Let me show you with graphics." He turned on the mini-projector and it focused itself on the whiteboard behind Frank's desk. The visitor opened a PowerPoint presentation. The first slide was a graph.

"You see the horizontal axis is distance in kilometers from the centers of the phenomenon that we deduced. The vertical axis is the ratio of the actual rate of these deaths divided by the expected rate, assuming that they are randomly distributed, taking into account population density and a couple of other minor factors.

"When we take the original list of unexplained deaths, we get this plot, which is pretty amazing in itself. The peak probability ratio is over 100. But we did some extra analysis. We went looking for deaths that were peculiar, but where autopsies hadn't been done. When we threw in those additional deaths, the peak is over 500. That's so unlikely that we should never have seen this by chance in the whole history of the universe.

Frank stared at the plots and then slowly asked, as if trying to work out the probabilities in his head, "What about all deaths whether explained, strange or unexplained? Are the statistics anywhere near this strange for those?"

The visitor nodded, "We thought of that. As a matter of fact we have a graph of that somewhere. I think it's in the appendix." He moved swiftly through the slides and found a graph that was nearly flat – as unlike the earlier one as could be imagined. "Look here, all deaths has only a small bump near the zero point."

"OK. You've sold me. There's something very strange going on here. Just where is here?"

The visitor switched to a web browser, showing the earth. There were a large number of yellow dots spread around the globe. "The dots are the locations of these centers of strange deaths."

Frank got up to the projection and pointed at a dot in the south of England. "Where is this one?"

"Interesting isn't it? It's the third largest center. I'll show you where it is." The area covered by the projection zeroed in on the south of England quickly.

Wendt stared and said, "That's Google Earth that he's using, isn't it?"

Brahms said, "You bet. They aren't shy about using home-grown apps."

The visitor had started talking again, "Actually, the site is within London, not more than 20 kilometers from this office."

Brahms beamed his smile again and said, "We just learned where their headquarters are. They're at the center of that map." Wendt whistled appreciatively.

The visitor was talking again, "We can't zoom in much closer than this."

Frank's head snapped around and he asked, "Why not? I know that Google has much higher resolution images than this."

"That's the rub, isn't it? We don't know why not."

Frank walked over to the IPad and took over control. He tried to zoom closer but quickly, he got an error message that the database didn't have higher resolution images. He asked, "What the hell is this?"

"We don't know and frankly, Google doesn't know either. We've spent a lot of time in video conferences with them. They're more mystified than we are."

Frank seemed to ask the room in general or maybe it was the universe, "Has the world gone crazy!"

Minerva laughed out loud. "Is that your doing, Brahms? The Boy Genius, indeed!"

The Boy Genius shrugged and said, "Not mine. I wish I could claim it, but I can't. I was thinking that it was maybe your doing."

Wendt asked, "Just where is that location, do you know?"

Brahms said, "We've been trying to figure out ourselves. It seems to be a department store."

Wendt finished for him, "A department store that's been under renovation for a very long time."

"Well, yes. How did you know?"

Minerva answered, "It's the location of the Old Ministry of Magic." Meanwhile the conversation was still going on in the video.

Frank was saying, "Well, what did you and Google try?"

"They searched backup servers for better resolution images. They couldn't find any. Then, they tried requesting new images. They all ended up being low-res images. We spent a whole day with them trying to get those hi-res images."

Frank was now pacing the room. Finally he looked at his visitor and asked, "OK, what else did you try?"

The visitor became more animated, seemingly warming to what he had to say. He seemed to want to prove that he'd tried every conceivable way to get what Frank wanted. He stood up himself and paced in a small circle. "Somebody had the idea of looking up maps in tourist guides to the city. The first thing that we tried was going to a large book store and getting a tourist guide."

Frank asked impatiently, "And?"

"And we almost didn't find out."

"What are you talking about? How could you 'almost not find out'?" Frank had stopped pacing.

"Well, we'd try to find the page that showed that part of London, and we couldn't seem to find the page."

'You mean the book was missing that page?"

"No, it wasn't that the page was missing; we just couldn't find it for the longest time."

Frank sat down again and leaned back, "OK. I know that you're sane. I know that you're making sense. I just have to figure out what the sense is. Keep going, and I'll try not to interrupt too often."

The visitor was patient. He went on, "Well, we kept trying and eventually, I was actually able to open to the correct page. What we found there was a map that looked like it had been smudged at one point—approximately right where the center of these unexplained deaths was.

It was clear that Frank wanted to say something, but he sat there licking his lips and trying to look away at the window to the side. The visitor went on, "We ended up getting all the copies of that book in the store, thinking that some wouldn't be smudged on that page. They all were.

"Then we tried other tour books and even other bookstores—all the same."

Frank finally couldn't hold his questions in, "Do you have a copy that I can see."

"Sure, I anticipated that." He pulled a small pocket book out of his left hip pocket. He handed it to Frank, who anxiously thumbed through it.

"Look, you were wrong about this copy. The page is missing."

"Look more carefully."

Frank thumbed slower through the book and shook his head in bewilderment. Then he arduously turned one page at a time, carefully inspecting the page numbers. Finally, he stopped. "It's here. And you're right. It is smudged. Why was it so hard to find that page?"

"I've absolutely no idea, do you?"

"No."

Frank said, "Well, you surely thought of other things to try. Why didn't you. . . " But he was interrupted by his visitor.

"Why didn't we just go down to the street and see what we saw? Maybe take a camera along?"

Frank twisted his face so that he was looking at the visitor with one eye only. As if that one eye could see more clearly than two, "This is a trick question isn't it. It should be obvious to me why you didn't, right?"

"It's no trick question. What's your idea about why we didn't do that?"

"I don't know. Maybe you were afraid of what you'd find if you went in person?" Frank said uncertainly—one of the few times that he answered a question uncertainly.

"Good guess. I think that was part of it, but it wasn't the main part. The main thing was that we couldn't remember for the longest time."

"You couldn't remember! How could you not remember? I don't have any trouble remembering."

The visitor pursed his lips as he considered how to answer, "Well, perhaps that isn't perfectly accurate. It's probably better to say that we seemed to think that we had so many other really important things to do that it slipped our mind almost as soon as we thought of it."

Frank thought about this answer and mentally decided again to allow the visitor more time to amplify.

The visitor finally commented, "You see, it's really strange. You can think about it as long as you have no intention of doing something, but as soon as you do, it becomes a different matter. The only way for you to understand is for you to actually try to go visit it. Let's take a walk down there."

Frank asked, "You mean right now?"

"Of course, right now. It'll give us a good appetite for lunch."

Frank stood up as though he were ready for a brisk walk, but he stopped and seemed to be in deep thought. He said, "We'd better bring a camera." He picked up the phone and said into it, "Connect me with the Equipment Room." There was a pause, "Yes, this is Frank. I want a good still camera. Wait, wait, no make that a video camera. Yes, easily portable. Yes, send it up immediately. Thanks." Then he turned to the visitor, "They'll be up very shortly and then we'll leave."

They waited and the messenger came with the camera. He handed it to Frank and said, "It practically works itself, just push the red button to record. There's pause and rewind. The controls are standard. It's auto-focus, auto exposure—everything except auto compose. Have fun." The messenger got headed for the door but as he was leaving, Frank suddenly said,

"Wait, would you mind sticking around while I practice with it. I don't want to lose the chance to video what I'm going to see." So Frank filmed the messenger and the visitor and then played it back, filmed some more and reviewed it. He erased some and recorded over that section. He was about to do some complex editing with it. The messenger was begging to be released to go back to his desk.

Finally, the visitor said, "You see what I mean? It's really hard to actually get going to see that site."

Frank was still fascinated with the camera and suddenly seemed to come to himself. "I guess so. You know, I was so absorbed by playing with that camera that I'd forgotten completely about going for a walk." He sat down and said, "It's crazy. I'm crazy. I can't believe that I couldn't do a simple thing like taking a walk. So what do we do?"

The Beat Goes On

Frank sat and thought. "Well, let's get hold of local law enforcement and get them to send a patrol in, Mickey."

Mickey shrugged and said, "I'm on it, but I don't think that they'll have any more luck than we do."

The next day Mickey met with a commander in the Metro Police Service. The commander thought it was a lot of time wasted, "We've not had a problem in that area in—well, since before we came. That's the last place that I think you'll find a band of rebel hosts."

Mickey answered, "Look, this isn't just me asking for a little help, I'm speaking for the Head of the Emergency Defense Org. We'll send in troops if we have to, but we'd prefer to use local forces that are familiar with the terrain."

The commander snorted but said, "Of course. I'll have the local Bobbies drive through the neighborhood of that department store a couple of times a night for the next few nights."

"I'd appreciate that. And, do you mind if they go in with helmet cameras so that we can watch them live?"

The commander eyed Mickey as though he were crazy, but just nodded.

That night, two Bobbies were assigned a car and helmet cameras. They were concerned that they were being reprimanded but the watch commander assured them that it was just a request that had come from the EDO. They'd shrugged to each other and decided to make the most of having a car rather than patrolling on foot.

Their first opportunity came about an hour after sunset. They were approaching the cross-street that would let them drive in front of the Main Entrance of the department store. They approached, turned onto the street and drove slowly along it. The taller, who wasn't driving said, "Boring. Nothing here. Just what we expected." As a matter of fact they reached the end of the block without quite realizing that they'd driven the block. Their patrol brought them back there about an hour later. This time though, their patrol car radio had squawked.

They didn't recognize the voice on the other end. But, it said that both their helmet cameras had failed when they were on the block in question. It requested that they stay on the radio and comment on what they saw as they drove the block. "Will do."

They approached the corner, turned it and the next thing they knew they were at the next corner and pulling away from the department store. The radio crackled to life and demanded, "We lost both your camera signal and your radio. What happened?"

Bolt, the driver, answered, "Nothing. This beat is as boring as life on the sunflower world. Nothing happens. Nobody has accidents. Nothing."

There was silence on the other end for a while, and then they just said, "Carry on," before signing off. The rest of the night went quietly.

The next day, the watch commander pulled them aside and said, "Change of plan for tonight. You two are back on your feet."

Bolt and his partner Range groaned. Range said, "We were just getting used to having a car. Are you sure we can't just keep it for the rest of the week?"

"No way. They want you to walk the street tonight."

Bolt sighed, "I suppose you mean, The Street, with The department store?"

"You've got it. And don't forget your helmet cameras."

Grumbling, they left for their beat. This time, it took them longer to reach the street. As they approached it, they talked about the stupidity of the commanders. "I don't get it at all. What's the deal with this street with this old abandoned department store?"

But when they reached it, they both found themselves reluctant to walk down the street. Each looked at the other and wondered if they could just get the other to take the hike by himself. Finally, they got a call over their personal radios.

"What's going on, you've been standing at the street corner for 15 minutes? Aren't you going to walk down it?"

Range answered, "Look, I don't like admitting it, but just standing here seems to get some of my host's memories jingling. I'm actually a little afraid that if I try to walk this street, I might revive my host's mind."

The watch commander said, "Get hold of yourself Range. Don't be silly. Have you had trouble with him before?" He asked suspiciously.

"I swear I haven't, but this is different. I've never felt any memories like these. There's a word that keeps coming up in the memories that I've never heard before—Spooky."

A strange voice came on, "This is Mickey of the EDO. What about you, Bolt. Does it feel 'Spooky' to you?"

Bolt pulled himself up a bit, "Not a bit of it, sir. But I have to admit that I'm not anxious to go down that bloody street myself."

There was some muted discussion on the radio, and then Mickey came back on, "Go ahead then, Bolt. Give us a running description of what you see and hear as you go."

Bolt said, 'Yes, sir. Range, keep an eye on me, you hear."

Range, relieved that he didn't have to walk that part of the beat said, "Sure."

Bolt started to walk down the street and then stopped, seemed confused for a moment and then described a slow circle as he turned and walked back to Range. As he got close, he commented, "Well, that wasn't so bad. Nothing to be concerned about."

Range said, "You know that you only took about ten paces, turned around and came back."

Bolt shook his head, like someone dazed and said, "Never. I walked all the way down to the end of the street, turned around and came back."

Mickey came back on the radio. "I saw you on Range's helmet camera. He's right. Just as you were about to turn around, we lost the signal briefly from your helmet camera. Then when you got back, it came back on."

Bolt shook his head, "That's crazy. I could swear I got all the way to the end of the street and then came back to this end."

Mickey said, 'That's OK. The two of you, just finish your beat. You don't have to walk past the department store."

Both officers expressed heart-felt thanks and went on with their beat.

Back at the police station, Mickey told the watch commander, "That's it with the Metro. I think we're going to have to bring in our own hardened troops. We'll keep you informed of when we make our own investigation so you won't get alarmed at heavily armed troops in your watch area."

The watch commander wanted to have another shot at the department store but he couldn't talk Mickey into it. The next day Mickey and Frank discussed their next steps.

Mickey was saying, "We've got to find the best unit in our forces and pick a few of them to go in."

Frank replied, "I agree, but I don't want anyone to get alarmed. Just a pair of troops. I like the way that one of the Metro coppers stayed at the head of the street where his helmet camera still worked, and the other went in."

"Just two? This seems like it requires more forces to me."

'Just two on the ground but I want a unit in the air in a helicopter close by the whole time. If anything goes sour, I want to be able to respond quickly and decisively."

"I second that. I ought to be able to pick a unit within a day or two and get them here and prepped. Any special equipment they should go in with?"

Frank thought a moment, "Let's try multiple communication channels—not just FM radio, but infrared and visible laser and whatever else you can think of. I want to see what the point man sees if it's at all possible."

Two days later, a crack unit of the 101st airborne had been airlifted in from the former US. They brought their own helicopters and other equipment. The commander met with Frank the day before the assault. Frank asked, "Do you feel fully knowledgeable about the mission?"

"I reviewed all your work on the flight over. You've been very thorough. I've not got the slightest idea what to expect. I don't understand why nobody is able to crack this nut, but if anybody can, it's us.

"But, I don't understand why you won't let me send in more than two men. I'd send in a whole platoon."

"No, it wouldn't make any difference if you sent in two or two dozen. If two can't do it, I don't think that a platoon would, either. And we'll still have your platoon to fall back on if two don't work."

"Well, it's your show. I'm just here to jump when you say to."

Two days later, they were ready. There was a command post set up in Frank's Conference Room with a dozen screens and the big projector screen showing the camera of the point man. The unit had just suited up and were on their way by helicopter to the general area. All were in the air except two who had gone to the police headquarters for the area. They were being taken to the target on the ground..

They met Bolt and Range and introduced themselves—George and Fred. Bolt asked, "Why human names?"

"The unit we're in is a crack tactical team, and every host in it is top notch. We decided that we needed to honor their hard work and ability by taking their human names."

Bolt formed a big "O" with his mouth but didn't say anything. But after a minute, he asked, "What's all the equipment you've got?"

George answered, "We've got urban camouflage on, a light pack with extra ammo, first aide kit, electronics pack. We're wearing hyper-kevlar body armor, helmet camera, radio, night-vision, and our piece."

Range said, "Piece? You mean your rifle? I've never seen a rifle quite like that. What is it?"

Fred smiled, "I'll bet you haven't. It's an M16 with sniper-scope, short barrel, banana clip."

Range laughed, "A short-barrel automatic sniper rifle? Who are you kidding?"

George said, "Nobody. This baby is accurate to 1320 meters. It uses very high velocity, depleted uranium rounds, and a very-high precision hand-milled barrel to get the accuracy."

Bolt and Range looked at each other and rolled their eyes. But George kept going. "Just get us to three blocks away and we'll hoof it, the rest of the way. Don't get any closer. I wouldn't want to mistake you for a rogue host."

They drove the rest of the way in silence. When they got within four blocks, Fred told them to stop and let them out. They got out and immediately found an alley that they disappeared into. Bolt turned the car around and left the vicinity to continue their patrol elsewhere.

Fred and George proceeded up the street silently and nearly invisibly. In the dark, their camouflage made it nearly impossible to see them at rest and they moved swiftly from point to point as they worked their way up the street using only infrequent hand signals to communicate.

They reached the head of the street. For the first time they broke radio silence. "Alpha unit at staging area."

A single word, "Acknowledged." returned.

They had a quick conference, "Who's going in?" Fred asked.

George said, "I see what the cop meant. It is spooky here."

Fred said, "I'll take that as me volunteering. Cover my back. See you in a few minutes."

George nodded and took a position behind a trash barrel with only his head showing around it. Fred headed down the street as quietly as before, commenting as he went tersely for the benefit of the Control Room, "Entered street. Nothing unusual in sight." After a few meters, his night vision went out. He said, "Shit" under his breath and hoped that the camera was working anyway. He continued on down the street continuing terse comments. "No lights or movement in the department store." "Feels like I'm being watched."

By the time he reached the middle of the block, he was convinced that some window in the building had unfriendly eyes behind it, but he had no glimmer of an idea which one. The street was possessed of an unearthly quiet. By the time he was half-way past the Main Entrance, he was sure that something was watching him from behind, but he didn't dare turn because he was afraid that if he saw it, it might attack.

On the other hand, he thought it might just not attack if it thought that he wasn't aware of it.

A memory bubbled up from his host. It was of a time when the host was a youth. It was summer. The clover – whatever that was – was just beginning to bloom. The host had been sitting on the ground drinking lemonade. He had been hot and thirsty and hadn't been paying attention to anything besides the cool, tart taste of the lemonade. Then he heard a buzz near his ear. He looked up and found that a bee was hovering near his glass just in front of his nose. Somebody had told the host that the way not to get stung was to remain passive and not attack a bee. The bees didn't want trouble. They were just attracted to sweet things. The bee slowly approached the host's nose. The host did his best to keep from moving. It had been excruciating to resist the temptation to smack the bee. The bee hovered and then pulled away from the host's nose. The host had relaxed.

Then the bee had reversed and approached the host again. However this time, it landed on the host's right ear. The host had gritted his teeth, but not being able to see the bee had been worse than seeing it. The bee took off. The host couldn't stand the tension. He swatted at the bee and it had stung him on the right side of his neck.

This was the bee all over again. He was close to the end of the street, but he couldn't resist the temptation to turn and look. In one fluid motion he dropped first to his knees, whirled around, brought his piece up and fell to the ground prone. As he was going prone, he thought he saw something flash ahead of him. He immediately squeezed off a series of shots on full automatic. Nothing seemed to move, so he jumped up and sprinted the short distance to the corner. As he did, his radio came back to life, and he heard voices shouting, "Who fired? What the hell's going on? Fred, George, answer."

Fred said, "Fred, I'm at the opposite corner. I fired. I think George is down."

A voice said, "Man down. Set down, and pick up George."

The helicopter pilot said, "No can do. The intersection is too tight there, not enough room. I'm landing at the opposite intersection."

With that the helicopter rotor noise rose to a scream above Fred, and he retreated to make room for it. In his earphone he heard the squad leader say, "First two out go down and find George. The rest set up at this end of the street and prepare to set up suppressing fire."

The first two men out ran down the street. But they'd not gone a third of the way before they slowed a bit and seemed to be looking around suspiciously. Then, one of them opened fire on the department store. He was firing at full automatic. Immediately his buddy opened fire too. As soon as the first's clip was exhausted, he fitted another one and opened fire again. The second did the same. They stopped after two clips and looked around quickly and ran down the street.

In the mean time, back in the Control Room, Frank was screaming, "What the bloody hell is going on there. Who are they having a firefight with?"

The two men reached George and their radios came back to life. "We've found George. He's taken a few shots to the body, but the armor seems to have stopped them. He's got a shattered left leg, though."

A siren sounded in the distance and the other soldier said, "I think we've got help on the way. I can see an ambulance coming. I think we should use it rather than try to get back to the copter."

A third voice said, "Agreed. Get George to the closest hospital. I'll meet you there after I get the rest of the unit back to the base."

Everyone remounted the helicopter including Fred. The ambulance arrived and a couple of EMT's got out. One of the soldiers said, 'I've already administered first aid. I've given him local NOPAIN and immobilized the leg. We're getting out of here right now."

One of the EMT's said, "Like hell we will. I've got to check this man out and make sure it's safe to move him."

The other soldier brought his rifle up and said, "Doc. We're going now. You can come on your feet or in a body bag. You choose."

The EMT's didn't say anything else on the way to the hospital.

The hospital room had a lot of people in it. There was the patient, two soldiers in battle dress, the doctor, a young woman who couldn't have been out of her 20's, a nurse, and just then three other men entered. One was dressed in civilian clothes, the others wore uniforms. One of them said, "EDO command on the deck." Everyone who was wearing a uniform snapped to attention, and even the patient straightened as much as he could.

Frank looked around the room. He spoke to the Doctor first, 'Do you and the nurse have to be here for this man's safety?"

The Doctor looked up at him and said, "Yes."

Frank said, "Are you really sure that I can't have a half-hour with him alone?"

The Doctor looked over at the patient and said, "I suppose he'll live without me here for the next half hour. I'll wait outside."

Frank turned to the standing soldiers, "Talk to me about what happened."

One said, "Sir, we came in to assist when PFC Bush was hit by friendly fire. We had to land at the opposite end of the street from him and run through to him.

"On the way, both my buddy," whom he nodded at, "and I became convinced that we were being observed by hostiles. We were passing a display window with an old manikin in it. I could have sworn that something moved in the display area. It was pretty, uh, 'Spooky' there. I turned and fired on the motion. My buddy followed my lead and we pretty much demolished the display."

Frank asked, "Did you boys get anything? I hear that you used a lot of rounds."

"No sir, not that we could tell and, yes, between the two of us, we fired off four bananna clips at whatever it was."

"Could either of you swear that there was something there?"

"No, sir."

"No, sir."

"I see. I heard that you boys were good. Is this typical performance for the 101st?"

"No, sir."

Frank nodded. Just then, the squad leader arrived. He looked around, sized up the situation, and simply came to attention. Frank turned to him. "Who are you?"

"2nd Lieutenant Mark Gravely, sir."

"Do you trust these lads?"

"Yes, sir. We've been in some action together. They've got cool heads. I wouldn't have sent them into this situation if they didn't."

"Hmmmm. All right, I believe you. We'll all talk more tomorrow. For the time being let's let this young man get some rest. What's your name?"

"PFC Bush, sir."

"You seem to be about the only one who kept his head about him."

"Permission to speak freely."

"Go ahead."

"All these guys performed well. You don't know what it's like on that street. It's like it's another world. A world that's definitely out to get you."

"Thanks, PFC." Frank turned and left.

Back at the office, Frank called a meeting. The staff was unhappy but came in during the late hour anyway. They filed in and sat down glumly. They had a feeling it was going to be a long session. Frank stood up and asked, "Just where are the centers of revolt that we know about?"

One of the aids said, "Well, that's a good question. Most of the tough ones are tough because we can't find them."

Frank asked, "Such as?"

"Such as – there is a lost regiment of the US "Mountain" Rangers. We're pretty sure they're somewhere in Afghanistan. Then there's a unit of the British Royal Marines. We've not got the slightest idea where they are. There are a couple of nuclear attack subs that we can't find and there's the USS Ohio—a nuclear missile submarine.""

Frank groaned, "OK. How many nuclear warheads?"

The aide winced and said with a voice that was a little wavery as if he weren't sure that the number was right, "250?"

"How many Souls could that submarine kill?"

"Well, it depends a lot on how the commander targets them." This was said with more assurance.

"Well, let's suppose that he wants to kill as many as possible."

The pain was evident in his voice as he said, "250 or maybe 300 million."

Frank stood with his mouth agape for a minute and then dropped into his chair. "You mean if I don't stop them, they could kill 4% of the population of this world."

The aide had a sort of grimace on his face, "Only if he's really trying."

"Right, I'll bet he won't be trying." Frank looked around at the Conference Room full of Souls trying to find some good in the situation and pretty much failing. He finally said, "Tell me about the place that we definitely know about that is tough."

There was a palpable feeling of relief at being able to say something definite and good. The aide went on, "Well, it's a base of the former US Space Defense Command under Cheyenne Mountain, Colorado, the former USA."

"You mean on Cheyenne Mountain?"

"No, I mean under. They have tunneled more than a kilometer into the mountain and hollowed out a fairly large cavern and filled it with communications gear, links to all the radars and satellites etc. that the US used to have. They've got living quarters, lots of food, defenses that could probably hold off a division for months. If you wanted to destroy it, you'd have to use dozens of nuclear weapons or battle your way close enough to the cavern to use tactical non-nuclear weapons. They've got air purifiers like in submarines and nuclear electric power. They could seal themselves off from the outside for a long time.

"As a matter of fact, that's exactly what they have done. But we're planning to wait them out. They've sealed themselves in and can't get out without opening the plug. When they do, automatic monitors will detect it and we'll be there before they can escape. We figure that in 18 to 24 months, we'll blast open the plug and go down and mop up what's left—IF anyone is left alive."

Frank was glum. "That's not soon enough."

"What do you mean?"

"I mean that when the Ohio surfaces, they'll be getting in touch, and the Space Defense Command is going to tell them to blow as many of us to what they call 'Kingdom Come' as they can. And they will. We'll..." he stopped and corrected, "I'll be responsible for the biggest massacre that this world has seen in all its bloody history. This race has a real genius for creating monsters—Adolf Hitler, Stalin, Pol Pott—but all wrapped together would be nothing compared to me. Hell, I'll be responsible for the biggest massacre in the history of our race."

Then everyone was silent around the table. Finally, someone asked, "Then you plan to try to fight our way into that base?"

"Have you got an alternative?"

"Well, we could use nuclear weapons to destroy the base." He didn't lift his eyes from the floor as he said that.

"How many nuclear weapons?"

"The aide conferred with an officer. They bent over an iPad and then looked up and said, "The optimum attack would be twenty 150 kiloton weapons." Then he added, "We think. There is a minority report that says that it would be more like four hundred 150 kiloton weapons."

Frank stared at him and then said, "Let's just split the difference, say one hundred. How much of the United States would be livable after you were done?"

The officer said, "Well, we think that east of the Mississippi would be acceptable."

Frank said, "Are you really suggesting that approach?"

"No, sir."

"Then, let's get started on a plan to attack and take control of the base."

The officer asked, "What are our priority objectives."

Frank smiled, happy to be able to give something other than painful alternatives, "First priority is capturing some the officers alive. If that isn't possible, then capturing the computers in operating order. If that's not possible, then just capturing whoever else we can.

"Now, get that plan to me within the next 2 days, and we'll start the campaign as soon after as possible." Everyone could tell that the meeting was over. They left as quickly as they could.

The Mine

They were seated around the video console room in the Shrieking Shack. Sally, Minerva, The Boy Genius, Pam Moertl, and Wendt. Getting the Minister of Magic out here was no small feat. She normally refused to leave what she regarded as the most secure spot in the world—Azkaban Prison. The threat that she would be left out of the decision-making for the most important problem that they'd faced yet was formidable. It was followed by a counter threat that the team at Hogwarts would be left out of the Ministry's decision making process. That might have led to a stalemate if Wendt hadn't gone personally to Azkaban to beg her to come.

Pam had insisted, "I have to come away with something. You've got to give me something to come."

Wendt had thought hard. What in the world could he offer her? He finally shook his head in defeat. "I can't think of anything to offer you."

She thought about it for a moment, though surely she'd already decided what she wanted. Then she spoke, "One favor—unspecified, non-negotiable whenever I want it."

Wendt rolled his eyes. "Come on? A blank check?"

Pam returned the stare, "a blank checker?"

"No, it's just a Muggle expression. It means no limits."

She smiled, "Right."

They continued the staring contest for several minutes. Wendt broke it, "Oh, come on. Even the Goblins asked for something specific."

Pam just shook her head. "No. Take it or leave it."

Wendt couldn't believe that she'd press an advantage at the risk of losing to the aliens. He finally gave in. "OK." And under his breath he said, "Asshole." She smiled.

So, she had been sitting in the Control Room of the Shrieking Shack as they watched the Boy Genius' video of the conference to attack the Space Defense Command Center. After it had finished playing Pam shrugged, "Is there anything we can do? Actually, is there anything we should do?"

Sally spoke first, "Anything we should do? Didn't you hear what they said about the people in that Command Center?" She stood up, not able to contain herself. "They're PEOPLE just like us. We've got to do something!"

Wendt added, "Besides that, the aliens think that these people will order a nuclear attack on the aliens. That could kill hundeds of millions of . . "

Pam broke in, "Hundreds of millions of aliens."

This time Wendt couldn't resist standing, "Many of whom also have real PEOPLE imprisoned." He started to pace, "Besides that, if we ever win the world back, we'll have tremendous amounts of radioactive fallout polluting the world for God knows how long."

Minerva asked, "And that's bad?"

Wendt just stared for a moment unable to speak. Then he just shook his head, "That would be a disaster for us."

Minerva replied meekly, "I was just asking."

Pam smiled.

The Boy Genius suggested, "Is there any way to get them out of there by disapparating or something?"

Everyone stared at him with different expressions on their faces. Wendt and Sally had hopeful looks. Minerva's look was puzzled. Pam's seemed to see him for the first time.

Minerva spoke first, "I don't know. I don't think anyone has tried disapparating from far below the surface. Just how far down is that Command Center, again?"

Wendt replied, 'A mile or so."

Everyone looked glum for a minute, and then Pam brightened and pointed out the obvious, 'Well, it's not our problem."

Everyone else stared at her. She went on, "We don't have access. We can't disapparate through an inch of ground at this range. It has to be someone in the States.

"All we have to do is send a message with details and it's their problem."

Everyone except Pam had a frown on their faces. She shook her head and said, "Well?"

Sally, still standing, put her hands on her hips, "We've got to do something more than that! Now, really!"

Pam, speaking with a "let's be reasonable" tone said, "Yes, you're right. We need to send them a message about this." And after a pause, "And it should be by personal courier. Who's going?"

Everyone else looked from one to the other and Sally, still standing, volunteered, "Well, I'll take it—but only if I have the authority to act as your personal representative in this matter."

Pam nodded slowly, "Yes, I suppose so." She turned to the Boy Genius, "Do you have some parchment?"

He shook his head, but said, "No, but I've got some good quality paper." He opened a drawer and pulled out several sheets and placed a pen on the desk next to her.

"Oh, I suppose it will do." She picked up the pen, trying to figure out how to get the ballpoint to work. The Boy Genius stood up, walked over, took her hand in his and forced her thumb to click the button at the rear of the pen. She smiled up at him and said, "Thanks. How do you get the point back in?"

"Push the button again; do you want a demo?"

She smiled again, "Perhaps later." Then she began composing a note. She roughed out the letter on both sides of one sheet, making corrections as she went and then took a fresh sheet and copied over. She folded it neatly and asked for a candle. Everyone looked at one another, and the Boy Genius stated the obvious.

"We use electric lights here. We don't have any candles."

Meantime, Minerva got out her wand and flicked it. A candle appeared out of thin air, "Oh, just use this, Minister."

Pam took the candle, lit it with her wand and dripped some wax onto the seam where the sheet was folded over on itself. She then touched her wand to it and the complex Ministry of Magic icon appeared in the congealing wax. She picked it up and handed it to Sally. "There you are."

Sally snorted, "Convenient of you to seal it before letting me have it. How do I know what it says?"

"Oh, don't be a goose. It just says that you are my personal representative in the matter of how to get the people out of the Space Defense Command Center. They're to treat you as though you were me, concerning this matter. Is that good enough for you?"

Sally nodded.

"Then let's go. Get yourself together and go to Azkaban. I'm going on there ahead of you. When you arrive, they'll send you up to the Auror Office. They'll see that you get to the American Auror Headquarters in Portland by port key. Now, I'm leaving this Muggle enclave." She got up and left the room muttering something about no parchment and no candles.

Sally commented, "Well, you have to say this for her—when action is necessary, she doesn't hesitate."

$\bigtriangledown$

The port key was a mop. Sally felt silly holding a mop and then had an even sillier idea. Why not mount it like a broom? She was just doing that when the mop and Sally disappeared.

She dropped to the floor, still mounting the broom in the center of a wide empty space in a large room that was otherwise filled with cubicles. When her head stopped spinning, she found that two men in robes were standing nearby pointing wands at her.

One of them said, "Drop the mop, then raise both hands very slowly."

She did so as best she could, dismounting the mop. Someone else back in the cubes was laughing like a loon. But the two pointing the wands seemed to be deadly serious. She raised her hands slowly, palms out.

"OK. Turn around so that your back is pointed toward me."

She did. She didn't know what to expect. What she got was frisked. He was doing it pretty efficiently until he started on the inside of her legs. She wasn't quite sure what triggered it, but the shock caused her to do three things at once. She slammed down on his instep with her heel, bent forward and grabbed his other leg with both hands and pulled. He fell backwards, and she rolled to the right, continuing to pull his leg and body between her and the other. His head hit the floor, and the impact stunned him, causing him to drop the wand. She grabbed it as it bounced up from the floor and pointed it at his throat.

But before she could say anything, a wave of rigor flowed over body and she was suddenly absolutely frozen in place. She could still hear the loon laugher keeping it up. She felt herself being searched pretty thoroughly.

After a minute, she heard one of the aurors say, "Shit. She's got a letter from the Minister of Magic in England."

The laugher stopped and she heard that voice say the first intelligible thing from his mouth, "Great. Well, I think we can trust an unarmed Muggle woman from the Ministry of Magic. Why don't you two go tackle something I'm sure you can handle—like a cup of coffee and a donut? I'll deal with her."

Her paralysis ended and she rubbed her sore muscles. He reached out a hand and helped her up. "Who was it who used the *petrificus totalis* spell on me?"

He bowed slightly, "Phil Pearson at your service."

She looked him up and down. He was a little over six feet tall with sandy hair, lank and a face that smiled with an upturned mouth only on one side. "Sally Harker. It's a unique pleasure."

"Do you need to deliver your letter to the Secretary of Magic?"

116

Sally thought a moment, "No. I can tell you what's in it and you can decide."

He asked her to explain to him first.

She explained about the Space Defense Command Center.

"Really? Are you sure? They're still in business. I was sure that they must have been infiltrated long ago."

"Yes. We have it on very good authority that the highest priority of the aliens is to fight their way into that facility and take it over. First, to capture at least some humans there; second, to capture the Command physically intact; and finally, to destroy it if there were no other option."

Phil nodded and thought. "So, you want us to evacuate them?"

"It's more complicated than that. There's a nuclear submarine that's still in human hands. It's a Trident sub and has missiles with nuclear warheads. We don't want them used." She smiled at him, "Funny. We and the aliens agree on that."

Phil couldn't help smiling, "I imagine so. They could destroy half the world and make the other half un-livable."

Her eyes popped, "REALLY?"

"Oh, probably that's an exaggeration, but it would be pretty messy for a continent or two for a good while."

He went on, "So, let's see, our priorities are, evacuate the Command Center:, then, if that's not possible, make sure that they don't send any 'Go' codes to the sub. and then, I'm not sure."

Sally smiled, "Do you have some tea?"

"Iced? Sweet or unsweet?"

"Neither, hot without cream or sugar."

He glanced around and said, "Come with me. I think I can arrange that." He took her to the "Break" room and emptied the pot of coffee, filled it with water and used his wand to heat it to nearly boiling. Then he rummaged in a cabinet looking for a tea bag. "It looks like all we have is green tea. Is that OK?"

Sally accepted it, and they walked back to his cube with a cup of hot tea, and Phil had a picked up a bottle of Diet Dr. Pepper. Sally asked how he'd gotten the Dr. Pepper. "Isn't that against the alien idea of generic junk."

He laughed, "Usually, but there were enough Dr. Pepper addicts around that it was just easier to continue making the branded version. Of course, it doesn't quite taste like the original. They pulled out all the trace carcinogens. The only version they make is diet, of course, with much less caffeine. Still . . . "

"You're an addict."

"Afraid so."

When they got to Phil's cube, he said, "We really need to get together a few Auror managers and the head. I don't want to sit in on any more meetings than I have to, repeating the same story over and over."

Sally asked, "And the Secretary of Magic?"

"Oh, God, I hope not. We'll never get anything done if he has to sit in."

He wrote a memo, requesting a meeting, used his wand to duplicate it, and sent them flying through the air. He shrugged and admitted, "We just have to wait now. By the way, we need to get you a place to stay. I'm glad you packed a bag."

He called over the wall to a neighboring cube, "Hey, Tom, do we have someplace that we could put a guest up for a while, here?"

A voice called back, "Just a sec. I'll check." There was silence for a few minutes. Then, "She could take the spot that the Japanese envoy had. He's leaving tomorrow, but nothing today."

Phil frowned and shouted, "Thanks." In a softer tone he said, "You can stay in my room tonight. I'll stay here tonight. God knows I've done that enough lately."

Sally seemed troubled and asked, "Why don't I stay here tonight, I don't want to put you out."

"Don't worry. I really have stayed here a lot. See." With a flick of a wand, a section of cubicle dropped down and revealed a thin mattress, pillow and thin blanket. Another flick, and it went up.

"I absolutely insist on staying here."

"Well, you can't. For one thing, it's against regs for an outsider to stay overnight, unsupervised."

"You made that up." She laughed.

"Not at all."

The responses to the meeting invite started coming back. Everyone had accepted the afternoon meeting. They went to the cafeteria for an early lunch. It was a late dinner for Sally. When they returned, they went to the meeting room and discussed the agenda. People started showing up before they were done.

When everyone had arrived, Phil introduced Sally as the personal representative of the Minister of Magic with full power to act in her stead. Sally's eyes widened, and Phil kicked her under the table. "OK." Sally thought, "I guess it's easier to ask forgiveness than permission. I'll go along."

He explained everything that she'd told him and opened the table to brainstorming. Sally raised a hand and was recognized, "Well, first, let me correct one thing. I think that our first priority is not getting the men out of the Command Center. It's keeping the Ohio from blowing up the world. The next most important thing is keeping the sub and crew safe.

The next most important thing is getting the Command Center crew back."

There was silence and then one of the managers asked, "So, you'd keep the Command Center crew in place to make sure that they communicate with the sub—even if it means that they fall into the hands of the aliens?"

She thought a moment and nodded slowly, "Yes. I guess it is. If they get in touch with the sub, then we try to get them out. If we can't. . ."

Somebody asked, "Do we ask them to commit suicide?"

"I don't know."

They set that aside and went back to brainstorm how to get the Command Center people out, or at least communicate with them. There were a number of ideas. Disapparation was suggested but no one knew if you could disapparate that deep in the ground. The suggestion was raised to experiment. But that raised the question of where to do it. No one knew of a deep mine that they could use for experimentation. There was a subcommittee appointed to do that. Sally and Phil were voluntold to do that.

Another possibility that was raised was using a port key. The problem was first, how to get a port key into the facility. As someone said, "If we could get the port key in there, we wouldn't need the port key to start with."

The possibility of using a *patronus* for communication was raised, and again, no one had every tried using a *patronus* that deep in the ground, so another subcommittee was appointed to investigate that.

The meeting ended without anyone requesting the presence of the Secretary of Magic. Everyone was happy at that. Sally was beginning to drag because her body clock was reading about midnight of a very long day. Phil agreed that she ought to get a full night's sleep and the next day they could begin their subcommittee work.

Sally woke up around 10 AM on her watch. Then she remembered that she had to adjust for Pacific Standard Time and realized that it was 2 AM. She tried to work in another couple of hours sleep and was fairly successful, but by 5:30 local time, she was done with sleeping. She got up, showered and dressed and decided to go up and let Phil have his room back. She found him still sleeping in his little cot. So, she just sat down in his chair and waited for him to wake up.

He eventually did and was a bit startled to find her sitting in his chair with her back turned to him. "Well, if you go to the other room, I'll get a little more dressed, go down, shower, and I'll be back so we can have breakfast."

The cafeteria's idea of breakfast was pretty spartan. You could have oatmeal or pancakes. You could have coffee or tea. Sally commented, "At Hogwarts, even in these parlous times, you can still get a scrumptious breakfast."

"Oh, sure. Rub it in. Well, at Hogwarts they've got house elves."

"Well, why doesn't our subcommittee start working? Got any ideas for finding a mine to experiment in?"

"Nope. But I do have an idea about how to find a place."

She was surprised, "You do?"

"Sure, we'll go to a cyber-cafe."

She stared at him in surprise, "You know about cyber-cafe's?"

"Sure, I do. Aurors have to spend lots of time among Muggles. We pick up stuff. And cyber-cafes are really useful for researching stuff. And speaking of useful. I have to admit that those special contact lenses that your Boy Genius invented are worth their weight in, well, worth a whole lot more than their weight in gold. Come up to my office and I'll get you a pair."

She smiled, "Are you kidding. I have my own. Just like American Express."

He looked puzzled, so she amplified, "You know—the commercial." He just shook his head.

"Oh, there used to be an advert about the American Express credit card. The phrase was, 'Don't leave home without it!'. I don't leave home without my alien-spoofing contact lenses."

Phil nodded, "I've got to remember that."

After retrieving Phil's contact lenses, they went to the large open area in the cubicle room, and he held out his hand to her. She hesitated to take it for a second. He cocked his head at her, "Afraid of cooties?"

She frowned, not wanting to admit her real fear. Her eyes locked on her shoes for a minute as though she thought they were unaccountably scuffed. She gathered her courage up and admitted her real terror. "We're going into the land of the ghosts."

Phil was puzzled but didn't want to admit that he was confused by the name. It dawned on Sally what his problem was. "Oh, you wonder why I call them ghosts?"

Phil smiled in relief at not having to admit his confusion out loud. "Yes, I was just wondering. . ."

Sally smiled. "Do you know what they call themselves?"

Phil nodded, "Souls, isn't it?"

Sally's smile grew, "Right-o."

He admitted, "I still don't get it."

Sally actually chuckled, "Don't you see? What is a Soul that isn't in its body?"

Phil frowned, "Well, you might say a ghost, but technically . . ."

Sally rolled her eyes, "Technically, shechnically. They might as well be ghosts."

Phil was not used to being contradicted on his own turf. "Look, they all have bodies – that is – except when they are traveling between planets."

Sally huffed and said, "Yeh, but they're not their own bodies."

Phil wouldn't give up. He said, "But they don't have bodies that are really their own."

Sally raised her nose up in triumph, "Exactly! They are permanently ghosts. So, we are going into the world that's packed full of ghosts – far more than Hogwarts has ever seen." She was silent for a moment as she thought about that. A frisson passed over her body and she added, "That's what scares me." Having said that, She realized that naming her fear had given her a certain power over it. She still didn't feel good about jumping into the center of a city of "ghosts" but she was ready to face it. Then she held out her hand and they clasped hands. She was in an alley with lots of garbage cans. He held onto her hand, "Follow me. The cafe is close."

She released his hand, "I guess I'm still a little nervous. I've been out among aliens but never in a large city."

He nodded. "You look super. No one will guess you're not 'one of them.' Just let me do the talking."

He led her into the cyber cafe. He waved at the man behind the bar. "Just two hot green teas. Thanks."

The waiter just nodded. Phil commented, "I'm a regular here." He led her over to a table with two chairs and a computer. He worked the computer as though he had been a knowledge worker all his life. He brought up a list of deep mines and they started researching each.

She asked, "It always unnerves me how these aliens just believe anything you tell them and will work for nothing." Phil changed his focus to behind her. She noticed and shut up.

The waiter was bringing the two cups of tea with a carafe of hot water. "Be careful. The water's pretty hot, Dave."

Phil nodded, "Thanks. Let me introduce a new friend, Dances-in-the-moon. You can call her Luna for short."

"Good to meet you Luna. How long have you been here?"

She thought furiously, "Oh, I just got to Portland yesterday, but I've been in England for a long time."

He nodded and said, "You should find the weather similar. I hope you enjoy the beautiful scenery. You should go up the Hood River sometime."

She was shaking a little and struggled to keep her voice steady. "Sounds like fun."

The waiter left, and Phil said, "You did just fine. If he'd been suspicious, I'd have used the *obliviate* spell."

"You're a dab hand with that computer."

"Thanks. We don't disparage the 'magic' of Muggles like most English wizards seem to."

They found a list of mines that weren't being actively worked. Sally suggested the Homestead Mine in South Dakota.

"Yeh, I agree. It's not been worked for a while and is really deep. There are lots of passages at different depths."

Luna said, "But I see that it was used for some kind of physics experiments after the mine was no longer being worked. Why didn't they keep that going?"

Phil laughed, "I don't pretend to understand science, but why keep an experiment going when you already know the answers. These aliens seem to know a whole lot about physics."

"I suppose. How do we get there?"

Phil brought up Google maps and checked out how far they were from the mine. "Well, we're not close enough to disapparate in one step. I suggest that we go to an intermediate spot like Denver first."

"You're the expert."

Phil got up, and Sally followed. As they left the cafe, which had begun to have a few more patrons, he spoke to the waiter, "Well, Dave, I'll see you around. Thanks for the tea."

"Come back any time. You too, Luna."

Her voice cracked a little as "Luna" answered, "I'm sure I will, uh, with Dave."

They returned to the alley and Phil held out his hand. This time, Sally was glad to take it and have the comfort of knowing that it was a real human's hand that she was holding.

They appeared on a wooded hillside. "I thought you said that we were going to Denver."

"This is just outside Denver. It's a spot in Estes Park that I like. The view is nice."

Sally nodded, and they took a few minutes to enjoy the view. Then Phil held out his hand, which she was happy to take it. They appeared on a hillside that couldn't have been more different from the one where they'd just been. The hillside had been stripped of all vegetation and was cut into giant tiers.

Phil said, "Well, I guess that we go exploring." They walked the barren hillside down to a cluster of buildings that they discovered were surrounding an entrance to the mine. The entrance itself was a shaft that had an elevator that ran down it.

She asked, "Do you suppose that this still is powered? How could it be?"

"Well, let's try. The aliens are essentially lazy. They wouldn't take the effort to disconnect power, they'd just put up a sign advising people not to enter the facility."

They looked for a way to start the elevator. Finally, Sally found it and pushed the button, "Well, that answers our question. We've got power." The elevator bumped to a start and went slowly down. They reached and passed the first level because they were both expecting the elevator to stop itself. Sally got the elevator going up again and this time stopped at the first level.

Phil opened the door and took out his wand. He lit it and they found a switch that controlled the lights. With lights, he said, "I'm on my way. Wish me luck."

Sally grabbed him by the arm, "Wait one minute. What are you doing? You're not leaving me down here alone."

He answered, "I'm sure not going to take a risk with your life by trying to disapparate both of us."

She wouldn't let go, "But eventually, you'll have to disapparate more than one person—perhaps a couple. Why wait to find out if it will work."

His jaw set. "But I'm not doing that experiment with you."

Her jaw set as firmly, "Well, what if you do die? I'm stuck down here in the middle of alien country. What good does it do me to be alive if you're not?"

"Oh, come on, you can get yourself to the surface. Just walk to Lead, South Dakota. You're a perfect little alien. As a matter of fact," here his jaw lost its set, "you're more perfect than any alien. You just tell the first alien you see that you need their car. Then you drive to Portland. Go to the mall and get in the phone booth. Easy Peasy."

She didn't lose the set of her jaw. "I will not do anything of the sort. I'm not letting go, like it or not."

He grimaced, "OK. You can disapparate with me, but not the first time. After the first time, you come along."

"Swear." She hesitated and added, "Swear the unbreakable oath."

"We'd have to have another wizard for that. I swear. Now let me go."

She did and he disappeared immediately and almost immediately re-appeared, "It's OK. It felt a little strange, but it's OK."

"Yeh, your clothes are covered with some kind of dust and what do you mean, strange. Disapparating normally feels pretty bloody strange to me."

"No, this was definitely strange. If you're ready, we'll both go."

She took his hand and they both disappeared. She couldn't tell what he meant by strange, but they returned and then took the elevator down to the next level. They got off, and he kept his promise. They both disapparated, and they both felt like it was definitely strange. They disapparated back and went down one more level. They weren't sure how deep they were, but she was guessing at least a couple of hundred feet.

Phil held out his hand and asked, "Ready."

"Oh, I've got a bad feeling about this. Are you sure that you want to try it?"

He nodded, "What is it, you English say, 'In for a knut, in for a galleon.'""

She nodded and said, "Yeh. Something like that." Then she took his hand. They reappeared after a noticeable period of time and both were coughing and hacking as though they'd breathed a lung-full of coal dust. At one point, Sally wasn't sure she'd be able to regain her breath, but she did. Phil shook his head. After a minute, he stopped gasping and said, "That's it. We were lucky to survive that. We can't go any deeper."

Sally nodded and just managed to choke out, "Bloody."

Then she said, "Let's get out of here before anyone investigates the power usage."

He shook his head, "We've got to turn out the lights below. I'm going to disapparate down the shaft to the elevator and bring it up."

He staggered over to the elevator, and she screamed, "No!" But he was gone. Shortly after than, she heard the elevator moving. Eventually he reached the surface, and held out his hand. He still looked pale but he said, "I know a little restaurant in Denver, that's still pretty good."

She took his hand, and they disappeared. This time it wasn't "strange". They arrived in an alley. They dusted each other off and checked for any obvious signs of strangeness. Finally, they decided that they were OK. They walked out onto the street and half a block to a pizzeria. Inside, there was a waitress who told them to take a seat of their choice and asked what they wanted to drink.

Phil asked for a Diet Dr. Pepper, "If you have it."

The waitress admitted that they did. She said that a lot of customers here, like it. She turned to Sally, who said, "I guess I'll try that too."

The waitress said conversationally, "Two DDP's coming up. My name's Chrysanthemum, but you can call me Chris. What's yours?"

"Oh, I've got a long name too, just call me Luna and this is Phil."

Phil immediately added, "She's too shy. Her full name is beautiful. It's 'Dances-in-the-moon."

She walked back to the kitchen and returned shortly with the drinks. Sally had been looking over the menu which seemed to be exclusively vegetarian Pizza. Chris asked what they wanted. Sally just impetuously said, "Oh, whatever is the most popular here."

Chris nodded wisely, "Good choice. The sunflower, cheese, and tomato is probably the most popular and the healthiest too."

They agreed. Sally thought that Phil looked beat out. But, he kept on the program, "I sure hope the port key team had better luck."

The next day, there was a stand-up status report. The port-key team had chosen an old salt mine near Lake Erie. They reported that port keys worked perfectly down to the deepest depth that they could go, a couple of thousand feet. They agreed to try it at the Homestead mine the next day. But Phil pointed out the dragon in the room.

"Do you have a way to get a port key down to our friends?"

Everyone was looking at someone else and nobody had an idea. The Head of the Aurors, Johnathan Elba, sent them off. The port key team was to test it at the Homestead mine and everyone else was to think about ways to deliver a port key. Phil and "Luna" went to the internet cafe and sat at a computer all morning, drinking tea and studying satellite imagery of the Cheyenne Mountain area.

Close to noon, Sally asked Phil, "It's spooky. The barista doesn't think it's funny that we spend the whole morning here?"

Phil smiled, "He assumes that we're good honest, law-abiding aliens and wouldn't do anything that even faintly smells of treason."

"Well, it's spooking me out. Let's leave and have lunch among real people. And besides, I've been thinking that we need to figure out what we're going to say to the Cheyenne Mountain people to convince them that we're for real."

"Yeh, I suppose somebody needs to do that. OK. Let's leave and have lunch."

They disapparated to the Reception Area. This time, the same guards were on duty. They stood back respectfully but with wands raised. "Take your contacts out and let's see those irises." Phil and "Luna" passed muster and headed down to the cafeteria, stopping at Phil's office to pick up some parchment and quills.

This time lunch was better than most breakfasts. There were fresh fruits and sandwiches—cheese, avocado, and various other vegetarian choices. They found a table by themselves and laid out parchments and started writing. It was a difficult task. Finally, Phil just balled up a parchment and threw it at the waste can. Sally had been watching and seemed zoned out.

"Earth calling Sally. Earth calling Sally. You there?"

She seemed to snap to. Then she said urgently, "Quiet!" Then she asked very deliberately and slowly, "What. . . did. . . you. . . just. . . do?"

He shrugged, "Made fun of you?"

"NO. No, just before that."

"Oh, I wadded up a piece of parchment that I would be ashamed for anyone to see and tried a free quaffle shot at the waste basket from short range."

"Right. That's it! Brilliant!"

He stared at her, "Well, sure, but just which was the brilliant part."

"The wadded up parchment. Do you know what that made me think of?"

"A stupid letter?"

"No. No. The parchment itself?"

"Sorry, kid. You've got me. What?"

"Didn't that make you think of a parchment tied to an owl's leg?"

"An owl's leg." Phil worried the idea, "You don't think that you could send a note past those aliens down into a mine shaft on an owl's leg?"

Sally flipped her head, "Why not? And for the matter of that, why not send a port key tied to the other leg?"

Phil kept worrying at the idea. "A . . . port . . . key . . . can . . . be . . . anything—large or small. I think you're right. But would they let an owl fly down through the tunnel?"

"I don't know. Why not find out?"

They continued working on text for a message to be tied to the leg of an owl. They took off in the afternoon when they thought they'd done their best. And too, they didn't know if the port key would work through a mile of granite.

The next day, the stand-up meeting had a hopeful report from the port key team, but they hadn't finished testing.

The following day, though, at the stand-up meeting they reported that they'd been able to use the port key from the deepest depth without much discomfort: the sudden difference in air pressure was somewhat disturbing to their ears but not intolerable. They immediately convened a full scale meeting.

The most wrangling was about the wording of the letter to be sent. Everyone was trying to imagine what the base commander would think. Everyone had a different idea. A rough draft was finally hammered out and another team was formed to come up with a design of the port key. They returned the next day with a port key design that was very clever. It was a simple ring that could be shrunk so that it fit snuggly around the leg of the owl, but could then be expanded to accommodate as many as needed to be transported back to their base.

Sally pointed out the one real problem, "Who's going to expand it down there?" The team's faces fell, and it was clear that that little problem hadn't been considered.

Then she supplied an idea. She bent over and untied her trainer and unlaced the shoe string. Somebody suggested that she was going to send a shoe down. She remained silent and stood up with the shoestring that she proceeded to wrap around her smallest finger. The eyes of all involved widened with the realization.

Some wag asked if she were going to send her shoestring down wrapped around the owl's leg. She shook her head in wonder, "No. I was thinking of a thing strong wire—like a piano string or a picture hanging wire."

With that, the team broke up and self-assigned tasks: procuring picture wire, producing a final copy of the letter, choosing an owl. Selecting an owl turned out to be a rather contention process. Should the owl be large and strong, easily able to carry both the wire and letter or small—easily able to avoid detection and capture?

The decision came down on the side of small and undetectable. Thus, they selected an elf owl—one of the smallest. So about a week after the beginning of the project, the owl was encumbered with the letter and small spool of fine wire.

Colonel Travis

The Space Defense Command security team had been beefed up with every enlisted man and woman who weren't absolutely necessary to monitoring the radio spectrum for signs of continuing resistance to the aliens. The aliens had recently become absolutely intent on capturing the post. After a few pointless attempts to talk them into surrender, the aliens had seemed content to wait them out and starve them to death. But then, suddenly, there had come a frontal attack. The squad that was kept on the doorstep to welcome visitors had noticed that the huge metal plug had become somewhat warm. They reported it up the line of command. The order had come back to drop back and try to keep from getting hurt when the door melted.

The door had eventually melted and the welcome committee had had to back off quite a distance to avoid the heat. The remnant of the door slowly cooled and while it was still pretty warm a robot had ventured in, promptly to have its head blown off. Then the assault had begun.

After the aliens had pushed the defenders past the first turning of the tunnel, the defenders had blown the ceiling out and they had some peace for a few days as the aliens tunneled through the thousands of tons of rock. They eventually cleared the passage, and the assault had renewed.

The commander of the SDC had called a staff meeting for 09:30. There weren't a lot of people at that meeting, just Colonel Travis, the electronics warfare unit commander, Arnold, the base security commander, George, the XO, and the Colonel's personal aide, Richards. Travis opened the meeting with the questions, "What's going on with the aliens?"

He looked around the room and found that everyone was staring at the papers in front of them except George. But no one offered an answer. "George, what do you think?"

George looked away from the commander's gaze for a minute. Then what he said was more a question than an answer, "They've lost their patience?"

There was more silence until the XO spoke, "I don't think they've lost their patience. These jaspers seem to have patience coming out their tails. I think something's happened and they need to get in here to learn something—either from one of us or from our files. I can't imagine what it would be, but it's got to be something—something real."

Travis looked around, "Opinions?"

No one had any further opinions except the security chief, "Whatever it is, they want it bad. They're willing to take lots of casualties to get it. That's not par for the course for them."

Travis nodded, "I agree. And when they want something that bad, it just makes me want to keep it from them all the more. So, I've begun to think about what we do WHEN they overrun us. Notice that I said 'WHEN' not 'IF'. Do any of you doubt that they'll over-run us?"

He looked around the table, but no one had anything to say.except the XO, "You're right. I don't want to admit it, because, one way or the other, it means that I'm sure to die—along with the rest of us."

The XO hesitated a minute and then added, "I suppose that means that we're not going to surrender the base. We'll destroy it before that happens."

Travis just nodded. George looked around and said, "That means that you'll want to get the W54 out of the vault in the armory."

The XO asked what he was talking about. Travis just nodded at George, who went on. "The W54 is a 250 mm shell that's been modified to include a small nuclear weapon. It's got a variable yield but the high end is 1 KT."

Travis asked, "Is that enough to completely destroy this base?"

George looked a bit puzzled and just shrugged but the XO said. "I think so. Just let me do a little math.

"The Hiroshima bomb was 20 KT and pretty much destroyed everything within a half mile radius of the blast point. The power of that bomb is twenty times greater than our bomb. That means the radius of destruction of ours should be about a third of the Hiroshima bomb—say 900 feet, about 250 meters. That ought to scramble the base pretty effectively." He hesitated a minute and then added, 'And really it ought to do a more thorough job than the Hiroshima bomb did there because a lot of the energy from that bomb just went up into empty space while we're sitting here in a natural reaction vessel. We're surrounded by billions of tons of solid rock that will reflect a lot of the energy back on us, not to mention collapsing and pulverizing whatever is left."

Travis said, "So you think there's absolutely no way that there would be any data left on the computers."

The XO looked around and didn't answer.

Travis asked in a slow querying tone, "XO? What is it?"

The XO grimaced, "Well, these are aliens. We don't know what they might be able to do. I can imagine that there might be little shards of computer memory left around, maybe more or less intact. It would be a monumental task. You'd have to literally sift through millions of tons of rubble looking for magnetic media shards and piece them together to reconstruct a memory chip or magnetic disk. A lot of the data would be completely lost, but who knows what would be left?"

Travis growled a low growl, "Can you think of any better idea." The XO was a little too theoretical for Travis' tastes. He'd argue a point into the ground.

The XO frowned and shook his head.

Travis went on, "OK. Well, George get that nuke out of the vault and bring it here. I want to be able to detonate it on a minute's notice."

George replied, "Yes, sir." He hesitated the minimum allowable time and said, "Permission to speak freely, sir."

"Go."

"Well, sir. I can't get that out without some people who work for me realizing that I've pulled the W54. I was thinking. . . " He trailed off and looked at the commander expectantly.

Travis finished for him. "You were just thinking that you can't keep something like that a secret on a base this size. Yup. I agree. I think that we've got to have a quick meeting of the entire base to announce that and what we intend doing." He turned toward the XO and said, "XO?"

"Yes, sir. I'll set that meeting up for change of shift. First thing tomorrow morning?"

"Sounds good. We'll pull the nuke right away then. Anyone else have comments?"

No one did.

The officer of the watch in the early morning shift was waiting for the change of watch expectantly. His replacement came into the office and they exchanged salutes. He said, "Well, Frank, I guess we're both going to the basketball court now. It must be pretty important to hold breakfast for it."

"Right, Don. Let's get out there and get this over and find out what's going on." They left the office and headed for the basketball court. He went on, "I bet that we're going to find out that the ET's have offered us a deal to get out of jail free if we give our word to not oppose them."

Don just frowned and said, "Don't make me laugh." They reached the basketball court that was snuggled between the Admin Building and the barracks. It would have been a courtyard except that two sides were open. The base commander was under one of the baskets, and everyone else was between the top of the "key" and roughly midcourt. The two watch officers found their way close to the front of the group of listeners.

Travis said, "I'm here to make a quick announcement, and I'll take a few questions. First, the announcement. I've decided that the new attacks that are happening are the result of our enemy deciding that we have something that they want very much. Well, we're not going to let them have it." Here there was a spontaneous cheer. He waited while the cheer died down. "And here's how we're going to do that. We're going to continue to resist until they get very close to the base. Then, when it's clear that the end is close. . ." Somehow it didn't seem so easy to announce as he thought it would be. He cleared his throat and said, "We're going to detonate a nuclear bomb to destroy the base and everyone in it." There was deathly silence then followed by Travis' request for questions.

Frank raised a hand and was recognized by the XO. He asked, "How soon do you think that will be?"

Travis nodded and said, "We estimate that it will be at least three more weeks. That assumes that they don't care at all about their casualties and clear the debris from the various explosive charges along the tunnel as quickly as possible."

Someone else was recognized and asked, "I've heard that dying of radiation sickness takes hours at least and is very painful. Is that what will happen to us?"

Travis looked over at the XO, who took a second to realize that he was expected to answer, "Oh, no. I figure that you'll be vaporized so quickly that you won't even realize that anything's happened." The questioner nodded. No one else asked any questions.

Travis finished up. "I know that some of you may want to go down fighting to the end, but if we do this, I'm sure that the aliens will regard their victory as Pyrrhic. Dismissed."

Frank and Don walked back to the office together. Don asked, "What's that Peeric victory thing?"

Frank chuckled a single time and said, "Oh, it's from Roman history. There was a country that was attacking Rome, and in a battle, they beat the Romans, but the commander of Rome's enemy named Pyrrhus declared that if he had another victory like that, he'd end up with an army of one."

Don laughed, "Well, I guess Travis is saying that we would actually kind of win with one of those Peeric losses."

Frank just scowled, "I think that was just for morale purposes. I don't think the ET's would care." As they entered the building, he said, "Hmmm. Come to think of it, I kind of hope he times it so the tunnel is jam packed with ET's before he sets that bomb off."

Then something happened that no one—defender or alien—had expected.

The alien field commander was trying to estimate the time until they took the next turning in the tunnel when a lieutenant interrupted his thoughts.

"Sir, I have a report from the forward brigade."

The field commander sighed and said, "What happened this time?"

"It was a bird, sir."

The field commander shook his head to clear his ears. He must have heard wrong. "Did you say 'a bird', Lieutenant?"

"Yes, sir. A bird flew down the shaft, past our position, and on down the tunnel."

"So?" As he waited for a reply, another thought occurred to him, "Could it have been a human-made robot?"

The Lieutenant thought several minutes, "I don't think so. The humans seemed to be firing on it."

"Really? They thought it was one of ours?" Then he thought about it some more. "It must have been a real bird. Could anyone identify the species?"

"It was pretty small. No one noticed it until it was past us. I don't think anyone recognized it."

He sighed again, "All right. I'll put it in the report, but the heavens only know what HQ will make of it."

As a matter of fact, HQ made nothing of it. They thought it was a practical joke.

The Lieutenant who was in charge of the defenders ordered his men to fire on the bird, but only one man got a shot off before it disappeared down the shaft of the tunnel. He then picked up his radio and paged the forward command post. They responded, and he announced, "Incoming. There's something that looks like a small bird, flying down toward you. I don't know, but I think it might be an alien robot."

The commander of the forward command post, ordered his men to stop a small flying object that was headed toward them. Several men got shots off but no one was close. The commander forwarded the message on. At the Control Center. several men were assigned to stop the bird or UFO or whatever it was. They too, didn't see it until it was flying over them. They quickly tried to track its flight and found themselves pointing their guns at the entrance to the Command Center. The bird was perched on the doorstep and seemed to be holding a leg out toward them.

The Sergeant in charge of the watch had his sidearm aimed at it, trying to decide what to do. Just at that moment the door opened and Colonel Travis stepped out. He commented, "Well, if I'd known that I was going to be facing a firing squad, I think I wouldn't have chosen this moment to take a little walk."

The Sergeant blurted. "Look out, there's a bird at your feet."

Travis looked down and saw the small owl on the doorstep. He started to bend over to examine it closer, but the Sergeant shouted, "Don't, it may be an alien device."

Travis said, "I don't think so. It's an Elf Owl, if I'm not mistaken. And it looks like it has something tied to each of its legs." With that he reached down, and the Sergeant had a real crisis of conscience. Should he shoot the bird while he still could or should it be investigated? His inaction decided the issue because Travis had picked it up and was saying, "Well, little fellow, let's see what this note is that's tied to your leg." With that the owl lifted its leg and Travis untied the note. He ignored the spool of wire for the moment.

"Well, boys, why don't you find a place to billet this bird and see if you can scare up a field mouse or two for it?"

The incredulous Sergeant acknowledged the command and took the owl from Travis and walked off toward the barracks.

Travis went back into the Command Center, entered his office and had his XO paged. In the meantime, he examined the letter. It was strange indeed. The direction was, "Commander A. Travis, Corner Office, Space Defense Command Center, Cheyenne Mountain, Colorado Springs, Colorado, USA." He unrolled the letter and began to read. While he was working through the letter, the XO knocked on the door. He had a unique knock. "Enter."

The XO opened the door and stuck his head in. "What you got?"

"Take a look at this."

133

He handed the letter over to the XO, who commented from the beginning, "Interesting address. You're pretty popular. Who knows your address so precisely that we want to talk to?"

"You've got to be kidding. No one."

"And, this paper. It's not paper. It's . . . You know, I think it's parchment." He was silent as he read the body of the letter. Then he said, "Well, it sounds like a practical joke. Where did it come from?"

"The leg of an elf owl."

"I don't remember that we had an aviary here?"

"We don't. The owl flew down the tunnel, evaded our defenses, and landed on the doorstep."

"Well, do you believe in magic?"

"I don't know. How do you explain it otherwise?"

The XO shook his head, "Well, I guess when you put it that way, I don't have another explanation. So, miniature owl flies past the fucking aliens, past three rounds of defenses, and steps up to you and says, 'Sir, message from the wizards who are still fighting the fucking aliens, sir.' No, if that's not magic, I don't know what is."

"I've been thinking of assembling the troops when we blow up the tunnel at the next turning point and reading this to them. We tell them that it's legitimate as far as we know and offer them the option of taking the port key to the wizards wherever they are. Critique?"

The XO sat for several minutes and then said, "Top of my head, you understand. I reserve the right to change my mind later. We've got several days to that point."

Travis nodded.

"OK. Then, here's what I think. We've got to keep command here as long as possible so that we can communicate with that sub and send them off to rendezvous with the wizards. After that happens, we all take the port wine key or whatever it is."

"But, it's set to go at a preset time. What if we don't make contact with the sub by then?"

"Oh, fuck. I guess we send a messenger with the port key and hope they can get another one to us before the aliens crack through."

"Yeh. I'll think it over. When the aliens round the next bend, we're going to have that meeting. Set it up.

The "outdoor" basketball court in the SDCC was full to the midcourt line that day. Travis had the troops assembled, including everyone from every shift. No one was minding the electronic listening post other than the XO. A few wounded were in the infirmary.

Travis stood before them trying to calm his nerves. He wasn't sure that he could read the letter to his troops and convince them that it was worthy of serious consideration. Possibly the fate of the world hung in the balance, and he hated to think that a failure of leadership at this point would doom the human race. He began.

"Ladies and Gentlemen, humans all, I have to admit that I'm as proud of you as any command that I've ever had. You do the human race proud." He scanned the faces, most of whom he could name without hesitation. They all seemed to justify the pride that he'd confessed.

"I think that we all counted on dying—sooner or later—in the service of our race and world. I know that every one of you has understood that and have made your peace with that certainty." Here he stopped. He was about to cross his Rubicon.

"A few days ago, an unusual event happened. An elf owl flew down the tunnel to our doorstep and landed. What very few of you know is that it had two things tied to its legs—a note and a spool of picture hanging wire.

"I believe the letter that I'm about to read to you that came off that owl's leg is the real McCoy. I want you to believe it too and take its message seriously. I can't imagine that its message is a hoax or a cruel joke regardless how bizarre it sounds. So, here is the text of the letter:

"To Colonel Travis and all non-magical people (Muggles as we call you) of the Space Defense Command, If you are reading this, then our owl has reached your base. We can't prove to you the truth of anything that we say, but we trust that you will see that this letter makes no sense if written by the aliens and makes the most sense in the world if written by your allies.

"Point 1. There is a Trident submarine, the Ohio, which still remains free of the aliens and is probably cruising below the Arctic ice." At that point there was a shout of joy from the men and women assembled. Travis even thought he heard someone call out, "Go Bucks!" He gave the crowd a moment to settle and then went on.

"This submarine must at all costs be kept from falling into enemy hands. It must also be prevented from firing its nuclear arsenal in revenge. There are better uses to put to that submarine and its armament.

"When you make contact, tell the captain what you know about the aliens and ask him to go to Hogwarts. He will know what we ask and why we ask that, and he will assure you that we are not aliens ourselves.

"Point 2. There is a way to evacuate you and your men. We've sent it along with the owl. It is the reel of wire. Unwind as much of it as you need so that everyone can grasp a section of it securely. At midnight on the fifteenth, it and everyone who grasps it will disappear from wherever they are and reappear at our Magical Law Enforcement office.

"Yes, Magic. It's real. It got this message to you, and we will use it and anything else that we can to defeat the aliens.

"Good luck and God Speed."

"It is signed, 'Head of Magical Law Enforcement of the United States, Chief Auror Officer, Jason Eldridge'

He folded the paper and put it in an inner pocket of his jacket. "I believe this document.

"The XO and I have decided to stay and fight the station at least until the Ohio makes contact. If that is after the fifteenth, we will continue to fight the station until the aliens break through. At that point, we will detonate explosives that will destroy this station and everyone in it."

"I offer all of you the opportunity to evacuate this post in order to fight elsewhere. You don't have to make a choice now. You can choose any time up until midnight on the fifteenth.

"That's all I have to say. Any questions?"

A hand was raised somewhere behind the front row. Travis recognized him, "What's your question, Airman First Class Rogers?"

Rogers stepped forward and crossed the midcourt line a couple of steps. "Sir, I've decided to stay with the command."

Then another man raised his hand and stepped across the midline. Then another and another. Shortly, you couldn't see how many or if there were any standing behind the line. And that was just fine with Travis.

A couple of days later, when the battle had resumed, the XO was in Travis' office. "Well, XO, what do you think is going to happen when midnight on the 15th arrives. Is anyone going to show up?"

"I don't know, but the feel that I get is that there isn't going to be anyone show up."

"Yeh, I agree. It's too bad."

"Why?" The XO had leaned forward on his chair so that he could catch what it was that had Travis worried.

"Well, if there isn't, I'll have to draft someone to go. As a matter of fact, I'm beginning to think that I have to do that anyway—just to be sure."

The XO rolled his eyes and said, "I'm glad I don't have to do that." Then he looked at Travis. The one look showed that they were having the conversation because he did have to do it. "I stand corrected." He thought and then asked, "Do you have any recommendations for selecting this messenger?"

Travis thought a minute and said, "I want you to pick the bravest man you can find."

The XO couldn't keep from asking, "Why the bravest? I know that I don't want to pick the man who is tempted to cowardice. To reward him would be unjust and a bad example, but why the bravest? Don't we need him here?"

Travis opened the drawer of his desk and pulled out a pipe and a very thin bag that contained the last shreds of tobacco. He slowly cleaned the pipe and then loaded it carefully so as to not lose a morsel of tobacco. Then he lit it slowly, leisurely. Finally, he said, "When the battle rages, almost anyone can find courage—the right man for the right moment. But it takes real courage for what this man faces: Not a single battle or even a long war, but the constant truth that he can't ever escape that each one of his comrades are gone forever. This man will have to face the dreams that will come at night of friends felled in battle that he escaped, of buddies whom he left behind to face a certain end. That man will need every bit of courage that he can muster to keep on living and fighting when all he knew and loved are gone."

The XO shook his head, "Well, that will give me something to lose sleep over." He asked permission to leave, which Travis granted.

As he turned to go, Travis said a single word to the XO's retreating back, "Tomorrow."

The XO turned back to Travis, "Yes, sir."

The XO returned to his office where he turned on his computer and pulled up a listing of all the personnel of the base. There was a neat electronic front page for each: years in service, age, rank, a history of assignments and a list of promotions. A few extended to further pages. There were ratings and reviews. They were all air force, so hardly any had been on the front lines of actions even though many had served in actions—the Gulf War, Mozambique, Afghanistan. Some had flown flights over countries that were potential enemies—spy planes.

There were medals that implied courage but Travis was right. The sort of courage that won you medals could be a one-time only thing that seizes a man and carries him to unusual heights. The more he looked, the less he believed that he could be confident of finding the truly courageous man.

In desperation, he picked three men who seemed to have evidence of real courage. He decided that he'd have to interview them before deciding. He picked up a phone and called the staff sergeant who served as his secretary into the office.

"Mike, I have three men's names on this sheet." He handed over the sheet. I want to meet them and talk with them. Set up an hour for each this afternoon, find them and get them in here.

The Staff Sergeant saluted, yes sired, and left the office. The XO wondered what he could ask them.

At one o'clock, the first arrived, Corporal Felderman. He was tall, young, athletic. He saluted smartly and stood at parade rest until he was ordered to sit. "Cpl. Felderman, I have a special assignment, and I'm trying to decide the best man for the job. You won't find out what it is until you draw the duty—if you draw the duty. It's an unusual assignment, and I want to understand the character of the men I'm considering before deciding.

"Tell me about yourself, your family, why you joined the service?"

He smartly recited the formula, "Sir, yes sir." He sat bolt upright with a back that didn't touch the chair back, nor did he lean forward at all. "I was born in Witchita, Kansas. My dad was retired Air Force. He started a dry cleaning business to keep busy. My mom, well, I have two mom's. My real mom divorced my dad because she couldn't stand the military life. I have a sister who stayed at home and still works the dry cleaning business. My mom married dad shortly after he started the business."

"Are you close to any of them?"

There was the slightest hesitation as he answered the question, "If you mean, do I love them? The answer is 'yes'.

"I joined the service because my dad loved the Air Force."

"You maintained RPV's for a while in Saudi Arabia, right?"

"Sir, yes sir. I was proud to keep the surveillance going for the allies in the Gulf War."

It looked like this was going to be a short interview, "Well, just one last question. How do you feel about your parents and sister?"

"I'll see those bastard aliens blown to kingdom come."

The XO thanked him and dismissed him. It was more than a half hour until the next arrived. He picked up the printout on this one. She monitored radio transmissions and tried to separate alien traffic from any remaining real human traffic.

She was ushered in, and when seated, the XO asked her the standard questions. Her family was broken. Her mother disappeared before she had gotten to know her. Her father had died of cancer a few years before. She entered the military because it was a place where she could excel as a woman and get recognition.

"Very commendable, Specialist Jones. You aren't married, I take it?"

"No, sir. I want to make Captain before I think about marrying."
She was reasonably good looking. It was impossible to tell how long her
hair was because she wore it in a tight bun at the back of her head that
wasn't visible unless you were beside or behind her. The hair was a dark
auburn. Her face was expressive when she chose to allow it to be, but it
was under tight control now.

The XO asked, "Do you have any close relatives?"

She thought a moment. "I'm not sure what you mean by close. I
have a cousin who I haven't seen since the aliens arrived. I don't know
what happened to her. Is she dead, was she able to go to ground and
avoid them or . . . " Her voice caught and she didn't finish her sentence.

"That sounds close to me. Do you have any other close relatives
or friends?"

"No, sir. All my other friends are here in this base."

The XO nodded and made a note on her printed dossier. She
asked permission to speak freely, "Can I fight at the end? I want to take a
couple of them with me."

The XO frowned, "I can't guarantee you anything. You've got
the most important job that we have—discovering the Ohio when it
comes up to communicate and make contact. I don't know where you'll
be when the end comes. If our job is done, everyone will be fighting,
until the Colonel pulls the trigger on the bomb."

She nodded, and he dismissed her.

The final interviewee was an Airman First Class. He was
medium height, had curly black hair that was short. His black skin was
the solid deep black that was impossible to mistake for Indian or South
American. He stood at stiff attention until ordered to sit.

"Well, Airman Nicholls, tell me about yourself. What do you
think is significant?"

"I had two brothers, seven cousins, six aunts and uncles, fifteen
nephews and nieces. We were a close family. There isn't a day that I
don't think of some of them. I miss them and will always try to
remember them just as they were before . . well, before I lost them." He
spoke about it almost nonchalantly and . .

Fred Nicholls, Freddie as his friends called him, always enjoyed the
holidays. It wasn't just that you had a day off from school but his family,
all his cousins and aunts and uncles, his two brothers, his mom and dad
all got together at one of the homes of the family. Usually it was his
Uncle Jerry's. He had a large single floor ranch style house with a large
yard.

It started in mid-morning and usually ran late in the night. In the late summer, the fireflies were out on the yard, and the random flashes of light always seemed to him to be like little fireworks. You never knew where they'd show up. It was always a delight to see them.

The morning was the gathering time as everybody brought their own specialty. Aunt Mary Jane made wonderful 'tater salad. Uncle Bob made homemade chocolates. His mom always brought two kinds of Jello Salad—lime with pears and plain cherry (but sometimes with real cherries). Aunt Millie brought pecan pie, but the most special was Uncle Jerry's barbecued chicken. It was to kill for.

After lunch, there were always games. For the cousins who liked board games, it was usually Monopoly. With eight players one game would go on and on all afternoon. Then there was always croquette on the lawn and frisbee throwing contests but he liked the croquet best of all.

In the evening, the leftovers were attacked with ferocity, and then in the evening, there were long talks around the dinner tables. There was the large dinner table in the Dining Room, that was the "Adult" table, and there was the huge round table in the kitchen that was the "Kids'" table. Of course, there were twice as many kids than could fit around the "kid's" table. So, it was only the older kids who actually sat at that table. Everyone else sat on chairs pulled up near the table or on the old sofa in the TV Room that was separated from the kitchen by only a low partition.

At the kids table in the evening, there were all sorts of stupid talk about who was better, Batman or Superman. Or there was the perennial debate about when Uncle Al and old cousin Terry, who was too old to sit at the kids' table, would get into an argument.

At the end of the evening all the kids hated the idea that the evening had to end. Even if the next day was a Saturday, like when the fourth fell on a Friday, no one wanted that day to end. Once he overheard one of the aunts at the Adult table say that the holidays with family was just like the banquet in the Kingdom of God. As a matter of fact, maybe it WAS the banquet in the Kingdom of God. He didn't know what the adults thought, but for him and his cousins and brothers, this was BETTER than the banquet of the Kingdom of God. Because didn't everyone say that the sinners of the world wouldn't be at the banquet? And where would that leave Uncle Al and cousin Terry?

Of course, there was the minority opinion that aunt Opal always talked about that the sinners and the righteous were together at the Banquet of the Kingdom of God. The sinners were on one side of this long banquet table,and the righteous were on the other. They all had their arms in splints so that no one could feed themselves, but could feed their neighbors. On the sinners' side, no one ate, and everyone complained about how selfish everyone else was. On the righteous side everyone served their neighbors, and everyone had all the good things that the banquet had to offer.

Anyway everyone was welcome at the Holiday picnics of the Nicolls family, even the uncle whom they almost never saw but was always getting drunk and lived over the hardware store in a little one-room apartment.

The XO was worried and asked, "Airman Nicholls are you all right?"

He seemed to snap alert again and said, "Yes, sir. Sorry, I was just thinking of old times."

"With your family?"

"Yes, sir. It won't happen again."

The XO nodded his head, "That's OK. Just don't let it happen when you're up on the front. And actually, I was wondering. You seem to care about your family a lot."

"Yes, sir."

"How do you manage, knowing that they're all . .." He didn't know quite how to finish. He finally settled for, "gone?"

Nicholls actually smiled and said, "It's not that bad sir. I have a lot of good memories that I'll never forget."

"OK. Nicolls, I've got what I want. You're dismissed. Return to your duties."

"Thank you sir."

The XO and the Colonel Travers were having lunch in Travers office. It was pretty boring. They'd had to dig into the emergency stores, which were considerable but pretty boring. The XO handed a file folder to Travers, "This is the one I chose."

Travers flipped through it and commented, "Interesting choice. No particular citations for bravery or courage. He's an AFC. Why did you choose him?" He quickly added, "I'm not second guessing you. I'm just curious how your mind worked it out."

The XO smiled, "It was really easy when it finally came down to it. He'd lost far more than anyone else that I'd found. He is already living the Hell that you talked about when you gave me this assignment. He literally has dozens of really close relatives that he's lost forever—at least according to his calculations. They're always with him but he doesn't just soldier through—he is actually pretty happy."

"Is he a latent psychopath?"

"Far from it, at least as far as I can tell."

"So what do you figure?"

"It's going to sound strange, but I think he's had a vision of heaven."

Travers lifted his eyebrows at that.

"Oh, I don't mean that he's some sort of religious mystic. I mean that he figures that he's already experienced what heaven must be like, and I think that he thinks that his family is there already. He's mourning at times, but I really almost think that his mourning is that he's not there with them."

The eyebrows went up again.

"No. No. He's not suicidal. He just longs for them all to be together again. That isn't going to change just because he's lost some more friends."

Travers nodded. "Well, I wasn't going to change your decision no matter whom you chose, but I think you've got the right man. And good thing too. We're not that far away from the fifteenth."

The morning of the fifteenth "dawned" as many others had with the dull rumble of gunfire in the distance. People had already taken to sleeping with earplugs to keep the noise out. There had been no sign of a signal from the Ohio. Travers and everyone else were afraid. They were afraid that the wire would work and afraid that it wouldn't work. There was an active pool. People were placing bets as to whether it would work, it wouldn't work, and the long shot possibility that instead of people disappearing and going to the wizards, a bunch of aliens would appear.

No one had, strictly speaking, forbidden off-duty officers and enlistees from being present when the "port key" was used, so everyone had been jockeying to be off-duty at midnight on the fifteenth. A few skeptics had earned quite a lot of money by selling their slots on the duty roster away from the midnight hour. Strictly speaking that wasn't allowed but was the commanding officers' prerogative, but the skuttlebutt had gone out that such swaps would be permitted if they were submitted more than a day in advance.

Travis figured that any diversion from the daily grind of battle and radio silence was worth it.

The current odds were running 2.5 to 1 that the port key would work as advertised, 1 to 2 that nothing would happen and nine to 1 that aliens would show up.

Just before lunch, Travis had called Nicholls into his office to assign him his duty.

Travis handed him a dispatch bag. "Airman Nicholls, your assignment is to deliver this courier bag to the wizards of the Auror Office."

Nicholls stared at him and then asked, "Permission to speak frankly, sir?"

"Granted?"

"Do you expect me to take that church key out of here?"

"Yes, I do."

"With all respect sir, I refuse. My duty is to stay here with my unit, risk my life, and die."

"Well, Mister. You duty is to follow my orders, and my order to you is that you are to risk your life taking that PORT key and carrying the message to the wizards that the Muggles of the Space Defense Command will send their message to the USS Ohio if it is humanly possible. Is that clear?"

Nicholls had come to attention, and he stood silent for several minutes. His face contorted into a mask of pain suppressed. When he finally spoke, his words were hoarse with emotion. "Yes, sir. That is clear."

"Dismissed. And I want you on the basketball court at 23:30 hours."

"Yes, sir."

He left the office.

Everyone except Nicholls was on the basketball court at 23:00 hours. There had been a last minute lottery going on around the number of people who would actually accept the offer to evacuate the base. Nearly everyone had wanted zero, but there were a small number of people who chose other numbers, such as one, two, three, five, and there even had been one person who bought eleven.

At 23:30 hours, Nicholls showed up, carrying the courier bag. It had been handcuffed to his left wrist by the XO. The XO had brought the bird with its spool of wire encircling its leg.

Nicholls reported for duty to Travers, who had instructed him to stand at center court, which would be kept clear. The XO brought the bird, which perched on Nicholls shoulder. "Nicholls, did you have parakeets as a kid?"

"No, sir."

"Why do you suppose the bird seems to like you?"

"You've got me sir."

The XO, grabbed a tiny knob that was attached to the end of the wire and pulled about three feet of wire out and handed the end to Nicolls. "Good luck. God Speed, as the wizards say."

Nicholls only nodded.

Travers announced, "All personnel will back off the basketball court. I don't want anyone hurt by whatever is going to happen in a few minutes." Then, he walked out to Nicholls and shook his hand. He told only Nicholls, "This isn't personal. You're just the best man I've got for this duty. I've used my powers as acting President of the United States to award you the Congressional Medal of Honor and everyone else in the command Silver Stars. That's what's mostly in the courier bag. There are also a couple of letters to the Wizards or Aurors or whatever they are."

"But sir, the President can't award a Congressional Medal of Honor."

"Considering that there isn't a Congress either, I'm acting Speaker of the House and President of the Senate."

Nicholls laughed, the first time that anyone had seen him laugh in the last couple of days. "You is THE MAN." Travers laughed too and they parted.

Someone started a countdown with about one minute left. By the end everyone, including Travers, was participating. When they reached zero, nothing happened, and then Man, bird, and courier bag lifted slightly into the air. They seemed to rotate rapidly and disappeared.

The XO commented to Travers, "Well, I'll be damned. You know, I bet that nothing happens in the pool."

"Well, XO, I was smarter, I took the number one in the lottery."

In the Mall across the river from Portland, the darkness was dissolved by the spinning apparition that landed with a thud in the center of the food court. Several robed figures approached it. One pointed a wand at him and said, "Look up and open your eyes wide."

He did as ordered. The figure with the wand set it glowing brightly, almost blinding the figure. The wand bearer said, "Looks good. Welcome to the Auror Headquarters of the United States of America. Before we go anywhere, we have to administer an oath to you."

Another wizard approached, and they administered the oath. The first wizard said, "Let me introduce myself. You can call me Phil. What's your name?"

"Can I get up now?"

"Sure."

"I'm Airman First Class Frederick Nicholls, but you can call me Fred. And I've got messages for you."

The Battle Won

Thirty-six hours later the plan was submitted, approved and the attack was to begin one day later.

The Command Headquarters had dozens of monitors and thirty seats. Frank insisted in camping out there until it was over. The planners had said that there was no point to remaining there because the destruction of the plug that blocked the tunnel would take hours and then there would be hours more waiting for the tunnel to cool enough to let soldiers enter it. But Frank had insisted on watching from the beginning.

The big military laser was set up about a mile away—just in case that the humans had any surprises for them. The big central monitor showed nothing particularly interesting. For the first ten minutes, the plug looked unchanged. There were glints of intense light off it as bits of it heated to incandescence and then disappeared as quickly. Gradually, it turned red as it glowed with the heat of the laser.

Frank had to admit that it was boring. He started reading reports but he was interrupted by an aide who said, "They're getting close to burning all the way through." He looked up, and there was a deep gouge in the mountain that he couldn't see to the end of from the camera's vantage point. Then suddenly, it was through and there was some applause in the room. There were still a couple of hours wait while the hole cooled.

After almost ten hours, the first units were ready to enter. They sent a simple robot in to reconnoiter but it only survived a few seconds. The few images that it sent out were underexposed and didn't really show anything interesting.

Frank asked, "Why not just fire some explosive rounds down the tunnel?"

"We risk collapsing the tunnel. Then we'd have to dig through with a much smaller laser. That could take a lot of time. Instead, we'll send in a couple of platoons of our best troops."

That was what they did. Each had a video camera on their helmets. They proceeded cautiously into the tunnel, and they proceeded for about 20 meters when the unfriendly fire started up. There was quite a lot of automatic weapons fire going both directions. The alien troops were pinned down, and they couldn't make any headway because they couldn't use any high explosive shells. They were taking a lot casualties.

"This is crazy. We just can't sit there and trade small arms fire with them. We've got to take a chance with higher powered weapons."

The division commander who was running the offense shook his head and said, "I suppose so." They brought up some rocket propelled ordinance. There were quite a lot of explosions but after a short while there the unfriendly fire ended. The tunnel looked intact. The troops advanced carefully with plenty of fire. They just reached the makeshift defensive location that had been destroyed. The lieutenant in command reported that the tunnel turned just at that spot. They began to move beyond the bend when there was a tremendous explosion, and they lost contact with all the troops in that area. Someone else came on the line and reported.

"They had explosives built into the tunnel wall at that point. They detonated them. There must be 30 meters of rubble between us and the other side of the tunnel.' There was total silence in the Control Room. Finally the division commander said, 'Bring up the engineers and get to work, clearing the tunnel and shoring it up.'

Frank got up without a word and walked out of the Control Room.

Over the next several days, there were advances and setbacks. The tunnel collapsed a couple of times. Not many were hurt, but it was discouraging. Frank stayed in his office watching the feed from the tunnel and reading reports. He summoned the commander to his office.

"I'm reading casualty reports, and I want to know how many Souls we've lost."

"Too many."

"How many too many?"

"Fifty-four."

"And how many hosts?"

"I don't know, certainly hundreds."

"You don't know! How can you not know? Have you no regard for them at all?"

The general was not repentant. "No, I don't. They're tools—means to our end of establishing the greater good for our race. No, I don't have much regard for them."

Frank couldn't stand to hear anything except daily reports of progress. There was progress—in fits and starts. The tunnel was being taken, one section at a time. There was a sort of grim cycle. They

146

succeeded in winning a turning in the tunnel. Almost immediately, when they advanced beyond it, explosives buried deep in the tunnel walls detonated and thousands of tons of granite dropped into the tunnel forcing them to excavate.

After they'd broken through, they were immediately under attack killing hundreds of hosts and some Souls. Then they fought their way down the corridor to the next turning in the tunnel and the cycle repeated.

Once, Frank had decided that he had to go to the Control Room in person and review their progress. While he was there a report came in from the tunnel. There was a low level commander talking with the Control Center. "We've discovered some IED's a short distance beyond the current bend in the tunnel."

The officer in charge asked, "We've not run into IED's before. Are you sure that's what they are?"

"Sure, they're on the surface of the tunnel. That's never been true before."

Frank asked the officer in charge, "IED?"

He laughed, "Yes, it's an acronym that the humans use for explosives that are planted at the last minute without much forethought. They are just "improvised". Get it, 'Improvised Explosive Devices'."

"I'd never run into the term before."

The officer in the field was waiting for orders. The officer in charge at the Control Room asked, "Do you think you can disable them or should we explode them by remote?"

"They're pretty simple. I think that we can remove them safely."

"Go ahead."

In the Control Room they could see from the cameras of the two soldiers what was going on. The officer who had been talking to them went along with a technician. They worked their way up the tunnel a couple of dozen meters and silently communicated with each other by hand signals. The tech worked his way up along the wall of the tunnel using some kind of detector. He stopped by a small device. He cut a couple of wires that came out from the device. Then he removed it from the wall and placed it on the tunnel floor. The tech repeated the process three more times.

Finally, the officer whispered into his microphone. "We've got all the explosives and have disabled them. We're going to work our way back out of the tunnel. Clear the route, I'd hate for one of them to go off and kill anybody besides us."

Frank thought about the—what was it the humans called it— "gallows humor" and breathed a sigh of relief. They proceeded about a dozen meters. Then their two monitors went blank and there was a flash of light and a crash of sound from another monitor. He turned and walked toward the door of the Control Room. The officer in command of the Control Room said, "Wait Frank, it's OK. The tunnel didn't collapse."

Frank didn't turn, he just kept walking out the door.

▽

After that Frank didn't return to the Control Room for more than a week. He read the reports and occasionally, asked an officer in to give him a summary. Finally, he checked his calendar and found that there were only a couple of days until the date that they thought that the Ohio would come out from under the ice. He called a meeting of his staff. "We're only four days from our deadline for de-activating the Space Defense Command center. What does it look like?"

His lieutenant reported, "We've only got one more turning of the tunnel to capture, then it's a straight shot into the Command Center."

"What's the chance of capturing it within 3 days?"

The lieutenant just shook his head.

"That's what I thought. OK. We don't have any choice, we'll have to destroy it now. We have to be 100% sure of succeeding and within three days. How do we do it?"

The staff looked around at each other with nobody wanting to give the inevitable answer. Finally, somebody said, "Only one way. Nuke."

"How big?"

That caused lots of discussion. There were a variety of opinions ranging from 10 Kilotons up to 1 Megaton. The answer depended on whether the humans exploded the charges that everyone was sure were at the final turning of the tunnel to collapse thousands of tons of hard rock between themselves and the nuclear weapon. It also depended on just how sure you wanted to be to destroy it completely.

Nobody wanted to commit to a specific number, so Frank solved that problem by simply saying, "One Megaton."

There was a glum silence following that. Then Frank asked how much of the West needed to be evacuated. There were even more arguments about that. One school of thought was that even a Megaton, buried so deep in the mountain would release very little radioactivity outside the mountain. Then there was the group that thought that the tunnel formed a perfect barrel for directing radioactive debris out of the mountain and in the general direction of Denver.

"How long would it take us to evacuate Denver if necessary?"

No one knew. There was no precedent in history—anywhere in the known universe. Frank took that badly. He started to give the evacuation order but there were objections. That would be terrible for morale. They should wait to see if it was necessary. It was getting to be too much for even Frank to bear. He gave the order. "Evacuate Denver. Tell them that there is a small danger from a radioactive leak at a former US military reservation, and it is being cleaned up." They set the time for the detonation—60 hours. They had to evacuate all military personnel except those necessary to continue the pretense of an attack. There were to be military aircraft ready to evacuate the few remaining soldiers at a minute's notice.

Frank began to haunt the Control Room. He spent every waking hour there watching the monitors showing the interior of the tunnel and the exterior. There was a constant hail of small arms fire going on. The sound had almost disappeared from his consciousness as time went by. The weapon had been transported from the military depot a couple of hundred miles north. It arrived in a plain truck without escort of any sort. He supposed that was perfectly safe. No Soul would think of stealing from someone else's truck, but what would the few remaining rebels not dare to do. In any case it had arrived safely.

The crew that had come along had unloaded something that looked roughly like a small garbage bin for an apartment building. He couldn't make out any details of the device. He supposed that there must be controls on the outside. They stopped at the mouth of the tunnel, and he stared at it, dumbfounded for a moment. There it was: a weapon so terrible that he had ordered the evacuation of a city almost 100 miles away despite the fact that the weapon would detonate deep under a mountain.

His reverie was interrupted by the officer of the watch who asked, "Sir, we need your go-ahead to place and use the device."

"Yes, the device. That's a good safe word for it. I suppose no one has surrendered?"

The officer said, "What a joker you are!"

"Yea. Well, let's play the big practical joke on those humans. Yes. You have my order, use the 'device'."

The officer pulled out an iPad and handed it to Frank, "It's just a formality but I need your signature."

"Sure, it's CYA all the way." He picked up the stylus and wrote his name in bold script. "If I'm going to do this, I don't want anyone else getting the credit."

Then he had a thought, "Do you know that two of this world's physicists who invented the nuclear weapon had a little bet the first time that it was used?"

The officer looked a little uneasy, "No, sir."

"Yes, they placed a bet just before the first test of the weapon. One bet that the weapon would ignite the nitrogen in the atmosphere and start a fire-storm that would destroy the world."

"No, sir. I didn't know that."

"True." He started to turn away from the monitors but thought better of it and turned back to the officer, "Don't you want to know who won the bet?"

He just stared at Frank, then decided that maybe it was a joke and laughed politely. Then he went back to the control panels and gave the order to proceed with operation Big Bang.

Frank thought to himself, "Well, I guess we do have a sense of humor here."

Several soldiers pushed the device into the tunnel, and one of the monitors showed a camera view from a helmet. It seemed that the action happened in slow motion. The giant dust-bin reached the final turn, and they stopped. One of the soldiers went down to his knees and scrabbled around the corner. After a couple of minutes a platoon of men rounded the bend in the tunnel and sprinted up the tunnel. The view turned chaotic as the camera-bearer was jogging, himself, and the camera jostled along. After about six minutes, they emerged out of the tunnel. The camera man ran up into a VTOL troop carrier. Its engines had been running, and another monitor showed one of the craft take off. The others were still taking on troops.

The officer of the day started a countdown, "Five minutes." The other planes took off. Another monitor showed a view from one of the evacuation planes. It had started to climb rapidly upward.

"Four minutes". The plane was still accelerating vertically to get a clear route away from the site.

The plane finally started to level off and fly horizontally. It was beginning to accelerate. "Three minutes."

It was possible to see it make some progress horizontally, but it couldn't be even a mile away from the tunnel. "Two minutes."

The plane was now accelerating away from the tunnel mouth, but it couldn't be much farther than two miles away. "One minute."

Frank swore, "Shit! Why aren't they further away?"

Then the monitor showing the tunnel mouth went white and then black an instant later. There was no sound from that monitor. After a seemingly endless five seconds, a blast of sound and debris swept past the plane. The scene jumped,and then the camera from that plane went blank. Frank shifted his view to another monitor. The view bounced around as though the camera was being swung around by a giant's hand. Finally the view stabilized. The pilot reported. "We lost one of the planes. The shock wave threw it into the mountain-side. I'm still not sure that I've got us under control,but I think we'll make it."

He did make it. The rest of the Control Room shouted for joy. Frank wasn't excited. People were slapping his back, but he just nodded and walked back to his office. When he arrived, his aide was waiting for him. "I heard it went well."

"Yea, we only lost one plane-full of troops."

"But they won't be sending any message out about using Trident missiles."

"Yes you're right. I just don't feel excited about killing so many people."

At the Ministry

The visitor leaned back and said, "We've been thinking about that quite a lot. It is possible to overcome this strange mental compulsion, but it takes constant practice and vigilance. Maybe we could send a robot in to try to get images and explore."

Frank nodded and said, "Yes. Did you know that we have military robots—hardened military robots? They can go into really tough places. Their electronics are well-shielded."

The visitor's mouth gaped open, "You're kidding—military robots. I can't believe that our race would even develop such a thing."

"Oh, we didn't. We inherited them from another civilization. I think they've only been used in a couple of extreme cases. We don't have any here. One's on a ship in orbit, but we can get it down pretty quickly. We'll have to do some training on it. There are no experts here."

The visitor said, "Let me know when it's here. I want to be on the team that uses it."

"You've got it."

▽

Brahms said, "You see what I mean? We've got to do something about this before they break into the old Ministry of Magic."

Minerva squirmed uncomfortably and said, "I think we've got to see the Minister. If the old ministry is to be a battle ground, she'll need to know and get somebody working on the defense. I'll send an owl to the Minister. We should be able to see her in a day or two."

Wendt said, "I agree. Well, Brahms, you've done it again. This is big. We'd better do some thinking about proposals to avoid a pitched battle."

Minerva sent her owl. She and Wendt went back to his quarters. They left the Boy Genius at the Shrieking Shack. He wanted to review some more videos before going to bed on the cot in a corner of the Control Room.

The next morning, a reply came from the Ministry. The Minister would see them over lunch that day. The next time that was open for an appointment was two days later. Wendt told Minerva, "This is definitely the time that turnabout being fair play is real. Let's go drag the Boy Genius to the Ministry."

Minerva agreed and so they showed up at the Shrieking Shack. They found Brahms watching video on a small monitor on a desktop in the Control Booth. He was wearing headphones and didn't notice when they came in. Minerva put a finger to her lips to signal Wendt for silence. Then she sneaked up on Brahms and pulled off his head phones and shouted in his ears, "Good Morning."

He jumped like a cat being pursued by a pack of hounds. Minerva said in her best innocent tones, "Did I surprise you Mr. Brahms?"

He said, "No. No. I was just thinking about you."

Wendt said, "Come on we're going for a ride."

Brahms asked, "Where to?"

Minerva said, "We're off to meet the wizard—or more accurately, the witch of Azkaban."

Brahms just mumbled, "Huh?"

Minerva said matter-of-factly, "We've got a lunch date with the Minister of Magic. Let's go."

Brahms objected, "But you surely don't need me. I'm just a lowly Muggle. Surely she'll not pay any attention to me."

"But you'd like to see her again, wouldn't you?"

"I don't know about that."

Wendt just said, "You're coming. Let's go."

So, they walked down the lane from the Shrieking Shack almost to Hogsmeade. Brahms protested all the way, but he had no choice. When they got to Hogsmeade, they went into HoneyDukes. Brahms asked, "What is this store,and why are we stopping here?"

Wendt answered, "This is. . ."

"A sweet shoppe," Brahms supplied. "What's good wizard candy?"

Minerva said, "Try some of Bernie Bott's Every Flavor Beans." She pulled out her purse and said, "Go buy a galleon worth of candy, and we'll be on our way." He went off browsing and asked as he did, "But why are we here, surely not because you have a sweet tooth?"

Wendt answered, "We're going to Azkaban by floo. This shop has a fireplace that's connected to the floo network."

Brahms asked, 'Wait a minute. Is traveling the floo network anything like disapparating?"

"It's pretty much except more disgusting." Wendt said.

"In that case, I'll just be on my way."

Wendt proclaimed, "Coward!"

Minerva caught him by the scruff of his neck as though he were a Weasley trying to pull a fast one. "No, you're coming with us." They went to the counter and paid for Brahms purchases.

Wendt commented. "It's considered good form to buy something from any shop that let's you use their floo connection."

"But what if you don't want to use the floo network?"

"That's why I'm buying," Minerva said.

Brahms asked, "But why the sweet shop rather than some other?"

Minerva dragged him over to the fireplace and said, "Not every fireplace is large enough to accommodate three at a time. HoneyDukes' is."

They walked into the fireplace, each man taking one of Minerva's hands. She had Wendt pick up a handful of floo powder and throw it down as she said, "Azkaban". They disappeared in a gout of green flames and walked out into the large courtyard of Azkaban. They walked to the Cafeteria and found a young man waiting for them. He greeted them and said, "Come up to the Minister's Office. You'll join her for lunch there. They went up the elevator to the 10th floor where they found the Minister waiting for them. The lunch was good. There was a Lobster mayonaise and crisp green salad.

As they ate, they began with light chatter. The Minister asked Brahms, "So, you're the famous Boy Genius?"

He reddened and said, "I hear that some people call me that."

She quickly said, 'I understand it as a compliment." She leaned toward him across the table and said, "By the way, please call me Pam."

The Boy Genius said, "Yes, ma'am."

She looked at him askance, and he quickly corrected to "Pam, ma'am."

She went on, "I really have heard wonderful things about you. Is it true that you can see what happens in all the offices of our enemies?"

"It's not just I. Anyone can come down to our Control Room and see what's happening there any time of the day or night."

She chuckled and said, "I hope no one can do that to my offices." Brahms turned slightly pink and said, "I'd never do that."

She put her chin on her joined hands and stared at him, "Really? Don't you think it would be interesting?"

Brahms opened and closed his mouth a couple of times trying to compose an answer and gave up. Then he tried to change the subject, "In a way that's why we're here."

She refused to be deflected, "To see me in my offices. Do you know that I have quarters adjoining my office? I spend almost all my time here—a virtual prisoner."

Minerva interrupted the tête-à-tête, "Brahms is right, we came here to tell you what we saw and heard from the office of the commander of the alien's forces."

Pam said, "But we can't talk business over the meal. It would ruin our appetites. We'll talk over dessert and coffee."

Minerva rolled her eyes, giving in to superior force. Pam turned her gaze back to Brahms, "I really think that I must visit you in your lair to see your wonderful magic." And she seemingly impulsively reached out and squeezed Brahms forearm.

His head leaned slightly forward and said, "You'd be welcome any time—day or night."

She said, 'Oh, I could never get away during the day, but I would sooo enjoy visiting you after the working day."

Minerva, disgusted, said, "At this rate we'll never get to dessert."

Pam simply turned toward her a minute and glared. Then she turned back to Brahms and said, "I suppose Ms. McGonagall is right. What did you want to tell me?"

"We discovered today that the aliens have a good idea where the old Ministry of Magic is and they intend to break in." Brahms' gaze was still fixed solely on the Minister.

The Minister's gaze turned harder in some indefinable way and she asked, "Is that really true, Mr. Brahms?" And before he could answer, she turned to Wendt and asked, "Can they do that? We have all sorts of protective spells on it still."

Brahms simply said, "Yes." Wendt amplified, "I think they might be able to. They don't have magic but they're brilliant, they have very advanced technology and they're determined. Oh, yes. They have lots of manpower too."

The Minister's gaze turned to Minerva in appeal, but she simply said, "I trust Wendt's judgment in these things. If he thinks that they can break into the old Ministry, I think they can too."

Pam muttered, "Shit. What can we do?"

Wendt said, "What do we stand to lose if they do break in?"

Pam looked around from one to the other—as if trying to judge if they could each be trusted. "Everything is there. At least, everything that matters. The historical records, the Department of Mysteries, the Hall of Prophesies."

Wendt thought and said, "I think there's only one thing to do—burn it down."

Both Pam and Minerva jumped to their feet and shouted, "No." in unison, but a blank stare came over Brahms face. Wendt knew it rather well. He was gazing into the future, thinking about all the possibilities—like a chess master examining all the important variations on the move that he was contemplating. His mouth gaped open, and he finally said, "Yes.

"Yes. It would work. And, if we're lucky, there'll be no suspicion about how it happened."

Minerva sat again but looked disgusted. She said in rather thick Scotch brogue, "Well, what do you expect from a Muggle. No respect for wizard tradition."

Pam had a worried look on her face, and she unconsciously took Brahms' hand in hers, "Brahms, do you really think that's the only way?"

He looked over at Pam and said, "Yes, Pam. All the other alternatives that I see just get us into more trouble." Then he put his other hand over Pam's hand that was holding his, "And if I understand anything about magic, I think that it will be possible to protect all those things that you cherish."

He looked into her eyes and said, "All of the offices of the Ministry of Magic are underground aren't they?"

Pam's smile returned, and she said, "Yes. You're thinking of burning down the shell of a department store that stands over the Ministry while keeping the Ministry safe."

"The department store. And yes, burn it down, protect the sub-levels from the fire, and make sure that the Ministry levels would not be exposed by clearing the debris of the fire. Is that possible?"

Pam looked over at him, and Wendt could have sworn that it was a look of rapt attention with which she regarded him as she said, "Oh, yes! I'm sure we can do that. As a matter of fact, we really need to get together and discuss the details. That would give me a chance to see your Shrieking Shack too. What do you say that I come by tonight!"

Brahms was dumb-struck. He finally gulped and said, "That would be wonderful. I mean, we really need to do that. I think the aliens are going to move quickly on the Old Ministry."

Wendt said, "Yes, we need to plan how we're going to. " At that point he stopped what he was saying because a well-aimed shoe had hit his shin and made him gasp. This gave Minerva an opportunity to observe that she was sure that they would consult others when the time was proper. Wendt merely said, "Ooooff."

Minerva went on, "I really don't need any dessert. I'm trying to cut back. Right, Wendt?"

Wendt massaged his shin and said, "Of course. I don't like coffee much anyway."

"Then we'll see you two later," Pam said as Wendt got up and hobbled off with Minerva. Wendt turned back and saw Pam give Minerva a wink with the eye not in Brahm's view.

As they left the apartment, Wendt commented, "I suppose you think that you've done a service for young love."

"There's nothing young about either of them."

"Well, then, mature love."

"I just thought that if they could be as happy as we are, the world would be a better place."

The next morning, Brahms didn't show up for breakfast. It wasn't very strange. He often spent days on end at the Shack working on some new hack to get into more of the alien network. But by the afternoon, Wendt thought that it was high time that he get a status report on the alien progress getting their war robot going. So, Wendt walked to the Shrieking Shack. He found the Boy Genius' chief lieutenant holding the fort down.

"Roberts, what's going on?"

"Oh, the aliens just got their toy-bot down from orbit and they're starting to put it through its paces. Would you like to see?"

"Sure." Roberts switched the view on his desktop monitor to one of the big monitors, and what filled the screen was something that fascinated Wendt. It seemed to be a strange amalgam of grace and stupendous power, of complexity with its multiple articulated limbs and multiple tool kits on the ends of them and of simplicity. The appearance of simplicity came from the fluid, economical movements that it used to achieve its objective. It was in a large, mostly empty warehouse, except that there was a jumble of strangely shaped crates and I-beams and who-knew-what-all. It looked rather like a game of pick-up-sticks but with two or three ton sticks.

It seemed to be searching for something, but it showed great patience. It took one thing off the pile at a time. Each was moved with transcendent delicacy whether it was a two-by-four or a construction girder. It seemed to be working its way into the heart of the stack but left a bewildering pile of things un-moved. It was such a fascinating display of dexterity and strength that neither of the men wanted to break the silence as they watched. Finally, it pulled an object from the heart of the stack. It was so small that they couldn't tell what it was, but the robot handed it over to one of the "trainers", dropping it exquisitely into the man's hand.

They both released their breath simultaneously and looked at each other. Roberts said, "It's hard to believe that that is a war robot." But just as he said that, the man who had received the object turned back to the machine and said, "Destroy the pile."

Almost instantly, the robot swung around and pointed one of its limbs at the stack and something happened. The center of the stack seemed to explode, and the pile collapsed to a much smaller pile.

Wendt asked, "Can we get a slow-motion view of that?"

Roberts said "Sure." He manipulated his keyboard and the scene re-wound to show the robot just before it had swung around. The motion was incredibly slow. Finally they saw what looked like a small white object greatly distorted by its speed flash across the screen. Roberts stopped the motion and reversed it, a single frame at a time. There were only two frames where it was visible. One showed the object elongated half-way to the target and the next showed the elongated object just arriving at the target.

"What was that?"

Roberts scratched the stubble on his chin and said, "You know what? That thing kind of looked like a golf ball."

Wendt agreed. Then, he asked where Brahms was. Roberts said that he'd not seen Brahms since the previous night when he was strutting around with the woman that he'd brought there—apparently, the Minister of Magic, if you could believe it. How Brahms had talked a classy dame like the Minister into slumming in their neighborhood, he couldn't figure.

Wendt allowed that love knows no logic.

Roberts said, "But that's all that the Boy Genius does know!"

"Oh, I think that Brahms knows a whole lot more about love than he did yesterday. Do you have any idea where he is now?"

"You've got me. By the way, I think that we'll start hacking into that baby," Roberts said while pointing at the screen.

Wendt had been about to leave, but at that last statement he turned back. "Look, I'd rather that you not try any hacking without Brahms being here to supervise. That thing is the product of a race even more advanced than these aliens. I think that it's quite possible that it might catch you at it."

Roberts squinted at him, "Come on, that race was defeated by these guys. They can't have been that great."

"Oh, they were that great—at least at technology. Let me remind you that these aliens are like a whole race of Riddles. They very nearly defeated us completely, and the book isn't closed by a long shot on this war."

Wendt walked back to the castle.

The Salamander

That night at supper, Brahms showed up for the first time that day. He had a big smile on his face, and he was whistling! He sat down beside Minerva and Wendt, who commented, "I can't remember you ever whistling. I didn't even think that you knew how to."

Brahms looked up from his plate that he'd been piling high with all sorts of food "Sorry, did you say something?"

Minerva looked at Wendt and just rolled her eyes. Wendt said, "Nothing important. But now I will say something important. We were kind of expecting to hear from you about details of having a fire sale at a department store."

Brahms said, 'Oh, that."

"Yes, Oh, that. What about it."

"Well Pam and I have it all set. We agreed that we would use a Dali something like that."

Wendt asked, "What? A Dali?"

"Well, it was Dali or Salvador or something like that."

Minerva perked up and lent toward Brahms, "Did you mean a Salamander?"

"Yeh, I think it was something like that—salvador, salamander, salle de bain, something like that."

Minerva looked over at Wendt and said, "He doesn't know what the significance of that is, and he's probably not in any state to talk seriously at the moment about it anyway. But that worries me. Salamanders are tricky creatures. Sometimes they're perfectly reasonable, and sometimes they're as bad as fire demons. If one of those things were to get out of control, it could burn down all of London before it was finished."

Brahms said, "Sure, I do. That's why we're using them. I figure that we can destroy that crazy war robot with it. I don't think an ordinary fire would do the trick."

Minerva looked at him again—carefully. Then Brahms said, "Oh, don't think that because Pam and I get along pretty well that I'm not thinking when I'm with her."

Minerva's mouth dropped open for a second and then she said, "Get along well together. Get along well together! You two are as loopy as Gnomes when you're together. Why would you think that you two could come up with a good idea when you're, you're. . ." Apparently, Minerva couldn't come up with the right verb, so she let the sentence hang.

Wendt said, "OK. Here's the acid test. Who's going to do this magic?"

Brahms said, "We're not morons. Do you think that I would volunteer Pam for that? She's a politician."

Wendt began to have a bad feeling about this, "Just who are you volunteering for this little plum of an assignment?"

Brahms said, "Well, I'm not supposed to tell before Pam gets a chance to talk to you two, but ."

Minerva echoed, "You two. Do you mean to say that she's going to ask us to do it?"

"Well, of course, who else would be better? Minerva you're a brilliant witch. And, Wendt, you're almost as smart as I am. And a damn site more practical."

Wendt grumbled, "I'd say you were pretty practical in this case."

Brahms went on, "Now, you two have to promise that you won't tell Pam that I tattle-tailed on her and please try to seem surprised when she asks."

Wendt said, "How can I act surprised when you didn't surprise me in the least by your announcement."

Brahms clapped Wendt on the back and said, "Oh, don't be a bad sport about it. It'll all turn out just fine. You and Minerva always seem to land on your feet in these crazy things."

"When are we getting together to plan this little campaign of arson?"

Brahms said, "Oh, I think that Pam's going to invite you to breakfast tomorrow, and she'll surprise you then. We'll spend the morning planning details."

"Thanks for the heads-up." Minerva said, as an owl flew into the Great Hall and landed in front of the three. It held out its claw toward Minerva, who removed the message. She said in mock surprise, "Oh, you'll never guess who wrote. Our dear friend Pam has invited us to breakfast tomorrow at her apartment at 7:30AM. And you'll never guess what. Brahms, you're invited too. What will I wear?"

She pulled a quill out of her purse and wrote a little note on the message. She quoted it as she wrote, "Dearest Pam, it would be a great honor and privilege to join you for breakfast tomorrow at your apartment." She rolled it up, tied it to the owl's leg and sent it on its way.

▽

The next morning, the three met at 7AM in the Great Hall. Minerva took both their hands and they walked into the fireplace. They came out as usual. Brahms seemed almost to be walking on air. He greeted Pam by kissing her hand. Minerva and Wendt just looked the other way. The breakfast was good, but the conversation was way too upbeat for half of the participants.

There either was nothing interesting about the breakfast or it was the most exciting breakfast you'd ever had depending on whom you asked;. After it was over, the real business began. They moved to a Conference Room. The attendees included a couple of Aurors and committee chairs in the Ministry in addition to the breakfast participants.

The meeting was basically an opportunity for the department heads to complain about being left out of the decision to torch the Ministry of Magic or at least the face it presented to Muggles. There was endless discussion of the reasons that it was necessary to do it and then to slowly extract agreement from each. Lunch came and went. Finally, the meeting ended, and the exhausted survivors went on to the true business of the day—planning the act of arson.

In this meeting there were only the happy four from breakfast and a couple of Aurors. One of them was Longbottom. Minerva and Wendt greeted him warmly. He kidded Wendt, as he always did when they met, about his abandoning Hogwarts in its Hour of Greatest Need.

Brahms had never seen this performance and thought it was genuine. He set out to defend Wendt. For example, he said, "Wendt was sitting in a jail cell when school started. He was under armed guard. How do you expect him to have gone to Hogwarts? And wouldn't the Carows just have sent him to Azkaban—if he were lucky."

Both Wendt and Longbottom laughed. "Sorry, Brahms, this is just a little joke between us that we go through every time we meet."

Longbottom added, "Wendt loves it."

"Oh, yeh. Just not as much as you do."

Wendt had not met the other Aurors before. For this meeting Pam was all business. She had to be, the Aurors were—except maybe Longbottom. The Aurors had been briefed about the program. For the most part they weren't very pleased.

The Auror, Jeffries, who was short, wiry, and looked like he spent most of the day in the gym or on the running track, did most of the talking. He summed up his position in one question—"Let me get this straight. You, Madame Minister, have taken the advice of two, two . . . Muggles and approve of this, this scheme to burn down the Ministry?"

Madame Minister answered quite calmly and coldly, "I've approved further exploration of this proposal. If there are no fatal flaws that are uncovered, we will proceed with it.

"Now, I'm going to ask the Auror Office some questions and you'll perform your duty and give me advice—which I may or may not follow. Is that clear?"

"Yes, mum," everyone in the room repeated.

"OK. First question, is it possible to limit the damage that a Salamander would do to one building and only the above ground parts and the first basement?"

Jeffries looked over at Longbottom and said, "That's why we've brought Longbottom along. He's our resident expert on Salamanders and other fire-based creatures.

"Well, Longbottom, what do you say?"

Longbottom was all seriousness, "Sir, I think that it is possible. You just have to lay out the limits to the Salamander at the start. Then they're reliable. The trick is to make instructions very clear. Like many magical creatures, it'll interpret your instructions with as much latitude as you permit. If you're not very clear, there's no telling what will happen."

Pam asked him directly, "Do you think that you could give a Salamander clear enough instructions to guarantee that it wouldn't do more damage than we want?"

Longbottom smiled, winked at McGonagall, and answered, "I know that I could."

She turned to Jeffries, "Do you trust him?" And then to Longbottom, "No offense intended."

Longbottom said equably, "None taken, ma'am."

Jeffries answered, "I'd rather not admit it, but where Salamanders and other fire creatures come in, I do."

Pam nodded and then said, "OK. How would you organize this operation?"

Jeffries had evidently been thinking about it because he started rattling off points: He'd have 4 observation posts on each of the four streets that faced the department store. Each would have to have someone who was good with *patronuses* because they'd use the *patronus* to communicate with the Command Center for the operation. They'd also have to have someone who was good at *obliviation*. Unfortunately, they were doing a lot of *obliviating* of memories these days because there were unwanted encounters of aliens with people, and the memory had to be *obliviated* from the aliens. They did have access to some contractors who could be brought in when there just weren't enough Ministry *obliviators* to go around. He would suggest one of them for this operation—probably the best there was. Who was it? It was actually a former professor at Hogwarts, Gilderoy Lockhart.

At that Longbottom gave a start and asked, "Is he out of St. Mongo's? I thought he was a hopeless case."

Jeffries said, "Yes, he recovered enough to resume a career as an *obliviator*. He was released a couple of years ago. I admit he has his little quirks like wanting to leave an autograph with everyone whose memory he *obliviates*, but beyond that, he's really pretty good.

Wendt commented that he'd seen him once since Potter left Hogwarts and he was convinced that he'd never return to society.

Jeffries went on and said that the Command Center should be in the Old Ministry itself. The team there should consist of Longbottom; who'd handle the Salamander: Wendt who would be in local command; and a backup for Longbottom who could handle the Salamander if necessary and be a general backup for everyone.

He said, "I think that Minerva should take that position. She's worked with Wendt a lot, knows Longbottom well, is a darn good wizard."

Minerva frowned and said, "Thank you so much for the recommendation. I will take the post; but what about Brahms. He should have a role in this operation."

The Minister immediately spoke up, "He can be liaison with me. I need to be aware of everything that's going on."

Jeffries stared at her a moment and nodded his head. "Very well. We'll provide assignments for the observation post and inform you of them immediately."

Pam wanted to know when they could complete the operation. Wendt said that since they wanted to do it when the robot was in the building, it'd have to wait on the aliens' pleasure. Pam frowned at that, but they were all stuck.

As a matter of fact, the operation started sooner than anyone really wanted it to. The next day, at Hogwarts, Brahms tackled Wendt and said, "Come, now. Fast!" The two of them sprinted all of the distance, well, a lot of the distance to the Shrieking Shack. As they went, Wendt complained about their not finding Minerva so that they could disapparate there. When they arrived, they hardly stopped to be passed through to the Control Room.

When they finally arrived there, Brahms huffed out between deep breaths, "The main monitor, Frank's office. Meeting coming up any minute. Subject—attack on the Ministry."

The aliens entered the field of view of the camera and sat around Frank's desk. He was angry. Nobody in the Control Room had seen him angry before. He was saying, "What do you mean that we're not ready to go after the London Nexus? You've been playing with that damn robot for days now. I've seen him going through his paces. He's brilliant. What are you waiting for?"

One of the aliens said, "Look, Frank. None of us has ever used one of those robots in the wild. Have you seen the operating manual? It takes up thousands of pages. The damn things are smart, but they aren't telepathic. You've got to give them precise instructions. When they're on a mission, they cut off all communications with the rest of the universe. They do what they have to do to accomplish their instructions, and you can't change them mid-course. It's all about preventing enemies from overriding their programming. So, you've got to have instructions that can handle all things that might come up.

Another said, "Right. I've been programming them the most. You make one little miscalculation, and they're off on some tangent that you might not be able to get them back from for days. We've got to have more time to practice with him."

Frank seemed somewhat mollified, but he was still curt. "OK. OK. How much more time do you need?"

"I don't know."

Frank's exasperation factor was getting higher. "Well, can you guess?"

The aliens all looked pointedly at any location other than Frank. They all found fascinating things on the floor, out the window, on the ceiling. Finally one of them said, "I think that we can be ready in two weeks." There were nods around the room, but none enthusiastic.

That gave them their timetable. There were technical details that consumed the rest of the alien's meeting. Brahms was fascinated as the meeting went on. Wendt dropped into a chair. He knew the time would come soon, but he'd not really dared to think that it might be so soon.

Minerva had apparently heard that Brahms was looking for them and had followed after them. She was still standing. She smiled and said to Wendt, "Well, we've got to get ready." She turned to Brahms and said, "Good, work." He absently nodded his head while his eyes were riveted to the screen.

About ten days later, Brahms had brought a piece of paper to Wendt's office. It had one thing, a time, written on it – 10 PM Wednesday. Wendt looked up and asked, "That's the date that they take the robot out for a stroll?"

Brahms nodded and said, "I watched their last planning meeting. They named the date and time. They think that they're going to get to the bottom of a lot of mysteries."

Wendt couldn't help smiling, "They can think that if it makes them feel better." He went on, "But we're going to teach them that there are more wonders in Heaven and Earth than are dreamt of in their philosophy."

Wendt added, "I hope."

They went to see Minerva in the Headmistress's Office. She seemed to have been expecting them. She had a freshly brewed pot of tea. She poured cups for them and asked mildly, "What brings you two young men to my office?"

Wendt said, "I've a feeling that you know perfectly well."

"If you mean that we've got to get ready for an assault on the Ministry, then yes."

Brahms shook his head sorrowfully, "How could you know – and with enough time to fix tea?"

Minerva smiled and said, "The Weasleys are not the only ones who know how to use extensible ears."

Wendt laughed, "You mean that you've had my room bugged?"

"I don't know what you mean by 'bugged' but I do know everything that goes on in your office – even when I'm not there." She said with a smug smile. "I've sent an owl to the Ministry. They'll have the Aurors here soon to plan our operation's last minute details."

The Ministry Aurors arrived the next morning. There were a dozen of them, and they set up their Command Center in Minerva's office. They explained that they wanted to be undisturbed, and hers was the only office with size and privacy for this sort of operation – especially with the grounds crawling with wizards and witches who were refugees. Wendt, of course, didn't mention the Shrieking Shack. It would be the end of his Control Center if they moved into those luxurious digs.

The Aurors set up a big bulletin board – about the size of one of the walls of his office. It had four big photos. Well, they were really like video screens showing the four sides of a large dilapidated building. It was actually the old deserted department store atop the old Ministry of Magic. They showed a live feed from the block where it was. In addition, there were still photos underneath the four live video photos. They showed the locations in adjoining buildings where there were Auror observation posts. There were Auror teams in each of them. There were other notes underneath those. There were photos of the Aurors manning them; there were duty schedules for the observer at each; there were little bio's of each of the Aurors – what their specialties were, age, years of experience and so forth.

Minerva and Wendt watched them set it up. When one of the Auror photos was posted, they both gave a start. "Isn't that Ginny Weasley?" they said in chorus.

One of the Aurors heard and said, "What? Oh, yes. Weasley, Ginevra Potter nee Weasley. She's good. I once criticized her in a team meeting and was the victim of a back-bogey hex. I could never prove it was her, but . . ."

When they had set up the big board, one of them materialized a big mahogany table and chairs. In the evening there was a meeting there, which Minerva and Wendt got to attend. As a matter of fact, they were the star attractions. The meeting was a planning session for the operation that they were going to run when the aliens attempted to break into the Ministry. Of course, the aliens didn't know that that was what they were doing, but the wizards did.

The general idea was that Minerva, Wendt, Longbottom and another Auror to be named later would man a local command post in the Ministry itself. The observation posts would keep an eye open for the Robot. When spotted, they'd inform the command post and Longbottom would deploy to the Department store level. When the observers saw the Robot enter the building, Longbottom would release the Salamander and would let it start a fire, but keep it strictly under control. The hope was that the Robot would be lured close to the fire, and then the Salamander would be allowed to start a real conflagration that would burn the department store to the ground destroying the Robot. Then the spells repelling Muggles would be released, and the aliens would conclude that the Robot had somehow caused the fire, hadn't been able to escape, and that the fire had destroyed whatever was causing the repulsion.

The Auror commander, Collin Baker invited questions.

Wendt asked, "Just how do we keep the fire from burning up the Ministry?"

"That's the job of the other Auror. We're looking for our best fire-suppressor. He'll keep the fire from flowing down to the Ministry."

"But, you've not found anyone, right?"

"Well, it's strictly a volunteer opportunity. We can't force anyone to take it."

Minerva sneered, "But you don't mind forcing us to take our stand in the Ministry."

Baker harrumphed and tried to look dignified. "But it was your idea. Surely, you believe in it enough to volunteer for it?"

Minerva just looked at him as though he were a 2nd year late for one of her classes. He tried to maintain his dignity, but it was a standoff.

Baker just finished weakly, "We'll inform you as soon as we've found someone."

He went on, "We want to put your team in place tomorrow afternoon at the latest. We don't want to be caught by a last minute change in plan by the aliens, right?"

Wendt said, "Right. Just how are we going to get into the Ministry?"

Baker seemed dumbfounded. Finally, he said, "Well, I supposed the floo network still goes there. Doesn't it?"

Minerva said, "I don't know. I guess we'll find out."

Longbottom rubbed his hands together and said, "This will be fun."

Wendt commented, "You know ever since your 7th year I've been very suspicious of your idea of fun."

What Happened in the Shrieking Shack

The day began quietly enough at the Shack, as the residents had been calling it. Monitoring all the miscellaneous activity at Alien Central was mostly filtering out all the pointless water-cooler talk from the significant. It was amazing how the aliens had taken up the leisure activities of their hosts. There was endless conversation about the all-England cup play that was coming up. There was an old saying that "Football is the Gentlemen's Game played by hooligans, and Rugby is the hooligans game played by Gentlemen".

Both sports had turned into gentlemanly games played by gentlemen as practiced by the aliens. Somehow no one came out of a scrum bruised, and football had become a non-contact sport, except for true accidents. And those accidents happened only very rarely. The Boy Genius (even Brahms thought of himself that way) had tried watching both Rugby and Football. He'd given up when he saw a goalie ask that his opponent, who had been in the box trying to head it in, be given a PK because the goalie had knocked him down. His opponent had insisted that he'd actually been offside and so shouldn't have a penalty kick. The B.G. had thrown a pencil that he'd been using to write C+ code at the Telly and had sworn off all sports until the last bloody alien was kicked off the planet—preferably by his favorite Rugby player, drop kicking him through goalposts and into a departing spaceship.

That morning had been boring until there was a knock on his office door. He asked the welcome diversion from boredom to enter. She did. That startled the B.G., who immediately pulled his feet off his desk and jumped up. He walked over to the tall, dark dark-haired young lady. "I don't think we've met. No, I'm sure that we haven't. I'm . . . "

But she anticipated him, "Nicolas Brahms, the Boy Genius; yes, I know your nickname. I'm Professor Sinistra. I'm here because I'm worried by something I saw last night."

"Really? What was it?" It seemed unlikely that she'd seen anything that would be worrisome around here—except maybe for the giant spiders.

"I don't know. It was flying—high and far away. I don't know what it was, and I'm afraid it was alien-made."

Internally, Brahms, shook his head but said, "Would you describe it, please?"

"I saw it silhouetted against the nearly full Moon. It was, well, do you have paper and pencil? I could sketch it." He handed her both, and she quickly drew a pretty fair representation of the surface of the moon. Over it superimposed a long thin pencil shape with some kind of tail. Then she drew another picture of the moon with a silhouette. But this time it was a very different cross-section with two surfaces protuding at about 90 degrees to each other. She said, "It seemed to turn while I was watching it and then looked like this."

That made Brahms stare. He said, incredulously, "That's a Raptor."

"No, I think it's some kind of airplane."

"No, NO. It's a U.S. Air Force plane called a Raptor. It's probably the most advanced airplane on the planet. I don't think that even the aliens have anything like it. They don't have to fight many battles in air. They don't need that sort of airplane. What the bloody hell was it doing flying within view of anyone here? How could it get here, with all the anti-Muggle spells?"

"It wasn't close. It was quite far away."

"If you saw it in that detail, how could it have been that far away?"

"I was watching through a telescope."

Brahms jumped up and laughed, "Don't you mean a crystal ball? Not really a telescope? I thought that you witches didn't do anything that smacked of **SCIENCE**?"

Sinistra stepped right up to him and stuck her nose right up to his and said, "I have a degree in astronomy from Princeton."

Brahms took a step back, "You mean Princeton as in Princeton, NJ?"

"No, I mean Princeton, Texas. Of course, I mean Princeton, NJ. Where's your degree from?" She was more belligerent than ever closing the distance between them.

"Well, the University of Edinburgh. If I may be bold, how did you get into astronomy—I mean, real astronomy?"

She harrumphed and said, "I got into **REAL** astronomy because I was curious about the stars and planets, and I didn't buy the centaurs' ideas about telling the future through the stars. The sort of future that you can see in the stars are things like the next transit of Mercury or the next solar eclipse."

Brahms laughed and said, "Well said! So, what do you do for a living? Don't tell me that you teach somewhere?"

She smiled slyly and said, 'Of course, I do. I teach here at Hogwarts."

"Now, I know you're kidding me. This school would never have a Muggle subject like Astronomy. What do you really do?"

"I really teach Astronomy—not Astrology—here at Hogwarts." She added, "You should come see my class some time. You might learn something."

An explosive, "Hah!" was all the response that she got out of him.

"Well, then, I dare you to come to my class and prove me wrong about anything I teach!"

"You're on. What will we wager?"

Sinistra didn't have a suggestion. Finally, Brahms said, "If I win, you let me take you out to dinner."

"What if I win?"

"Then I let you take me out to dinner."

"Somehow, that doesn't seem quite like a legit bet."

"Well then, you come up with something better."

She twisted her face into a sort of caricature of concentration but she finally said nothing and shrugged.

"Done then. Where do you want to go out to dinner?"

She laughed, for the first time of the day. "Well, there really isn't that much choice. If times were normal, we could disapparate to London and pick from a thousand restaurants. As it is, we have to be satisfied with a choice of the Three Broomsticks, The Hogshead or Madame Paddifoots."

Brahms laughed and said, "Quite a selection. Maybe we rethink our wager."

Sinistra said, "Oh, no you don't. You're not backing out now. And we don't have to go to one of those three. London will be back again. And we can go to a real restaurant. I'll tell you what. I'll take you to the continent and we can go to a Bistro in Paris or a Taqueria in Seville or a bar in Denmark. What do you say?"

Brahms said, "I'll do the taking around here. That's the terms of the bet. So when is your next class?"

"Before then, I'm worried about this Rapture thingee. Why are they flying in this area? How can we know when they are? How can we defend ourselves?"

Brahms scratched his chin. He got up and paced. He examined his shoes. Finally, he said, "Do you have telescopes?"

"Yes, only one of any size. The rest are large-field low-power telescopes that the students use. In class."

"Good, we can use those to scan the skies for unfriendly flying objects."

"Oh, UFO's," she said.

He laughed again. "Yes, I suppose so, though most Muggles wouldn't call them that. We'll have to move them here where the electronics that we'll attach to them won't be disturbed by magic. We'll scan the horizon. I think that there won't be any that will fly overhead—unless they already have an idea of where we are and program some to fly over this area."

He called in an assistant and instructed him to find some LCD cameras that could be fitted to telescopes. Professor Sinistra and he discussed moving and setting up telescopes near the Shack. They decided to do that right away. Professor Sinistra and Brahms went to the Astronomy Tower. There was no one up there at that time of day. When they arrived at the top of the tower after a trot up the flight after flight of stairs, they were exhausted and dropped onto a couple of stools. She picked up her wand and flicked it at one telescope. It lifted off the floor and floated off toward the stairs and disappeared down them. She flicked the wand at another one. It followed the first. And so on.

As he followed the telescopes with his eye, he followed the line of sight back to the wand and the hand that directed it. "Will they find their way down to the Shrieking on their own?"

'Oh, I suppose so, but we should accompany them down. But we don't need to rush it, just follow them and make sure none goes astray."

"So, we have a little time to talk?"

"Certainly, but what do you want to talk about?"

"What would I talk to you about! Oh, what about Princeton? What about astronomy? What about America? What about music for the matter of that? There are probably a thousand questions that we could talk about." And so, they talked about her interest in astronomy, about how her father encouraged her to follow it wherever it led—even if it led to a Muggle University. He didn't anticipate that it would lead to the States, but he even forced a grin when she told him in a transport of ecstasy about being accepted to the great American Muggle University, Princeton.

She told him about her trip there by floo powder to the Leaky Cauldron and then by Muggle cab to Gatwick and then by Boeing 707 to JFK in New York and then by Muggle bus to Princeton New Jersey and then by Muggle cab to her dorm.

She told him about the beautiful little town of Princeton, of meeting people who actually were friends of Einstein and John von Neumann. She told him about taking day trips to New York City and

171

seeing concerts at the Kennedy Center and meeting American witches and wizards in Greenwich Village. She talked about almost being recruited to work for Bell Labs in New Jersey.

She wondered, "Where would I be now if I'd taken that post?"

Sobered by the thought Brahms said, "I hate to think." That thought silenced them both for a bit, and then she said, "I suppose that we ought to go see what's happened with the telescopes."

With that they looked up and realized that the sun had set, and the sky had turned dark. They stared at each other for a moment, and Brahms asked, "How'd that happen?"

"Oh, we were both just wool-gathering and it snuck up on us."

"Are you hungry?"

She laughed and said, "Famished, but the Great Hall is closed for the evening, I'm sure."

"Have you ever been down to the kitchens?"

"The kitchens? Oh, you mean where the house elves are?"

"Yes."

"No, I guess I haven't. Have you?"

"It was one of the first places that I found when I got here. You don't really mean that you've never been there?"

She harrumphed, "Well, certainly not. They were off limits to the students when I went to school here, and as a teacher—well, I never missed a meal."

"Then, you've missed an important part of your education. Let's go." He grabbed her hand and led her a merry chase down the many flights of stairs to the basement level where the kitchens were. When they got down to that level, he slowed down, and she was able to catch her breath and speak.

"Are you sure that you want to interrupt them? They're probably almost finished cleaning up from Supper."

"Come on." He opened a door, and they went inside. There was a large clean modern kitchen with stainless steel everywhere. There were work tables, ovens, grills, There were house elves everywhere. One of them noticed them and said, "Oh, hi Brahms. Who's your friend?"

"She's one of the professors. Professor Aurora Sinistra, I'd like you to meet, uh. . . Don't tell me. It's . . . Babou, right?"

"Yes, sir. What can we do for you? Are you looking for a late night snack?"

"Actually, we missed supper and thought you might have some left-overs."

"Of course, of course. Sit down at that table. I'll have a couple of plates for you *momentito*."

As they waited, Sinistra complained that Brahms hadn't told her anything about himself. He agreed and began to tell her a bit of his

172

history. He told about growing up in Anglesey, about his father who had driven a lorry at an RAF base, about his mom who had taught at a local private school. He'd gone to a traditional University. As a matter of fact, he'd not learned his trade at any University. He'd always been a genius (boy) at computers. He'd program cash registers and business computers for small businesses in the area to earn money. Before he'd finished 6th form, he had a consulting business and had done some hacking for fun. He'd had to stop at that point for some explanations.

Sinistra wanted to know what hacking was. He'd answered, "Well, it's hard to explain if you don't know anything about computers. Tell me what you know about computers."

Sinistra had said, "Well, when we were at Princeton, I programmed a super-computer to solve some astrophysical problems—like simulation of motions of clusters of stars, but I've never heard of computers like that being used in cash registers or small businesses. It seemed like you had to have a national laboratory budget to have a computer."

Brahms laughed so hard that he almost couldn't breathe and he certainly wasn't able to protest that he wasn't laughing at her. However, she didn't take it so kindly. She finally pulled out her wand when it was apparent that Brahms was having trouble breathing.

That sobered him up pretty quickly, "Don't jinx me, I wasn't laughing at you."

She was still cross, but said, "I was just afraid that I'd have to give you artificial perspiration or something, so I was going to use a spell to give you a serious mood to stop the laughing."

"Good. I was afraid that. . . that . . . oh, never mind. But I really wasn't laughing at you, I just had a mental picture of the sweet shop in my home town using a CRAY 9000 to figure the value-added tax on a bag of gum drops." At that she started laughing as well, tears coming to her eyes.

She said, "I see what you mean."

At that they both noticed Babou standing there with two plates of food. She quickly asked, "How long have you been standing there with our food?"

"Not, long Ms."

"I'm so sorry that we didn't notice you. Here let me take those." She quickly relieved him of the plates that had grown cool. He seemed to realize that and tried to take them back but Sinistra was not having any of it.

She told him not to worry and just "toddle off", which he eventually did—not any too happy. She asked Brahms to keep going.

"Anyway, I had my own personal computer." He saw her puzzled look and said, "It's a very small computer. Not very powerful but able to do basic calculation types.

"Anyway, I used my personal computer to do hacking." Again the puzzled look. "Hacking is the art of deducing how computer programs work without seeing the code they use to solve problems."

"Computers solve problems? I thought they created them." She said it with a perfectly straight face, but Brahms knew that she was kidding him. He gave her a stare that told her that he wasn't taking any of that kind of kidding.

Brahms went on, "I spent a lot of personal time developing my hacking skills. I mostly worked my way into public websites like charities, bulletin boards, CERN. I just poked around to see how people organized their computer networks.

"Then I got miffed about the French and worked my way into some of their defense systems. I learned quite a lot about how people defend computer systems by hacking the French. They eventually detected me and complained to the British. They actually came in by force with no warning, banged down my front door, confiscated my computer and records, and threw me into a high class military prison for a while.

"Eventually, someone with a brain realized that I could be of great service to Queen and Country if I were working for the 'good' guys defending the computers from the inside rather than hacking in from the outside. So, they cut me a deal. I would be released on probation, but I would have to work as a consultant for MI-5 for as long as my prison term would have been if I'd gone to trial. I'd have to work for galley slave wages and I couldn't tell anyone what I'd done."

Sinistra stared at him, "But you're telling me! Aren't you?"

"Oh, yeah, I'm telling you but several things happened between then and now. First, I performed a great national service for Queen and Country."

Sinistra frowned, "What was that?" She quickly added, "Oh, I know, you can't tell, it's a national secret."

"No, I can tell. I found Tom Riddle."

Sinistra gasped and stared even harder at him, "You what! Why didn't you inform the Aurors where he was? You could have saved a lot of grief for a lot of people."

"Oh, the Order of the Phoenix didn't want me to. They were right, too. He and Potter had to have it out, and I'd just have gotten in the way although at the time I was anxious to get in the way."

"What else happened?"

"Oh, yeah. I got knighted for that little service."

"Really, then you're Sir Boy Genius." and she laughed at her own joke.

"No, I was forbidden to tell anyone that I was knighted. It kind of takes the fun out of it you know."

"And yet, you keep telling me these things."

'Well, you're kind of special. I never even told Wendt about that. Anyway, the aliens came and the British government isn't exactly around, so I feel like my honor doesn't require that I keep my word to a dead institution."

By this time their meal had gotten really cold. They ate and talked. Neither really noticed the cold food. They decided that they couldn't wait until the next day to get to work on their project, so they immediately walked down to the Shrieking Shack. It was pitch dark out. Even though Sinistra had her wand lit, she stumbled a couple of times, and she ended up having to hold Brahms' arm most of the way there.

Along the way, they ran into a few wayward telescopes that had got caught in the fence that surrounded the Shack. When they got to the Shack, they found the night crew on duty. Brahms asked for a status report and was told that there was not much going. The aliens were still dithering about when the assault on the Ministry should happen.

"Well, keep an eye on it. We want to give them as good a warning as we can at the Ministry. Say, do you know if we've some good CCD's around?"

The night crew rolled their eyes but merely said, "Sure. In the store room on the 2nd floor." As if he didn't know that perfectly well.

Sinistra said, "I guess I've been out of big time astronomy too long. I suppose that Coupled Charge Detectors are as common as computers these days."

Brahms shrugged and said, "Yes, you have been. We're going to build ourselves a telescope grid." He led her up to the 2nd floor; they found about a dozen CCD detectors; and they took them to a workroom on the first floor. He had Sinistra bring in one of the telescopes, and they set to work attaching the detector to the eyepiece of the telescope.

"I wish that my telescopes were better quality, but we weren't exactly planning to build a detector grid when I bought them."

Brahms wasn't sorry at all. "They're fine. As a matter of fact, they're almost perfect. They are low magnification, have a wide field of view. They've even got clock drives. I'm thinking that we set them up as though we were at the North Pole. We point them close to the horizon and the clock drives move them around the horizon."

She said, "I get it. They scan the whole horizon. They could pick up almost anything flying. IF they can detect those sneaky planes."

Brahms scratched his head, "Sneaky?"

"Sure isn't that what they call planes that can't be detected?"

"You mean stealthy planes."

They experimented with the clock drives. Standard clock drives would turn the telescopes around the horizon in 24 hours. They needed it to be much faster.

"You're right. That's really slower than I want to go. I'd like more like 10 minutes. We'll have to see if we can speed them up considerably." With that, he immediately opened up one of the drives and started to fiddle with adjustments in it. They tried quite a number of things. They finally settled on his hacking the computer that regulated the clock. It turned out to be easy (for him) to change the period of the clock once he got into the operating system of the computer. They experimented with one of the drives, changing the period and timing how long it took to do one complete rotation.

They had completely lost track of time. It was really long past midnight. So, he invited her to take a cot. She blushed until she realized that he didn't intend to share the cot. Then she discovered that that was as disturbing to her as the alternative.

▽

The next day, he insisted on getting a CCD camera working on a telescope, so they worked on that. That went pretty quickly. Sinistra pointed out a problem. "We can't set the telescopes up here. The ground is irregular, and we're on a hillside.

They thought about that problem for a while, considering going to the top of a ridge and placing the telescopes. The problems with that were many. Getting the telescopes and themselves up there being not the least of them.

Then Sinistra had an idea. "Let's set up on the lake-shore. It's pretty flat. The horizons are all pretty low, if you pick the right spot. It's easy to get to."

That allowed them to move on to another problem. How would they get the signal back to the Shack for signal processing? And how about power?

They decided to break for lunch and discovered that it was a lot closer to supper time. Sinistra insisted that they go back to the castle and wash and change clothes before supper and then re-attack the problems. Brahms reluctantly agreed but on the walk back to the castle made an interesting discovery. It was still necessary to steady Sinistra with his arm even though it was broad daylight.

Supper was always a crowded, hurried thing since Hogwarts had become a haven for refugees. Everyone ate in shifts, and the benches were always crowded. Fortunately, there was plenty of good food. The house elves had outdone themselves in making meals hospitable to the many guests who piled in for meals. Sinistra and Brahms had to squeeze in together in a small space left by a group of goblins. They had been none too happy to share their table with a wizard and—was that a Muggle?

Brahms put a good face on it. He said, "Well, good evening gentlemen."

The goblin next to him said under his breath, "What's good about it?"

"Well, we're here enjoying these most excellent foods. We're all walking around directing our own footsteps without having an alien under our skins—literally. It's a beautiful day outside."

The goblin just turned toward him and stared as if to say, "How stupid could you be?"

The goblin finally said, "I suppose you're a Muggle."

"Yes, you're right. Brahms at you service."

The goblin was too flabbergasted to do anything but mumble, "Oggbar at your service."

"Good to meet you. Allow me to introduce my associate, Professor Sinistra."

The goblin seemed to be drawn along into a conversation despite himself, "Professor. What are you a professor of?"

"astronomy."

Oggbar considered that answer a moment and said, "I suppose that's kind of a strange thing for Hogwarts?"

"Not at all. Astronomy has always been part of the curriculum here."

"Well, I suppose that you don't have that much to lose, being holed up in this overcrowded, remote, cold frontier town like this. Whereas we left all the gold and vaults of jewels and wonderful art back unguarded in our bank." He finished by looking down at the plate in front of him, seeming to wish it were a plate of jewels instead.

Brahms patted him on the back and said, "Oggbar we've all left things behind. Most of my friends are dead or as good as dead."

He shook his head and said, "Our wealth is as good as dead. Our beautiful artwork—lost, lost."

Sinistra asked, "Artwork? I didn't know that the bank owned artwork."

Oggbar looked up at her in amazement and asked, "You don't know about goblin art?"

"I've heard about goblin swords and shields. I've heard that they're comparable to the finest art of wizards. But somehow, I just find it hard to understand shields as works of art."

Oggbar seemed to see her for the first time. "Surely, you've heard of the sword of Griffyndor?"

"Of course, I guess I knew that was goblin-made   I only saw it once—when Longbottom used it to kill that awful snake of He-Who-Must-Not-be-Named."

Brahms corrected her, "Tom Riddle."

"Oh, yes. But I can never quite get used to calling him that. Anyway, under the circumstances, I didn't really get to appreciate its beauty as I suppose I should."

"Yes, that sword was an exquisite work of art. It's the height of the art, but most goblin swords are really wonderful. The shields can be just as spectacular. You really should see a few. Both the swords and the shields are not only beautiful but extremely useful. They have fought terrible battles and never grow rusty or loose their edge."   With that Oggbar caught himself almost smiling as he described the wonders of goblin armory. He came back to himself and finished. "But you'll never see any of them. They're buried in the vaults of Gringotts, and we'll never get to recover them."

Brahms stared at him without seeing him for a few minutes as he thought over a possibility. He came out of the reverie with a question, "Oggbar, would you like to have a chance to use those swords and shields?"

Oggbar frowned and then growled, "What are you talking about? We don't have them, and there's nobody to fight."

"No one to fight. We may have to defend this castle to the last man. Hand to hand combat toe to toe with the aliens. Wouldn't you prefer to go down fighting to just surrendering?"

"Of course, but we don't have any of those weapons. We had to leave Gringotts too quickly. We couldn't go down into the deep vaults."

Brahms asked Sinistra, "Isn't the floo network still working?"

Sinistra said, "Of course it is. Oh.. . . I see. You're thinking that the goblins could go back by floo to Gringotts and take their time. They could bring back the weapons and . . and. . What?"

Oggbar said, "And Prepare! Train! We'll teach those aliens what it is to take on a regiment of trained goblins in goblin-made armor."   A fell light seemed to burn in his eyes as he contemplated what the coming battle would be like. "Yes, bring on the aliens."

Sinstra almost gasped, "I suppose that we could take some goblins through the floo network to Gringotts."

Oggbar said, "Oh, no. Not directly to Gringotts. We closed off all magical ways to enter Gringotts. We don't want would-be robbers to get ideas. We'll have to go into a different business near Gringotts."

"Well, we've got to get somebody higher up than us to sign off on this idea." Sinistra was saying and she could hear Oggbar growling again. "But I don't think that'll be hard."   She added under her breath, "I hope."

Brahms said, "We've got some things to do tonight, but tomorrow, we'll start working on it."

Oggbar's growl subsided. Sinistra and Brahms left the Great Hall, and she breathed a sigh of relief as they left the hall. "I don't know what we should hope—that we don't have problems or that we do have problems."

"Yeh, I know what you mean. Those guys are scary enough unarmed. I'm afraid to imagine what it would be like having them running around and dueling with swords."

They went up to the Shack and they attached a charge-coupled detector to one of the telescope's eyepiece mount. They checked the signal coming out and connected it to a port on the image processing server. The server processed the signal and provided a display on one of the monitors. "Good," Brahms said, "Let's put it in place."

"How are we going to connect it to the server all the way to the lake?"

"That's not so hard," Brahms said. "The aliens have provided us with the key. They've got a first rate data cable." He reached into a drawer and pulled out a small spool of wire. "This spool contains 10 kilometers of cable."

Sinistra stared at the small spool. "That's not possible."

"Oh, yes it is. It's a wonderful invention. Signal loss is at the quantum limit, and the cable itself is flexible, strong, and light." He thought for a moment. "As a matter of fact, it's dangerously strong and thin. We can't just lay it on the surface for someone to trip over—or worse. Perhaps, a set of flags along the route?"

Sinistra said forcefully, "Not needed. I'll excavate a trench for it to go in. It doesn't have to be deep does it?"

Brahms was amazed, "You could do that easily? We've got kilometers to go, you know."

"Sure. And cover it up after us."

"Wonderful. Let's go right now." He led her outside, where he found and opened a junction box where the cable providing them internet access connected with the wiring of the building. He connected the cable to an available port, and Sinistra started a trench close to the junction box. He laid the cable in the shallow trench as Sinistra covered it over as they went. It took them 2 hours to reach the lake and find a good flat spot to place the telescopes. Sinistra had sent one telescope ahead of them—the one with the CCD camera. They placed the telescope and attached the cable. Then they trotted off to the Shack. They ran up to the Control Room and found the night shift on duty.

Brahms took an empty console and searched for the signal from the telescope. Sinistra was bending over his shoulder fascinated by the process. He found it and displayed the static picture on the screen.

"Now," he said, "I'll turn on the clock drive." He did, and the image started to shift slowly to the left.

"And now, for fun, I'll turn on the image processing engine and. . ." he was entering some commands into the interface, ". . . have it search for changes other than the steady progression of the stars." After doing that, a watch box appeared on the edge of the screen. "This will display any anomalies that the image processor picks up. Let's go get some tea."

They went down to the cafeteria and heated some water in the microwave and brewed some tea in a couple of cups. They went back up to the Control Room and sat down for a minute to admire their handy-work in action. They had hardly sat when the watch box on the display started flashing and a neat small red circle enclosed a fairly bright point of light that was moving against the background of stars. Brahms exclaimed, "What the!" Almost immediately, there was a red dotted line extending from the object off the edge of the screen, and the watch box showed the projected closest approach to the Shack.

"That things going to go almost directly overhead!" Brahms jumped up and said, "Come on." He ran down stairs, went down the hall, and stopped at the metal door that had a keypad on the wall next to it. He rapidly keyed in 12 digits, and the door popped open. He stepped inside and returned quickly with a stinger missile. "That thing's going almost directly overhead. Let's go out and be prepared to give them a welcome if they come too low."

They ran back to the Main Entrance. The guard shouted after them, "What the bloody hell are you doing?"

Brahms replied as they passed on the run, "Keep a watch on the door. I'll let you know if we're being invaded." Once they got outside, they found an open spot that had a good view of the sky. Sinistra had pulled her wand and was at the ready.

She said, "It's too big a coincidence that the first night we find something."

He just stared into the sky and after a few seconds pointed, "There it is about 45 degrees over the horizon. It'll be overhead in 40 seconds at this rate."

She just said, "Shit." and raised her wand.

It was on a trajectory that was taking it directly over Hogwarts. Brahms raised the Stinger launcher and felt a bit silly. What could he do against a Raptor if that was what it was?

It went nearly overhead and kept going without the slightest deviation from its course. Sinistra said, "I think that was a satellite."

Brahms stared after it until it disappeared below the opposite horizon. "I suppose you're right. We'll have to program it to figure out what are satellites and what are airplanes."

"Why?"

"Because we can't do anything about satellites." He hesitated and reflected, "Can we? Could you shoot down a satellite?"

She pondered a moment and, bemused, said, "I don't know. I've never considered the possibility." They walked back toward the castle and she said, "I don't think so. But, tomorrow is another day. Let's go to bed." He stared at her for a moment, but she didn't seem to realize that what she'd said was at all unusual. They had just reached the gates of the castle. He bid her good-night, and they separated.

The next day, he was up too late for breakfast again, but this time he ate alone. He searched half-heartedly for Sinistra but without luck. However, he noticed that the goblins all seemed to be in a very good mood. He decided that he didn't have time to go to the Shack and get anything useful done before lunch, so he hung around talking to anyone who came within range, killing time before lunch.

One of the people that he was killing time with was the groundskeeper and his apprentice. He said "hello" to them, and the apprentice immediately started talking.

"Hello, Mr. Brahms. Have you noticed the goblins today?""

"Well, yes. I have. They seem to be in a very good mood. Do you know what's going on, Dudley?"

"Yes, sir, I do. They're talking about forming an army. They seem to think someone is going to supply them with a horde of goblin-made armor and swords."

Brahms internally said, "Uh, Oh." to himself but nothing out loud.

Filch amplified, "I don't know what kind of moron would give them the idea that they could form an army and would help them get weapons, but I think they must be mad."

Brahms hmmed for a few minutes as Filch went on and on about the stupidity of the idea. Finally, the B.G. excused himself, saying that he had an appointment with Professor Sinistra. That was sort of true. He headed out for the grounds but was stopped by a tap on his shoulder. He turned and expected the worst—Oggbar asking when they were going to go to Gringotts. He found instead Dudley Dursley.

"You're the one that suggested forming a goblin army, am I right?" He quickly added, "Don't worry, I won't tell Filch if you are."

Brahms smiled and said, "I'm afraid I am. Pretty bone-headed, eh?"

"No, sir. I think it's a great idea. I can't imagine any fiercer fighters than goblins, and I'd like to see them make mince meat of those aliens." His voice caught a moment. Then he went on, "My mum and dad didn't make it here. I tried to bring them without letting them know what was on, you know, in case." He stopped abruptly and seemed to be concentrating on his feet. Then he looked up and said, "Let me show you something."

"Sure, go ahead."

He pulled out a wand. It was extremely simple. Brahms had seen a fair number of wands. Most were fairly ornate. Nearly all had some sort of ornamentation—even if it was only a fancy handle that had been added after the wand had been purchased. This one was different. It was a cylinder somewhere between 8 and 9 inches long. It had been polished to a high sheen, but the wood just looked like ordinary wood.

Dudley looked at it long and hard as though making a difficult decision that concerned it. "This is my wand. It was made by Mr. Olivander. I once swore that I'd never use it."

Brahms could tell that there was something special about it—something that he wasn't saying. Finally, he said it, "I've never seen a wand more powerful than it. When I first held it, I could feel the power coursing through my hand up my arm and into my heart. I decided then that it was a wand that was so powerful that I was not the man to use that wand in anger—that no man was that man—that that man was God. But I kept it with me ever since this wand chose me. I've used it off and on for minor things – like . . . Oh, you know, moving a desk down to my office. Now, I want to use it – really use it." There was a fire in his eyes that made him blink.

He could hold back the tears no longer. A few lone tears rolled down his face, and he looked up at Brahms. "Now I'm scared. I want to use this wand so badly that it's a need that burns inside me. I'll break that promise that I made. I want to use it to smash the aliens to so many pieces that you could never find enough of them to fill a teaspoon. I want to find every one and slice them to ribbons." The intensity of his words was in his eyes. They seemed none-the-less to have an appeal in them—an appeal to Brahms to save him from that terrible fate.

Brahms couldn't face those terrible eyes. He looked away and said, "Dudley. Come see me at the Shrieking Shack sometime—not today, but soon. We'll talk about your wand."

Gringott's

The next day at breakfast, Brahms found Sinistra, who was quite willing to be found. "Sinistra, what do you think of putting together a little expedition to Gringotts?"

She nodded contemplatively, "I suppose that we've got to find a 'softie' to approve the project and recruit a few wizards to help."

"Well, I suppose George Weasley is always up for this sort of thing. How about Ron?"

"It's a little risky including them both, but who knows?"

They approached the Assistant Head of the school, Professor Slughorn. He had his doubts about approving the adventure but Brahms argued vigorously for it. "Look. We've got the goblins agreeing not to sell us out, but this is the sort of thing that might get them positively on our side."

Sinistra added, "And it's not as if it's dangerous. We'll go by floo directly to Diagon Alley. No aliens have a hint that it exists. We won't even go through the 'Leaky Cauldron'. We'll go directly into a shop close to Gringott's. We'll stay low. Nobody will even know that we've been."

Slughorn was teetering, "Yes, but if you get into trouble or worse—hurt, how would I ever explain it to Minerv . . uh . . Professor McGonagall?"

"We'll be taking along some wizards who've seen lots of action and know how to handle themselves in a tough spot—the Weasley's."

Slughorn perked up, "You mean Bill and Percy?"

Brahms sort of said rapidly under his breath, 'Uh. . Ron and George."

"Well, if you got the sensible Weasleys, then that's just fine."

Both he and Sinistra beat a rapid retreat before Slughorn had a chance to reconsider. Outside his office in the dungeon, they slowed down and said, "Now all we have to do is convince Ron and George to go."

As predicted, George wasn't a problem, but Ron took a little convincing. "What are you thinking of? I had an awful time the last time we tried breaking into Gringotts. I can't imagine the goblins would let me come within a hundred miles of the vaults."

George said, "But Ron, the Goblins are going to be helping us break into Gringotts, we're on the side of the Angels."

"Right. We were the last time too, but we almost got fried by dragon fire and buried alive in a vault and who knows what else might happen the next time."

Brahms said, 'Look, Ron. We really need you. This could make a big difference in the war against the aliens."

Ron looked down at his feet and finally said, "All right, but you have to promise me that I won't have to go in the vaults."

George said, "Sure, Ronnie. No problemo. You can stand guard outside."

▽

They picked up a third wizard who had worked in Flourish and Blots back when Diagon Alley had been the shopping mall of wizards and witches rather than an abandoned wreck. The Goblins were sending ten goblins, led by Glorblatt and Oggbar. They had discussed what hearth they would use to enter Diagon Alley. The Owl Emporium that was close to Gringotts was suggested. The Goblins themselves favored someplace down Knockturn Alley, which would put them more out of view and would allow them to arrive and leave with lights and attract less attention.

They finally agreed on Bourgan & Burke's. It was close to the entrance to Knockturn Alley and would allow quick access to the bank. They also agreed that they would have an early breakfast and leave at first light. They arranged for an early breakfast from the Hoggwart's house elves. Everyone agreed to an early bedtime, but no one succeeded.

When their alarms went off, everyone swore that they'd never let themselves stay up late again and secretly knew that they'd never keep that promise. They met in the kitchens, where the house elves had set up two round tables of eight places each. There was one place that stood empty. Brahms asked one of the elves about it.

"Why do you set a place where there is no one?"

The elf said, "It's good . . uh . . what do you Muggles call it? Karma?"

"Yeh, I guess we do call it Karma. But why do we need good Karma?"

"You're going into danger aren't you?"

184

Brahms looked around and decided that the house elves were safe to talk to about their little adventure. "Yes, but how do you know that?"

"When people gather early for breakfast for no reason, you know that the reason is danger."

The meal, of course, was good. There were lots of carbohydrates, and the elves had packed a lunch for each. Even the Goblins had thanked the elves, and then they marched up to the Great Hall. Just as they entered the great hearth, someone ran up to them. She was shouting, "Brahms! Brahms! Don't leave just yet."

It was Sally. She arrived and handed Brahms a back sack. He looked at her quizzically. She just shook her head negatively and said, "It's for good luck. Don't look at what I've packed for you until you get there."

She turned and left.

Brahms noticed that Sinistra had his arm clutched in her left hand. "Don't take it with you, whatever it is."

"Sally's pretty smart. I think I'll hold on to it." He threw it over his shoulders and cinched it tight. She took his arm, and everyone else took floo powder. They appeared in a much darker and danker floo, going through single file. The first was George. He lit his wand, looked around and said, "Looks clear to me." Bourgan & Burke's had never been a cheery place, but with no human habitation in months, it was even dustier and mustier than it normally was. There was very little daylight that made its way in, and they worked their way through the shop mostly by wand-light. The front display windows were grimy, and George, still leading the way, declared he'd have to stick his head outside to see what the alley looked like.

He opened the door and walked out. The people inside could see him slowly turning from left to right. He declared, "It looks OK. Come on let's go."

They left the shop to be watched by the former Flourish and Blott's employee. The rest slowly walked up the sloping street toward Diagon Alley. As they approached the wider more open street, they none-the-less felt no safer. They stayed close to the walls of the alley.

When they were onto the main street, they stopped and stared about them. Ron was the first to speak, "Bloody Hell! I've never seen the place look so empty. It was bad when Riddle was in charge, but at least, there were a few people on the streets and a few shops open. This is just plain 'spooky'."

Everyone seemed to agree. They walked slowly and softly as if afraid of awakening whatever it was that had caused the street to be abandoned. They were mostly silent, but Sinistra commented to no one in particular, "The summer that Riddle took over the Ministry, I spent a lot of time out of the country. It was an awful time. When I came back to get ready for the next term at Hoggwarts, I went to Diagon Alley to get some robes and a few books. The first thing I noticed was that Florian Fortescu's ice cream shop was empty. I asked Madame Malkin what had happened. I couldn't imagine Diagon Alley without him. I never went to Diagon Alley without stopping for an ice cream.

"She just shook her head, and I knew that I'd never see him again in this life. This is just about as bad."

By this time, they'd reached the bank, one of the older Goblins ascended to the Main Entrance and put the finger tips of his forefingers of both hands on the double doors – one hand on each one. The doors opened silently inward, and he smiled a satisfied smile. They quickly entered the bank and closed the doors behind them.

Glorblatt signaled them to gather around him. He said, "All right. We need one wizard to go down with us. The other wizards and Mr. Brahms will remain here to guard the door. Mr. Weasley, you'll accompany us down to our vault."

Ron Weasley's eyes widened until they looked like pie plates. "Me? Why me?"

"We need a wizard, and you're a wizard."

Ron Weasley looked around at the other wizards and Brahms in silent appeal, but George just said, "Come on Ron, you've seen more of the vaults than any of us. It just makes sense."

"Not to me, it doesn't."

But, Ron gulped and turned to the Goblins. Five of them broke off and walked toward the entrance to the vaults. The other five remained at the entrance to Gringotts. It turned out that they'd decided to run a sort of conveyer belt operation. The five Goblins who were going to the vaults would take turns bringing armor up to the main floor. The other five would carry the armor to Bourgan and Burke's and through the hearth to Hogwarts. Goblins there would take the armor on to their camp.

As they walked down the halls toward the tram system, Ron looked around, hoping for a diversion that would slow their progress to the vaults. He noticed lots of art work—the human kind, paintings and even a few statues. He commented on it.

Gorblatt said, "You like it. We have some of the finest Muggle art in this building." He pointed at a painting and said, "That's a Reubens." A little further along, "That ship was painted by your English painter Turner. I think it might be my favorite in the collection."

Ron stared at them and asked, "I thought that you Goblins thought that all Goblin creations properly belong only to Goblins?"

Gorblatt agreed.

Ron went on, "Well, then, what about these Muggle paintings? Where do you stand on the ownership of them?"

Gorblatt just stared at him. "We own them."

A quizzical look came over Ron's face but he only said, "Interesting."

Ron and two Goblins rode one tram down to the lower vaults and the other three rode another. The tramway was as light as it ever was, which was to say that it was practically impossible to see anything outside the beam of the headlamp of the tram.

They reached the bottom of the tramway, and they found a large door that led back into the wall of the cavern. Glorblatt took Ron by the hand and led him to the vast door. He said, "Mr. Weasley, please take this." He handed Ron, a rectangular parallelpiped about 3 centimeters by 10 centimeters.

Ron asked, "What's this for?"

"Do you see the indentation in the door that matches this?"

"Yesss." Ron was rather reluctant to admit that he did.

"Just insert it into the recess with the line running length-wise matching the line in the door."

"Why should I do that?"

"Just do it, Mr. Weasley."

Weasley looked down at it and decided that "in for a knut, in for a galleon." He placed it into the recess, and for a few seconds nothing happened. Then a line appeared in the vault door and flashed briefly bright red, and a crack appeared in the door. It rapidly opened, and the door fitted into a recess in the walls that showed no sign that a door could come out of it. The interior behind the door immediately lit with fairly bright indirect light.

Ron gave a sigh of relief and just remained standing outside the vault. Glorblatt said, "That's all. You can go up to the surface with the first load of armor."

Ron asked, "What was that all about?"

"Oh, we wanted to make sure that the defenses of the vault didn't kill the first person to open it before we went in."

Ron just stared and exclaimed, "You what!"

"Don't just stand there. Pick up a couple of suits of armor and get moving."

"A couple of suits of armor? Those things must weigh a couple of stone apiece."

Glorblatt shook his head and said, "Goblin armor is both strong AND light." So Ron stepped forward and pulled a couple of sets of breastplates, grieves, mail shirts and shields and lifted them with surprising ease. They were indeed light. He followed a couple of other Goblins who went to one of the trams and loaded it with themselves and their armor and they shot to the surface.

When they arrived, the Goblins proceeded directly to the door where they handed their loads to the waiting Goblins there, who took the loads and rushed off toward Knockturn alley. Ron did likewise. Then George said, "We were wondering if we'd ever see you again. What was it like down there?"

Ron said, "Did you know that they were going to use me as a guinea pig to find out if the person opening the vault door would get fried or something?"

George said, "Hadn't the slightest. But better you than I, bro."

"Right. Well, the next time, you're going down first."

Ron went on, "If you've seen one vault, you've seen them all. This one was filled with armor. You've seen some typical stuff—lots of jewels. Shiny chain mail. All the usual stuff."

The wizards and the Muggle spent lots of time just waiting for the seemingly endless stream of Goblins laden with armor to end, but it never did as long as they were there. Around noon, they asked the Goblins if they were going to stop for lunch. However, the Goblins just stared at them and said, "We can always eat, but we've never brought the armor out of the vault before."

Ron had already broken into his lunch and was enjoying a beef pasty. Between bites he said, "You don't mmmm know what you're mmmmm missing."

The Goblins didn't waste their breath talking to Ron but were either shuttling to Bourghan & Burkes or down to the vaults. Eventually it began to get dark, and Ron was not the only one to express the desire to get back to Hoggwarts before it got really dark. The Goblins just said, "We've got to get more armor out before we leave."

Finally one shift did not return to the vaults, and Brahms asked, "You're done emptying the vaults?"

Gorblat arrived with another load and he said, "We're done. Please help us get the last of this armor to B&B."

Everyone took some armor, and they walked as hastily as they could in the failing light. They could see wand-light in the shop. When they arrived, most of the Goblins had already left. They all trooped into the hearth, and Brahms and Sinistra were the last to leave. He held her back a moment and asked, "Those Goblins seemed plenty intense about that armor. Do you think that we've done the right thing?"

She just shrugged. They then walked into the hearth and out into the Great Hall at Hogwarts. The last of the Goblins were scurrying out the door, and there was not a scrap of armor left in the hall. The last shift of supper was just being finished, and all the wizards of the little trip shuddered as if to get the smell of the trip off them. They chose an empty table where they sat. A couple of platters of food materialized, and Ron said, "I guess we're lucky that they waited supper for us." Then he immediately dug into a chicken breast he'd taken off one platter with one hand as he ladled some beans onto his platter with a serving spoon.

George laughed and said, "It's good to see that my little brother hasn't lost his appetite."

Ron answered through a mouthful of mashed potatoes, "How could I lose my appetite when I've been through such trials!"

"Brother, you wouldn't loose your appetite if you were hanging upside down by your toes."

"Exactly my point." he responded

Just then Sally came up and asked Brahms, "Did you have to use my backpack?"

Brahms' eyes widened, and he said, "I completely forgot that I had the backpack with me. I wonder what was in it." He picked it up off the floor behind him where he'd laid it when they'd got back. He opened it, and immediately his mouth dropped open. "Are there hand grenades in there?"

"Of course. You don't think that I'd go anywhere dangerous without them?"

Goblin Armor

The next couple of days, Brahms took it easy. He stayed at the Shack and got people to bring a plate of food down to him. He reviewed tapes of interesting conversations that the team had culled from the security cameras. There was nothing really important.

One day, he decided that he should have breakfast at the castle. He went up, had breakfast, and strolled slowly toward the Shack. He went past a field that was quickly filling with Goblins in armor. He smiled at the way that the little bodies were dressed for war. He noticed that there was one Goblin sitting on the sidelines, completely out of the activity. He walked over to the Goblin and asked, "Do you mind if I join you?"

"I suppose not. You're the Brahms, aren't you?"

"My name is Brahms, yes."

The Goblin looked up, pointing its long nose directly at Brahms's nose. "You're something of a hero here."

"Really? Why?"

"No wizard would have done what you did for Goblins."

Brahms took a deep breath and considered reminding the Goblin that there had been several wizards along on the adventure. He also thought about the fact that Goblins were stubborn, and therefore, maybe he ought to be gracious and simply accept the praise.

He shrugged and said, "It seemed like the right thing to do. You guys deserved it. What's going on here?"

The Goblin sighed and said, "Military training. I so wish that I could take part, but I'm too old and feeble to do it."

Brahms sat with the Goblin for a few minutes as he watched the training session go into full swing. There were little one-on-one battles that seemed to be bound to kill someone, but the armor seemed to be invulnerable, and although lots of Goblins were knocked over, no one seemed seriously hurt. He decided that he'd try to cheer the Goblin up, "Well, it's good to see such enthusiasm, but you know, if it ever came to a real battle with the aliens, they have weapons that would make short work of this Goblin corp."

The Goblin swung around on Brahms quickly and said, "You don't know what you're talking about. Goblin armor is unequaled. I don't care what the weapons of the Enemy are like, they couldn't stand against Goblin armor."

Just then Brahms realized that someone was standing behind him, and she was speaking. "Modern weapons—even Muggle weapons would cause a slaughter." It was Sally.

He immediately stood and said, "Allow me to introduce, uh. . . Sorry, what is your name?"

The Goblin had also stood and said, "Farhok." A gleam came into his eyes and he asked, "Would you like to place a small wager on that?"

"I don't want to take your money."

"Oh, we'll see whose money is taken by whom. Would you stand a hundred galleons?"

Sally sensed a trap and said, "Let's say fifty."

Farhok said, "It wouldn't be interesting for less than 75."

Sally laughed and said, "Done. How do we test it?"

"Very simple. I'll bring my armor to the Shack tomorrow at dawn, and we test my armor against your weapons."

She smiled and said, "A sort of duel at dawn."

Farhok said, "Precisely." Then he turned his back on them and sat, completely oblivious to them.

Brahms said to Sally, "I guess we should go. I think that you need to rest up for tomorrow."

"Rest up my eye!" And they walked down the hillside toward the Shack.

The next morning Brahms was awakened very early for the 2nd day in a week.

He went down to the Great Hall on the outside chance that there might be some food there. Instead he found Sally. She had her backpack slung on her back, and she waved at him as soon as she saw him. They proceeded out toward the main gate and as they left the castle, they ran into Farhok. He was wearing his armor.

They met, and Farhok asked where they'd go for the duel. Brahms offered the hills behind the Shrieking Shack. Farhok had no problem with the suggestion, so they all walked toward the Shack and then through the grounds and on behind the Shack. They walked into the hills for about 15 minutes, and then Farhok suggested that they stop. No one objected, so they set up for the duel.

Farhok asked, "Well, young woman, where's your weapon?" with something of a sneer.

Sally un-slung her backpack, opened it and pulled out a clear plastic bag. Farhok asked, "What's that?"

She opened the bag and pulled out the parts of a gun. As she assembled it, she said, "This, my friend, is the ultimate choice of freedom fighters and soldiers who can't count on regular supply lines. You can drop it in snow, sand, mud, a pond, then pull it out and fire it without a snag. It's the Kalyshnikov AK-47 with sniper-scope and banana clip." She was quick—not the 20 seconds that she'd once claimed, but considerably less than a minute.

Farhok said, "Whatever. Let's get started. Where do you want me to stand?"

Brahms said, "What do you mean stand? Where are we going to put your armor so we can do some target practice?"

"Put it? It's right where it needs to be, on my back."

Sally said, "Look, Farhok, I can't just take aim at you and fire. It would be murder, literally."

Farhok looked back and forth between them and shook his head. "My Great-Great-Great-Grandfather fought the Goblin wars, and wore this armor, and came out without a scratch. I'm not better than he. I'll stand in it."

Sally looked between Farhok and Brahms and ended on Brahms with a look of appeal on her face. He said, "Sally, come over here."

She reluctantly came over and said, "What?"

He whispered, "Look, how good a shot are you?"

"Pretty good, why?"

"Why don't you just fire a round into that shield of his? Look at the way he's holding it. The edge extends well beyond his body."

Farhok shouted to them. "Are you forfeiting?"

Sally looked over at him and said, "Just give us a minute."

She looked back at Brahms and said, "That just might work. It would save face for everyone, and when the round goes right through that shield, he'll see sense."

"OK. Do it. And if you have to miss, miss away from him."

"You bet." Then she turned to Farhok and said, "OK. Get ready."

Brahms dragged Sally behind a large rock and said, "Safety first."

Farhok seemed to set himself determinedly and said, "Do your worst."

Sally rested her elbow on the rock and took a deep breath, held it, and gently squeezed the trigger. There was a solid clang, and she jumped up and trotted over to Farhok. Brahms asked, "Did you hit the shield?"

"You heard it ring, didn't you?" When they reached Farhok, they examined the shield and saw no sign that anything had hit it.

Farhok smiled broadly and said, "I said, do your worst. What was that? I didn't even feel it."

Brahms told Sally to set the Kalyshnikov for semi-automatic and fire off a half dozen rounds. She agreed and set herself again behind the rock and there were five clangs, but nothing seemed to have happened otherwise. They went to examine the shield and found no marks.

"Well, I could make good use of those galleons."

A determined look came into Sally's eye and she said, "Let's try one more time."

Brahms asked as they got behind the rock, what she was going to do. She said, "I'm going to turn on full automatic and fire the rest of the clip into that shield."

She placed herself, set the rifle on the rock, took her deep breath, exhaled slowly, squeezed the trigger, and held it until it stopped firing. The first part of the burst knocked the shield out of Farhok's hand, and the rest hit him square in the midriff. He was knocked over by the impact. She and Brahms leaped from behind the rock, Brahms shouting, "Damn it! You've killed him."

She reached him first, but he'd already started to get up. He exclaimed, "That's better. I was beginning to think that you didn't have anything."

Brahms noticed that there was some blood seeping from his chain-mail. "Farhok, you're bleeding."

Farhok looked down at himself and asked, "Where? I don't feel. . . " Then he noticed the spot of blood. He pulled the chain-mail up and revealed a white shirt underneath that had a spot of blood. He pulled that up and what appeared to be a scratch about an inch long showed itself. Brahms stepped closer and examined the chain-mail.

"There's a bullet shard protruding through a link."

Farhok laughed, "That's just a scratch. I do worse to myself shaving. Is that the best you've got?"

Sally stared at him a moment and said, "Do you really want to try something worse."

Farhok just laughed.

"That does it!" She reached into her backpack, rummaged a bit, and pulled out something. Brahms immediately recognized it.

"That's a hand grenade!"

"You bet it is."

"But you can't use that. We've got no control of it!"

Farhok snarled, "Bring it on!"

"Look, Farhok, you don't know what you're asking for. These things are mean, and they're not clean."

193

"This is a duel. No quarter asked."

This time Sally pulled Brahms aside, "We're stuck. If we don't do this, we'll lose all the face we have gained over the last month." He had to admit the justice of that.

"OK. But let me lob the grenade. Maybe we can keep him fairly far away when it goes off." He returned to Farhok and said, "This weapon is designed to be thrown at the enemy, and it's designed to bounce around so that the enemy can't pick it up.

"So, here's what we're going to do. I'll practice throwing it once so that we can get the range of how far I can throw it. You'll go place yourself where it lands. I'll come and get it and return here. Then, when you're ready, I'll throw it toward you."

Farhok seemed to be enjoying this part, "And I'll catch it."

Brahms frowned and said, "If you can." Then he threw it as far as he could. All three trotted over to where it finally landed, and Farhok picked it up and handed it to Brahms.

"Thanks." He and Sally headed back to where they had been standing. Before they got there, Farhok called, "Any time."

Brahms muttered, "Great." under his breath. He looked over at Sally who shrugged. Then he pulled the pin and lofted it. As soon as it left his hand, he dropped behind the rock they'd used for cover before. He lifted his head above the rock in time to see the hand grenade land a couple of feet from Farhok, who had been running toward it to catch it. It took a crazy bounce and Farhok went running after it. Brahms just shook his head in disbelief. Farhok almost got to it, when it exploded. He was thrown a couple of feet into the air and landed on his back.

Both Brahms and Sally leaped the rock and ran toward Farhok. This time, he didn't get up and both had a sinking feeling in the pit of their stomachs. Brahms, lifted his head and tried to find signs of injury. Farhok shook his head and moaned softly. Then he said, "Well, that's more like it. I felt that!"

Both Brahms and Sally released long-held breathes. Farhok seemed to realize that Brahms was holding him up and looking him over in a worried way. He shook himself off and got to his feet. "Well,' he said, "If that's the best that you can do, then I think I win the bet."

Sally made a sound that might have been a laugh or a sign of relief and said, "That's right. I've got to admit it."

They all started walking back to the Shack, and Farhok said, almost under his breath, "You were really worried about me, weren't you?"

Sally answered first, "Well, of course, we were worried about you. I don't want you to die or even be seriously hurt!"

Farhok thought about that for a moment in silence as they walked and then said, "I don't think many wizards would have felt that way." Then after several more minutes of thought, he said, "I know something's going on."

Brahms asked, "What do you mean, something?"

"Well, I know that Wendt and McGonagall have been planning something, and I think that you, Mr. Brahms, have been involved."

"You must realize that I can't talk about it. IF there were something going on."

"Well, let's just suppose that there is some kind of battle or attack being planned. Let's suppose that you have some influence on the planning."

"OK. Let's just suppose. So what?"

"I want in."

"In?"

"Yes. IN. I want to be part of it. I want a shot at those things. I want a chance to lop a few heads off." He hesitated and completely stopped walking, which forced Brahms and Sally to stop and turn to see him. "I want a chance to show those so-called Goblin leaders that they can't treat me like I wasn't worth dirt."

Sally turned and started walking again. Brahms continued to look at him. "I won't promise anything."

"That's all I want."

They walked the rest of the way in silence. When they got to the Shack, Farhook reminded Sally of the bet. She went in and got her purse. She pulled a bag out and slowly counted seventy-five gold galleons. He smiled wickedly and swaggered off toward the castle. Sally asked, "Well, what are you going to do?"

He looked after the receding figure. "I don't know."

Later that day, he found Wendt and McGonagall at lunch. They were sitting at an otherwise empty table. They were deep in conversation and Wendt had just taken McGonagall's forearm in his hand to emphasize a point. He asked, "Do you mind if I join you?"

They answered in unison, "Yes!"

"Thanks, I will." He sat across the table from the two and asked, "Do you know a goblin named Farhok?"

Wendt answered, "No. Go away."

"Thanks. He wants in on your little adventure."

McGonagall said, "I don't care what he wants. This is strictly a two person adventure we're having just now, and you're not invited either."

"I'm serious."

McGonagall got a glint in her eye and said, "I'm not kidding either."

"He wants in on your Ministry mission."

That got Wendt's attention. "He knows about that?"

"I don't think he knows any details, but he seems to know that something's going to happen. He figures its going to involve some sort of battle and he wants to be part of it."

"Shit. I wonder how many others know that something's going on?"

McGonagall said, "I think that it would be impossible to keep the fact that something's going on secret in a small community like this with everyone packed in so close.

"You know, if we don't let him in, he may start talking about it. If he's in, we could make sure that he doesn't say anything."

"You mean the unbreakable oath?"

"Of course. He'd take it to be in on the mission."

Wendt shook his head, "I've got a bad feeling about this. You start letting outsiders in, and it never ends."

But Farhok found Wendt and asked about the mission. Wendt explained the conditions for acceptance for the mission. Farhok was reluctant to agree to take the unbreakable oath. Wendt said, "It's very simple. You either agree to take the unbreakable oath, and you become eligible for the mission—whatever it is. Or you don't. In which case, we part company, and I'll thank you not to pester me any more."

Farhok looked at the ground and thought furiously. "Let me think. Why do you want to have me take the unbreakable oaths?"

"We want our activities to be truly secret. You surely understand that."

He shook his head, apparently disbelieving, "I have to say that the Goblins never have had secrets in war. We act openly and attack when we can. We fight without hidden ideas."

"Maybe that's why you lost the goblin wars of a couple of hundred years ago. Think about it. We've not got much time. I'll need to know tomorrow."

They parted. The next day at breakfast, Farhok arrived with a grim look on his face. All he did was to stand before Wendt and nod. Wendt said, "The Shack. Tonight at 8PM."

That night, Wendt, Minerva and Farhok gathered at the Shack, and Brahms ushered them into the Main Floor Conference Room. Minerva had Wendt and Farhok clasp hands and said, "Goblin Farhok, do you swear that you will not reveal anything that you learn about the operation that will be described to you tonight to anyone who is not part of the operation until after the last alien has left this planet?"

Farhok repeated, swearing. As he said these words the threads of fire surrounded their joined hands, and they kept constricting until

Farhok was convinced that any slightest misstep would be his last. "I know to the bottom of my gut that I can never break it, and any serious try to would kill me."

Minerva said, "Yes, it's a binding magical contract. I'm sure that you understand the binding part now."

Brahms said, "Now that you're in, we'll show you what we know." He turned on the overhead projector and showed them all the video of the alien robot. Farhok stared at it, mouth agape.

"What is that thing?" he asked in wonderment. "How did the aliens make it?" And after a minute, "Any goblin would give his right arm to be able to make one of those."

Brahms smiled and said, "Yea, we bloody well would too. We call it a robot and that's what the aliens call it. It's a product of one of the races that the aliens conquered. I have a feeling that no alien understands the technology that goes into it. Only aliens who are controlling whatever creatures created that thing can make more."

"How do they control it?"

"In a way, they don't. It's intelligent and seems to take instructions. It figures out on its own how to do what they want it to do. As a matter of fact, we've seen it disobey direct orders in order to achieve what the controllers wanted it to do. The rules are pretty complex that it uses to decide what its controllers really want it to achieve rather than what they simply ask it to do. I've got a feeling that it's sort of a double-edge sword. If you use it, you can't be absolutely sure it'll do what you really want. We're pretty damn lucky there's only one of them in our solar system."

Wendt said, "That's what we're going up against. Do you still want in?"

The Goblin's eyes retained their hungry look. "Are you kidding? This just makes me want in all the more."

"Well, you're in." He turned to Brahms and said, "Show him where we're going." Brahms moved on to the next slide.

"Do you recognize this?" There was a picture of an old drab multi-storey building seen from the 3rd or 4th floor of a building across the street from it.

"I think so. That's the old Ministry of Magic building, isn't it?"

"Right. The aliens have identified this as a target to attack. They think that there's something funny going on there."

"Well, there is. Or there used to be. That's old news. Why do you care if they attack it?"

"If they find their way down to the lower level of the Ministry, they'll know that there's an organization around that they know nothing about—a big organization. We don't want them to know that.

"Also, we think it's a chance to destroy that robot."

Farhok's face fell. "You'd destroy that. But, it's. . . it's . . . well, beautiful."

Brahms said, "Right. Too beautiful. Too capable to be in the aliens' control."

Farhok shrugged and asked, "Can I have the remains after we destroy it?"

Brahms rolled his eyes. "I don't know if we can dare to do that. Even destroyed, it might have a way to signal the aliens and let them know where the remains are."

Minerva said, "We're not precisely sure when we're leaving, but it will be soon. If you still want to come, you'd better be ready to move quickly. We'll take the floo network to the Atrium of the old Ministry."

There was no answer from the Goblin other than the gleam in his eyes.

The next day, as soon as breakfast was over, the four who were going to the old Ministry packed their belongings. Wendt, went to his office, opened the locked drawer and pulled out a box of bullets. He opened his purse and shoved it in, wondering if he should put another box of bullets in. He pulled out the gun and checked the action and the clip. He made sure that the safety was on and removed the clip. Then he put it back in the purse. He grabbed his old duffel bag that he always used for traveling, threw a couple of shirts and several changes of underwear and socks in. He looked around the room and his desk. He thought of the other contents of the locked drawer. He thought about taking the bottle of Dewars whiskey that was hidden at the bottom of the drawer. He decided against it. There was something that felt final about this examination of his office and its contents.

Before he left, the maintenance man, Filch, showed up. Filch grasped Wendt's hand in a firm grip, "Wendt, I brought something for you." He held out something suspiciously long and thin wrapped in a brown paper bag. "I hear this is a dangerous job."

Wendt couldn't help smiling at the thought of what Filch would think was useful for a dangerous mission. "Well, if it wasn't before, it certainly will be now. I suppose if worst comes to worst, I could toast the aliens before I die." And he poked Filch in the ribs. Filch grimaced and said, "Now, I'm serious. This stuff isn't to be left for any aliens. If they have you cornered, don't you let them have any of this. You finish it off."

Wendt chuckled, "Sort of mutual assured destruction—the whiskey and me."

Filch scratched his head and tried to puzzle out that comment.

"Oh, don't worry about it, Filch. It's an old joke—a bad old joke."

But Filch wouldn't give it up. He leaned his head over so that it almost lolled on one shoulder as he struggled with the comment. "I just don't know," he finally said, as though it were a weighty issue that needed all his mental faculties, and the outcome would decide the course of world affairs. After staring for a while, he just turned slowly and walked away. When he reached the door to Wendt's office, he turned and said, "Just, remember, guard that with your life." He then strode purposefully through the door and didn't turn back again.

Wendt couldn't imagine why Filch would be so cautious about the rock gut that he called fire whiskey. Wendt slowly unwrapped the bottle and discovered a bottle of Johnnie Walker Blue Label. It was the domestic US version— some claimed it was aged 60 years although Johnnie Walker doesn't quote an age period. He wondered how Filch had gotten that. He wrapped it up carefully in the original paper bag and then wrapped it again in a t-shirt that he was planning on packing in with the rest in his duffle bag. He picked it up and glanced around the office wondering if he'd ever see it again and closed the door behind him. As he walked down the hall, he looked around at the walls, seeing them as if for the first time. The amazing old castle that had survived so many years and seen such tumultuous events—especially recently, but still looked as though they'd had nothing more exciting happen to them than hosting a medieval orgy or two. He thought of all the people who had died here even just while he had worked within these walls. Whatever happened, it looked like he wouldn't be one of them. More likely, he'd die someplace else, fighting the aliens.

As he approached the Great Hall, he saw Minerva striding toward him, her traveling bag hanging by its strap from her shoulder, as if it were an overlarge handbag. When she got close enough for easy conversation, she asked, "Ready to go?"

"I suppose so. Hey, does everyone in the castle know what we're doing?"

"Probably not. Who is it that knows and surprised you?"

"Filch. He just saw me off at my office. He gave me a little going away present that defies everything I understand about him. It was a bottle of Johnnie Walker Blue Label. He never drinks anything but fire whiskey, and he never spends any more than a galleon on it. He didn't say anything about my going off and probably never returning, but I can't imagine his spending anything like what that cost him if he didn't know that this might be my last trip."

"This Johnnie Walker Blue Label is expensive?"

"Yes, and it's darn hard to get outside the States."

"You know it's practically impossible to keep secrets around here in the best of times, and with the place being packed to the rafters, it is simply impossible."

Wendt took her forearm and pulled her a bit closer and lowered his voice, "Do you think this is a dangerous thing we're doing?"

She leaned her head back a little so that she could look directly in his eyes, "Let's see. We're going to use a Salamander to set fire to a building that we're in and in the mean time battle one of these alien "tobors" or whatever they are that are maybe immune to magic. No, I don't see why that would be particularly dangerous."

"When I was packing, I had this spooky feeling that I was never coming back to the office."

"Well, you know, you're not."

"You couldn't have kept that little piece of information to yourself, could you? I suppose you're thinking of firing me—so I won't return to my office."

"No. I mean that I'm thinking of a promotion for you after we get back."

"Oh, I thought you'd be moving in with me."

"Well, there's one virtue about this little job that we have to do."

"What's that?"

"If we're going to die, we'll be dying together."

"That's one of the million things I love about you: You always have a way of looking on the bright side of things."

"Yeh. Well, I'm not the only one."

Just then Longbottom was hurrying out of the Great Hall and broke into a trot when he saw them. "Come on, you two. You'd think that you weren't looking forward to this little adventure."

Wendt frowned at Longbottom. He was having way too much fun with this, "Oh, no. I'm having the time of my life. As a matter of fact, it'll probably be the last time of my life."

Longbottom clapped him on the back and said, "I love your sense of humor."

"Yeh. But it'll probably get me killed some day."

Longbottom grabbed Wendt around the shoulders and steered him toward the Great Hall, and the three of them went in. They approached the fireplace where Farhok was standing, waiting, and Longbottom said, "I'll go first. I'll just make sure everything is OK and I'll pop back right away." Minerva nodded. He stepped into the fireplace, threw down a little floo powder, and spoke, "Old Ministry of Magic". He disapparated in a flash of green fire.

They waited for his re-appearance for several minutes, which grew to ten and then twenty. Minerva wanted to follow him immediately to see if he'd had a problem. Wendt grimaced but said nothing. He held out his hand to Minerva and they walked into the fireplace. Farhok was right behind them. His armor was clinking slightly, and Wendt found himself wishing that he'd refused Farhok's request to come. Wendt closed his eyes. He found that that lessened the disorienting wrench of being blasted into a new location. Nonetheless, he stumbled a bit as they landed on the hearthstones of the fireplace. Wherever it was. He opened his eyes, but for a moment wasn't sure that he had, because it was pitch black wherever they were. He started to say, "Minerva." But she had just lit her wand. They peered into the darkness. As their eyes adjusted to the light, more things came into view. The long line of hearths, the large Atrium was dimly visible—at least the near end. But where was Longbottom?

They were about to step out of the fireplace when a light appeared in the distance. Wendt whispered stridently, "Nox". Minerva took the hint and extinguished the light at the end of her wand. Wendt pulled her down to the floor and against the wall of the fireplace. He pulled his purse out of his pocket and opened it to get the Glok out. He held it in both his hands extended, ready to squeeze the trigger if necessary. Minerva had her wand extended as well. They waited silently in the deathly stillness of the great room.

Minerva whispered, "Do you suppose it's Longbottom?"

"I hope so."

The light slowly grew in intensity, but that was the only way that it was clear that it was approaching. Wendt whispered, "Be ready to send us back if it's not Longbottom or if any of us senses something wrong." He could hear Farhok drawing his sword.

Minerva silently opened a small pouch, removed a little floo powder, and held it in her left hand. Finally, they heard a sound that could only be whistling. Minerva, still whispering, said, "It's Longbottom."

"If you think so, I'll get up and go out to meet him. You stay here."

She just snorted and said, "Like Hell."

He got up and called out, "Longbottom, why the heck didn't you come back sooner?"

Longbottom's voice returned, "Have I been here a long time?"

Minerva's voice sounded behind him, "Way too long. We were worried about you,"

Farhok said, "I wasn't worried."

Longbottom replied, "I've been fine. Everything seems fine here."

Minerva lit her wand again, and the combined wand light was bright enough to get a decent look at the Atrium and the Hall of Hearths. Wendt asked, "Where do you want to set up our base camp?"

Longbottom said, "In the Auror's Office. It's on one of the upper floors, and the Head of the Aurors has an office with a view out onto the Atrium." Everyone agreed to the idea, and they made their way to the Auror's Office. They discussed whether or not to activate the lights or the elevators. Finally they agreed that the less evidence there was that anyone was present, the better. So, they spent quite a bit of time searching for stairs. There had never been a need to use them, so nobody knew where they were. Finally, Longbottom found an almost hidden door that had the word "Stairs" printed on it. They were locked, but Minerva made short and silent work of the lock.

Longbottom whistled respectfully. "In a different life you would have made a decent burglar."

Minerva said, "In a different life, we wouldn't have to be burglarizing the Ministry of Magic."

Wendt muttered, "Let's just stick with the life we've got."

They walked the stairs, and for the first time since they'd arrived, it seemed like there was enough light for normal purposes in the stair well. Longbottom was trying to remember how many floors above the main entry level the Auror Office was. He finally decided it must be five. On the fifth, they stopped and opened the door. Longbottom stuck his head out cautiously and looked up and down the hall. It was clear. They went in the hall and tried to find the entrance to the Auror Office. Minerva wanted to split up to search the floor but Wendt forbade it, and they worked their way down the hall. Longbottom wanted to stride forward rapidly as though he were home. Both Minerva and Wendt and even Farhok forbade it. They had searched most of the floor when Longbottom muttered, "Damn."

Both Wendt and Minerva exclaimed, "What!"

"Oh, it's nothing. I just realized that the proper floor is the next one up. Let's get back to the stairs." They mounted the stairs, and this time they were on the right floor. They eventually found a door with the Auror's Office plaque and the Auror's seal, a shield with a circle circumscribing an equilateral triangle, containing a vertical bar. Longbottom unlocked the door using an unusual key consisting of what looked like a large "jack" from the child's game of jacks.

Wendt grabbed the door before Longbottom had finished opening it. He swung it back so that the seal could be seen again. He asked Longbottom, "What is this seal?"

Longbottom shrugged and said, "Oh, it's just the Auror seal."

Wendt asked Minerva, "Isn't that the sign of the Deathly Hallows?"

She stared at it in the wan wand light, "I do believe it is. I'd never really paid attention to it before. Longbottom, why is that the logo of the Aurors?"

Longbottom scratched his chin and said, "I honestly don't know."

Minerva looked at him with mild disgust, "Don't the Aurors teach their recruits anything?" Longbottom shrugged, and Minerva asked, "Don't Auror recruits have any curiosity?"

"Not about ancient runes."

"That's not an ancient rune. It's a symbol of a . . a . . I guess it's a faith." Wendt said. "Would you agree, Minerva?"

"Oh, that's an interesting question. Now that we know that the Deathly Hallows were real or, at least, had real objects that had properties that were similar to their reputed properties, I suppose we can't exactly call it a faith or belief. They're established fact."

Longbottom showing some impatience muttered, "What are you two talking about?"

"Oh, the Auror seal looks a lot like the symbol of a group of people who believed in the existence of a trio of objects that gave their possessor power over death."

He snorted, "Now, you're just being creepy."

Wendt said, "No. No. Your buddy Potter owned them for a brief span of time. They were the Cloak of Invisibility, the Wand of Power, and the resurrection stone. Just ask him about them."

Farhok said, "They were probably Goblin-made."

Wendt said, "No. They weren't the sort of things that Goblins ever made. They supposedly were made by the Peverall's—an ancient family of wizards of whom Harry Potter may be the last descendant."

Longbottom seemed to take real interest, "Yeah. I saw the Invisibility Cloak. Er. . . Well, I saw him wearing it. Er, . . I knew he was invisible, and he said he had a cloak of invisibility."

Wendt stood for a moment silently and then said, "Yes, that Cloak, it was supposed to be perfect. No one could see you if you were wearing it."

Minerva said, "Yes, that's right, so?"

"So, Moody or the faux Moody, once claimed in my hearing that he saw Potter – actually saw him – using his 'Mad Eye' once at Hogwarts when Potter was wearing it. I can't think of any reason for Moo. . that is Crouch to lie about that. What do you think?"

She looked up and slightly to the left as she considered. Finally she said, "I don't know. The Hallows were made by real, ordinary people. It seems like they could be imperfect. But . . ." she trailed off in thought.

Wendt said, "Yeah. If they were imperfect, how could they give their owner power over Death?"

Longbottom ended his long silence by declaring, "Now, you two are really creeping me out. Let's stick to normal scary things like that robot. Come on. Let's set up camp in the office."

That seemed like a good suggestion to everyone, so they went into the office. They brightened their wands and took a quick reconnoiter of the large open room with dozens of cubes. Longbottom took them to his cube. He opened a drawer and pulled out what looked like a coal oil lantern. "I keep this here in case of emergency." He touched it with his wand and it glowed brightly, giving off a yellow glow that in some way lent a warm, comforting feel to the whole room.

Minerva opened her handbag and pulled out four cots and blankets and even a couple of small pillows. "Set these up. We'll need to get a good night's sleep in."

Longbottom said, "Good thinking Minerva. Glad that you were on top of things. I didn't think about having to sleep." She turned a deep shade of vermillion and said softly, "It was nothing special."

Longbottom showed them around the office. There were restrooms that even had small serviceable showers. There were ice boxes. There was a food vending machine. Then he said, "Now, I'll show you the 'holy of holies'." He led them to a handsome mahogany door, which he threw open to reveal a large paneled room. The light from the large room filtered in dimly. Longbottom lit his wand, and they could see the room better. It had leather sofas, deeply cushioned armchairs. Most were uphostered in yellow, but there was one grand one in red. The massive desk faced into the room but behind it was a large window with dozens of panes. It wasn't possible to see what it looked down on.

Longbottom said, "Sit. I'll close the door and turn out my wand. There's usually enough light coming from the fountain that your eyes will eventually be able to see the Atrium. They took seats and Longbottom extinguished his wand. And indeed, their eyes did adapt. After about five minutes, they could see a faint light coming from the fountain, actually from the pool below it.

Minerva asked, "I didn't realize that the pool was lighted. Where does the light come from?"

Longbottom was nearly invisible, but was it a trick of light that it seemed that his chest expanded a bit? He said, "They're luminous fish, lanterneye fish. I suggested that the pool be stocked with them."

Minerva simply said, "Amazing."

There was only barely enough light available to dimly make out the walls of the Atrium, the row upon row of office windows that faced out on the Atrium. Longbottom was sitting in the chair behind the desk and had swiveled around to look out the window. He swiveled back and said, "This is the office of the Head of the Aurors. Pretty impressive, eh?"

Wendt said, "Very impressive. Have you ever been here before?"

"Sure. He interviews every applicant himself—here. I was scared stiff by the office when I was interviewed by him."

Minerva asked, "And now?"

"And now, I'd like to have this office myself one day. My mom was on a fast track to management when. . ." He paused and in the profound silence, Wendt thought he heard a catch in the voice. He finally said, "When Lestrange. . ." He simply stopped there.

Farhok apparently didn't know about the Longbottoms who had been tortured by Deatheaters because he asked, "What happened to your Mom?" Everyone remained quiet, and he looked from one to another. Finally he said, "I guess it's a secret."

Longbottom said simply, "No, it's not a secret. A Deatheater tortured my Mom and Dad to the point of death and then let them live. They never recovered fully."

Farhok just stared at him and said, "Bad, I suppose."

No one said anything for an eternity, and then Longbottom simply got up and walked back into the room of cubicles. Farhok immediately followed. Minerva and Wendt remained for a few minutes and then joined him. The room was still lit by the light of the lantern that was trying to be cheery and warm but that seemed a lot cooler. Wendt glanced at his watch and commented, "It's time for a good night's sleep. How will we know if something happens in the night?"

Longbottom said, "Oh, one of the Aurors that are watching will send a *patronus* in here and it'll wake us up."

"I don't think that I've ever had that honor."

"Just hope that it isn't Ginny that sends her *patronus*. She has a knack for finding some disgusting thing to do if you don't wake up right away. I remember one time that I was on a rotating watch. Her *patronus* went inside my ear and shouted for me to get up. If you've never had someone shout at you from within your ear, you've not had one of life's truly infuriating experiences."

Wend said "Thanks for that cheery thought."

They set up the cots and turned the lantern down to the level that it was little more than a night light. They made sure that all the doors were closed and secured. Minerva and Wendt set up their cots in one office next to each other, and Longbottom used another cubical nearby. Farhok set up in another cubicle. Minerva whispered in the dark, "This would be very romantic . . ."

Wendt finished the sentiment, ". . . if I weren't thinking about the possibility of being awakened by someone shouting from inside my ear." But he pinched her lightly on her thigh, and she giggled. He commented, "How can a grown woman giggle?"

Minerva asked, "How can a grown man pinch like a school boy?"

"Oh, and how should I pinch?"

"Like a gentleman and a scholar."

'All right, I'll pinch you like a gentleman and a scholar."

"Then you won't pinch me at all." She giggled again. From the nearby office, a tired voice said, "Come on, you two. You sound like a couple of school kids. Let's just get some sleep."

The next morning, they had breakfast in the Auror Office that overlooked the Atrium. The first day, it seemed like camping out. Then as they talked about what was coming up, it seemed more like being in prison with a life sentence. They quickly realized that they had better plan their actions when the aliens came for them. So, they spent several hours talking about plans.

One of the first actions they took was going up to the sub-basement of the "department store". It was a back room where inventory had once been stored. That had all gone. Longbottom, when he was being briefed by the Chief Auror, had learned of a way to get to the sub-basement through a trap door that connected the top level of offices of the Aurors to the sub-basement.

The top level of offices had a janitor's closet. In the closet was a rope ladder that became rigid with the touch of a wand. They climbed, Longbottom first, Minerva next, Farhok then Wendt last. He declared that he should go last because he was a gentleman and would catch any of the others if they slipped. And, Longbottom should go first because he was a gentleman and would be the first to die if something terrible was waiting for them. Farhok didn't say anything, just claimed his spot.

Minerva replied,"Gentleman, my eye! You just want to be the first one down if something bad is waiting for us."

They climbed up the ladder and emerged in the sub-basement. It was full of what appeared to be packing crates. Longbottom explained that they were empty and were there as "window-dressing" to help conceal the trap door that led up from the Auror Offices. Minerva and Longbottom lit their wands, illuminating the large room in a bright actinic light that seemed too bright but that left lots of areas barely visible. There didn't seem to be anything but the packing crates, so they chose a direction and walked off, hoping to find a stairs to the basement.

Longbottom spotted them first, and they pondered for a moment whether to go up with wands lit or not. Wendt finally decided it by commenting, "If there's something up there waiting for us, they already can see our wand-light in this pitch black. We might as well have the advantage of light ourselves."

Longbottom whispered, "Better still, let's blind them with a really intense burst of light just before we go up." No one objected, so he led the way, with his wand unlit. When they neared the top of the stairs, he stuck his wand above the level of the floor and bent his arm out over the edge of the floor and said, "*Lumos Ultima*." There was a flare of light that was almost blinding even reflected from the walls of the next floor. He then said "Nox" and the three went over the top lit by Minerva's wand. They scanned the area in more or less normal wand light. Wendt had his Glock drawn, safety off and raised at the ready. Farhok had his sword drawn. There was no apparent danger. The basement was nearly empty with only a few cardboard boxes here and there. Minerva commented, "Boring."

Longbottom said, "The next level is the main floor of the department store. Do we go up there?" The question hung in the air for a long moment and Wendt said, "I don't see a reason to. Longbottom, can you control the salamander from here?"

Longbottom thought a moment and said, "I don't see why not."

"Then we're done here." Minerva said. "Let's get back to the Ministry."

They worked their way back down the stairs and found that it wasn't so simple locating the trap door back to the Auror Offices. All the packing crates looked pretty much the same. They searched for what seemed like an hour but finally, Wendt said, "It's over here."

Longbottom said, "Are you sure? It looks like any section of floor." And then they all noticed the pattern of footprints barely visible in the dust. There were four sets heading away from the spot. They had to use the lock opening spell to get it open but nothing more serious. They worked their way down to their base camp and then discussed what they'd seen.

Minerva observed, "I didn't realize there was such a short distance between the Ministry and the subbasement. If we burn up the department store, can we really keep it from setting the Ministry on fire?"

They pondered that for quite some time. There were various ideas about how to protect the Ministry from catching on fire. Minerva suggested a shield charm. Longbottom thought that it would protect from flames but the heat itself would leak through.

Wendt said, "Sure, the infrared radiation would go straight through without . . " He was interrupted by Minerva, who said, "You made that up. Didn't you?"

"No, it's God's truth."

"God's truth. Sometimes I think you make these things up just to see how gullible I am."

Longbottom chuckled and said, "You two are like an old married couple."

Minerva said, 'Old, I give you."

Wendt said, "But I won't. You're as beautiful as the dawn of the world."

She laughed, "And as old. So, Mr. Smarty, what's your idea?"

Wendt thought for a moment. Minerva started to say, "See, I told you so." when he shushed her and said, "Wait, I've got an idea. Just give me a minute.

He got up and started pacing, "What about this. Those crates in the sub-basement."

Longbottom nodded and said, "What about them?"

"They're empty aren't they?"

"That's what they tell me. We didn't open any of them or even try to lift them to see if they had anything in them.

"Well, suppose that you filled them with water?"

"You mean right now?" Minerva asked.

"No, after we get the signal and you go up to start the fire."

Longbottom thought about it for a bit and then said, "Well, I suppose they'd hold water for a while, but I think they'd start to leak right away."

"They wouldn't have to hold water very long—just until the fire reached down to that level. Then when they started to catch fire, they'd burst and fill the sub-basement with water. It just might work."

Minerva scratched her forehead. "Could you fill them quickly enough?"

"With your help, I think so."

Wendt nodded and said, "I think you might want more crates. Do you think that you could conjure more?"

Minerva, still concentrating, said absently, "Sure, duplicating objects is child's play. Where you get into trouble is things like food, gold, silver, a few other things. Water isn't a problem either."

She stood and paced a bit, herself, "What I'm uncomfortable about is the amount of water that we'd need. We've no idea how hot the fire would get."

Wendt said, "I think that putting a couple of feet of water in the sub-basement would be enough. There's not much that will burn down there. The walls and ceilings are concrete and steel—not much to burn there."

Longbottom suggested going up and filling a crate or two to find out how long it would take and how waterproof the crates really were. They climbed up again with much more confidence this time. They picked a crate near the outer wall and filled it with water. They watched it for a half hour. At the end of that time, a little water had begun to seep out of the crate—not through cracks but seemingly permeating the wood and sweating out. In the mean time they had begun duplicating crates, stacking them on top of each other until there were only a few aisles through the piles of crates. They went back to the original crate and found that it had lost a little water, but not much. There was a small pool of standing water around the crate.

They then went back down to their base camp and were shocked to see that it was already 4PM. They'd missed lunch and hadn't realized it. Then they were famished and magically cooked a three course meal complete with key lime pie for desert. As they sat and finished off desert, they talked about the next day. As they talked, Minerva noticed a light outside the door. She shushed the others and put out the light with a wave of her wand. "Look, there's something outside the door." Wendt and Longbottom and Farhok got down on their knees and drew wands and Glock and sword.

The light seemed to move away. Everyone sighed, their muscles relaxed, Minerva whispered, "What are we going to do?"

Longbottom said, "We've got to find out what that is. You know it could be a *patronus*. We should be hearing from the watch teams sometime soon. This is our first real day here."

So they went out looking for it. They left the room and found the source of the light was outside and seemed to be a *patronus* shaped like a horse. They began to approach it, still with wands drawn. Wendt had put away his Glock, figuring that there was nothing it could do against that object, whatever it was.

It seemed to see them almost immediately and approached. The voice coming out of it was indeed Ginny Weasley's, "Well, it's taken you long enough to find me. Where have you been?"

Longbottom recovered his voice first, "We're camped out in the main Auror room on this floor. Why didn't you just come in?"

"Well, how'd I know where you were? But here's the current status. Nothing unusual has been happening. No sign of the robot. No sign of aliens. They seem to have the area blocked off, but we don't see any sign of barriers or signs"

Wendt said, "OK. Let's make this the regular time that you show up for status. And now you know where to find us when the robot does come. Any word from the *Boy Genius*?"

"Who?"

"You don't know what we call Brahms?" Minerva asked.

"Boy Genius? How'd he get that name?"

"Well, it's a long story, but if you saw the Shrieking Shack now, you'd know."

The voice took on a certain stridency as she said, "What's he done with the Shrieking Shack?"

"Well, he's made it livable. You really haven't heard?" Wendt asked.

"No. And if he knows what's good for him, he'd better return it precisely the way it was after this is all over."

Later, Longbottom commented that somebody had better pass that info on to Brahms. "I'd really hate to have his uh misfortunes on my conscience."

Minerva nodded wisely and said, "Yes. I've seen her when she is uh unhappy with someone. It's not a pretty sight."

Longbottom added, "I can't blame her. The Shrieking Shack is a Hogwarts landmark. Without that what would the upperclassmen have to frighten the 1st years with?"

Minerva added, "And an occasional 4th year, hummm?"

Wendt said, 'Oh, I see, the Forbidden Forest and the Bloody Baron and Hagrid's brother and Festrals and the Headless Hunt are not enough, eh?"

Longbottom shrugged and rejoined, "There were loads of other stuff when I was there. Blast-ended scrouts and Tom Riddle and Hagrid's pet dragons. The list goes on and on."

Minerva walked back to their base camp with everyone following and said, "We'd better get some sleep when we can. We've no idea when the aliens will be coming." Everyone reluctantly agreed to that. Farhok insisted on standing watch. He drew his sword. Wendt informed him that he wouldn't be relieved, but Farhok was determined to stand a watch or two anyway.

The next day started as calmly as the previous one had. It was beginning to seem like they might have a lengthy boring wait for the excitement that was coming. Wendt pulled Minerva aside and asked her, "We've not heard a peep from the Boy Genius. What do you suppose is going on?"

She took it a completely different way, "Well, it's about time. I've been dying for some 'action'. What have you been thinking?"

It took a minute for Wendt to understand her point. Then he said, "Well, you've got a good question there. Better than my real question, actually." And he kissed her. The kiss, that started not particularly passionately, had a great deal more feeling before Minerva was done. After a little friendly groping, Wendt brought her back to his question.

She glanced around to see if Longbottom was in earshot. "Your question is pretty good itself. You're right Brahms can be pretty anal about following things up. I wonder if he's found something else of interest and hasn't been following the Great Robot Adventure. I think that we should get in touch with him."

The day had been wearing on and "night eventually came. Night, but a night which was only distinguished from day by the almost inaudible clicking of Wendt's mechanical watch. They had meals and thought about the coming confrontation. As "night" neared, they prepared for another unsatisfying sleep. As usual, Farhok insisted on doing watches during the night. This day he had napped through much of the afternoon in preparation. He camped out in the Head Auror's Office with no lights on and only the light of the luminous fish to break the pitch black of the Atrium.

It was a little past midnight when Farhok was shocked to see that there was suddenly more light in the Atrium. He squinted and looked again carefully to be sure that his eyes were not playing tricks ,but there certainly was more light. Furthermore, the source of the light was moving because the uneven illumination was visibly changing as he watched.

A grim pleasure came over him. Here was an opportunity to prove his worth on this expedition. He rose and headed out the office silently so that no one would be disturbed. The supple Goblin armor didn't make the slightest noise, he thought proudly. As he walked past the cubicles where the others slept, he thought about how unprepared the others were for surprises. He reached the door to the outer hall when. . .

When the little Goblin jumped involuntarily because the voice of the Auror Longbottom said, "Going for a midnight stroll, Farhok?"

Farhok's shoulders slumped, and he decided that there was not going to be a Farhok-the-Hero moment He slowly turned trying to put off the moment and said, "I saw somebody with a light moving around near the Atrium. I was just going to investigate."

Then he heard what he feared most. Minerva asked, "And you were just going off without backup?"

He shrugged and said nothing. Wendt was stumbling up, sleepily. Farhok prepared himself for the inevitable group party this was going to become. He was right. It was quickly decided that everyone would investigate together. They all went back to look out into the Atrium to see if whoever it was was still nearby. Whover it was, was. Then they went out to search for their visitor. Longbottom led, Minerva brought up the rear, and Farhok and Wendt were in the middle.

Wendt had his ridiculous pop-gun out, and the wizards had their wands drawn, of course, and Farhok had his sword out. They decided to take the stairs. Longbottom had his wand lit, but the light was constrained to almost a pencil-thin beam. They opened the door to the stairs as silently as they could, but it squeaked. They haltingly made their way down the stairs and eventually reached the Atrium level.

When they opened the door with all light off, they discovered that the intruder had either left entirely or had left the Atrium area. Farhok thought, "This is it for the evening. If he's left, then we could spend the whole night—or even days searching in the dark for a non-existent invader." After a while, he said as much. They decided that they would search the Atrium area and work their way up the levels to the Auror Office. If they found no one in any of those offices, they'd call it a night, but set a watch to be on duty continuously.

The going was slow. Most of the doors of the offices were locked. Some yielded to the *Alo Ahora* spell. Some didn't. Longbottom opened one of the doors and took a step in. He immediately dropped to the floor silently. Wendt could see nothing. He dropped to the floor outside the office and tried to see something in the dark that was only slightly relieved by Longbottom's glowing wand.

Farhok immediately leaped over Longbottom, his sword drawn. He too fell to the ground, motionless. Wendt fired off several shots about the room from the outside, more hoping to get a reaction that might reveal the location of their assailant than hit anything. Minerva crept up from behind and nearly scared him to death by tapping him on the shoulder. "Shit, I almost shot you. Have you got any ideas?"

She whispered in his ear. "With those shots, I'd have expected to get some reaction if it were a person. I think it must be some kind of automatic spell. Unless our visitor were the owner of this office, I think that there's no one in there. Let's pull Longbottom and the Gobin out and see if we can revive them."

Fortunately, Longbottom's legs extended over the threshold and Farhok's body had mostly fallen on Longbottom. They slowly dragged Longbottom out, and the Goblin came with him. At one point, Farhok's right arm snagged on something, and they were afraid they might not be able to get him out. However he moved enough so that his body extended over the threshold, and then he could be pulled directly rather than being pulled by friction with Longbottom's body.

Once out, Minerva immediately diagnosed the spell that had dropped them as *petrificus totalis*. She quickly reversed it. Longbottom's only comment was "Why is it always me?" And they went on their way, being more careful for a while.

By the time they reached the 3rd floor, they had again thrown caution to the wind and were actually opening four doors at a time, cautiously sticking a hand in, and declaring the office clear after a quick search. They reached their own floor and hesitated a moment wondering whether to search offices on their floor. Being bone tired with tension by that time, they decided not to. They opened the door to the Auror Office, not noticing light leaking under the door. Longbottom, who went first, as usual, immediately went to his knees on the floor when he realized that the light in the room wasn't theirs. Wendt tripped over him. Farhok had his sword out and leaped over the two, running into the office, sword flailing.

Minerva just said, "Damn" under her breath and then used the *Revellio humanum* spell that showed a person close to the Head Auror's Office. Wendt had his Glok out and shouted, "Come out or we're coming in firing."

Then a familiar voice said, "It's just me, 'Georgy Porgy.'"

Minerva disgustedly said, "George Weasley, what the Hell are you doing here?"

He rounded a corner and said, "I've just come to help."

At Sea

The Captain was on the bridge of the Ohio class nuclear sub. He looked over at the XO. "Go to periscope depth and deploy."

The XO gave commands to bring the sub gradually to 15 meters depth and raise the periscope. It was purely routine. No one was expecting anything but a ho-hum check-in after being under the Arctic ice for three months. They'd been out of contact for that whole period. The sub came to periscope depth, and the captain scanned the horizon 360 degrees. "It's clear. Raise the electronics mast and let's check-in."

The electronics mast raised, and the communications officer worked the console. After a moment he reported, "Sir, there's a message from Atlantic Command."

The captain raised his eyebrows momentarily before regaining command of his face. "I'll take it in my cabin." He left the XO in command and went to his cabin, where he opened the laptop and logged in.

He opened Outlook and saw a priority message that had been encoded. He clicked to open the attached message and entered his personal ID, password and the ship ID and password. A web browser opened, and there was the message. He stared at it for a couple of minutes. He closed the browser and reopened the message. He read through it twice. Then he got on the phone to the bridge.

"This is the captain. Please send Mr. Wainwright down to my cabin."

The captain watched the sweep hand on the watch to see how quickly he would arrive. It was 38 seconds. Apparently, Wainwright had figured it was urgent. He was right.

Wainwright reported. The captain told him to sit. He swung the laptop around so that the XO could read it. "Take a look, and tell me what you make of this."

Wainwright read the message through twice and then said, "Sir, are you sure this isn't a prank of some sort?"

The captain simply shook his head.

Wainwright went on, "This is the craziest order I've ever seen." He quoted, "Report to Bridgeport Naval Station for decommissioning." He looked up at the captain and added, "What the hell is this all about? Have you heard any scuttlebutt about our ship being de-commissioned? And why in the middle of a deployment? Is there a war going on, and we didn't hear about it?"

The captain said, "I don't know anything, Wain. This is as much a surprise to me as it is to you. You haven't heard anything have you?"

Wainwright shook his head. "Do you think there was a war, and we lost?"

The captain stared off toward the corner of the cabin. Then he turned back to Wainwright. "I don't know. If we were at war, we'd surely have been given attack orders through the ELF system. But," he hesitated as he seemed to be searching for the right words, "I think that we'd better do a little research before we do anything."

"Are you going to acknowledge receipt?"

The captain smiled and swung the laptop back toward himself. "Yes, I am." Then he began typing and read aloud what he was typing. "Message garbled in receipt. Please resend." Then he entered passwords and ID's and sent the message. "That will probably hold them for a little bit. Let's do a little research." He invited Wainwright to move his chair so that he could see what he was doing on the laptop. He opened another web browser and keyed in the URL for CNN. The page came up, and the two of them stared at it.

The captain said, "That's the gall-derned strangest headline page I've ever seen."

Wainwright read through the headlines aloud, "Hurricane in upper Atlantic. Cancer Cure rate reaches 98%, US World Cup team defeats Brazil in Regional play, German Bid Wins next Special Olympics location. What the hell is going on? Where's the real world news?"

The captain agreed and suggested trying some other web sites. They tried Google News, Yahoo News, *The Times of London*. They were all the same. There was nothing that would have made the front page before they went under the Arctic ice. As a matter of fact, those very headlines were found on all of those web sites.

The captain suggested, "What foreign languages do you know, Wain?"

Wainwright shrugged and said, "French, Spanish, a little German."

"Let's try the frogs. Do you know a website to bring up?"

"Let's try *Le Monde*. That's a world class paper."

The captain did a Google search for *Le Monde* and immediately found the website. He turned the laptop so that Wainwright could read it without craning his neck. "What do you see?"

"All the same junk on the US news websites." He fell silent as he scrolled through the home page of *Le Monde.* Then his mouth dropped.

"OK. Don't hold out. What did you see?"

"This is absolutely crazy. I don't believe it."

"Don't believe what!"

"Unless my French has completely failed me, this article says that the French and English World Cup Soccer teams played a Regional match yesterday. The French won."

The captain broke in, "What's so strange about that?"

"Just listen to what this article says. 'The French and English were tied at the end of regulation time. They played two golden goal overtimes."

The captain interrupted again, "What's 'Golden Goal'?"

Wainwright felt like rolling his eyes but restrained himself. He decided he'd have to explain all the fine points of soccer as he went. "'Golden Goal' means that the first team to score a goal wins immediately. Anyway, there was no 'Golden Goal' in regulation overtimes. So they go to PK's,' He hastily added, "PK's are free shots that a player gets to take from about the 20 yard line. The goalie, and this is important, can't move until the player taking the PK shoots.

"Now, this game, the French won via PK's 9 to 7. The final winning play happened when the French player kicked and the goal shot was blocked by the English goalie. The referee ruled that the goalie had moved before the kicker had. So, he got a 2nd try. The French player complained that the goalie hadn't moved before him, but he was overruled and had to kick again. That one he scored on. The French coach after conferring with his player protested on the field, but the British goalie insisted that he'd moved first. Later the French team appealed to FIFA, the international Soccer organization. Their appeal was denied. The French then threatened not to play in the next round if the game weren't replayed. FIFA stood firm. The latest was that the French Foreign secretary was going to bring the issue to the United Nations."

The captain said, "That sounds pretty strange—that the frogs are so insistent on fair play, but . . ."

Wainwright shook his head, "It's not strange; it's impossible. It would be like the Chicago Bears winning on an overtime touchdown over the Green Bay Packers in the NFC championship, which was disputed because the receiver had stepped on the line, and the Bears had insisted that their receiver had been out of bounds. But then, the Packers had insisted that he'd been inbounds. And then, the Bears threatened not to play in the Super Bowl."

"No shit?"

"Absolutely no shit!"

The captain leaned back again. "Maybe, this is a hoax or some sort of frog joke. Let's check somewhere else."

"OK. Let me find the web site for the RTF."

"RTF?"

"French TV and radio."

He found the website, and they listened to the live news feed. Wainwright listened and said, "Same old Shit." He listened some more and then said, "This is it. Sports. Yes. Yes. Same old story. The French radio reports it just like *Le Monde*. This is real."

The captain stood and paced back and forth in the small cabin. About three paces, turn, three paces, turn. Finally, he sat down again. Meanwhile they hadn't stopped the radio feed. Wainwright said, "Wait a minute! This is stranger yet. The French report that an interstellar ship has just landed at Orly Spaceport."

"What do you mean, spaceport?"

"That seems to be what the French means. I've never heard the word before, but. . . Yes, it says that the ship contained a shipment of 10,000 aliens."

"Oh hell. What's going on? Have we been invaded by by. . ." He didn't finish the sentence but Wainwright did—aliens.

They just sat a while staring at each other. Finally, the captain said, "It looks like that is it for us, doesn't it? That would explain the crazy orders and..." But he never finished the sentence because the phone rang. He motioned to the XO to answer the phone.

He did, listened, and then hung up, "There's another priority message come through." The captain whirled the laptop around to face him. He opened the message and said, "Same message and they want an answer right now."

Wainwright asked, "What are we going to do?"

"I can't believe I'm saying this, but I think we're at war, and I may well be the ranking surviving officer in the US Navy. I guess I've got to plan our strategy. Do you agree?"

Wainwright said, "I'm glad you said it and not me. But, yes, I agree. What kind of acknowledgement are you going to send to the Atlantic Command?"

The captain seemed to come to himself, He started keying. "Message received, acknowledged, understood, and execution begun."

"What are we really doing?"

"Get up to the bridge and submerge. Find a thermocline and put us below it. Then assemble the commissioned officers. We've got to do some thinking. Make it for one hour from now."

The XO left for the bridge, and the captain got out a legal pad and started making notes.

▽

There were about a dozen officers in the Officers' Mess. The captain waited until everyone was there and then entered the mess. The call went out, "Captain in the mess." Everyone leaped to their feet and snapped to attention.

"At ease, gentlemen." Everyone sat and bent their attention on the captain. "Gentlemen, we are at war. Unfortunately, we may be the last surviving force of the US Navy – the last ship." There was a sudden hubbub that quieted quickly at a look from the XO.

"Yes, it's possible that I may be the acting Secretary of the Navy, if not a higher officer. The XO will confirm everything I'm telling you. We are convinced that the enemy is a force of aliens from another star system.

"I know, it's hard to believe, but we've seen pretty clear proof. The XO will provide details later. For the moment, I want to let you know what we're up against. It seems to be a very insidious enemy that can, in some way, take over the bodies of humans, and impose their will or even possibly, completely replace the humans they inhabit. We'll be making a general announcement to the crew shortly. Until then, I want to enlist your help in thinking through the problem we face.

"When we surfaced, we were given orders to go to the Bridgeport Naval Station for decommissioning. I suspect that's happened to all naval forces. This may mean that the only attack subs out there are still run by humans or just don't exist. That would be lucky for us, but I don't think that we can count on it. So, our first goal should be making contact with any remaining resistance forces, including those of all foreign powers. Once we know about the resistance, we can plan our next steps. I'm now going to open the floor to questions and suggestions.

The missile officer rose and asked, "We've got quite a lot of nuclear firepower here. Do you intend to use any of it?"

The captain had feared that question, but knew it would come, "That would be our final option. And we certainly can't use it now without a lot of good intel to base firing decisions on."

Another officer stood. The captain addressed him, "Mr. Gallagher."

Gallagher, the Chief Engineer asked, 'How do you intend to find resistance forces? I think I'd be really reluctant to answer any radio signals from someone who claimed to be resistance."

"Mr. Gallagher, what do you think?"

"Look for signs of battle. Do we have access to the intelligence satellites?"

The XO said, "Not a bad idea, but, frankly, I'd be afraid to try to use the satellites. They probably could trace where the user was located."

Then the XO looked at the captain and said, 'Permission to speak frankly."

"Granted, of course."

"I think we both know a force that likely is still resisting if anyone is."

The captain groaned, but he said, "Yes, I think that I know whom you're talking about, but we'll not discuss them here. After this meeting, come to my cabin to discuss your idea further."

The rest of the meeting was spent answering questions that didn't have answers, like what kind of technology do the aliens have and what do they look like and how do we know when a human is really an alien?

The captain's cabin was cozy but it seemed large—too large for comfort. Both the occupants wished that they could make it smaller—so small that the aliens would never find it. The captain said, 'Where do we go to find the wizarding community? As far as I know there are only two places. One's in the North Sea and the other is on the northern coast of Scotland. But I don't know how to get closer than a few dozen miles without wizard help."

"You're right. We need wizarding help. The only thing that I can think of is to pick one, go as close as we can manage, then surface, and just cruise up and down, and hope that they notice us."

The captain snorted, "Wain, that's what I was sure you'd say, but don't we have anything better?"

"I can't think of anything."

"Great. Then go up and set sail for the coast of Scotland. It's closer. It won't take too long for the aliens to figure out that we're not on our way to visit them. Then we'll find out how much of the military apparatus of the Navy that they left intact."

"You mean that you expect them to send out search planes and maybe attack subs?"

"They'll send out everything they've got. We've got two dozen nuclear missiles at our command. That would make for a lot of dead aliens, if we used them."

"And we'll be sitting ducks cruising up and down the Hebrides."

"Well, we'll find out just how good we are pretty darn quickly if your friends, the wizards don't find us first."

The captain dismissed the XO, who went directly to the bridge to get the course laid in and the ship on the way.

The helmsman laid the course in and set the auto pilot after asking for the speed. The XO answered, "What's the best speed we can make without announcing our presence too loudly?"

The helmsman said, "Between 15 and 20 knots."

The XO said, "Pick a number and make it so."

"Aye, sir."

The captain was on the bridge when the navigator announced that they'd reached their co-ordinates. "Take her up, Mr. Slaughter. Level off at periscope depth" He spun the periscope around and said, "Clear. Raise the electronics mast and scan for aircraft."

"Clear."

He addressed the XO. "Come to the surface, send a watch up with binoculars to look for aircraft, surface ships and . . . and." He couldn't quite bring himself to say the word "wizards". He just ended, "whatever else shows up.

"Cruise up the coast to Loch Dubh at 5 knots and then inform me when we arrive."

He left the bridge. After he'd gone, the navigator said to the helmsman, "Just what are we doing?"

"Trying to attract attention, I guess."

"Then why did we cruise here as though there were a dozen Chinese attack subs after us?"

"You've got me."

The XO had moved over close and broke in on the conversation, "Belay that talk gentlemen."

After about eight hours of cruising, the XO knocked on the door of the Captain's cabin.

"Come."

The XO said, "We've reached Loch Dubh."

"I know. We've got to turn her about and cruise back down to our starting point and, . . , oh hell, I'll come up and stand this watch. Get some sleep. I've got a feeling that when things start to happen, they'll happen fast. I want somebody fresh on the bridge."

He went up to the bridge and gave the commands. The watch on the sail changed a couple of times. There was nothing to see. When they reached the starting point, all light was gone in the sky. The captain ordered the boat to submerge and head out to deep water to find a thermocline to hide under. "Wait until local sunrise. Send for me. Then return to this point. Come to periscope depth and check for any threats. Is that understood Mr. Carter?"

220

"Yes, sir."

"Oh, yes. Get the XO up here at that point as well."

"Yes, sir."

The captain returned to his cabin and wondered if he'd be able to get any sleep. Ordinarily any captain at sea can get to sleep quickly when necessary and awake even quicker, but he wasn't a captain at sea. He was an admiral at least. Maybe he was actually the Secretary of the Navy.

The phone rang once. Before the ring ended he was up, clear-headed and reaching for it. In the interval between the first ring and the second ring that never happened, he picked up the phone and said, "Yes."

"We're on the way to station, sir."

"Thanks, Carter, I'm on my way. Is the XO?"

"Called you first sir. He's next."

"Good."

The captain reached the cabin in near-record time. Carter reported that he'd scanned the surface. Nothing was in sight.

The XO entered the bridge as the brief report ended. The captain said, "Get a look with radar."

The report was negative. The captain ordered the boat to surface and to get two lookouts up to the sail and to turn off the radar as soon as they were up. He ordered the cruise of the previous day repeated. The navigator asked, "Sir, including the return at the far end of the course."

"Yes, Mr. Bart."

Both the captain and the XO stayed on the bridge for the full course to the far end and then when they came about for the return as well. At one point, the XO asked the captain if he could buy him a cup of coffee.

"Of course, Mr. Wainwright, I'm always ready for somebody else to buy." There were smiles around the bridge but no laughter. Everyone knew that the unspoken question was really, "Can I talk with you in private."

They reached the officer's mess and sat in the otherwise empty room. "What is it, Wain?"

"How many times are we going to cruise up and down waiting for somebody to find us?"

"You mean, how much of a chance are we going to take that it's the aliens who find us?"

"Yes, sir."

"After this return trip ends, we'll go back under that thermocline from this morning, and we'll give the crew a rest for a shift. Then we'll go to the North Sea site."

"Yes, sir. I think that's the better hope anyway." The Captain nodded.

On the sail, the sailors who were on watch were straining their eyes on the horizon, when suddenly there was a sound from immediately below them. One, Seaman Bielski, looked down and shouted, "Ben, look."

While they were in the mess, the intercom sounded. "Captain to the bridge. Captain to the bridge."

We Went Fishing for a Trout and Caught a Whale

Sinistra and Brahms went back to the Shack. When they arrived, the crew on duty had news for them.

"There's something brewing with the assault on the Ministry. There's a meeting at Frank's Conference Room for this noon. We think that this is IT."

Brahms looked at them incredulously, "IT. How can it be IT.? Surely we should have more warning?"

The crew leader, Samuels. said, "Haven't you been reading our emails? They've had several meetings planning the details of the assault. They just hadn't set the date. It was looking to be today or tomorrow."

Brahms leaped into an empty chair and logged onto a console. Sure enough, there were a bunch of notes with titles that should have grabbed his attention. What the hell had he been doing the last couple of days? Oh, yeh. He'd been distracted. He looked up at Sinistra who had a worried look on her face. She said, "Nick, what's this all about? Assault on the ministry?"

He compressed his lips, thinking hard. "OK. Sit down. Let me think. Sinistra, suppose we had to get a message to the real Ministry right now. How could we do it the fastest?"

She remained standing. "Well, the fastest would be to go there ourselves through the floo network, I suppose."

"OK. Stay and watch this with me. Then, when we've learned exactly when the attack is, we've got to get to the Ministry right away so we can warn them."

She sat down next to him and put her hand on his right elbow lightly. The lightest of touches was still felt and he swung around, surprised. Just then, Samuels interrupted them, "There are people entering the Conference Room" and the view on the big screen showed them filing in.

▽

Frank sat and said, "Better get comfortable, this could be a lengthy affair." He turned to someone and asked, "When does the assault begin?"

The answer was, "We've not got the robot in place, quite yet. I think the trainer's giving last minute instructions. Let's say about half an hour."

"Good. It'll be after noon. We might get lunch in if we eat right now. I don't think I'll be much in a mood for lunch once the action starts."

With that, Brahms leaped up. "Come on Sinistra, we've got to get to the nearest floo. Where is that?"

She was on her feet before he'd started to speak, "Come on! It's in the Great Hall." She ran out the door, closely pursued by Brahms. He almost lost his footing on the stairs but regained it. They waited impatiently at the Main Entrance as the guard fumbled, letting them out.

Brahms was panting a little but asked, "How long to the Great Hall?"

"I've never run it. Maybe ten minutes at this pace."

All Brahms could gasp was, "Shit."

They dodged around Wizards and a few Muggles who were walking the path. When they reached the doors of the castle, Brahms glanced down at his watch and swore—15 minutes already. They sprinted down the entry hall to the Great Hall doors. Fortunately, they were open. They ran through, in the hearth, and both Sinistra and Brahms grabbed hand-fulls of floo powder. Sinistra laughed, "What are you doing with floo powder."

He just shrugged and said, "Go!"

They disappeared in a green flare and found themselves looking out the hearth at the interior of Azkaban prison. They ran out. The person at the Reception Desk asked, "How can I help you?"

Brahms blurted out, "We need to see the Auror team that's running the operation at the old Ministry."

The receptionist was flustered and just spluttered. Sinistra interrupted and said, "Where's the Auror Office?"

She responded to that question, "Third floor. Take the elevators at the . . . " But the two of them were off at a run and didn't hear her plea that they take visitor badges. There was an elevator just starting to close. They ran in, hand-in-hand and punched the 3rd floor button. The elevator seemed to have been designed for hospitals because the door slowly

224

closed, the lift started to rise slowly, the door crept open at the 2nd floor, and closed as slowly. It crawled up to the 3rd floor. By this time Sinistra had her wand out and was ready to blast the door open, but Brahms restrained her, and they squeezed out before the doors were half open.

They looked around for a directory sign and finally found it on the wall next to the elevator. "Auror Offices 350 through 375." They guessed a direction to start running and quickly found that the room numbers were declining through the 330's. They turned and dashed down the hall in the opposite direction, dodging wizards and witches. At 350, they threw the door open and bounded in. Brahms looked at his watch— 25 minutes. The Auror at the Reception Desk asked, "May I see your visitor badges?"

She was reaching for her wand when Sinistra, who still had her wand out said, "Don't. We need to warn the team at the old Ministry that the aliens are coming in minutes. Where's the, the," She couldn't think of the name.

Brahms asked, "Where's the Control Room for that operation?"

The reception witch said, "I'm sorry, without ID, I can't tell you anything."

Brahms said, "Shit." He looked around to see if there were anyone around that he knew. Just then, the door opened behind them. They turned to see who it was.

Pam Moertl's eyes widened at the sight she saw. She adapted quickly and came to the side of Brahms and asked, 'What brings you here?" as she slipped an arm through his and started to pull him aside.

Brahms said, "No time for that Minister. We've got to warn the team at the old ministry that the aliens are coming any minute now."

She hesitated for a moment trying to take it all in. Then, she said, "Right, come with me."

The reception witch tried to object but one look from Moertl had her sitting back on her heels silently. They walked briskly down the internal hall, and she touched her right index finger to a pad on the wall next to the door. It opened silently, and they all went in. There were tables and a large map of the old Ministry on the wall that was something like a white board. There were a couple of people standing next to the wall talking quietly. They turned when the door opened and one said, 'Well, it's good to see you Minister. What can we do for. . ."

He never finished the sentence. The minister rapidly said, "Can it, Argo. The aliens are coming right now for the Old Ministry. Get the word to the team lead. We'll just sit and enjoy the show."

Argo looked to a woman with a shade of hair that Wendt would have called strawberry-blond had he been present. She immediately, walked to a desk, picked up a wand and what looked like a bronze knut, and tapped it with her wand. The knut turned red and then glowed green

225

for a few seconds. She looked up and looked between Argo and the Minister, trying to decide which to report to. She finally decided on the Minister, "Done, Minister."

The minister asked, "Who's on duty right now at the local Command Center?"

The witch looked down at a notebook and said, without looking up, "Ginny Weasley."

The minister looked up and said, "The Weasley woman. She's talented but a little unpredictable. But, she's good in a fight. We're probably lucky."

Ginny's coin turned red and vibrated. She pulled it out of her purse and said, "This looks like the real thing." She touched it with her wand and it turned green and stopped vibrating. "I'm sending my *patronus* over. Get ready for the *patronus* from the Auror Office.

Bill, who was sitting at the window with omni-occulars said, "Ready. I've got eyes on the street."

Ginny's *patronus* flew out of her wand and went through the window and flew across the street into a window in the old department store. It swiftly flew downard through floors and then sub-basements and into the old Auror Office. There were five there in the office having lunch.

Ginny's *patronus* landed on the table between them and a strident female voice asked, "George! What are you doing there?"

George smiled, "What a pleasant surprise, sis. What brings you here?"

"What brings me here is the aliens who are siccing the metal monster on you all in a minute or two—if not less. Again, what are you doing there, George?"

"Oh, I figured that they could use some help here, having to depend on my little sister to give them warning. And it looks like I'm right. Did you say one or two minutes?"

"Get out of there George. I don't want to have to come over there and jinx you."

Longbottom was up and throwing his backpack on his back. "I'll just be on my way, while you two have a little family reunion, shall I?"

Farhok jumped up as well and since he never took his armor off, he was ready to go. "I'm coming along with you Longbottom."

"No you're not!"

"You'll need help. I'm with you."

"No, you're not!"

Farhok's expression was as stern as any of them had ever seen Farhok wear. He asked, "How are you going to stop me."

MInerva said, "Oh, bother. Let him come Longbottom. But, Farhok, if you screw anything up, I swear that I'll come up there and eviscerate you myself!"

The two almost ran off, but Ginny's *patronus* looked away and said, "OK. The thing's on the street and heading for you. Don't go yet Longbottom. I want to let you know what to expect. Bill, what's it look like." She fell silent for a moment and then resumed.

"The thing looks like an an arachnamanchula. Big. Not harry and. . . " She hesitated again and then picked up. "Something just happened. I think it went through the shield around the Ministry. It stopped for a second and then a silvery thing suddenly appeared around it. It was that way for a couple of seconds, and then the silver thing turned transparent. The interior is sort of blurred, but it looks like it has a shield charm around it. But it just keeps going. It doesn't drop after a few seconds. It's sort of groping its way down the street, but it seems to be getting used to walking with that shield thing around it. It's going at a normal pace now. You'd better get moving. I'll be up with you in the sub-basement when you let the Salamander go. We'll have another *patronus* in your Auror Office to let the rest of you know what's going on."

George said, "I'll just pop up with Longbottom and his new buddy and keep them company."

Ginny swung around and said, "You'll do no such thing, George Weasley. Don't make me tell your buddies there what you middle name is."

George sulked a little and said, "Ginny, you sound more like Mom every day."

She laughed and said, "Sticks and Stone's, Georgy. Sticks and Stones."

In the mean time, Longbottom and Farhok had left the room, and Minerva had got her wand out. Ginny's *patronus* had left as well.

Minerva looked around at the other two and said, "Well, this is it, gentlemen. I guess we should get ready for the worst."

George looked around as if Ginny might still be able to see him. "Your buddy the Boy Genius thought you might like to have this." He pulled his backpack up on the table and pulled an assault rifle out of it and a fabric belt with a number of hand grenades hung from it. Then a couple of extra clips of ammo and several boxes.

Wendt said, "A friend in need is a friend indeed George. You may just be a lifesaver."

George said, "Well, in all fairness, I should add that the B.G. also said that he thought none of those would be much good against that thing, but he thought that you would take comfort from having them."

Wendt replied, "I really could have gotten along perfectly well without that last comment."

"Oh, no need to thank me."

"Then I won't."

Shortly after that another *patronus* showed up. It looked like a doberman pincer. "I'm in the command post with Ginny. I'll keep you up to date if anything interesting happens."

George said, "You'll be pretty busy then. I think that just about everything that happens from here on out will be interesting."

"Maybe you're right. The thing just tore the doors out of their frame up above you without seeming to exert itself in the least. It's on its way in and it just disappeared out of our sight."

By this time, Longbottom and Farhok were opening the trap door and climbing up into the sub-basement. Ginny's *patronus* was next to him and said, "The thing just entered through the Main Entrance above us. Better get that salamander going."

Longbottom finished pulling himself up and looked around. "I think that I'm going up to the basement. I want to make sure that that robot thing doesn't have a chance to escape before I release this baby." He patted the side of his backpack.

Farhok was strangely silent, but actually got out in front of Longbottom.

Ginny said, "Don't take any unnecessary chances. I've lost too many friends as it is in the last several years."

Longbottom shrugged and said, "Not to worry."

He lit his wand and proceeded to the stairs to the next level. He climbed rapidly and caught up with Farhok who seemed to have amazing night vision. Ginny whispered in an insistent hiss, "We don't know where that thing is. I'm trying to get another *patronus* into play to follow it, but we don't have another person available to run another *patronus*."

"We'll know when the thing arrives." By this time, he'd reached the basement, walked to the middle of the room, and pulled out a glass jar that seemed to have a smouldering fire inside it. They could hear a sort of scrabbling sound that seemed to be coming from the floor above."

"Come on, Longbottom, let the thing go and get out of there." the *patronus* said.

"Not, just yet."

Farhok seemed transfixed nearby.

"Damn stubborn Longbottom. I can see why the Carows hated you back at Hogwarts."

"Oh, I thought that was my most endearing quality. Everyone seemed to like it back in the old days."

"Well, back in the old days, you were using it against Riddle, not against your friends."

By this time the scrabbling sound was quite noticeable and there was a dim light that shown near the stairs. Longbottom said, "I'm putting out my wand, I don't want the thing noticing it. Farhok, come over here." But he didn't move either.

Ginny hissed, "Then give it something real to notice—that Salamander."

Longbottom just tscc-tscced and crouched watching as the light near the top of the stairs grew stronger and stronger.

Ginny hissed even softer, "Longbottom, get out of there right now. That's an order."

"Don't get excited. I just want to see the whites of its eyes."

There was a creak from the stairs as if a heavy weight had just descended on them. Ginny's voice had a strident insistence in it, "Go. Now." Then the front legs of the thing appeared, lit by the transparent shield that surround the thing.

Ginny's voice was a suppressed scream, "Neville Longbottom, get out of there, NOW!"

Farhok was still standing near the center of the basement. As soon as the robot had descended completely, it shown the light around and noticed Farhok. At that moment two things happened. Farhok drew his sword and started to charge the robot. In response the robot after a second of watching Farhok run toward it, turned the shield on to full power. It turned a bright silver and Farhok swung his sword in a wide arc that intersected the silver shield. In that instant, there was a sort of explosion. The goblin was blown backward, and the sword was shivered into at least a dozen shards.

Longbottom didn't say anything, but lowered his wand and opened the jar. The Salamander was a ruddy red thing of vapors. When it left its prison, it was held by Longbottom's wand. He said a few words to it that weren't in any human language. Then he released it. It scuttled along the floor, almost like a serpent, searching out anything flammable, setting little chips of wood and paper on fire. The light from the Salamander seemed to excite the robot. It ran down the steps and slowed as it saw the Salamander. The Salamander saw it and ran toward it.

The robot stopped in its tracks and waited as the thing approached. When it reached the shield and started to slither through it, the shield seemed to drop back suddenly and became perfectly reflective and quite bright.

Ginny shouted, "Now, Longbottom."

Longbottom took the opportunity to do something Ginny didn't expect. He ran over to the goblin who was still lying on the floor, scooped him up, and ran toward the stairs, which was also toward the thing, but the shield maintained its perfect reflection. He passed it quickly and started down the stairs, but the silver shield dimmed slightly. When it realized that the Salamander couldn't get past the shield at that lower power, it quickly turned and started toward the stairs to the lower level. The salamander, went off in another direction toward the wooden columns that supported the next level of the building. It leaped onto one, and it instantly burst into flames. The salamander scrabbled up it and attacked the wood floor above it.

Meanwhile Longbottom had reached the floor below and was hiding behind a barrel about a third of the way into the sub-basement. He was trying to think of a way to attack the thing that was bounding down the stairs. He began to wonder if his wand would do any good against it. It seemed to know just where he was. It was going deliberately directly at him. Then an idea occurred to him. He raised the wand and the barrel next to the thing exploded. Water went everywhere. It didn't seem to bother the thing other than the thing seemed to be slipping and sliding a bit.

It was only a couple of barrels away when suddenly the ceiling above the thing collapsed onto it. That didn't seem to bother the thing a whole lot. It shrugged the pile of concrete and wood off itself and then it was moving again. Longbottom looked around for the source of the diversion and saw that George was back at the trap door, standing and throwing another curse. This one struck the bright shield and bounced off. All the diversions gave Longbottom a chance to run back to the trap door. He was most of the way there when he noticed how bright it had become in the sub-basement.

He looked around and saw that the light was coming in from the floor above, and he could see that the entire ceiling of the floor above was on fire. The thing had seemed to notice too because it had stopped pursuing him and had turned and was running back to the hole in the ceiling that George had apparently created. It leaped up to the next floor as though it were taking a single step. It was then lost in the collapse of the ceiling of the floor above. The last that George and Longbottom saw of it as they lowered the still unconscious Farhok through the trap door was burning timbers flying as though they were matchsticks.

In the Auror Office of the old Ministry, Minerva was asking Wendt, "What are you doing with that thing?"

"I'm trying to figure out how it works."

'You mean you don't know how it works!"

"That's what I mean."

"You seem pretty casual about it."

"Oh, I just think that Brahms is right. That thing is going to look at this assault rifle and laugh."

"Great." She turned to the *patronus* and asked, "What's going on up there?"

'We don't know. The Salamander's loose but it didn't seem to make much of a difference to that thing. Apparently, the building's on fire. We can see smoke coming out the windows of the department store.

"Oh, here's something from Ginny. Apparently, the fire has got the thing worried. It's trying to escape from the building.

"Now, it's got the Salamander attacking it again, but this time is different. It's having to deal with a few thousand tons of burning beams and debris. Apparently, it's had to slow down considerably to keep the Salamander and fire off of it and is making only very slow progress toward the main floor.

"The heat must be really intense, the steel girders are bending and softening. The thing has practically stopped. The shield thing is a perfect silver reflector, but it seems to be contracting as though it's harder and harder to keep the fire out. It's started moving again slowly.

"Wow!"

Minerva and Wendt both exclaimed, "What is it?"

"Just wait a sec.

"OK. The shield thing completely disappeared, and the thing started running like hell. It was tossing girders out of the way like Blodgers, but the Salamander was on it. It suddenly sagged and slowed and then dropped just a dozen meters from the exit from the building. The rest of the building has collapsed, and Ginny can't tell what's happened to it."

In the Conference Room at Buckingham Palace, they watched video from a dozen cameras spread around at various places—none of them less than a couple of blocks from the department store. They watched the robot enter the building.

Frank pounded the table with his fist, "I wish that thing would communicate with us. How I would like to see video from it right now."

Somebody said, "That's the robot. It's put its shield up so that it wouldn't be attacked. It usually cuts off all communications in that situation."

Frank just shook his head. Everyone else had a glum expression. Nothing happened for quite a while. The tension in the room grew—all the more because there wasn't anything that made sense to be said.

Finally someone tried a joke, "These humans have a saying. 'No news is good news.'"

Frank looked up at the woman who'd said it and just stared. Her eyes dropped and she mumbled something about humor being good medicine.

Frank looked up at the screen again and said, "Isn't that smoke coming out of the 2nd floor?"

Somebody switched the view to infrared. "You're right. There's a hot spot at the south end of the building."

Somebody else said, "Maybe it's on the offensive. Maybe it's found something or somebody."

Frank said, "I'm beginning to think that it's more likely that something's found it."

The smoke soon began to billow out of a broken window. The infrared display was a bright orange at points.

Robbie asked, "Do you think it's time to send in fire trucks or something?"

Frank looked at him and said, "Sure. Let's do it." And he crossed his fingers. Shortly they saw a couple of fire trucks turn the corner in one of the displays, and then they stopped abruptly as though it had hit a barrier. He went on, "I was afraid of that."

The firemen got out, even though they were two blocks from the fire and seemed to be milling about aimlessly. Meanwhile the fire kept growing and seemed to engulf the whole building as though it had been made of tinder. Parts of the structure began to collapse. Then the entire structure above the first floor gave way and descended into the center of the building.

Frank looked around and said, "If you can, get a forensic team in there." No one said anything. He looked around and in a voice that seemed on the edge of breaking, "Do it now! See what's left of our wonderful robot. I'm going to my office." He got up, left the room, and everybody else looked around.

Somebody said, "What just happened? It's not possible. I saw that thing do things that I couldn't believe were physically possible. I saw it deflect 50 mm. depleted uranium cannon shells as though they were snowflakes."

Somebody else just looked at him and left the room. He was left standing there alone, staring at the fire control team hosing down other buildings so that they wouldn't catch fire.

In the Auror Office under what was left of the department store, everyone had met and were drinking toasts of pumpkin juice. Even Farhok lying on an improvised cot seemed happy.

Minerva said, "To George, who saved Longbottom."

George said, "To Longbottom, who justified my coming."

Longbottom said, 'To me for trapping that thing in our basement."

Farhok asked plaintively, "Isn't someone going to toast me?"

Longbottom said, "Right. To Farhok for nearly getting me killed."

Farhok's face fell, but he didn't say anything.

Wendt raised his cup and said, "To getting us out of here."

George asked, "Haven't you been having a wonderful vacation here?"

Wendt just stared at him and said, "Sure, but it's time to get back to work."

George said, "Spoilsport."

Minerva said, "We've got to get Farhok back to the hospital wing of Hogwarts to treat his injuries."

Farhok looked around and suddenly realized that his sword wasn't in sight. He asked, "Where's my sword." Everyone looked at each other and the silence grew long. "What happened to my sword!"

Wendt said, 'I'm sorry. When you attacked the robot, you struck its shield with your sword a terrible blow. It, well, . . ."

"What happened to my SWORD!" He practically screamed the last word.

Wendt went on, "It was shattered by the blow you struck the robot with." He turned to Longbottom, who just shook his head. "I'm SO sorry, Farhok. It's just completely gone."

Farhok looked from face to face, "It's just lost. I dropped it. It must still be up there. Someone help me find it." He looked to Longbottom, whose face fell.

He said, "Farhok, you were lucky to survive yourself. It was a terrible creature that you attacked. I couldn't believe my eyes. There's nothing left of your sword."

Farhok screamed a terrible wail, "Nooooo! I must go up and find it."

George bent down next to Farhok and said, "I was up there. It was terrible. There was nothing anyone could do. The fire was like a storm. Everything was ablaze. There were thousands of tons of girders and concrete and dust falling everywhere. The fire is probably still going. You'd just be committing suicide trying to go up."

Farhok seemed to accept the inevitable. He shook his head that was now bowed down. He said, "It was my great great grandfather's sword. He used it in the Wizard War. No one in my family has ever let it be harmed. I might as well commit suicide."

Longbottom said, "We've got to get moving if we want to get Farhok treated at Hogwarts."

Wendt looked at him and asked the room in general, "We should try to move him without disturbing him. Can we keep him immobilized? Do we have anything we can secure him to the cot with?"

George said, 'Farhok, lie down straight. I'll keep you still." Farhok didn't say anything, but did lay flatter and stayed still. George pointed his wand at Farhok and said, "*Immobilis*."

Minerva nodded approvingly and said, "Come on. Let's go." She took her wand and levitated the cot with Farhok on it. They gathered up their belongings and started out toward the elevator. They reached the Atrium level and headed for the hearths.

They all walked down to the Atrium, and Wendt looked into the pool at the luminous fish. He nodded and then joined the others at the hearths. He took Minerva's hand, and they walked into the hearth and out at Hogwarts in the hospital wing.

Madame Pomfrey approached them and asked, "What's this then?"

Minerva said, "We've got a wounded Goblin here. He doesn't seem to have much other than bruises and contusions, but we don't know about internal injuries."

Wendt added, "He was knocked unconscious. He may have a concussion."

Pomfrey nodded and said, "Well, we'll sort him out." She took her wand out and released the *Immobilis* spell and asked, "How did you do this?"

The goblin remained silent and then said, "I don't want to stay here. Nobody should know that I was here."

Pomfrey said, "Well, you've entered my hospital wing, and nobody leaves the wing until I release them. But take him into my room. I'll make sure nobody but I will treat him."

They carried the cot into Madame Pomfrey's room and she said, "It's just as well. We don't have any open beds available anyway. I'll sleep on the sofa of my office.

"No visitors at all and with a little luck he can be out of here in a day or two."

Turning to him, she looked at him and said, "To be on the safe side, we'll treat you with skelegrow just in case you've got any cracked bones."

Farhok wailed, "No skelegrow! I know a Goblin who had to take that. It was terrible!"

Pomfrey turned back to the others and said, "Out of here, all of you. I'll let you know, Minerva, when I release Farhok."

They all left Pomfrey's quarters and George commented. "I think he ought to be proud of what he did, and all he wants is for nobody to know about his bravery."

Wendt said, "He's lost a valuable family heirloom. We've all got to respect his privacy. As far as we're concerned, we don't even know Farhok."

Longbottom spoke in a low voice that was almost silence, "I think I know how he feels."

The Loch

The captain responded on the intercom, "What's up."

The bridge reported that somebody was on the deck.

"What the hell. Get the master-at-arms up to the bridge. We'll be up there."

The XO and the captain sprinted up to the bridge. They arrived, and the captain talked on the phone to the conning tower., "What's going on up there?"

Bielski answered, "There are two people who suddenly appeared on the deck. They want to come on board and speak to the captain."

"The hell they do. Tell them to stay there, and we'll have someone to escort them in momentarily." He turned off the phone and looked for the Master-at-Arms. He gave him orders. "There are a couple of people on the deck. Bring them aboard and take them to the Officers' Mess. Take along a couple of your seamen armed with assault rifles. Treat them as hostiles. If they crack a smile, you've got permission to shoot them."

As the MA left, the captain turned to the XO. "Get the camera feed from the Officer's Mess going up here. Then go in, and interrogate them. Find out what they're up to."

The XO asked for permission to speak freely, "You know that they're almost certainly wizards. How could they get on the deck if they weren't?"

"That doesn't mean that they're not aliens too. I'll be watching in my cabin. When you're satisfied with what they're up to, join me, and we'll discuss what to do."

"Yes, sir." The XO waited until they were on board and then headed down to the Officer's Mess. When he arrived, he found the two "guests" sitting at a table with two armed seamen holding their pieces at the ready. He carefully chose a spot out of the line of fire and separated from the MA.

"OK. I'm laying down the ground rules. I ask the questions and you answer. If you make me nervous in any way, I might just have these gentlemen shoot you. Understand?"

The man answered, "Yes, Mr. Wainwright."

Wainwrght tried not to show a reaction, but it was not easy when a total stranger called out your name. "Since you think you know my name, let's start off with yours."

The man answered, "I'm Nicholas Brahms, formerly a consultant with the SAS, and this is Professor Sinistra of Hogwarts School of Wizarding and Witchcraft. We're here to see if you are aliens or not."

Wainwright took a pace toward their guests, "You are wizards?"

The woman answered, "I am. Mr. Brahms is a Muggle. We saw your ship in our telescopes, and we hope that you're not aliens. It would make us feel a lot better if you could prove that you aren't."

Wainwright couldn't stifle a brief chuckle, "You're not the only ones. But first, how did you get on deck without being seen?"

Brahms answered, "We disapparated here. I know you've heard of that—maybe even seen it in action."

"You claim a lot of knowledge about me. Just how do you claim to have this knowledge?"

"Wendt told me about you and some of your adventures. You had some magic demonstrated by Fred and George Weasley on-board this ship—maybe in this room. Would you like a repeat performance?"

"Not yet. And if your lady friend or you touch anything that looks like a wand, the Master at Arms is going to put a couple of rounds in you.

"How do you prove to me that you're not aliens?"

Brahms looked around the room trying to find some hint of an idea how to do that, and then he had a thought. He looked back at Wainwright. "If we were aliens and wizards, we sure wouldn't be sitting here talking about how we need to prove we're not aliens."

Wainwright nodded at the armed seamen. "Maybe you're concerned that you wouldn't be faster than those two?"

"Oh, think. We wouldn't have been standing on your porch knocking at your door if we were aliens."

"Maybe."

Sinistra asked, "How do you prove to us that you're not aliens?"

Wainwright smiled, "Your argument works both ways. We wouldn't be standing here palavering if we were aliens, we'd force you to do whatever aliens do when they take people over."

Brahms scratched his chin, "But we sure wouldn't worry about being shot, if we were about to be attacked in some other way."

Wainwright grimaced, "Stalemate."

Wainwright turned toward the door, opened it, started to walk out and turned back to the MA. "If they twitch a muscle before I get back, don't hesitate."

"Aye, sir."

Wainwright went to the captain's cabin and was admitted, "Well, what do you think sir?"

"It looks like we should take his challenge."

"What do you mean?"

"Let this Sinistra prove that she's a witch and that this Brahms really knows Wendt by having him specify the same magic spell they used on me that time."

Wainwright said ruefully, "I see that you aren't volunteering for doing a repeat performance."

"No, I want to be a spectator this time. If it pans out, then I'll come in and we'll all talk."

Wainwright returned to the mess and said, "OK. Prove that you're a witch, Ms. Do what your friend tells you to."

Brahms looked at her and smiled, "Set him upside down in the air."

Wainwright said, "Wait a minute." He turned to the seamen. "She's going to pull out a wand. It's all right. But if anything strange happens other than my turning upside down. Shoot them. They're probably the two most dangerous people you'll ever meet."

Then he turned back to Sinistra, "Go ahead." She pulled her wand out of her sleeve and didn't speak a word. Then, he was suddenly upside down with his feet almost touching the deck above. "I'm satisfied. Let me down, and then slowly, carefully put your wand on the table. Then roll it gently away from you to the opposite side of the table and sit back, moving slowly at all times." She did that. In a moment the door opened, and the MA spoke sharply, "Captain in the mess."

Nobody came to attention, but the captain wasn't surprised. He immediately said, "As you were." even though no one had come to attention. He walked over to the table and bent over the wand but didn't touch it. Then he sat opposite them.

"Well, you seem to be legitimate. Do you have a way to prove that we are?"

Brahms immediately answered, "Yes, sir. We do. You'll have to take the unbreakable oath. As a matter of fact everyone on the ship will have to."

The captain was immediately wary, "What is this oath and what makes it unbreakable? And how does that prove we're not aliens?" Then he quickly added, "I see. We swear that we're not aliens."

"No sir. The unbreakable oath is unbreakable because you die, if you try to break it. And we don't ask you to swear that you're not an alien. It actually immunizes you from being taken over."

"How is that possible?" Wainwright asked.

"It's pretty simple. You swear not to reveal any information to an alien. If you do, like you would if you were taken over, you and the alien die. Then. There."

The captain whistled, "Pretty effective. Kind of hard on both the alien and human if it happens."

Then he added, "OK. I buy it. Everyone takes the oath. Period. I'm ready. Administer it."

Sinistra got up and walked over to the captain, picking up her wand as she went. Brahms walked around the table and stood next to him, "Stand up, please. Grasp my forearm."

The captain did. Sinistra wordlessly tapped their arms with the wand, and the fiery ropes entwined their arms as Brahms spoke the oath and the captain took it. As it ended, the captain released a breath that he'd held almost thoughout the spell. "Whew. I was just a little uncertain how this would end up. I'm glad to still be standing here.

"Does the whole crew take the oath next?"

Brahms said, "No, we've got to get this boat under cover before the aliens notice it—if they haven't already. Let's get it into the Loch where our protective spells will keep it from being observed."

The XO said, "Then let's get up to the bridge and get moving."

Everyone followed the XO up. The MA who had drawn his sidearm came last. On the bridge, the captain gave the order, "Helmsman, take your direction from our guests." He turned to them and said, "You can watch the monitor that shows the view from the bow. Please use Port for left and Starboard for right in your directions."

Sinistra said, "You're really pretty close to the inlet to the Loch. Just do a 90 degree turn to the ri . er . . starboard."

The helmsman said, "There's nothing but cliffs there, sir."

The captain asked, "Yes, I can see. What's going on?"

Brahms said, "It's the defensive spells, you can't see the Loch."

The captain said, "Let me guess. Only Ms. Sinistra can see the inlet to the Loch, right?"

Brahms nodded.

The captain asked, "OK. That means that Sinistra has to give orders to the Helmsman and we all hope that between them, they can get us into the Loch."

The XO said, "I think that's true. Do you think that you could give directions to the helmsman about how to steer the boat to get us into the Loch?"

She shrugged, "I think so. Do we have any choice?"

"Give up?" Brahms asked.

"I'll try."

So, she sat in the seat next to the Helmsman, and they talked through the kind of directions that he needed to help him steer the boat. Finally, they agreed that they could start. They took the boat in a big circle as a trial, and then they lined up the boat with the inlet of the Loch. Sinistra was satisfied, and they started to accelerate toward the Loch. As they got closer, Sinistra saw that they were out of line, and she had the helmsman steer to starboard 10 degrees. They had over-corrected. She had him go port 15 degrees. That was too much. They came back 20 degrees to starboard because they were now getting really close to the Loch. At this point, the captain ordered the boat to full stop. The momentum they'd built up was too much. The XO shouted, "Emergency reverse!"

The ship slowly came to a stop only a couple of hundred meters from the cliffs. The captain was unhappy. "XO. Come with me to my cabin." The XO grimaced and followed him.

In the cabin, the captain asked, "Well, do you have any ideas?"

The XO scratched his ear. "Well, we could sit out here and practice with the lady directing the helmsman. We could try a different helmsman."

Then he said, "Permission to speak frankly, sir?"

"Granted."

"Well, I think that she would do better if she could steer herself directly. She appears to be smart and capable of learning quickly. Actually having her hands on the wheel could help her get a feel for how quickly to steer."

"I don't like it." He got up and paced, mumbling to himself and finally said, "OK. Let's try your idea."

They returned to the bridge and the captain asked Sinistra, "Would you try the helm yourself?"

"You mean steer myself?"

"Yes."

"Yes." Sinistra echoed, "I'll try."

"OK. Mr. Kelsey, relinquish the helm to Ms. Sinistra. You'll remain to give her advice."

This time they pulled out to sea again. She asked, "How do I control the speed?"

The captain said, "Just say whether you want to go faster or slower and I'll give the command."

She nodded and said, "Then, slow down a little."

The captain said, "Ahead one quarter." Then he amended that, "No make 20%."

240

The ship gradually slowed, and they approached the cliffs. She steered to port and then starboard and then back again. They were less extreme motions, but she shook her head and said, 'No. It's not right. Stop her.'"

The captain nodded approvingly. "Full stop."

"Do you want to try again?"

"Yes."

"Mr. Kelsey, take us out to sea again, and then let her take over."

They went out several kilometers, and then she had the helm again. This time, she went even slower. They could barely see the cliffs come closer. This time, the steering was less violent, and the XO found himself rooting for her to take them in.

But again, as they got close, the steering turned more and more violently. Kelsey urged her, "Don't oversteer. Just take it slow and easy." She calmed some, and the oscillations to port and starboard lessened, but finally she had to say, "No. It's not good."

They went out to sea again, and this time, there was noticeable tension on the bridge as they approached the cliffs. Everyone held their breaths as they came closer and closer to the cliffs. There was more than one quickly suppressed word of encouragement. The captain looked over to the XO as they reached the point of no return. If she decided to stop to try over again, it would have to be now. The moment passed and everyone stared at the monitor that showed the view of the cliffs rushing up. The radar man had begun a distance countdown. "200 meters. . . . 150 meters. 100 meters. 50 . . . 20 . . 10 . . " The collision alert had been sounding from the point that they'd reached 150 meters. The XO was expecting a grinding collision. But Sinistra didn't say anything. Then the cliffs turned black. After a few seconds the monitor cleared and they could see the Loch.

Everyone released their breaths, and the captain said, "Mr. Kelsey take the helm. Full stop. Congratulations on your first successful piloting of a boat, Ms. Sinistra. Would you and Mr. Brahms please come down to my cabin for some discussion?"

In the captain's cabin, it was crowded with the captain, the XO, Sinistra and Brahms. The captain was to the point, almost to the point of brusqueness. "Well, what's the story in the realm of magic? Who's in charge? How do I get to see him or her?"

Brahms took the question. "Imagine the British government without a military. New Scotland Yard is known as the Auror Office. The Prime Minister is the Minister of Magic. She's got a bit more power than the Muggle Prime Minister—and not just because she can do magic."

"What's her name?"

"Pamela Moertl."

"How do I get to see her? Is she located here?"

Sinistra took that one. "We can probably arrange a meeting once the Head gets back from, . ." She hesitated not knowing how much to reveal. She finally finished weakly, ". . .from a mission.'

The captain immediately jumped on that, 'Head? Head of what?"

"Headmistress of Hogwarts School."

"Oh." He was disappointed. "Well, are all your leaders women?"

The XO spoke for the first time. "I can answer that. And really, you should be able to as well. When we were involved with wizards the last time, the heads of departments and so forth were all men."

Brahms went on, "I think people thought that men had bolluxed it up the last time round, so they have been appointing women to a lot of leadership posts since."

"Well, how soon can we see the Minister of Magic and start to help toss these aliens off-planet?"

Brahms said, "Well, we really don't have to wait for the Head to return to put you in touch with the Minister. She'd probably like to get to talk with you without the Head being involved."

The XO asked warily, "Why's that?"

"Because I think there's some sort of competition going on between the two of them. I'm not sure what it's about, but it seems to me like the Minister thinks that the Head may want her job. There seems to be a tradition of that. The politically 2nd most powerful post in the country seems to be the Headmaster of Hogwarts."

Sinistra looked archly at Brahms and said, "I think it may have more to do with plain old competition for some guy."

The captain thought the conversation had gone plenty far enough that direction, so he interrupted. "Well, anyway. I want to see her as soon as possible to establish where we are in the chain of command and what we can contribute to the effort to oust the aliens." He hesitated and then went on, "You are interested in doing that, right?"

"Oh, yes. We want to do that."

The captain let out a sigh of relief and nodded. "OK. Then let's get down to more immediate priorities, like where can we get hold of some supplies/ We're not tight at the moment, but we're cut off from our normal supply chain. I want to make sure we have access to food and other supplies. Who's in charge here while your Head is away?"

Sinistra said, "It's the Head of Slytherin House, Professor Slughorn."

"Well, I'll need to see him. When do you think that we can arrange it?"

"We'll disapparate over there and arrange for a meeting as soon as possible. Do you need to arrange for people to be off the ship?"

"Why?"

"Well, you've been at sea for months—I suppose underwater, surely your people need relief from life on ship."

"Oh, they'd like shore leave, but we were only about half-way through our tour of duty when this happened. So, they can get along quite nicely for a couple of more months on the boat—more if they have to."

Sinistra shrugged and took Brahms' hand. "Are you ready to return to the castle?"

Brahms nodded and with no more ad-do, they disappeared with a pop of imploding air filling the spot where they had been standing. The captain turned to the XO and said, "Wain, I don't think that I'll ever get used to that way they have of popping in and out."

▽

Slughorn invited the captain and XO to visit the castle. Brahms said that he could spare a room with a couple of cots if they would feel more at home in high-tech surroundings. They took Brahms' invitation.

Shortly after they arrived, while they were still unpacking their duffels in their Spartan room in the Shack, they realized that they were not alone. Both the XO and the captain swung around to find the window in the west wall was open, and an owl was sitting there regarding them. It had what appeared to be a letter in its beak. When they noticed it, it leaped into the air, flew over the captain's head, dropped the letter, and flew out the open window.

"I could have sworn that window wasn't open when we came in."

"Yea, Wain. I agree." He looked at the direction on the front of the envelope, which read, "Captain, USS Ohio, The Shrieking Shack, The Storeroom on the 2nd floor." He commented, "Well, that owl is well-informed." He opened the envelope, took out the letter and handed the envelope to Wainwright. The captain scanned the letter and commented, "We're invited to meet with Slughorn tonight in the Teacher's Lounge and from there to the Ministry of Magic to discuss the consequences of our sudden arrival. So is Brahms. This says that Brahms can show us the way. I suppose we can't refuse."

So, a couple of hours later they found themselves walking in the company of Brahms up the hill toward the castle. They could see the fields of tents and the Quidditch Pitch, the groups of people, apparently practicing magic. There were people riding brooms overhead in formation. Brahms commented, "Pretty amazing, eh. I'd never have guessed that they could be so organized."

The captain asked, 'This is organized?"

"Sure, you should have seen the refugees when they first arrived. It was chaos."

They arrived at the Teacher's Lounge and found a party of people waiting. Slughorn introduced the heads of houses: himself, the Headof Slytherin; Prof. Flitwick, the Head of Ravenclaw; Prof. Sprout, the Head of Hufflepuff; and Professor Rolanda Hooch, Head of Gryffindor. He introduced them and then finally, Professor Sinistra arrived. She apologized, "Sorry, I'm late. I had to finish some lesson plans."

The officers were opposite each other, and each had heads of houses on either side. Brahms and Sinistra sat opposite each other. Slughorn and Hooch were at opposite ends of the table. The meeting included dinner. Table talk during dinner was light—about the weather, the latest quidditch match results, the ports of call that the Ohio had visited. What were their favorites and so forth. Coffee and tea appeared on the table, and the talk changed. Slughorn asked what the captain brought to the table.

The captain said, "As a vessel of war, the Ohio has one purpose—to frighten any enemy with the terrible vengeance that it can deliver. It is a failure in this situation. It hasn't frightened the enemy, and I'm not entirely sure that it can actually deliver the terrible vengeance that we promise."

This admission of weakness surprised all around the table. Slughorn interrupted, "But surely you can do something. Why is it that you are powerless?" He hesitated, seeming not to want to admit his own ignorance. "And what is the nature of that power anyway?"

"It is based on the thermonuclear weapon. A small device about the size of that briefcase over there. . ." the Captain pointed at Slughorn's leather case. ". . . contains enough energy to vaporize a one kilometer circle in a city and kill most people at a much larger distance.

"There are about 250 such bombs in the Ohio. They wouldn't be much use if we couldn't deliver them to distant targets safely—at least safely to us. We have 24 rockets on that boat that can deliver those weapons as far as 10,000 kilometers away."

Slughorn gulped, "That doesn't sound like you are powerless."

The captain went on, "That's not the full story, though. Our enemy crossed at least hundreds of light years of space to get here. They routinely take off from the planet, circle it, and land. They travel throughout the solar system with ease, as far as I know. I can't believe that they couldn't detect our rockets and destroy them before they reached their targets. If we can't deliver them, we might as well be armed with broadswords."

Everyone was silent for a moment. Then both Sinistra and Brahms opened their mouths to speak at the same time. After a little silent interplay, Sinistra yielded to Brahms, who said, "What if you could deliver accurately those warheads without fear of interception—and more precisely than your rockets could?"

"Well, then, we'd be a formidable force indeed, but how could we do that?"

Brahms nodded his head toward Sinistra, who said, "If those bombs are no larger than briefcases, they could be carried into a city by wizards disapparating into the center of the target, dropping the bomb and apparating out again."

Everyone was silent again. The idea of a single person carrying a weapon of such destructiveness into the heart of a city and leaving it to detonate and kill hundreds of thousands or even millions of people was almost hideous beyond imagining.

Finally, Slughorn said, "I guess I hadn't conceived how big the stakes that we're playing for really are. You could destroy every city of any size in Europe with the weapons in that ship."

Wainwright spoke for the first time. "But that assumes that we can actually remove the warheads from the missiles and activate them outside the missile. Captain, do you think our missile techs could do that?"

The captain thought a moment and said, "I'm sure that they can remove the warheads. Whether they can separate the components of the warheads and rig the triggering mechanism to accept commands from new controllers that we'd build, I don't know."

Brahms said, "I've got a crew of electronics and hacker geniuses. I would be willing to bet that we can."

The captain asked, "We're guests here. Professor Slughorn, would you approve of our doing that on your property or would we have to leave if we intend to go forward?"

Slughorn shrugged in denial, "I can't make that decision. It would have to be the real head when she gets back or more likely the Ministry that would have to make that decision."

Everyone seemed to be relieved to be able to put that decision onto the shoulders of someone else. They finished the coffee and tea, relatively happy that the decision was at the least one for another day and probably someone else's. Slughorn insisted that the guests take a room in the Slytherin house, which they accepted.

That night, they all stayed in Hogwarts. The next day, Slughorn joined the officers of the Ohio at lunch, "How did you spend the night?"

Wainwright said, "I have to admit that it was the best night's sleep that I've had in months. How about you captain?"

"True. Of course, the last couple of months we've been sleeping on narrow, hard bunks—when we've gotten sleep at all. Still, having a 4-poster bed with a thick blanket and cool, clean night air is a luxury."

"Wonderful, wonderful. We've got an appointment for 2PM— lots of time to spruce up and get ourselves down to the New Ministry of Magic." He pulled a couple of corn beef sandwiches off the pile on the platter in front of them. "Help yourselves. These are marvelous sandwiches."

The rest of the officers took handfuls each and fresh cups of hot coffee and started munching. The captain ate moderately and asked Slughorn, "Is there anything special we should know about protocol when visiting the Minister of Magic?"

Just then Sinistra and Brahms showed up at the table and took seats on the same bench. He asked if there was any news about an appointment to see the Minister.

"I was just starting to tell the captain. We've got an appointment this afternoon. We'll make a decision on how to use your weapons—or if we do. You two are included because you were instrumental in getting the ship into protection."

Slughorn said, "It's time to go to Azkaban." Slughorn invited the captain to take his hand. The captain looked at his XO, who was also offered a hand by Flitwick.

Wainwright said, "I think this is necessary for us to travel." He took Flitwick's hand and followed him into the hearth. Flitwick picked up a handful of green powder from a bowl near the hearth. They entered the hearth. Flitwick spoke one word, "Azkaban" while he threw the powder down, and they disappeared in a flare of green sparks.

The captain said, "Well, I suppose there's not an alternative, is there?"

Slughorn shook his head, and they walked into the hearth.

When they arrived, the captain commented, "This is an unpleasant way to travel."

Slughorn agreed.

The captain and Wainwright walked out first and looked around. The captain said, "I always wondered what it looked like in here when we broke in. And now, I've become a regular visitor."

Sinistra said, "It looks a lot better than it did then." What had been the exercise yard was set up as an atrium. The place was well-lit, and there was a reception desk. They checked in, and the receptionist commented that there had been a lot of Muggles coming through lately.

Sinistra added, "Yeh, they let just about anybody in here these days. I remember when you had to get an invite from the Wizengemot."

Brahms introduced the Muggles to the Minister and the Aurors that accompanied them. She asked the captain, "The Ohio. That was the ship that was involved with the rescue of people from this very prison, wasn't it?"

"You're quite right. I often wondered what the interior of this place was like when we were preparing for the assault. I never hoped—or feared—to see the interior. This is something of a homecoming for me." He looked around and continued, "Rather nicer than I expected."

Pam commented, "Oh, by the way, of course, it wasn't quite this pleasant when it was a prison."

They went to a smaller conference room. It was much more elegant than the typical ones. There were well-cushioned, leather chairs, a mahogany desk, an espresso machine, a leather-bound notebook at each seat.

The Minister motioned them to sit. She was 100% business. She smiled at Brahms, who was placed by the place-cards next to her. The captain was on her other side. "I've met with my advisers, and we'd like to use your vessel's uh capabilities to convince the aliens to leave our world."

Pam asked how they had avoided being captured by the aliens. The captain's answer was, "Simple, we were under the ice of the Arctic ocean on an extended mission as the conquest proceeded. They thought that after we emerged, they could simply order us back to port and take us easily.

"However, they didn't count on how much the world had changed under their control. It was almost immediately obvious when we surfaced and began to be suspicious of the orders that we were given that it was a very different world that we were returning to than the one that we left.

"Pretty quickly, we decided that we were all that remained of the United States of America. That resulted in my having the unenviable promotion up many pay grades to be the acting President of the United States. Wainwright here is the acting Vice-President. God help us."

Slughorn commented, "So, this is a meeting of state."

Pam reflected and said, "I guess it is. Let me be the first to welcome you, Mr. President."

Pam then asked THE question, "Just what can you do to help us defeat the aliens?" Her manner was that of a scholar posing a purely academic question, but there was cold earnestness, an intensity, in her voice that belied the scholarly pose. It was a question that troubled her.

She turned to face the captain directly and said, "You occupy an unusual position. You are a visiting head of state, but you are also here seeking asylum and assistance yourself. I clearly can't force you to co-operate with our ideas, but I certainly want to encourage you to."

The captain smiled, "You're right. I have an unusual position. I suggest that you simply make your proposal and be open to our suggestions. I think that you should for several reasons. As you say, you really can't force us to use our capabilities if we choose not to. But beyond that, we may have technical knowledge that would change your proposals if you were aware of it. Also, we may simply have a good idea or two ourselves. Please proceed."

Pam outlined the idea of her advisers. It amounted to blackmail. They would threaten the aliens with annihilation if they refused to leave. Of course, it might be necessary to prove the reality of that threat before they would believe it.

"So, you want to threaten that we will go to nuclear war toe-toe with them if they don't surrender and leave?"

Pam shrugged, "That's about it."

The captain nodded. "Well, I don't have a better idea, but I do have some suggestions. First, they know what nuclear weapons you have access to. They know the inventory of weapons that the Ohio has. They are formidable, but even if we were to use them in the most efficient way possible, we couldn't kill more than, oh, say 250 million or so people. That's only a couple of percent of the population of the world. They might just call your bluff."

Pam's mouth opened in surprise and horror. She said, "But you're talking about millions of people. No! Hundreds of millions of people. That's hideous. Even Volde , er , Riddle with all his deatheaters only killed a few thousand people. What you're talking about is insane."

The captain looked over to Wainwright, who nodded and said, "Madame Minister. You were probably not involved much in the war against Hitler, but tens of millions of people died in that conflict. It's entirely possible for people to do—and accept—such hideous casualties."

Pam body seemed deflated. "But surely, we wouldn't just do that if they refused."

The captain said, "No, certainly not. But I think that we need to be prepared to prove to them that we are capable and willing to do that if necessary."

One of the Aurors said, "We just thought that they'd surrender if we threatened that."

Wainwright said, "I'm afraid that it just doesn't work that way in the Muggle world. I wish we could assure you that nobody would get hurt, but it's just not there."

Everyone was feeling like there had been some sort of group loss. Finally, the captain asked, "Then we have your permission to prepare some nuclear weapons and make them available for use against the aliens?"

Pam seemed to be in a reverie. She woke from it and said, "Oh, yes. Of course. Let us know when you have weapons ready. We'll need training on how to use them, of course. Oh, one last thing—when do you think the first batch will be ready?"

"That's hard to say, but I think a week or two will do it. We want to be very careful. We'd hate to repay your hospitality by blowing your school to kingdom-come."

"That couldn't really happen, could it?"

"I'm afraid it could."

On that cheerful note, the meeting effectively ended. There were mutual civilities, but all groups felt like they had sold some part of their humanity. They just hoped it wasn't for a mess of potage.

On the way back to Hogwarts, the captain started discussing what they'd need to make the weapons. The discussion continued when they reached Hogwarts.

The Cave

The captain laid out what he needed. First, he needed help removing one of the Trident D5 missiles from its launch tube in the Ohio. That had turned out to be a very scary proposition. The missile had to be raised very precisely vertically until it cleared the missile tube hatch.

Professor Slughorn called for help from wizards who had lots of experience with the *leviosa* spell. Since a Trident missile weighs 58 metric tons, it was necessary to get several capable wizards to lift the missile. The planning included choosing a spot that was flat and could accommodate the 15 meter length of the missile. Once a spot was chosen on the shore, the Ohio was maneuvered as close to that spot as was feasible while leaving some clearance under the sub. That took a day.

On the chosen day, the four wizards and the four backups went out on boats to the sub. The massive hatch of Launch Tube 6 was raised, and the wizards came on board. The four primary ones counted down to raising the missile. Zero was reached and . . .

The CPO who was in charge of the operation heard the trident missile scrape the sides of the tube, and he shouted, "Stop. Stop. Let it down easy." The wizards did their best, but there was more scraping, and there was a definite ring of metal on metal when it hit the base of the launch tube.

"God-damn it," The CPO was lucky the captain hadn't reached the deck and didn't hear the invective. When the captain did reach the deck with the XO, there was a hurried conference with all concerned.

The XO spoke first, "That scraping sound must mean that the net force on the missile isn't directly through the center of gravity and true vertical. The forces have to be nearly perfectly balanced, or we'll rip a hole in the tube and maybe in the missile itself."

The captain asked, "Is ignition of the fuel possible?"

The XO shrugged, "I don't know. Nobody's tried rupturing the casing of a missile to see."

The lead wizard of the team asked, "Just how perfectly straight up does this thingee have to go to prevent scraping."

The captain looked at the XO, who looked at the CPO, who shrugged, "There's practically no clearance. They're meant to fit snugly. There's high pressure gas that provides pretty darn precise thrust that is straight along the bore of that gun."

There was discussion and finally they agreed to try again. This time they'd apply force very slowly to see how straight they could make it by going slowly. This time, they applied their spell slowly. There was no movement for a minute, and then the missile started moving very slowly. It wasn't long before the tube began to squeal.

"OK. OK. Let it down—slowly."

They did, and the squeal subsided.

"OK. What next?"

The XO asked, "Could we remove the warhead with the missile still in the tube?"

The CPO shook his head, "No. You have to have access from the side to release the warhead."

The captain said, "We could try another missile."

The chief of the wizards said, "I think the problem is that we're not providing the same force from each wizard. We probably need to try different combinations of wizards to find the closest matches."

The XO said, "Look, we've got 8 wizards, that's 70 combinations of 4 at a time. We'd better get going if we are going to finish today."

So, they started the laborious task of replacing wizards one at a time. They quickly got confused because 70 combinations are a lot to keep in your head. Finally the XO, made a chart and they started testing systematically. Each combination tried lifting the missile. Each time the missile started squealing sooner or later. They had not gone through half the combinations when it was noon. They decided to take a long lunch break to allow everyone a chance to unwind before starting up again.

They all crowded into the Captains Wardroom for lunch. The cook had prepared sandwiches and tomato basil soup. The sandwiches were good, and the soup was superb. Some of the wizards declared it was a meal worthy of the house elves of Hogwarts. Then they took some time to get acquainted as a way of allowing some more de-compression before returning to the nerve wracking work of trying to lift the missile. It turned out that the CPO had a cousin in England who knew the sister of the Muggle husband of one of the wizards.

Then came the awkward discovery that neither the cousin nor the sister had made it to any sort of safety. That ended the lunch break prematurely. Everyone wanted to get back to work.

In the early afternoon, they were rewarded by a combination of wizards that was able to get the missile ¾ of the way out of the tube before it started squealing. The CPO looked to the XO who looked to the captain, who just shrugged and said, "Keep going. If the hatch is damaged beyond repair, we just will have to limp to our home port on the surface. IF we ever get back there."

Miraculously, the missile came out without any serious damage being done to the tube and none to the hatch. It closed and appeared to be tight. Meanwhile the wizards propelled the missile slowly toward the shore. It flopped a good bit as they tried to lower the nose faster than the tail. It did eventually come to rest without too much of a bump.

The captain congratulated the XO, CPO, wizards, and the chef. They declared it a day and left the missile lying on the beach.

$\triangledown$

The next day, a far smaller party arrived at the beached missile, which looked slightly in the early dawn light like a beached whale. There was the CPO, who was carrying a tool kit. There was Brahms and the XO.

The XO asked the CPO, "Is there anything else you need?"

The CPO answered, "Well, I need my tools, which I have. When I've removed the warhead, I'll need someone to help me transport it to the cave where we're going to work. There, I'll need lots of light."

Brahms said, "No problem, as soon as you are ready, we'll get a wizard or two to disapparate us to the cave. We can provide an electric generator and some really bright work lights when you need them."

"That sounds good." He hesitated and said, "There's one other thing. I've been trained removing the warhead, and I don't think that will be a problem, but . . . ."

The XO smelled a problem brewing. "But?"

"But, I need the manuals for opening up the warhead and removing the individual devices. That means I'll have to take them off the ship. I think that's strictly against regs."

The XO laughed. "Is that all. No problem. Permission granted."

The CPO continued, "That's not quite all."

The XO's face sank and he said, "And?"

"And I'd like permission to discuss them with Brahms' crew so that we can build a new triggering device for the bombs."

"I've got to discuss that with the CO. But you won't need that permission for a while, right?"

"Oh, no."

"Good, then get moving."

The CPO set about the process of disconnecting the warhead from the missile. The bolts were pretty straightforward. But after they'd been removed, there were data cables that had to be disconnected. That was ticklish. There were several color coded cables that had to be disconnected in the right sequence. The CPO worked them through several times until he was sure that he was doing them in the right sequence. Then, he did it for real.

By the end of the operation, he was sweating profusely, but all connections were severed. They took a break while Brahms went to find a couple of wizards to help with the disapparation. They arrived and one wizard disapparated himself and the device. The other took the three Muggles and himself.

When they arrived outside the cave, the plan was that the wizards and the CPO would go in with the lights, and they'd choose a specific spot to disapparate the warhead to before they actually took it into the cave. Brahms and a wizard went for the generator and lights. They set up the generator and got it running. Then they took the lights into the cave and set them up.

One of the wizards asked why they didn't just have a wizard light his wand inside. The XO answered, "Well, if something goes wrong, and the bomb goes off, we only want to lose the CPO."

"Oh." That was the end of the discussion.

The wizards and the CPO chose a spot to disapparate the bomb to, and they moved it there immediately. Then the CPO came out, his face as white as ashes. The XO asked what had happened. The CPO said, "There's a little problem. There's a large dent in the warhead casing. We didn't see it before because it was under the warhead the way it was sitting, but when we disapparated, it twisted, and its easy to see."

"Is the casing broken?"

"No. It's intact, but something inside may be broken."

The XO sat down and sighed. "We've got to have a conference with the CO on this one."

They disapparated back to the ship and tracked down the captain. They went to his ward room, and the XO explained the situation. The captain grimaced and asked, "OK. Mr. Green. What's your evaluation?"

"I've no idea. The contents may be unharmed or one or more of the devices may be broken."

"Chances of an explosion if we try taking it apart?"

"You've got me. I'm not rated to do anything we're doing next."

"XO, what's your evaluation?"

"Well, we've got a couple of options. We could try extracting another missile and hope that we have better luck. Personally, I don't think we'll have much more luck.

"Second, we could go ahead and try opening this one up and see what happens. I think we might have a non-nuclear explosion, but I think it's unlikely that we'd have a nuclear detonation.

"Third, we could give up and try to think of something else."

The captain asked the CPO, "Are you willing to try to go ahead. This is strictly a volunteer operation from here on in. I wouldn't order anyone to keep going on this assignment."

The CPO didn't hesitate, "In for a Penny, in for a pound as they say around here. "

Brahms couldn't resist commenting, "Actually around here, the phrase is more like 'In for a knut, in for a galleon'."

"Whatever."

"Let's take off the rest of the day, and we'll let you sleep on it, Mr. Green. If you're still interested tomorrow morning, we'll go ahead."

The next morning, they met again, and the CPO was still a "go". They disapparated to the cave. They were about to all enter the cave, when the CPO turned and held up his hand. "This is a one-man operation from here on out." No one was happy—either with staying out or with the possibility that they might be inside.

The CPO went in with his tool set, and they turned on the generator and the lights. He began to open the warhead casing. It was hard to get off because of the dent, but he was strong enough to force it. When he did and got a good look at the contents, he swore silently. One of the devices was broken. It was bent, and there was a large gash along the side exposing the interior.

He made a snap judgment in that instant. Later, he had a lot of time to wonder if it were the right one. In the meantime, his one goal was to remove all the warheads that were whole and get them out of the cave. The first one that he tackled was painfully slow. He had to refer to the printed diagrams multiple times before he removed a bolt or disconnected a cable. The second was slow, but he only referred to the diagram once per connection. By the fifth, he was hardly looking at the instructions.

Outside, the wizards, Brahms, and Wainwright had nothing to do, but they didn't find the time boring. They mostly paced. One of the wizards asked why they stayed away from the cave mouth. Wainwright casually answered, "Oh, if one of those dozen bombs go off, there will probably be a chunk of the cave wall blown away around the entrance." The wizards took a couple of large steps away and one of them asked, "But what if more go off? Wouldn't it be better to be further away?"

Wainwright answered, still casual, "Oh, no. If only one goes off, we can probably disapparate away quickly and survive, but if more go off, even if we don't get killed immediately, we'll probably die in a few hours of radiation poisoning. I'd rather go quickly than spend the last hours of my life throwing my guts up."

The two wizards looked back and forth at each other and said nothing.

Finally, the CPO came out dragging one of the devices. They started to approach him, but he waved them off and said, "No. Stay back. One of the devices cracked open. I want to drag the rest out. These may be contaminated. You'll have to get someone with a radiation meter here to check them out."

Wainwright said, "We'll help you get them out."

The CPO shouted, "No, sir. I'm already exposed. You mustn't be."

He went back in and started dragging the rest out. Everyone else stayed well clear. When the 11th came out, he staggered over, and Wainwright said, picking one of the wizards, "You're going to disapparate him and me to the ship. And you," indicating the other," bring Brahms."

They reached the ship. When they did, Wainwright shouted up to the lookout, "Get the surgeon up here on the double. We need to get this man to Sick Bay. Then inform the captain that we're back." He then had a second thought, "Brahms, go get somebody who can check out those devices for radiation and get them somewhere safe. Then come back here."

"Yes, sir."

Brahms and the wizard disappeared. The surgeon appeared on the deck, and they helped Green down to Sick Bay. The XO explained what had happened on the way. When they arrived in Sick Bay, the surgeon gave him a shot of granulocyte colony-stimulating factor and a potassium iodide pill right away. Then he used a radiation counter. He commented, "You don't have any radioactive material on your skin or clothes. Are you sure you were exposed to radiation?"

Green pulled his badge out of his breast pocket and just said, "Look at this." It was a dosimeter.

The doctor commented, "It's 100% saturated. Yes, you've been exposed.

"I want you to stay here in bed and rest. We'll keep an eye on you. You'll probably have a hard time keeping food down for a while. We'll stick with liquids until we know better."

Then he turned to the XO. "Come on. We need to have a discussion with the CO."

The captain was in his stateroom with Brahms. When the XO and the surgeon arrived, the captain announced, "The devices were not radioactive, so radioactive material probably didn't escape the 12th device. How's Mr. Green?"

The surgeon said, "He isn't showing a lot of signs of radiation sickness, so I don't think he got a gigantic dose. His dosimeter is maxed out, so he got at least 20 rem. If he'd gotten anywhere near a thousand, he'd have obvious symptoms now. So, I'd say he's got somewhere from—oh—25 to 500 rem."

The captain asked, "So, what does that mean for his prognosis."

"Well, if he got the high end, he'll probably be dead in a couple of weeks. If it was somewhere in between, say 100 or so, he'll probably survive for a year, maybe two. Now, if it was near the low end, it depends a lot on his genetics. If he's not got much genetic susceptibility to cancer, he might live out a more or less normal life. If he's not so lucky, maybe he'd have a couple of years to dozens of years."

"We can find out easily enough how much radiation it was. We just send someone in for a minute or so with a dosimeter. We pull him out as soon as the dosimeter starts to register. How long it takes will tell us a lot."

The captain thought about it. "Does it make any difference to his treatment whether he got a lot of radiation or a little?"

The surgeon thought for quite a while about that. "I don't think so. We'd do pretty much the same thing, but surely he'd want to know which it was?"

"Let's let him make that call. Can he have visitors now?"

"I don't see why not."

The captain and the surgeon went down to the Sick Bay where the captain asked the CPO, 'How do you feel, Chief?"

"Not bad sir. This medicine may be worse than the sickness." His face belied his bravado. He asked the surgeon, "What's it look like?"

The surgeon gave him the same speech he gave the captain—unvarnished.

"Well, Chief Green, you've got a choice. We could send someone into that cave for a minute or so and find out how much radiation you got and then make a pretty fair guess as to how much time you've got left. What do you think?"

"I wouldn't want anyone to risk himself for me."

The surgeon said, "It wouldn't be much of a risk. We'd monitor his radiation and pull him out long before he got much."

The CPO didn't hesitate, "Well, sir, when I signed on for the service, I didn't know what might happen. I could be in harms way and not live for very long, or I could retire after thirty and see my great-grandkids. I didn't know then and I think I'd just as soon not know now.

"But I do want to keep working on this assignment, win, lose, or draw."

"You've got it, Chief Green."

"Thanks, sir."

"Take it easy. We'll get you back on the line as soon as we can."

They left, and on the way back to the Wardroom the captain stopped and said to the XO, "God, I hate that part of my job."

"Everybody does, sir."

Back at the Wardroom, they discussed what to do about what was left in the cave. They decided to seal the cave and leave whatever was there, there.

Brahms went back to Hogwarts and went to see the Healer, Madame Pomfrey. He told her what happened and asked if she had any magic for the situation. She said, "Tell me more about this radiation sickness?"

"Well, imagine getting a really bad sunburn. That sort of thing can cause skin cancer. You do know about skin cancer."

"Of course, young man. Do you doubt my qualifications?"

Immediately Brahms was on the defensive, he quickly said, "No, no. I just wanted to be sure that we were talking the same language." She seemed to be satisfied, so he went on, "Anyway, this kind of radiation penetrates all the way through a person's body and causes the same sort of damage throughout your body."

She leaned back in her chair and stared into space for a few minutes and then leaned forward and spoke resolutely, 'In a case of those sorts of burns on the surface, we'd normally use ditaney and I might use it topically, even in this case. We can't have him take it orally. But, in a solution that penetrates the skin, it might do him some good."

"Do you think that we might talk to the surgeon?"

Here she shuddered and said, "What an awful idea! Do you think the surgeon would permit me to treat him with a solution of ditaney?"

"Probably not, but I think the captain would let you do it, if the patient agreed."

She got up and said, "Then, I've got to get to brewing. I'll want to consult professor Slughorn for recommendations. In the meantime, please give him my condolences for being treated by a 'surgeon'." She said the word with obvious distaste.

In the meantime, the surgeon decided that he'd done all that he could do for Green who wasn't in significant pain, so he released his patient for duty. Which allowed Green to find Brahms and get started on the next step of converting the weapons for their use. This required devising timers that could be used to detonate the devices. Green brought all the documentation that he had on the devices to the Shrieking Shack. He started reviewing them with the technical group that Brahms had assembled.

After the first session, he'd asked Brahms, "Can I see the devices?"

"Sure, they're down in the weapons locker." They went down to the basement level, and Brahms had to ask Green to turn the other way as he entered the entry code for the vault door of the weapons locker. It swung open, and the CPO stepped inside.

"Well, I'm impressed. You have quite a little collection of weapons here—everything from sidearms and hand grenades up to Mark 4 nuclear devices."

"Thanks. I'm particularly proud of the international flavor that we have. For example, we have some AK-47's over there."

Within a couple of days, Green, with some help, had built a prototype detonator-timer for the Mark 4's. One day, near the end, speaking to Brahms, he wished that he could do a full scale test of the timer. Brahms looked at him askance, "That's a good idea, but I just don't know where we could do that test."

"Oh, I know, but you know, after spending so much effort, you just hate not knowing whether or not the thing would work—especially when you may not survive to see it used for real."

"I'll talk to Professor McGonagall and see if I can get her to agree to a test. But I wouldn't hold my breath."

The Heroes Return

"Uh, excuse me."

Minerva and Wendt practically jumped back into the hearth. Wendt looked around and found the Boy Genius and . . . and Professor Sinistra sitting in guest chairs in her office.

Minerva regained her voice quicker than Wendt, "What are the two. . hmmm. . . two of you doing here?"

Brahms said, "Well, there's sort of a situation that's come up."

Wendt frowned and stared at him. "Situation? Is there something that you," and he corrected himself, "you two have done that we need to know about?"

Brahms answered, "Well, it's really good news—just unexpected. You see, well, we have some unexpected guests."

Minerva said, "Sinistra is this some doing of yours?" with a suspicious tone, acquired years before from pranks that Sinistra had pulled.

"Oh, no. no. It's just that, well, Nicky should tell you."

"Nicky is it? Well, Nicky, speak for yourself."

Brahms stood up and said, "Well, we had installed some cameras to search the skies for unfriendly aircraft, and they actually found, well, a submarine."

This time Wendt recovered his voice first, "A submarine—just cruising up in the skies, I suppose?"

"Well, of course not."

"Then I suppose in the lake."

"No submarine could get up into the lake without wizarding help. We detected it on the open ocean."

"I see. Just cruising on the open sea above the surface I suppose, getting a suntan."

'No, sir. They were actually trying to be found—by us. They are in the Loch now. Their officers are down at the Shack. I told them that you'd be back in a couple of days. They were most insistent on seeing you."

"Interesting. Me in particular?"

"Oh, yes, you." Sinistra said.

"Well, let's not keep them waiting any longer."

On the way to the Shack, Wendt tried to imagine who would ask for him by name and what ship could possibly be sitting in the Loch. They reached the Shack with him burning with curiosity. The officers were waiting in the one Conference Room in the Shack.

The door opened, and he found Commander Wainwright and several other officers—some of whom he recognized and some he didn't. "Wain, how in the world did you get here? I guess I was afraid that you'd been lost—maybe sunk and dead, maybe worse."

Wainwright said, "I think you underestimate the Ohio. It would take more than a few. . . well, I'm not sure what they are, but it would take more than a few of them to sink us."

"Thank God. I've got a million questions: How did you get here? Are you sure you've not been traced?" He was interrupted almost immediately

"Wo, wo. We've our questions too. First, you probably know a whole lot more about what's going on in the world than we do. Your wizard buddies wouldn't give us any intel that we didn't absolutely need until you arrived. How about filling us in on the state of the world?"

Wendt turned to Sinistra, "Have all these people been given the unbreakable oath?"

"First thing."

"OK. Then, we'll fill you in with as much as we know—which may not be a whole lot more than you know." Then he gave them the Reader's Digest version of what had been happening in the world, the last couple of months.

"Shit, I thought it must be something like that, but it seemed so fantastic that I held out some hope that there was some other explanation than what we could imagine. I hardly knew what to hope for. As it is, we're not traitors but I'd rather be a traitor and have the world not ruled by bug-eyed monsters from Antares than the way it really is."

"Well, it's good to have you with us. I'm really glad. It's nice to have a nuclear sub in your hip pocket for emergencies."

Somewhat surprised, Sinistra asked, "You two know each other?"

Wainwright replied, "Oh, we go back a long ways. I guess it's been years at least."

Wendt nodded and said, "Yes, that sounds about right."

Sinistra said, "That would be during the Great War."

Brahms was trying as hard as he could to keep from laughing. "Sorry, I was just thinking of that trick that you pulled on the captain with George and Fred to convince him that magic was real. We repeated it on Wain to convince him that Sinistra was a real wizard er witch."

Sinistra frowned at him, "Let's be sure we keep that straight, eh?"

Minerva asked, "How did you get here?"

Wainwright said, "That's a longish story, but I don't mind telling it."

Brahms said, "I'll get us all some tea. Anybody want coffee?"

No one did, so he left, and Wainwright started his story. He told about being under arctic ice for months and finally surfacing to discover that the world had gone through a sea change. He added, "No pun intended."

"None taken." Somebody said.

He went on, telling about trying to decide where to go to look for resistance, their cruising up and down, hoping to be found by friendly wizards, but being afraid of being found by aliens. Then, when they were close to giving up, they were noticed.

Sinistra and Brahms took over from there. They had set up the telescope array, looking for alien aircraft, but they had found the submarine instead. The automated image scanning software had picked up the submarine on the horizon at the entry point of the Loch into the Arctic Ocean. They hadn't believed it when they'd seen it. Brahms was convinced that it was an alien craft, but Sinistra had insisted that they investigate.

Minerva asked, "Why were you so sure that it wasn't alien?"

'I don't know. It just seemed all wrong for the aliens. They seem to be much more creatures of the air than they are of the seas. They wouldn't need submarines once they'd conquered a world and maybe not even before they'd finished."

Brahms went on. "So, we agreed to disapparate onto the deck and see what we could find out. There was a watch on duty that spotted us, but not until we'd banged on the side of the submarine. They were scanning the horizon and didn't expect anyone to show up on the deck.

"After they sent an armed group of men out, they took us inside, and we were questioned by the captain and Mr. Wainwright. They didn't have a good way of proving that we weren't aliens. Of course, we had a way to prove that they weren't, but that didn't help them.

"Finally, Mr. Wainwright just declared that we must be non-aliens because, with the powers of wizards, why didn't we just use the imperious curse or any of a dozen other curses? The captain bought the argument and then. . ."

Wainwright interrupted, "And then they had to convince us to take the unbreakable oath. I'll tell you that I was pretty nervous about it. I was even half-scared that I wouldn't pass. But, of course, it went fine."

Brahms went on, "So, we agreed that they had to get the sub into the Loch, where it would be protected by the magic charms from detection.

"We had a problem though. Nobody on the crew could helm her through the loch. The only person on-board who could see the loch was Sinistra."

Wainwright went on, "So, we gave her a crash course in helming. We got her first of all to just sail straight for a bit to get some confidence up."

Sinistra said, "MY confidence. It was everyone else who was shaking in their boots the whole time I was at the helm.

"They had me steer 'her' straight ahead for miles and miles. Then they had me make a gentle turn to the left."

"Port." Wainwright supplied.

She ignored him. "The boat turned very slowly. As we turned, I could see the land start to come around to being straight ahead and I saw the Loch. Slowly the boat came to where I was pointed straight into the Loch, but they kept me turning. I wanted to go straight in, but nooooo. Nobody would trust me.

"Then when I'd done a 360 degree turn, they had me doing another port turn. We'd just finished 180, and then we did a right turn."

"Starboard."

"Yeh, yeh. We did another 180 and I was wondering if we'd ever get into the Loch."

Wainwright said, "It's kind of hard to steer a big ship of any kind—especially a sub. So we wanted to get an idea of how she handled her before taking a chance with flying blind into a narrow loch."

"Yeh. Yeh. Anyway, they finally decided to take their hearts into their hands and let me steer it into the loch. So, I brought the boat around, got us lined up pretty well with the loch, and headed for it."

Wainwright said, "Sinistra's giving the expurgated version. She missed the opening of the Loch a couple of times."

Brahms said, "We couldn't see anything except cliffs, and we were headed straight for them. We were slowly approaching the cliffs, and it felt like being in a slow motion collision. We just kept going, and the cliffs kept getting closer. Finally, I don't think anyone could just keep watching as we seemed about to hit the cliffs. I forced myself to keep my eyes open while the tv monitor that we were watching turned blank. Then the terrible crash that we were all instinctively expecting never happened. Then after a few minutes the screen cleared, and we could see the loch."

Wainwright said, "We all breathed for the first time in about fifteen minutes, and then it was all over. Bart took the helm back, and we dropped anchor when we were about a hundred yards off shore. We've been there for several nights waiting for your return."

Wendt said, "OK. We're glad you're here with us. I hate to be greedy, but what can you do for us?"

Wainwright said, "Well, we've got 24 missiles. No, actually 23. We extracted one. We can cruise the world and still have lots of power left. We've got a crew that's smart a-sea or on the ground. What do you need?"

Wendt scratched the 5 o'clock shadow on his chin. "Could you dis-assemble that missile and pull the individual warheads out and be able to use them?"

One of the officers who hadn't spoken yet said, "We've already gone through that. If you were to mosey down to the weapons locker, you'd find a bunch of Mark 4 nuclear weapons."

Wendt just said, "Oh."

Minerva said, "Oh, oh."

At the Ministry

The door didn't open, but somehow there was a white apparition that appeared in the doorway to the Minister's Office. She looked up, and said, "Oh, come on in Horace. I was never one of your favorites, but I did all right. You needn't fear anything from me."

The *patronus* fully entered the room and announced, "We are ready to act, and Minerva, that is the headmistress, would like you to come to Hogwarts to a meeting to discuss details and timing."

Pam stared at him. She asked herself why in the world Minerva would want to exert her power at this time. It must be that she wants to do something that Pam wouldn't approve of and wants to be on her own ground when they discuss it. "Well", she thought to herself, "it's probably time to have it out with Minerva. Why is it that Hogwarts Heads always seem to want to be Ministers of Magic or at least to lord it over the true Minister?"

Aloud, she said, 'Oh, I suppose so. Why does Minerva insist on being so tiresome?"

Slughorn could only fumble out, "You're invited to lunch tomorrow and to the rest of the afternoon."

She looked down at her calendar. There was only one meeting, and she thought she could cancel it without much problem. "That would be just fine, Horace. Tell the Head that I'll be there ready for one of the famous Hogwarts Great Hall feasts."

He nodded and the *patronus* disappeared.

▽

The next day, Pam, her personal secretary, and one of the deputy heads of the Aurors met at the great hearth in the Atrium and walked through into Hogwarts Great Hall. Slughorn met them and invited them up to the

Teacher's Lounge where there was a selection of sandwiches, mayonaises, fruit salads and vegetable trays waiting.

"Well, Minerva, I must say that you know how to entertain. Let's lunch. I don't believe in talking business over a good meal. It so tends to upset the digestion, don't you agree?"

"Completely, Pam. You and the other guests should go first and then we'll join you."

The lunch was enjoyed, and no one's digestion was ruined. There was very little talk except for the occasional monologue of Professor Wendt, telling about the adventures in the old Ministry of Magic and the monumental fire that leveled the faux department store that had used to be above the old Ministry. After everyone had finished dining, Minerva began, "We have something we want to show you." She signaled toward the door. A wizard entered carrying something like a very thick fishing rod carrier. He lifted it with a groan and placed it on the table before Pam.

Pam stared at it and asked, "What is this?" And immediately added.with wide eyes, "Oh, this is. . . is . . ."

Minerva smiled, almost smirked, "Yes, that's one of the weapons that the good captain brought us."

Pam realized how lucky she was that the meeting hadn't happened at Azkaban, She said, "This is really it. If it . . uh . . what is it that these devices do anyway?"

Wendt filled in, "Explode."

"Yes, if this exploded right now, what would happen?"

Brahms said, "Well, let's see. All of Hogwarts—the castle, the Quidditch pitch, a big chunk of the forbidden forest and maybe even Hogsmeade—would disappear never to be seen again."

Pam's mouth opened involuntarily, and she tried to mouth a word or two. Finally, she just said, "When is it that you want to use it?"

Wendt hesitated and then said, "WE don't want to use it—ever."

"Then why the hell did you go to such lengths to put the thing together?" She was getting exasperated with them.

"We want them to give in, but if they don't, we want to be ready to demonstrate why they should."

Pam was suddenly struck by a different perspective. It was like the first realization of personal mortality that one has. It was sudden. It was frightening. It was depressing. It was over in a blink of an eye. But in that blink, she thought of all the refugees that were within shouting distance. She thought of their degradation, of the Muggles, of every human being on the planet. She even thought of all the Muggles who had been attacked and essentially killed. She felt welling up in her something hot and violent—the desire for vengeance. She looked up at Wendt and pointed down at the thing in front of her, "You must use this for Vengeance sake."

"No, Pam," Minerva said, "We don't have to, and we hope that we never will. We wanted you to feel the terrible power that is in our grasp and see that it is too terrible to use—except as a final, desperate deed."

"Then what are you going to do?"

Wendt stood and began to pace the length of the table looking at each person seated there. "We're going to scare them to death. We're going to take over their world-wide news service at the height of prime time and threaten terrible things if they don't agree to evacuate the world."

"And you think they will—just for the asking?"

"We're going to be pretty darn scary. We're going to take over the entire broadcasting building. Keep everyone out while we broadcast and give them an ultimatum."

Minerva took up the story, "We'll require them to meet us at a remote Pacific island—a couple of representatives from them who will be empowered to go to Nihoa Island to negotiate."

Pam asked, "And just how will you get there?"

Wainwright said simply, "The United States Navy will provide transport. We will sail to the neighborhood of Washington State in the United States, and our negotiators will disapparate there probably from the Auror Office in Vancouver, Washington. We'll get there by Port Key with your permission, Madame Minister."

"Well, you've got it all figured out, don't you? I suppose I should be thankful that you've been doing your homework." She looked around and found that everyone was waiting for permission to go ahead. So, she said,"OK. OK. Now, get this thing back to whatever dungeon you keep it in, and let me get back to Azkaban."

At the Shrieking Shack

The phone rang, and Brahms picked it up. The guard at the Main Entrance asked if a "Dudley Dursley" was expected.

Brahms said to send him up.

Dursley knocked on Brahms' office door, and Brahms asked him to come in. Dursley said, "You said that I could come."

"Yes, I did. Please sit down." Brahms offered him tea or coffee but Dursley didn't want any. "Dudley, have you heard of the Deathly Hallows?"

"No sir."

"Well, they are a trio of magical artifacts that are said to hold the key to mastery of life and death. One of them is said to be a wand of power far beyond any other wand."

"Do you think this wand is that Hallow? Wait, no, it can't be. Olivander himself made this wand."

Brahms wasn't quite sure where he was going with this himself, but he kept going. He knew that sometimes he just had to talk through an issue, and a solution would come to him in the talking. He hoped that would happen this time. "Many people—including Harry Potter—believe that Potter had the three magical artifacts—including THE wand after he fought Riddle for the last time.

"I wondered at that time and afterwards, if Potter really did. The other two objects were an invisibility cloak and the 'resurrection stone'.

"But, the wand that Valdemort had didn't seem to be an especially powerful wand. It was beaten by several wands—including the wand that Professor Dumbledore wielded in his battle with Grindelwald. Then too, Riddle had it in his battle with Potter, and it certainly didn't defeat Potter's wand—although it was something of a draw.

"Just so, with the invisibility cloak that Potter had. It was formidable, but Mad Eye Moody built an artificial eye that could see through it. The fake Moody who was a teacher a Hogwarts one year told Wendt that himself.

"I think the resurrection stone was probably the real thing. At least, Potter claims that he used it to resurrect his parents and godfather once for a short period of time.

"I think that you may have the real wand of Power."

"But you've never seen it work, and I told you that Olivander made it."

Brahms closed his eyes in concentrated thought. Then he said, "You mean that Olivander said that he made it. Do you have any proof that he was telling the truth?"

Dursley had his turn to concentrate on his answer. "No, I don't." He rushed to add before Brahms could speak, "He seemed perfectly believable when he told my family and me that. I don't think he was lying. And, believe me, I've had a lot of experience with liars and detecting them. I could tell you stories from my youth gang days that would. . ."

Brahms quickly said, "Yes, yes. You don't need to go into details." He then considered for a while before saying, "I don't think that you would be so scared of it if it weren't an extremely powerful wand— probably much more powerful than the wand that Potter had after defeating Riddle."

Brahms hesitated again and then asked Dudley, "Would you reconsider using it against the aliens?"

"Do you think this wand is the real wand of the Hallows?"

"I think it may be, but my belief or disbelief doesn't matter. Whether or not it is, I think that you have a responsibility."

Dudley shook his head and said, "Maybe. I want to talk with someone about it."

Brahms asked, half-afraid of the answer, "Just who would that be?"

Dudley answered, "Why, my boss, of course."

Brahms was afraid to ask the next obvious question, "Just which boss is that?" He decided to leave it unasked. After all, it might be Minerva rather than his immediate boss, Filch.

Dudley finally said, "Is that's all?"

"Sure. But please come again when you've decided."

Another Day in Paradise

The day began at Hogwarts with the change of the guard at the perimeter of the grounds. In Haggrid's hut, there was the small group of people who were very careful to do no magic while they were inside. Outside, a gasoline-powered generator hummed providing the only place (other than the Shreiking Shack and the USS Ohio) within 20 miles that had electricity. It powered a satellite dish, an HD TV, various kinds of radio equipment that could pick up transmissions in virtually every part of the EM spectrum where people had once broadcast and a stereo system. This time the occupants were monitoring a broadcast of what had once been the BBC. It was now known as the World-1 TV network. The news was droning on as usual about production quotas, sports events that hardly anyone really cared about, and weather forecasts.

Haggrid said, "I've never heard such miserable codswallow since Valdemort was running the show."

"Well, when we get to the right moment, you'll be very entertained by what they'll be broadcasting." Brahms said.

Haggrid harrumphed. He'd insisted on not knowing exactly what they would say. His view was that you could predict everything that the network usually broadcast. He wanted to be surprised for once.

The popular 18:00 news show was coming up. One of the most appealing aspects of this show to aliens and humans alike was the eye-popping beauty who was broadcasting the news at that hour. The aliens seemed to be not entirely immune to human hormones, though even they couldn't explain why.

She walked onto the set and to the news desk. The aliens were quite aware of the appeal of the finely turned ankle that she presented. She began reading the news off the teleprompter. She was not just beautiful, but the alien buried deep within her brain was both quite smart and capable of using the innate intelligence of the beauty that it rode. She had already started ad-libbing as she read the first story. Suddenly, she and her co-anchorman slumped to their desks.

Wendt said, "OK. This is it. Wish us luck."

Wendt, McGonagall, and three others walked outside and proceeded about 100 meters from the Hut—the minimum distance that you could go and not have magic interfere with the electronics in the Hut. As they reached that distance, they held hands and disappeared.

Inside the Hut, the TV screen showed nothing for forty seconds, and then two people walked into the field of view of the TV. The TV changed focus point and the two people who were moving each kicked one of the co-anchors off their chairs and sat in their places.

The woman seemed to take over where the beauty had left off. She was shorter with greying brown hair and was wearing a funny pointed hat. She said, "In a late-breaking development, the satellite network studios have been taken over by a small group of humans. They have an important news announcement for the aliens who have occupied the Earth. For this, I turn to my co-anchor. Professor X."

She turned toward the other person, and the camera pointed toward him. He said, "Humans have been very patient in responding to the invasion of the Earth. That period of patience ends today. This building has been taken over by humans temporarily because we are – no pun intended – humane. We will not attack and kill all aliens on the Earth, just because we can. We intend to offer the alien invaders an opportunity to retreat from the Earth forever without casualties. However, our patience is not infinite. We will remove aliens from Earth forcibly if we have no alternative. For details of how this will happen, I turn the show over to Mistress Q." He turned his head toward her, and she began to speak as the camera panned toward her.

"Invaders of Earth, the way that your retreat from Earth will be accomplished is your decision. We are prepared to negotiate a peaceful exit for you. We will begin negotiations one week from today.

"If you choose to negotiate, you will send two representatives to a place at a time to be specified by the humans of Earth within a week. These representatives will be empowered to negotiate all details of your withdrawal. If they fail to appear when and where required, a small reprisal will happen. If they come and are unable to negotiate for any reason, a medium reprisal will occur. If they attempt to kill or capture the human negotiators, a serious reprisal will be exacted – possibly in Paris, possibly in Beijing, possibly in New Dehli, possibly in London.

"You will receive only one additional warning. If you fail to negotiate in good faith twice in a row, all aliens will be removed from the Earth by the fastest method we have." She turned toward her co-anchorman. He stared directly and intently into the camera which caught well his intense determination.

"Some of you are well-versed in the human poet, William Shakespeare. As he said in one of his plays, 'If tickled, do we not laugh; if pricked, do we not bleed; if wronged, shall we not revenge?'

"We will be merciless as you have been merciless."

With that the screen went blank.

Frank had caught the broadcast. He always did. He picked up the phone and dialed the home of Jes. He came on the line quickly and said, "Boss, I saw the broadcast. That's not some grotesque joke is it?"

"You're the one who should know about jokes. Is it?"

"No, sir. I'm not responsible for it, and I can't believe that any Soul would be."

"Agreed. Well, get a meeting set up tomorrow morning—early." He sighed and wondered for the thousandth time how it was that he had accepted this job.

The next morning at 7AM sharp, the advisers and Jes and he were in the Conference Room. "OK. Let's start with the obvious questions—how was it done?"

The man who had been Head of the Surete service and had subsequently become the Head of Security for the Souls when he had become the host for a like-minded Soul said, "We've not got the foggiest idea. But we do know pretty well what happened.

"At 6:05PM, plus or minus a minute or two, all hosts and Souls fell unconscious in the building—not just the floor that the broadcast happened from, but the entire building.

"By 6:07PM, security forces were dispatched to the building. They never arrived. Every driver claims that he simply couldn't find the building. They claim to have driven within a block or two of the building, but they hadn't the foggiest notion where the building was until 6:25PM, when suddenly every one of them realized how to get to the broadcast building.

"By 6:31PM, the first of the security forces entered the building. They found receptionists and camerapersons and broadcasters and technicians and everyone who was in the building unconscious. Within 4 minutes, they all began waking up.

"We took them all to the hospital where they were examined overnight and released today. They had every kind of scan and blood analysis done that we could think of, but there was nothing abnormal and nothing worth noting in their blood chemistry or nervous systems—either Souls or hosts.

"They are going back to work today. I'm lost."

Jes said, "Thank you, Security." sarcastically.

Frank asked, "OK. Let's hear the military side. Can they do what they threaten?"

The military liaison got up and stood at attention as he reported, "It's impossible. We control air and space. They'd have to drive a bomb into a city. And our security will be heightened. We'll detect any weapon before it gets into any city."

"Well, do they have weapons?"

"We've lost a Trident nuclear submarine, as you know. It does have something like 250 thermonuclear bombs."

"And if they could deliver those, how many Souls could they kill?"

"It's a very rough estimate, and it depends on how they decide to deploy them, but. . ."

Jes broke in, "Just tell us how many people."

"Well, we think about 250 million to 400 million people—if they were trying for maximum casualties."

Frank's face fell, and he said softly, "Almost half a billion Souls. It would make the butchery that these humans inflicted on themselves seem like Amateur Night at the Rialto."

Someone asked, "What did you say, sir?"

"Oh, it's a phrase from somewhere in my host's memory. Do you think they'd do it?"

Several voices said, almost in unison, "No, how could they? Even if they had the capability."

Frank looked around the room, "Search your memories—those of your hosts. Search them! Do any of you doubt that they are capable of that level of atrocity?"

There was only silence in answer.

Frank said, "We have so little time! We've got to co-operate, at least as far as going to negotiate with them."

Jes said, "Surely given some time, we can figure out where these people are. Just give us some time. Stall them as much as possible in negotiations."

Frank turned to him and stared directly into his eyes, "Will you take responsibility if they decide we're being dishonest with them?"

Jes just stared back. Someone else said, "Surely, they can't keep hiding forever."

Frank looked at her and said, "You tell me where they are then."

He went on, "No. We have to meet them and be prepared to withdraw if we can't negotiate another way or find them."

The security chief said, "Well, it may take them longer than they think to set up this meeting."

Frank looked back at him and said, "One of my favorite pieces of host literature has a character who answers a statement like that by saying, 'Go ahead and think that, Jane, if it gives you comfort.'"

The meeting broke up, and the only new "to do" was choosing the negotiating team.

The next day, the evening prime time news broadcast was interrupted again as before. The two people who appeared on camera seemed to be the same two. She said, after kicking the newswoman out of her chair, "We will meet the alien negotiating team at Nihoa Island in the Hawaiian Island chain at 1PM local time five days from today. For details of the scheduled meeting, I turn to my co-anchor, Professor X."

Professor X. took over, saying, "You will send a negotiating team of two. They will be able to make binding commitments on behalf of all aliens. They will arrive on the island no sooner than 12:30 PM local time. They will come unarmed and without support staff. Any attempt to harm or sequester the human negotiators will be treated as an act of war, as outlined in our last broadcast.

"The negotiators will be prepared to leave the island no later than 4PM local time, the same day. Please don't neglect any of these details. Now, for a final word of encouragement, Mademoiselle Q."

The camera shifted back to Minerva who said, "Remember, the key to successful negotiating is understanding the relative strengths and weaknesses of your negotiating partner and being prepared to accept the consequences of whatever position you take.

"As we humans say, 'Be there or be Square.'" With that word, the screen went blank.

Jes and Frank had taken to having dinner together and watching the nightly news. Frank said, "OK. How long will it take us to get our team there?"

Jes considered and said, "I'd say 2 hours to get to the Hawaiian Islands. Then probably, they'll have to travel by air to the closest inhabited island and go by helicopter to this Nihoa Island. Say another 24 hours. We don't have any aircraft carriers in the area, so it'll all have to be run by helicopter from islands. We'll probably have to send one helicopter out with the team. It will leave immediately to go back to the support island. Then, we'll launch a 2nd helicopter to pick the negotiators up about 4PM."

"How are they going to get there?"

"Well, they do have a nuclear sub. They could be submerged off the island and send them over by small boat."

"I can't think of another way, but that just doesn't seem right. It's too risky for the sub. How are they going to get to that meeting?"

"Maybe they won't. Maybe they're just proving their superiority by standing us up?"

"I don't know, but I don't think so. Well, regardless, get our two negotiators going. I don't want to have to substitute someone at the last minute."

"Right."

While this conversation was going on, the USS Ohio was sailing under the surface of the Pacific about five hundred kilometers off the coast of Washington state.

In an abandoned mall in Vancouver, WA. a mop appeared out of thin air with two people clinging to it. One of them spoke, "Minerva. I have to admit that there is a certain low cleverness to the way that wizards keep inventing ever more painful ways to travel."

"Oh, shut up, Wendt."

This exchange was witnessed by several Aurors at their office and a widow who had begun the long trek that Minerva and Wendt had been traveling. One of the Aurors made introductions. He began with the widow. "This is Mrs. Joyce Longbottom. She discovered the aliens the evening that her husband, Frederick died.

"Mrs. Longbottom, this is Professor James Wendt and the Headmistress of Hogwarts school of Wizarding and Witchcraft, Minerva McGonagall."

The widow held out her hand and said, "It's a pleasure to meet the people who are going to avenge the death of my husband."

Wendt and Minerva shook hands with her uncertainly, and Wendt took the task of disabusing her of her misapprehension that they were going for revenge. "Madame, I have the good fortune of not being able to understand your pain. I have not lost any loved ones in this war—yet.

"I don't want you to misunderstand our goal. We first and foremost work to free the Earth from the scourge of the aliens, but if we can avoid deaths on all sides, we intend to. If vengeance stands in the way of throwing these aliens off the planet, we will not seek vengeance. But, I'm honestly afraid that there will be blood shed before we are done."

The woman spat in his face and said, "This is what I think of avoiding vengeance."

The American Auror Phil said, "Mrs. Longbottom, we honor your husband and will do anything we can to give you peace concerning his death."

Mrs. Longbottom thought a moment, "Yes. I'd like to go along with these Brits to the negotiation. I want to look these aliens in the eye."

Wendt said, "Ma'am. We can't allow you to be present at the negotiations. I'm sorry. We have given our word."

Her lips tightened into a thin line. Then she relaxed and said, "If I can't go to the negotiations, can I at least be along on this subsea thing that will take you there? You owe me at least that?"

Wendt and Minerva looked at each other and she said, "Mrs. Longbottom, please allow me a few minutes alone with my partner to discuss this."

They left the room and stood alone in the hall. Minerva said, "We owe her at least that and probably much more."

Wendt shook his head and said, "I've got a bad feeling about it. She's going to get in trouble. Who knows what she'll do. I don't blame her for wanting to do something terrible to the aliens. I feel that way frequently myself, but we can't just go along with her on this."

Minerva said, "What can she do? There will be a half dozen good wizards on the ship. We'll keep her under watch."

Wendt shook his head again, "Think of what she could do on a sub, if she took a mind to."

Minerva just said, "We can use the unbreakable oath."

Wendt didn't have an answer for that. So, he agreed.

They went back to the Auror Office and Wendt said, "You can come along, but you have to take the unbreakable oath, swearing to not get in the way of our mission in any way and not to harm any of the crew or passengers of the submarine."

Mrs. Longbottom thought long and finally agreed. The Auror Phil administered the oath and made it very stringent. She was sweating hard when she finished the oath. Her only comment was, "You're hard people."

Minerva said, "You've got to get your things together within the hour. One of the wizards on the sub will be here and will take all passengers back at 2PM."

She nodded and smiled. "I've been preparing for this for some time." She opened her handbag and said, "Everything I need for a month is in here."

At two on the nose, George Weasley appeared at the door of the office and said, "Knock, knock. Who's here?"

Wendt said, "We've got an extra passenger. Mrs. Frederick Longbottom."

"Mrs. Longbottom, this is our ticket to the sub, George Weasley."

George asked, "Any relation of Neville?"

"Not that anyone knows;"

"Well, Mrs. Longbottom, its a pleasure to meet you."

"And you, Mr. Weasley." She had become a calmer, almost friendly person now that she knew that she would be along for the ride.

"Is everyone ready to go?"

Wendt picked up his duffle. Minerva picked up her overnight bag and Mrs. Longbottom simply stepped forward. They took hands and they disappeared.

They arrived on the deck of the Ohio. They were immediately ushered below and the ship dropped below the surface in minutes.

A seaman accompanied them to their cabins. It was decided that Mrs. Longbottom and Minerva would share and Wendt had to give up his berth with Minerva to share with George. The rest of the wizards bunked with crew.

Minerva and Joyce had a little girl-to-girl talk once they settled in. Minerva said, "OK. This is a very uncomfortable way to travel. It already stinks here, and I'm assured that it's only going to get worse. We will eat with officers, but you can't expect house-elf cooking. Don't expect any special treatment. There isn't any for anyone. Clear."

"Perfectly."

The next couple of days were uncomfortable in ways that the last time that Wendt had been on this ship hadn't been. The last time, there was a smaller crew, and everything had seemed less crowded. There were drills to go through, and everyone on-board was unified in purpose. There were no women passengers until after the raid on Azkaban.

This time, everyone sensed the tension between Mrs. Longbottom and the other wizards. Her presence was a damper on conversation in several ways. No one wanted to talk about the English Longbottoms to avoid offending the American Longbottom. Everyone suspected her of wanting to sabotage the mission and so didn't want to talk about it if she were around.

The captain and officers became aware of this split in the wizarding community from the first mess when Mrs. Longbottom was introduced to the officers. Fortunately, they were quickly on station where they intended to disapparate to the island in early morning. Because of the strange results of disapparating through water, both Minerva and Wendt wore swimming gear and carried their clothes in waterproof bags. The plan was for them to change back into swimming gear when they disapparated back to the sub.

They gathered in the missile room. Minerva was very nervous about wearing a bathing suit, but she admitted that she didn't really have a choice. Wendt was not much less nervous. It was approaching an hour after sunrise, which was when they'd agreed to go. The XO was in attendance. The captain was not. The XO gave the countdown to H hour, and on the count of zero, the two disappeared from the submarine.

They appeared on the island. It was not much more than a barren rock. They were wet, but not soaked. They opened their waterproof bags and pulled out towels, dried off, and changed. At first, they were a little self-conscious because they were naked on naked rock with no shelter at all, but after the first few minutes, they laughed and exchanged a kiss and a hug and helped each other towel off and change into dry clothes.

Minerva then materialized a table and chairs, got out the papers that had been prepared for the meeting outlining their bargain position, and waited. It was quite obvious that no one could sneak up on them there—except by magic. So they had a little breakfast that they had brought along and sat down to wait.

Brahms had been sitting in the Teacher's Lounge with Sinistra. They were on a couch near the hearth where a comfortable blaze was going. They were talking and sitting in silence from time to time. Brahms had just put his arm around her shoulder and squeeze a bit when the door flew open, and one of his tech's had run into the room shouting, "Mr. Brahms are you here?"

Brahms got up and announced his presence. The aide said, "Hurry, you've got to get back to the Shack immediately."

Brahms' face fell, and he started to trudge off. However, Sinistra popped up and asked if she could come along. Brahms brightened and said, "Sure." as his assistant shook his head "no" vigorously. That sealed it. Brahms said, "Let's go."

While they ran down to the main floor, Brahms asked the tech what was going on, but he refused to say. That spurred them all to run the faster. They got to the Shack and ran up the stairs to the Control Room. Inside the team was larger than normal. One of them looked up when the door opened and announced, "You just missed it, but I'll replay it." He rewound the video and started afresh.

The tech commented, "You see the two men getting off the commercial jet? They're the two negotiater team from the aliens. The video from the CCD camera at the hangar isn't great, but we have a positive ID.

"You see they're walking out to the military helicopter. Now, watch!" He went silent, and the video showed about a dozen heavily-armed military trot out on the tarmac after them and board the helicopter after the two."

Brahms exclaimed, "But they're breaking their agreement."

The tech barked a laugh and said, "No, really?"

"We've got to do something. Can we get hold of the sub?"

The tech picked up a clip board with a schedule on it. "It's too late. If they're following schedule, they're already on the island with no means of communication, and we can't get hold of the sub anyway. It's submerged. We'd have to have access to an Ultra Low Frequency antenna to reach them there. And we just don't happen to have one of those in our hip pocket."

Brahms looked around desperately, appealing to everyone he could see including Sinistra, "Isn't there something we can do? Think!"

Everyone was silent. He scanned the figures in the room and there was no change. "Come on. Something. Anything. Something crazy."

The tech just shook his head and said, "Minerva and Wendt are sharp and resourceful. They'll come out OK."

Brahms just shook his head and said, "I hope."

On Nihoa, Wendt and Minerva were whiling away the time as best they could. Wendt was reading a novel on his cell phone—now otherwise useless. As a matter of fact, it had been useless for a very long time. He'd set it to airplane mode to keep the aliens from honing in on it. Minerva had pulled the *Daily Prophet* from a couple of days ago and was working the crossword. She commented, "I have to admit that the *Times* has a better crossword."

Wendt just smiled and kept on reading. Gradually he began to notice a distant, deep "Whump, Whump, Whump." He realized that it must be a helicopter approaching. He looked up and pointed in the distance and commented to Minerva that their guests were arriving. She put down her paper, and they both watched the small dot slowly grow and become louder.

They straightened the table and cleared off the surface except for papers and pens. The helicopter got closer and closer and finally landed about 100 meters away. As they watched, the blades slowed until they could be observed individually. They had to hold the paper and even the pens in place. Finally, a hatch opened and two people got out. It was hard to make out details at that distance, but details didn't matter, because they were not the last to get out. They were immediately followed by several more. And it was clear that several were holding rifles of some sort.

"Shit. Get down." Wendt shouted. They both dropped to the ground and he took her hand and asked, "Do we go?"

However, Minerva never answered. Almost immediately, they heard another sound behind them. They could identify that sound. It was someone disapparating. Wendt shouted, "Good old George. Always there in the nick of time." None the less, he pulled the Glock from his purse, and Minerva pulled her wand out.

But everyone was surprised by what happened next. Simultaneously they heard a female voice cry in a tone that made it a curse, "*Avadra Kedavra*." And at the same time, two of the men were thrown back. The voice sounded again. By this time, Minerva and Wendt whirled around to find Mrs. Longbottom firing curse after curse in the general direction of the helicopter. No one was moving in the vicinity.

Minerva rolled toward her and knocked her down. She grabbed the wand out of her hand and shouted "no!" Wendt reached her shortly thereafter, clasping both women in his arms and shouted, "We've got to get out of here before they decide to do something drastic."

Minerva disapparated them. They were all drenched when they appeared on the missile deck of the sub. The surprised crew members wrapped towels around them, and the CPO asked what had happened.

Wendt said, "All the wheels came off. Minerva, keep that mad woman's wand, and let's find a wizard to watch her while we report to the captain."

The captain found them. Or rather, a seaman did and took them to the captain's cabin. He asked them point blank, "What the hell happened out there?"

Minerva said, "We were hoping you would tell us. All of a sudden Mrs. Longbottom appeared on the island and started cursing people. We don't know if she killed all the aliens who had come but she sure didn't fail to for lack of trying."

"So, that's what happened. The officer in charge of the Missile Room reported that she showed up in the Missile Room and then disappeared—literally."

Wendt said, "In all fairness to her, she showed up just as an alien helicopter showed up and disgorged a bunch of troops. She started using the killing curse, and we don't know what would have happened if she'd not been there. We might have ended up doing the killing."

The captain was still hopping mad, "God damn it! You told me something like this wouldn't happen."

Minerva said, "We told you that she couldn't do anything to jeopardize the mission. I don't think that she did. I think it was shot from the start."

"Then what do we do now?"

Wendt scratched his head and said, "I think they've called our bluff. We've got to get back to Hogwarts as fast as we can. So, you get us to disapparation range of the Auror Office in Washington as quickly as you can and then return to Hogwarts yourselves."

Minerva looked between the two, "Does this mean that we have to do something devastating to a city?"

"I suppose so. But we've got some time to think about what we're going to do."

The captain got on the phone to the bridge. "Is the XO there? Good. Put him on. Wain, see if you can find us a thermocline to get under and turn on the juice. I want to get to our rally point off the US coast at maximum speed." He then turned to them and said, "What are we going to do with that Longbottom woman?"

Wendt said, "Oh, I don't think that she's any danger to do anything stupid now. But we'll go down and talk to her."

They left and went looking for George, with whom they'd left her. They found him in the Enlisted Mess. They dismissed George and sat down opposite her. Minerva said, "OK. Tell us about it."

She looked exhausted. She was still a little wet and had a towel around her shoulders. "I just couldn't stand that I hadn't been able to save Fred. I had to have revenge."

Wendt asked, "How is it?"

"Oh, it's not worth much. I had a rush when I could attack those . . things . ." She said the word with as much disgust as a human can put into a word. Then she went on, "But it doesn't last long once it's over. Can I just go to our cabin? I need to sleep."

Minerva nodded and they let her go.

The trip to the place where they could disapparate seemed to drag on and on. They weren't anxious to be home and have to face the problems they would have there, but they had been in the cramped quarters of the sub as long as they wanted to be. Especially Minerva wanted to be rid of her roommate who would only sit on the bunk and stare at the bulkhead.

They arrived at their destination finally, and the three who had disapparated onto the ship left along with George. They arrived at the Auror Office and were greeted by the night crew. When they parted from Longbottom, Minerva told her, "No one has to know what happened on the ship—and off, but if we hear that you've gotten into any more trouble, we'll tell the whole story."

George, Minerva and Wendt took the mop handle and disappeared, reappearing at Azkaban. The Minister was waiting. She said, "We're meeting. Now. I want a full report."

George asked, "Which is it you want? A full report? Or, now?"

She had already turned and was headed out the door and the three followed her down the hall to her private Conference Room. Shortly after they arrived, the Head of the Auror Office showed up. Without further word, they sat, and she leaned forward. "OK. Give. My dear friend, Mr. Brahms, wouldn't give any hint as to what was going on. You know, I thought we used to have such a close relationship, and now he won't give me a brass knut."

Minerva said, "I don't know that he was all that devoted to you, but we can tell you what happened." Then she turned to Wendt and nodded.

He rolled his eyes and asked, "Why is it always me to give the bad news?"

Pam just snarled slightly and said, "I don't care who gives it, just give."

Wendt sighed and said, "Well, our threat didn't scare anybody. They landed on our deserted island with a bunch of military. That by itself was a wheel off the cart, but we might have been able to talk them out of doing anything rash—like hanging around, but then." Wendt stopped there and wished that he smoked a pipe. It would be great to have a diversion to give him a little time to think over how to say the next part. Of course, Pam was impatient. But, good old Minerva came to the rescue by picking up the story.

"You see a witch from America—the first one to report the invasion by aliens—came along on the sub and then at the last minute disapparated to the island. As soon as she landed and the military started showing up, she started . . uh . . using the forbidden curse to start killing them right and left."

"Oh, shit. Were there any survivors?"

"Well, we didn't exactly hang around to find out how many survived and how much fire-power they had. We disapparated immediately."

"Great!" She leaned back and stared up at the ceiling. No one else had anything to say. She then leaned forward and said, "I guess that we don't have any choice. We have to keep our promise, don't we?"

It wasn't exactly a question, but Wendt wanted to pretend that he misunderstood and started to say, "Well, we could get in touch with them and let them know that someone on our side went round the bend, and we'd like to try again."

Pam just glared at him and didn't even say a word. The Head of the Aurors, seeming to be thinking out loud asked speculatively, "Just how large a city do we have to destroy?"

Minerva tried to interject a word of moderation, "Look, I have to point out that every single alien that we kill is also a human death. I really think that we should try to figure out a way to do something without killing any Muggles."

Pam practically sneered, "How can we possibly do that?"

Wendt said, "Wait a minute. There may just possibly be a way."

Everyone stared at him, and someone asked, "Just how could we possibly do that?"

"Just a minute. Let me think. I may have an idea."

There was silence in the room again and after a minute, Wendt, speaking slowly and haltingly asked, "Is there any time that aliens are around without being inside a host?"

Pam simply said, "Give me a break!"

The Auror chief said, "Now, wait a minute. They come from the stars, right?"

Everyone agreed.

"They don't have hosts then—at least, most of them."

Everyone agreed.

"Then when they come down to the planet, they don't have hosts."

There was a dawning awareness that spread through the room. Wendt nodded, "Sure, they come down in shuttles. They travel in little vacuum bottles that keep them at liquid helium temperatures. There are at least thousands of them on a shuttle, probably tens of thousands." Everyone nodded.

"Then, we need to get ourselves a shuttle schedule."

Wendt said, "And I know just the person to get that schedule."

In the end, it turned out that anybody could get the schedule by reading the newspaper or internet. They discovered that the next shuttle carrying some substantial number of aliens was to leave Orly Spaceport within a week.

There was an operational meeting at Hogwarts the next day. After some discussion, it was decided that since the aliens didn't publish precise launch times, and indeed, didn't plan precise launch times, they should have a local—a French wizard—deliver the device. So, the decision was made to have Madame Maxine of Beaux Batons Academie suggest a French wizard who was familiar with Paris to deliver the device. They sent an owl to her The next day she requested that they come with the device, prepared to train the wizard.

The next day, Wainwright, the CPO who knew the device, Brahms, Minerva, and Wendt walked through the hearth of the Great Hall of Hogwarts and emerged in La Grande Salle de Beaux Batons. The CPO was carrying the device. They went to a smaller room and the CPO opened the leather case and began explaining how the device timer worked. The French wizard who was to use it had no questions. He said that it was "tres simple."

The discussion centered around how the device would be used. There was a group, the Hogwarts group, which wanted the device used as soon as possible with maximum caution after they started loading aliens onto the shuttle. Their position was that it was perfectly fine to disapparate next to the shuttle, drop the bomb off and disapparate out as fast as possible.

Then there was the Ohio group who wanted the weapon deployed when it would do the most "good", namely just before take-off of the shuttle. They wanted the agent to observe the launch site and try to put the device on-board the shuttle as soon as possible just before launch. If it could be worked, possibly even disapparating on-board just as lift-off started, drop the bomb off and head for the 'hills'. Strangely enough this group included the French wizard, Gaspard de Nuit, who would actually be doing the deed. He seemed to be very anxious to make an impression on the aliens, and to have the shuttle explode in flight seemed pretty impressive to him.

The French position (excluding Gaspard) was that the thing must be done with both safety and impressiveness in mind. Their position was that the device should be placed at night so that an explosion would have the widest visibility. Madame Maxine was sure that the guard of the aliens would be lowest at night when no one was working on the ship.

The Ohio position won out for the simple reason that the person who was actually to place the device favored that position and refused to cooperate otherwise. Minerva and Brahms weren't happy, but they had to admit that Gaspard had big advantages. He spoke French like the native that he was. He had good knowledge of the area and could find a place of concealment to observe the loading of the shuttle more easily than anyone else. He was willing. So, the Ohio plan was adopted and the device was turned over to Gaspard with much insistence that he treat the weapon and the assignment with respect and great care.

Another Day in the City of Lights

The sun had just set at Orly Spaceport. A wizard was standing on the grounds of the Ville de Vissous overlooking the airport with a pair of omni-occulars. He had been watching the loading of the shuttle. It had almost finished. He felt sure that the shuttle was going to take off very shortly, and if it were to be this shuttle, he'd want to disapparate the device there in only a few minutes.

He'd been afraid that the *stupides anglaises* or the even *plus stupides americaines* would decide at the last minute to abort the mission. He had been watching the spaceport for several days. The cycle of the days had become very clear after the second day. A truck would drive up beside the shuttle. Several people would unload the crates of alien canisters from the truck and carry them into the shuttle.

There was never more than an hour between deliveries. Then, on the first afternoon, there had been the long gap at the end of the day. He had agonized over the reason for it. Were the aliens done loading the ship and would it lift off without its little extra cargo that he would deliver? Or was this just the end of the day and deliveries would resume the next day?

It had been the latter. After a long sleepless night of indecision, the deliveries had been resumed the next day a little after 8 AM.

But now, there had not been a delivery for over an hour. This must surely signal the end of the loading process, and the launch could happen any time. He had sent the signal by the silver sickle in his pocket. He was requesting permission to disapparate to the ship under his cloak of invisibility, enter the ship with the thing that the "Boy Genius" called the "device", and set the timer.

He felt the vibration of the silver sickle in his pocket. He pulled it out, afraid that it would be "*ALLEZ*" and afraid that it would be "*RETOURNEZ*". He took a breath and opened his hand. The inscription on the coin read, "*ALLEZ*". They'd chosen to go then. He immediately pulled his wand and tapped the coin. The inscription changed to

"D'ACCORD'". He opened the briefcase that sat beside him. There was a simple keypad and digital display. He pressed the asterisk and entered the code and then pressed the pound sign. The digits lit up "00:00". He then pressed zero, zero, one, zero: ten seconds and the pound key again. The display lit up with the numbers. He closed the brief case and lifted the omni-occulars to his eyes again.

"Merde", he thought to himself. They had already closed the cargo hatch and pulled the gantry away from the shuttle. He only had a few minutes, at most. He picked up the briefcase and twisted.

The next moment he was in the dark cargo hold itself. It was a terrible chance that he was taking that he could disapparate into the ship. He lit his wand. Then he opened the briefcase. At that moment the engines roared into life. The ship began to rise as he found the # key and pressed for five seconds. He made sure the count down timer was counting down. Nine . . . Eight. . . . Seven . . . Enough! He twisted again and appeared outside a tavern in Brignogan. As he appeared he said, "exploser la Vengeance".

▽

In a room in Buckingham Palace with a southern exposure, Frank was reading another disturbing report about deaths in Afghanistan. He was tired of hearing all the bad things that were happening. And now, his people had screwed up, and there was some terrible vengeance that was coming. Well, the time limit was almost up and nothing had happened—so far.

He was absently watching the night sky over London when he noticed a bright star rising. There was something strange about it, but he couldn't think what it could be. It was changing color but that wasn't unusual with stars near the horizon. Then it struck him. The star was rising in the south where no star should rise.

Just then, there was a crash as the door to the room was thrown open. He turned and saw his chief aide, Jes, run into the room and grab the remote for the TV. He turned it on and switched to the news channel. The speaker came to full power quickly. The scene was the two news leads talking about a late-breaking story.

". . . in late-breaking news there was a tragedy at the Orly Spaceport this evening. The following video has graphic violence. . ."

He asked Jes, "Orly?"

Jes only nodded and pointed at the screen. The announcer was going on. "This video was taken by various security cameras on and near Orly."

Then the screen showed a normal shuttle rising from the pad being tracked by an airport camera. It rose for several seconds and then the view flared white—the entire screen solid pure white for an instant, and then it turned black. The commentator said, "The next short video is from another camera on Orly but at a greater distance." It didn't track the rising shuttle but showed a long scene of the spaceport and the shuttle rising at first slowly and then accelerating out of view of the camera. Then there was another white flare that rapidly came down from above and engulfed the entire spaceport. Finally, there was another video that showed Orly from a great distance. It was apparently a street security camera. The camera didn't even show the rising shuttle but it showed the flare of the explosion that came from the sky and obliterated the entire airport and neighboring suburbs. The camera survived the blast and showed a classic mushroom cloud rising above the spaceport.

The female commentator had obviously been crying but now had controlled her reaction and was introducing someone. "We've been able to contact Dr. Renard, a distinguished physicist at the Physics Institute of Berne, formerly Switzerland. Dr. Renard, I want to thank you for being available to talk with us about this tragedy. Would you please interpret for the audience what happened at Orly this evening?"

Renard was obviously not in the studio, but was speaking from an office somewhere. He said, "Well, first of all, let me tell your audience that what they just witnessed was the explosion of a weapon based on hydrogen fusion. The humans who created these weapons called them nuclear bombs, which was not an entirely bad name for them. As you can see, they are terrible weapons, but the worst part was not just the immediate devastation caused by releasing that much energy, but the long lived radioactive debris left and scattered to the wind."

The male commentator asked, "How could this happen? Was the shuttle struck by some sort of missile?"

"It must have been. I can't believe that the security procedures of . . ."

Frank asked Jes, "Is that true?"

Jes shook his head and said, "No, sir. We've just looked at the radar recordings. Nothing was flying within ten miles of that shuttle."

The female commentator said, "Do you believe this is the revenge that the rebel humans spoke of?"

"No, I don't see how they could have gotten hold of nuclear weapons from the small stockpiles that are left. They are guarded as carefully as anything in the world."

Then there was a voice that sounded from off-camera, "But then again, that's exactly what happened. We" and two humans, both recognizable to nearly everyone in the world strode onto the set of the show, "are responsible. We don't make idle promises."

The woman who had just walked onto the set interrupted and said, "Oh, you people in the control booth. Don't cut us off. We'll just have to take over and run the cameras as we have done before if you do. And I can't promise that you'll all survive."

The man picked up where he left off, "The good people of the newscast have not told you that almost 100,000 aliens died who were on the ship. Another couple of thousand who were working at Orly died and a few hundred died who were in close-in suburbs. Many, many others were injured.

"We will contact you soon to specify the next time and place for negotiation for your withdrawal from our planet. I promise you that if the terms of the next meeting are abrogated in the slightest, the vengeance will make this incident seem mild."

Without further comment, the two walked from the set. The two commentators looked at each other in shocked surprise and simply said, "We'll be back in a minute after this public service message."

Frank turned to Jes and said, "All section heads to the Conference Room ASAP. Let me know when they arrive. Damn, it wasn't my fault. I didn't order that fool to try to try to capture them."

Jes just turned to go and at the door before leaving said, "I know, boss. I know it won't happen again. Nobody would dare take that kind of chance."

Frank just grimaced and Jes left.

Half an hour later, the Conference Room had all section heads except one, and Frank decided to start without him. "OK. No comment on my part is necessary. Talk to me. What do we know? What do we suspect strongly? What do we guess is true?"

There was a babble that broke out. Frank allowed it to proceed for about five seemingly interminable minutes, and then, he said, "Around the room, clockwise from me."

The one next to him shook his head in the negative. The next man said, "It wasn't a missile. There wasn't anything in the sky."

The next said, "Orly security is absolutely sure that no one walked the bomb onto the tarmac. They'd have been detected long before they got to the ship."

Frank said, "Well, just how do you think the bomb got to the ship?"

He just shrugged and shook his head.

The next man said, "The scientists have analyzed the radioactive debris of the bomb blast. The weapon was probably about 250 KT to 300KT. It was manufactured at the Pantex Plant near Amarillo, TX. It was part of a series that were built for Trident missiles that were launched from Trident nuclear submarines. We think it was on the USS Ohio when it began its last cruise."

Frank interrupted, "Could it have been launched from a sub. . ."

The man interrupted back, "No. Those missiles flew above most of the atmosphere. We'd have detected it if it had been launched from a sub. And more important, the Trident missiles were armed with half a dozen to a dozen warheads. Only one detonated. It couldn't have been from a Trident."

Somebody else said, "Did you notice that they managed to kill a lot of Souls while killing virtually no humans?"

Nobody else had anything to say. Frank looked around and said, "Well, let's see what we've got. A warhead that was built for a Trident missile, but it wasn't delivered by a Trident missile. As a matter of fact, no one has an idea how it was delivered. And we have a Trident missile sub wandering around and no one has an idea where it is.

"What about that question? If we don't know where it is, does anybody know where it's not?"

Another aide said, "We've been trying to find it, but we haven't had a real need to find submerged vehicles on other planets. We have to depend on local technology. These submarines were always very hard to find—especially the nuclear missile subs."

Another aide said, "We have reactivated a set of hydrophones on the Atlantic floor. They were used to track submarines in the Atlantic from the Arctic Ocean to the Antarctic. We found the people who used to operate them. They've searched the Atlantic for any sign of the Ohio. They have not found any submarines."

"So, it could be just about anywhere in the oceans of this world that cover ¾ of the surface of the planet?"

The aide said, "Except the Atlantic."

Frank just stared at him and said, "I don't agree. These humans are far too resourceful."

After scanning the room, he asked, "Suggestions?"

Jes, who hadn't said anything so far said, "I suggest that we co-operate fully with them so long as it doesn't involve actually moving anyone off-planet."

Frank shook his head. "I think it's gone beyond that. If we don't learn something about them before very long, we're going to have to surrender and pack up and move out. As a matter of fact, I want you," looking straight at Jes, "to form a working group to figure out how quickly we can withdraw and what we'll need to do that."

Everyone stared agape at Frank. But he went on, "Don't be surprised. If we don't find a vulnerability that we can exploit against them and find it soon, I think we're done on this planet."

One of the aides said, "No kidding. When I saw that nuclear weapon go off, I thought, 'That's it for us.'"

Frank said, "Well, besides preparing for that possibility, everyone else will pursue more evidence that this event provides us. Can we track them down from some mistake they made? Get out of here and formulate ideas and we'll meet tomorrow to brainstorm what we can do."

The next day at 8:30 AM they had a status meeting. There was no bright spot, but Jes raised a point. "We've put off all shuttle flights—even suborbital—until there is a. . ." He stopped, lost for a word or an idea.

Frank said, "Yeh, until what?"

"Well, maybe we could start up again—cautiously?" He ended on an upward hopeful lilt.

Nobody else said anything, waiting for the only word that mattered. Frank finally said, "I can't think of anything better to do. But,' he hesitated for a moment for emphasis, 'NOBODY and I mean NOBODY will be on board. The first few shuttles should be landing absolutely empty. That released the pent-up tension and everybody contributed ideas. It was finally decided that the first landing should be at Heathrow spaceport. That was too deep in the city for another nuclear attack. Surely. It was decided that the next landing would be the next day—late, but in full daylight. After the meeting ended, Jes was actually optimistic. "That does it. I think we'll be alright after we get that shuttle down."

Frank grunted and went back to his office.

At the same time, there were a group of people standing and sitting at monitors in the Shrieking Shack. "You see Wendt. This is a great opportunity. If we can bring that shuttle down without nuclear weapons, they'll be totally demoralized."

Wendt looked at the Boy Genius, "Yeah. That ought to be as easy as pie."

Brahms said, "OK. I admit that I don't have a good idea, but damn it, we've got wizards. That ought to be as easy as pie for them.

"The shuttles come down pretty fast and break at a full G until they land at a standstill. We could probably only disapparate somebody on one in the last, oh, 15 or maybe 20 seconds. They'd practically be on the ground by then."

Minerva had been silent for a while and said, "I don't think that we could use a jinx until it was even closer to the ground than that."

Sinistra asked the group in general, "Don't those submariners have something they could shoot a shuttle down with?"

289

Wainwright, who was the only one there representing the Ohio said, "Well, speaking for this submariner, I can tell you that we don't have anything that could touch it. You'd ideally want to get it much higher before it had braked much. Coming down at a klick or so a second would make quite an effect on the ground."

Everyone looked around and somebody joked, "Well, we just have to appoint somebody who's not here."

Wendt twisted his head so that it was tilted half-way toward his left shoulder. "You know that's not such a bad idea. I actually have somebody in mind."

Sinistra said, "You wouldn't do that to someone. Would you?"

A twisted smile came onto Wendt's lips—or maybe it was just the effect of still having his head tilted. "You know I wouldn't force someone to take on a tough assignment—strictly volunteer, but I think I know someone who wouldn't mind volunteering. And I think he's got some talents that would make him a good candidate."

Everyone stared at Wendt and no one seemed to have an idea of whom Wendt was thinking. Finally Wendt said, 'Minerva. You know perfectly well who I'm thinking of. He doesn't like the idea of using his powers. He's maybe even afraid of them..."

Her eyes opened as wide as pie plates. She stared at Wendt for a minute and finally said, "That would be cruel." Everyone else was pressing them to say who it was.

Minerva cut through the babble and said, "I forbid you to talk with him or anyone else about him until you and I have talked this through thoroughly."

Wendt said, "You know I wouldn't do that." But he stopped and reconsidered, "OK. Let's sleep on it and see if we can come to agreement tomorrow."

Somebody else said, 'But you've got so little time."

Wendt said, "Minerva's right. We do this right or we don't do it at all." With that the two of them left the room, and then the Shrieking Shack and headed for her room.

The next day, they had breakfast at the Common Room but didn't see the person they were looking for, so they went down toward the dungeons. They found their way to the office of Argus Filch. Wendt was on good terms with Filch and simply opened the door without knocking. They found Filch and his apprentice sitting around Filch's desk with their feet up on the desk, drinking something out of mugs that might have been mistaken for coffee.

Filch saw Wendt first and started to reach for the lower left drawer of his desk where he kept a variety of beverages, but just in time, he noticed McGonagall. He immediately dropped his feet from the table, and amended the question that he was going to ask. He said, "Professor, would you have a little nip of . . . er. . . coffee with us? And of course, you as well, Head?"

By this time Dudley had his feet firmly planted on the floor and was trying to look inconspicuous. That would have been a hilarious effort if the situation were less serious. McGonagall said simply, "We've no time for that now. Listen carefully. We have a request for Mr. Dursley. Filch, go do some of your duties somewhere else."

Wendt interrupted, "No, I think I'd like Mr. Filch to stay if he will." Filch beamed and shot a glance at McGonagall, who rolled her eyes at Wendt and said something under her breath that even the sharp ears of Filch couldn't make out. Wendt went on addressing Dursley, "Mr. Dursley, we have a very serious request for you. It's terribly important to the defense of our planet, and I'd like to be able to order you to do it, but in view of your expressed opinions, I can only ask you respectfully to do it.

"There's an unmanned alien shuttle that is set to land at Heathrow spaceport in about 10 hours. We'd like to make it crash. We think that you are the only person who can do that. We'd like you to agree, but it is completely up to you. If you refuse us, we'll not ask you again. As a matter of fact, there probably isn't time to set it up even if you changed your mind later."

They all turned to look at Dudley, and the one who looked with the most amazement on his face was Filch.

Dudley lowered his head and said, "Professor, you know how I feel about using magic that way. I don't think that I can help you."

Wendt's expression didn't change at all. He had been steeling himself for those words, and he didn't let his panic show. He only nodded and turned to leave the office.

But then Dursley raised his eyes and turned them towards Filch, "Can I, Mr. Filch?" Filch was startled to find himself consulted, and his face showed it. Still, he regained control and said, "MISTER Dursley, you can do anything you choose to, and you don't have to answer to me or the Head." Apparently, Wendt was in a third category yet.

Dudley looked back to Wendt and asked, "What do I have to do?"

Minerva immediately began reciting the steps. They would have to find a sturdy tripod, probably from Professor Sinistra that would hold a large pair of Omni-occulars to which Dursley's wand and a powerful laser could be attached. Dursley would have to practice aiming the whole rig at a fairly fast-moving shuttle from a really long distance using the laser to mark where the beam of the wand would intersect the shuttle. They would use levitated flying objects to simulate a shuttle descending at high speed. He'd practice firing the wand at the flying objects. When he was reasonably good, they'd disapparate to a field outside London where they could see the shuttle descending and not be interrupted.

Dudley's jaw dropped as they went through the steps. Finally, he just said, "You lot are crackerbox."

Minerva said, 'I suppose you're right. So, let's get started without further wasted time."

They went out to the Quidditch Pitch and set up. George helped by bewitching a blodger to rise straight up in the air a couple of kilometers and releasing it. At first, Dudley just used the omni-occulars to find the blodger. When he could usually find it and track it fairly well, they added the laser. Brahms contributed a high-power industrial laser. Nobody asked him where he found it. That actually made finding the blodger a little easier. It shined bright red when the omni-occulars were pointed at it. Then finally, they added the wand, strapped to the laser so that they were parallel.

Dudley practiced doing the spell whenever the flash of red appeared in the omni-occulars. The first few times, the beam completely missed the blodger. But a minor adjustment to the attachment of the wand to the laser fixed that. Then Dudley vaporized all the blodgers they had to work with. They then moved down to Quaffles. They quickly disappeared.

Finally, George said, "You've got it. We're ready." And he high-fived Dudley. But Dudley said, "I want to try something else." No one knew what he was talking about. Dudley sighed and said, "Aren't you forgetting a piece of Quidditch equipment?"

George caught on slightly before the rest. "Come on Duds old boy, you can't mean to say that you want to try a snitch?"

Dudley nodded.

George shook his head, "Well, don't forget that I warned you." Then he released the snitch from one of the sets and sent it flying straight up. Dudley tried tracking it with Omni-occulars without much success. He fired off a couple of shots and brought nothing down. He then looked at George and said, "Another."

"Well, it's your funeral." And he released the snitch. It flew straight up. But this time, Dudley seemed to be able to keep his eyes on it. He tried a couple of shots and then lost it again.

"Another."

George said, "Well, I have to admire your determination if not your stupidity."

The snitch shot up. This time George didn't try a spell on it to make it at least start straight up. But it was as if that spell had been getting in Dudley's way. The first spell blasted it to pieces. Dudley asked for another and another. They all ended on the first or second spell in blinding flashes.

Everyone was speechless, including Dudley who seemed to be stunned. Finally Wendt said, 'Well, we have no time to lose. Let's go."

In the Situation Room of Buckingham palace, Frank sat watching the various screens. One showed a shuttle undocking from the space station and begin to descend. He asked superfluously (because he knew the answer), "How long to landing?"

A bored tech answered, "About 15 minutes—maybe a hair less depending on weather."

They watched the ship shrink as it distanced itself from the space station. Eventually the view became better at a different monitor that was a telephoto view from a ground station. The ship was, as usual, descending tail down. It was slowing steadily as it descended. He knew that it was breaking at about 5 G's at max and would quickly ease up to about 1 G. The digital display superimposed on the image of the shuttle descending showed that it was about 50 Km. above Heathrow. As it descended, he felt better and better about its chances. It was about 30 Km from the Earth's surface when a tech said, "That's strange."

Frank got a big lump in his throat. "What?" he croaked.

"Oh, the ship should have executed a small correction to its velocity. It's probably nothing." Frank's heart sunk. He wondered how long it would be before the certainty that something was wrong would hit. The tech exclaimed, "What the . . ."

Frank looked up and saw on the monitor that the shuttle had begun to tumble. He didn't say anything.

The tech let out a long-held breath and said, "No, it's stabilizing. That gave me a scare. . ." Then he stopped in mid-sentence and Frank looked at the monitor again to see that the ship had indeed stabilized, but with the nose pointed straight down.

Frank sprang into action, "What's going on?"

"I don't know. I'm trying to take manual control of the ship, but although I'm getting some telemetry from it, I don't seem to be able to control the engines or the stabilizers or anything below the mid-ship point."

'Where's it going to hit?"

A 3D map of London appeared on a screen, with a red trajectory line that ended near the west perimeter of Heathrow. Frank asked, "Can we destroy it before it hits?"

The tech just shook his head.

"How much energy when it hits?"

The tech just said, "It'll happen in 10 seconds. Not enough time to ask the computer."

The last five seconds passed in silence. Then there was a flash that blinded the camera that had been tracking the shuttle. The monitor switched immediately to a different camera that showed the fireball of what appeared to be a nuclear explosion.

Frank screamed, "We didn't have any weapons on that ship, right?"

"No, sir. It was empty. That was just the release of a lot of kinetic energy." He keyed a couple of commands into the keyboard and said, "According to the computer, it was about 1KT. It would look a lot like a small nuclear bomb."

He looked over at Jes and asked, "I don't have the heart to look at the network. You do it and get everyone up to the Conference Room as soon as you can."

"Yes, sir."

That evening, the team was eating Chinese in the Conference Room. There was a buzz of conversation. Frank finished his Moo Shu chicken and said, "OK. Let's have it. Around the room."

"We've verified—no nuclear weapons. It was just the kinetic energy of the falling spacecraft and residual fuel. The engines apparently shut off when the ship flipped nose down, so there was a good bit of residual fuel that exploded. It hit about 200 meters from the perimeter of Heathrow and dug a hole about 50 meters across and 30 meters deep. It started some fires outside the perimeter and knocked a couple of houses down. Fortunately, no one was seriously hurt, although several families are without homes at the moment."

The next man said, "We were lucky. If that had hit a kilometer further west, we'd have had thousands of deaths and many more serious injuries."

Frank sniffed, "Luck my foot. There was nothing of luck involved."

Someone said, "The humans haven't claimed responsibility for the event."

Frank looked dangerously at him, 'They don't have to. All of London saw, felt, and heard the explosion. They know that it was purely the 'goodness' or 'generosity' of the humans that kept that bigger tragedy from happening."

Someone else said, "We've been trying to figure out what happened. It seems that there was a sudden event that cut off control lines in the shuttle and caused the ship's computer to lose control of it. Then it was just inevitable that it would settle in a stable fall with the terminal velocity of the ship determining the amount of energy that would be released when it hit."

Jes said, "They're thumbing their noses at us. They're showing us that they can do that sort of thing anytime, anywhere at their will. And we can't do anything about it."

"Great. Is it true that we can't do anything about it?" He looked around the conference table. Nobody said anything. "OK. I guess that settles it. We can't do anything about it. What does that mean?"

The military liaison said, "I think it's clear. We're finished here. I can't protect the population, and the humans have threatened to do terrible things if we don't cooperate."

Jes shook his head and said, "It's interesting how your values change as time goes on. There was a time when I thought a terrible thing was a tornado hitting Fort Worth, United States and killing a hundred people. Now . . ." He just let it hang on the air.

Frank looked around the table, "Anyone disagree?" There was a long silence, and he said, "Qui tacere consentira."

There was a general look of puzzlement around the table and Frank translated, "In an ancient, dead Earth language that means, 'He who is silent consents.'"

As if to underscore the truth of that adage, the room remained deadly quiet. Frank said, "Then I'll say what no one else will. All that is left for us is negotiating the terms of surrender.

"So, let's get a couple of things straight first. I'm issuing an order effective immediately. If anyone does anything to harm, disturb or insert a Soul in a human, I will personally kill that Soul, its immediate superior, it's superior, and everyone up the chain of command below me. Is that understood?"

Everyone muttered, "Yes."

"I didn't hear that. What did you say?"

There was a chorus of "Yeses."

Frank went on, "Jes, I'm frequently fairly subtle in the way I say things. Would you please interpret that order in your own words?"

Jes gave an involuntary chuckle and said, "Sure. What the boss just said was that if anyone in the entire world gives any human a hard time or so much as an evil glance, then he will personally track that Soul down whether it's got a host or is in a thermos on its way to Aldebaran and rip it out with his bare hands. And he won't stop there but will track down everyone the Soul knew and repeat the operation. Does that cover it Frank?"

Frank nodded and then Jes went on, "Any questions?"

The military liaison asked, "What if the Soul is just acting in self-defense?"

Frank started to open his mouth but Jes interrupted him and said, "Let me take that one boss."

Frank nodded, and Jes continued, "The boss will personally see to it that the Soul involved will wish that the human had succeeded in killing him."

Jes asked, "Any other questions?"

No one had any.

"In that case," Frank said, "I'll expect everyone to be working on how we withdraw safely from this god-awful world. Prepare contingency plans for the following situations and any others that you can think of. First, we withdraw on our own timetable. Second, what's the very shortest timetable that we could withdraw under? Make no assumptions—just how do we get off in the minimum time without loss of life?

"Oh, I suppose one assumption," Frank added, "Just that we don't have hostile fire.

"Third, that we do have to retire under hostile fire. What's the minimum deaths that we can achieve."

They were dismissed. As they left the room, Jes and one other were left. The other asked Jes, 'You were just kidding to break the tension, right?"

Jes stared at him for a moment as if trying to decide what tack to take in answering the question. Finally, he said, "I'm going to tell you a story in answer to your question. It's a true story. It's about the boss, and it tells you something important about him.

"It's from the other planet that we were on and lost. We were in a base together at the boss's office. What happened only he and I know. I don't know if he's told anyone, but I sure haven't."

The other sort of edged away and said, "Maybe you oughtn't tell it then."

"No, you need to hear it, and maybe it's a story that needs to get heard generally.

Jes sat on the conference table and started. "We were in his office on the base when there was an attack. It was a fierce battle. And one of the natives actually reached our office, even though it was the most heavily defended spot in the base. It was using another native that had a Soul in it as a shield. Those natives were all brilliant and had quick reflexes. Nobody wanted to shoot the live shield with a Soul in it, so it managed to get to the door of our office and break through.

"I was young, inexperienced; and I froze. Frank grabbed up a weapon sort of like the assault rifles of this world and immediately started firing at full automatic into the native hostage with a Soul in it. He had no hesitation.

"I picked up on what was happening. Despite all the slugs going through that body the alien was still getting off some shots and was ducking most of the bullets. I figured that Frank would need more ammo quick, so I tossed my assault rifle on to the desk where he was standing and none too soon. He ran out of ammunition. He immediately grabbed my gun and opened fire. He was almost too slow. The alien got off a couple of clear shots and almost got us. But then Frank was firing again, and the alien was ducking. I immediately reloaded Franks assault rifle. He ran out of ammo and switched again.

"This time the alien finally fell. Frank just kept firing into his body. I finally woke up and realized that Frank was not going to take any chances, so I started to reload again, but not soon enough. Fortunately, the alien was dead.

"About thirty seconds later reinforcements arrived, and they stood gaping at the two of us standing over the dead natives and the dead Soul, not knowing what to make of it."

The aide interrupted the story to ask, his voice full of incredulity, "Let me get this straight. There was a wild native without a Soul—let's call him A—who was using another native who happened to have a Soul in it—let's call him B—as a shield?"

"Right."

"And the wild native, A, didn't care that the other native, B, was going to die as a result?"

"You've got it."

The aide exclaimed, "Had they no decency at all! To use a fellow person that way is . . . is . . ."

"You've got it. Now, any Soul who accidentally or on purpose breaks this new rule will be treated just as that Soul was who had the misfortune to get used as a shield by the native A in our little story. The Soul was an innocent bystander, but . . .

The other just said, "Shit."

Jes replied, "Exactly. I'll bet that you never used that word before."

"Right, I always looked down at humans who 'swore'."

"Then it's a good thing that I told the story. People who work with Frank ultimately learn a lot."

Several hundred miles away, in the Shrieking Shack, there was a group of people watching the meeting in the Conference Room. Wainwright said, "Well, that about fixes it for the aliens. Are you going to go give them another fireside chat?"

Wendt looked around the Conference Room, "Not yet. I want them to keep stewing in their juices for a bit. Besides, we need to find out how quickly they can get off the planet when they put their minds to it before we give them a target date. I want to know what that 2nd scenario date is."

Minerva said, "You know that there are lots of wizards and witches—not to mention goblins who'd like to see a whole lot more of those shuttles blown away like we did the first. I don't think that they'd be right, but there's a lot of sentiment to make them pay for what they've done to people—Muggles and Wizards alike."

George asked, "And just why is it that we're being so kind to them, hmm?"

Wendt looked directly at him and said, "George, they might be able to help bring back a lot of their victims. It's not a fair trade—all of their lives for some of ours, but you want for them to avoid despair.

George had a grim smile on his face, "And why would that be? I think that despair might be a good thing for them to experience."

"Despairing people do desperate things. We don't want them tempted to desperate acts, but I think that they can do a little stewing before we relieve them of their worst fears.

"Also, you don't want us taking chances with the lives of people like the Dursley's, do you?" With that question, George fell silent.

Wendt hadn't noticed, so he went on with his argument. "And frankly, I have to agree with you, I think that a big dollop of despair might be a good experience for them—a taste of what they dole out every day, but we just can't afford that luxury. Revenge is a dish best served cold. It's way too cold for our health."

George looked away and his voice quivered a little. "It's hard to believe I could forget that they are Muggles. And I'm so happy that Sally made it here."

"There are lots of Muggles like her that we'd lose if we let the desire for vengeance overcome us."

George shook his head and said, "You're right. I give up."

They ended up deciding to wait for the aliens to decide what was the quickest that they could get off the planet before paying them another visit.

After the meeting was over, a few people hung around the Conference Room talking in small groups. Wainwright stayed to talk with Wendt. "Who is that Sally that George seemed so concerned about?"

'Oh, it was someone who worked at the SAS control while we were fighting Riddle. She was my secretary. George and Fred both sort of had a crush on her. In the end, Fred won out. Of course, he died before Sally and he could do anything about it. George has always had a sort of soft spot for her. Even though he and Angelina eventually got married and are happy together as far as I know, I think he still has an occasional heart throb for Sally. After Fred's death it was so obvious that she was mourning him that George didn't try to do anything—but I don't think that he can entirely forget her. He succeeded, as you can see, to put her out of mind for quite a while, but all it takes is a mention of her, and it brings him up short.

"I have to admit that I sort of took advantage of that to get him thinking straight again."

Wainwright nodded wisely and said, "I suppose everyone has someone like that—someone that it just never worked out with, but the thought of her kind of knocks you for a loop if the name comes up unexpectedly. In my case, it was Mary Lou Conalt. We were in high school together. I asked her out to the Jr.-Sr. prom. She was nice about it, but turned me down flat. Every now and then, I run across the name and a lump forms in my throat. How about you?"

"Oh, it would be all my life were worth to tell you who that is for me."

"But you do have one?"

"Of course, I have one. Do you think that I'm completely heartless?"

"But what about Minerva?"

"She's the love of my life, but you know perfectly well that no one can be completely devoted to one person."

Wainwright chuckled, "I know that and you know that, but you'd better not let a hint of that get out to Minerva. I hate to think of what you might end up as."

"Right."

In the Conference Room at Buckingham Palace, the meeting had begun and the Shuttle Fleet Commander had started the status review, "We've got a number of possibilities for how quickly we can get off-planet.

"First, the best way is just to let the normal rotation off-planet work and not allow new immigrants arrive. As you know that process would take about 15 to 20 years." He swiftly raised his hands in a defensive posture as if warding off the arguments, "I know, I know. That's not practical in this situation. I'm just raising it for comparison sake to show you how much we can speed this up."

"The next best thing would be to call back the ships that have already left and could return to pick up refugees. It would take a half year for the ships to stop their momentum, then another half year to accelerate to speed, and then another half year to break to enter orbit. Say it took 6 months to get everyone loaded and up to orbit. That makes a total of 2 or 2 1/2 local years. Pretty darn impressive, I say."

Frank frowned. "Not good enough."

"Right, so the next best alternative is not very pretty. But we've been clever, I think."

Frank was still frowning, "Just get on with it, and stop patting yourself on the back. You just might break your arm."

"Right. Well, we asked ourselves where could we put ourselves temporarily while waiting for permanent resettlement that would be low-maintenance and safe.

"It would have to be close but pretty hard to find if the locals ever tried.

"Our answer was deep craters near the South Pole of the moon, where the sun never shines and radar from earth doesn't reach either. We could build simple structures to shield the vacuum bottles from meteorites and cosmic rays. Solar flares wouldn't reach there.

"Nobody would have to stay there longer than the usual twenty-year cycle time. It would probably be a good bit less. That would be safe."

Somebody asked, "How long to evacuate our Souls that way?"

The shuttle commander seemed pained, "Well, we could evacuate 200,000 per shuttle fight. It would take 40,000 flights. We have a shuttle fleet of a little over 100, so it would only require 400 flights. I think we could do two a day. So, maybe 6 months or so."

Frank nodded slowly, "That pretty impressive. Could we do better?"

"Well, we've been racking our brains for better ideas, but there's just this one half-baked idea. We could put vacuum bottles into middle altitude Earth orbit—say 40,000 KM. altitude. We could put them in orbit there in sort of net things that would keep them from floating all over the orbit. We'd still eventually move them to the moon, and it'd still take the same amount of time to place them in the deep craters, BUT we could get them into this lower orbit much faster—maybe 10 times faster."

Frank interrupted, "That would be in 20 days—less than a month?"

"Right. I have to admit that I'm pretty nervous about the idea, but if we had to, I think we could make it work."

Frank turned to the chair of the news organizations, "Any word from our friends, the humans?"

"No, not a word. It's getting spooky. We've been putting out commercials trying to encourage them to get in touch. Not a nibble so far."

"Great. Anybody have any ideas?"

The Senior Genius

The Souls sitting around the table were silent. Frank said, "OK, let's tackle another question. How safe are we in mid-altitude Earth orbit? Can the humans hit us there?"

The military liaison stood and said, "We're perfectly safe. We have automated laser defenses that would shoot down anything that left low Earth orbit."

Frank just shook his head. But, an older Soul rose and stood. Frank said, "Yes, Dr. Yi what do you think?"

Dr. Yi, paced around the table so that he was directly facing Frank and had the whiteboard behind him. He began, "As far as the military is concerned, that's true. However, there's a very strange nature to this planet and its inhabitants that no one can quite understand. Prior to our invasion. . ." He was interrupted by a gabble of conversation. But he waited until it stopped and went on, ". . . Yes, invasion is the correct word—especially from the viewpoint of these hosts. Before our invasion, the technology that this race demonstrated was far inferior to ours. Oh, they could put a few nuclear weapons up to the synchronous orbit that is proposed, but the military is quite correct: they could easily be shot down. This civilization could even—in a pinch, as they say—could put some nuclear weapons into the deep craters near the South Pole of the moon, but they'd not get anywhere near their target before being destroyed.

"However, there's a second technology working here. It's subtle and hard to find, except when it wants to be noticed. The nuclear weapon that destroyed the shuttle at the Orly Spaceport was a product of the pre-invasion technology. As a matter of fact, we can name the place and almost the time that it was manufactured. It almost certainly came from the USS Ohio submarine." He stopped for emphasis and then added, "But it wasn't delivered by a missile, and we have no idea how it was delivered. As a matter of fact, we have no idea where the USS Ohio is— even though we've been searching for it with all our resources for weeks.

"Oh, it's theoretically possible that it was delivered by quantum teleportation, but the technology of this world had only teleported a few measly photons prior to our arrival. Even the most advanced technologies that we've encountered only teleport information and photons—not kilograms of matter, intact, and ready to detonate." He finished with a ferocity that seemed to match the nuclear weapon that he was describing.

He turned back to Frank after having parceled out his attention throughout the room and was almost gentle, "Frank, not even your race of geniuses—that is, the ones that you fought—had accomplished that.

"Then consider the destruction of the second shuttle. We've no idea at all how that was done. There was a laser beam scattering off the surface of the shuttle for a few seconds before the disaster, but that couldn't have been what destroyed the internal controls of the ship. Again, we have purely normal pre-invasion technology coupled with this bizarre technology that far exceeds anything that we dream of doing.

"So, to answer your question—is deep Earth orbit safe? I have to say that it's every bit as safe as craters on the Moon, but whether that's as safe as houses or as safe as Afghanistan, neither I nor anyone else can say."

There was nothing more useful that came from the meeting, and Frank dismissed everyone with instructions to continue detailing plans for plan two and three. Just as everyone was rising, he cleared his throat and added, "Just one more thing. Please think about anything that the humans may ask us to do before leaving." There was a general sigh of resignation to one more impossible task as people left the Conference Room.

▽

At the Shrieking Shack, this latest meeting resulted in quite a lot of glee. The team that watched the meeting live immediately broke into excited discussion. The consensus was that the battle was over. So, they merely had to walk up to the person they called "Frank" and demand whatever they wanted.

Minerva immediately brought everyone down to Earth with one of her patented "Harumph"s. "Well, do you all suppose that our work is over?"

There were generally negative sounds made as everyone settled down. "So, what are our next steps, she asked?"

The Boy Genius said, "Well, we stay with the program. We demand a meeting to deliver instructions, and this time, I suggest that we name the people that we meet with. We tried dealing with whomever showed up the last time, and you see how that turned out. Let's not fool around. We meet with the top people. Let's name Frank and Jes."

Sinistra agreed, "Yes. They've not shared their names before. It ought to be a shock to them that we know who they are."

There was general agreement with that, but there was general disagreement about who should go this time. Risking leaders like Minerva and Wendt seemed questionable. But they would not be gainsaid. They wanted to be present to rub it in someone's face that they didn't give a damn for the possibility that the aliens could do something to them, and there was a lot of sentiment for defying the aliens to try to do their worst.

This time around there were other people who wanted to go. The Headof the Auror Office wanted to go. There were some quick owls exchanged back and forth between the Minister of Magic and Minerva, but in the end Minerva won out, pointing out that two on two was the perfect match-up for such a meeting.

Before the exchange was over, Pam had pointed out that she herself might just usurp the right with the Head of the Auror Office to do the negotiating. Minerva had pointed out that it was still a dangerous undertaking. That had tipped the scales. It was to be Minerva and Wendt.

The news anchor at World News Central was looking over the stories that were on the script for the nightly news. She looked over at her co-anchor and for at least the hundredth time over the last couple of months had crossed her fingers and said, "Not tonight."

He smiled and said, "Couldn't be tonight. I've got a good feeling about the broadcast." She had nodded and then quickly got out her compact to check the hair that might have been mussed by the over-enthusiastic nod. The set manager caught her attention, nodded, and held one finger up. One minute. She looked over at her co-anchor, smiled and soundlessly mouthed the question, "Ready?" He nodded back.

The manager started the seconds countdown with four fingers. She took a deep breath and prepared her standard greeting. When the countdown reached zero, she counted silently, "One Mississippi" and started the greeting, "Good evening. This is Kyla with my co-anchor, Robby." She looked over at him, and her greeting died on her lips. She saw two figures walking around a camera, seemingly from nowhere. She maintained her poise enough that she only silently mouthed, "Oh, shit."

The two figures walked up to Robby and her. The woman said, "We'll be doing the news tonight. Why don't you two go over behind the director, and enjoy the show?" This was the first time that she'd actually not been knocked unconscious by this pair. Her mouth gaping open, she got up, as did Robby and walked backwards toward a side entrance to the studio.

The man sat first and said, "We're going to try this a little differently today. The normal crew can stay at their posts, provided that they don't try to interfere with the show. I have to warn you, if the show is interrupted or the show isn't broadcast as normal, we'll take over with our own crew and broadcast ourselves. Oh, yes. If that happens, the people in the room won't broadcast another show—ever."

Kyla looked around and saw that suddenly there were a dozen people in the room who were wearing capes of some sort and whom she'd never seen before. She leaned against the wall and hoped that nobody tried anything crazy while she was in the room.

The woman was going on, "Good. Then lets' begin with tonight's big story." She picked up a sheet of paper and held it as she spoke, as though she were reading from it. She never glanced at it, so she obviously wasn't. "In late-breaking news today, the representatives of the humans of the planet Earth have arranged a meeting with the highest-ranking leaders of the invading aliens to negotiate the prompt withdrawal of absolutely all aliens permanently from the Earth. This meeting will occur in three days at the top of Mount Evans near Denver, Colorado, USA. The human representatives will be my associate and I." Here she looked over at the man. She reached out her hand and Wendt squeezed it briefly.

He took up the narrative. "Representing the aliens will be the two leaders who like to call themselves Frank and Jes. They will be prepared to name dates certain, when the first aliens and last aliens will leave the Earth.

"They will come alone, driving a Red Miata convertible with the top down. Well, there's no accounting for aliens' tastes, is there, Q?" He looked over at Minerva.

The woman answered, "No, there certainly isn't. I figured them more as '99 Yugo types."

"No one will approach the mountain closer than five miles for two days before the meeting. Any attempt at breaking these requirements or at harming the negotiators will be answered with the most terrible retribution that you are able to imagine."

The woman picked up the narrative, "On the light side of the news, there is a report that a shuttle-full of aliens departed the Chenai Spaceport today for deep space, and they were NOT vaporized in a nuclear explosion. You just never know when those crazy humans are going to show mercy to their oppressors."

Wendt said, "Well, I think that's it for the Good News Hour tonight. Join us in a couple of days when we find out the answer to the question that's on everyone's tongue, 'When are the aliens going to pack up and leave for good?'"

With that the two cloaked figures stood, walked outside the view of the cameras and Kyla couldn't see them anymore. She looked around and found that they'd all disappeared. She looked over at the manager and he signaled for her to return to the news desk. She and Robby returned and sat. She looked at the teleprompter with the stories for the night. She glanced over at Robby and said, "Let's go on with the show." Then she turned to the camera pointed at her with the red light on and said, "I guess we can't top that news, but in the top of the news tonight, the Department of Energy reports that energy usage last month declined 45% from the same month last year. Congrats to all you Energy conservers out there. . . . "

At Haggrid's hut, there were several people crowded around the Telly. Sally Harker said, "That's my boss. He's always got something funny to say when the chips are down."

Haggrid added, "Yea. And Minerva was in there with a couple herself. I thought I was going to choke when she talked about those crazy Muggles . . er . . humans."

At the Buckingham palace Conference Room, Jes said, "Well, we're in for it now. How in the world did they know who we were?"

Frank said, "Oh, I'm not surprised by anything now. But it's not so strange. It's almost impossible to keep most things secret. I guess we just have to live with our fifteen minutes of fame."

"I hope its more than fifteen minutes. I'm just afraid that we'll be the first on their retribution list."

"Well, we've got to get moving. Pack. I want to be in Denver not later than tomorrow evening." In point of fact they were in Denver by noon the next day. They had a small entourage—a couple of technical experts, the Shuttle Fleet Commander, and the military liaison in the group. They borrowed a car from the car loan agency but they had a little trouble finding a red Miata. No one manufactured Miata's anymore. They were not quite energy efficient enough, and there weren't many Souls who enjoyed driving enough to justify continuing to manufacture the car.

They put out an announcement on local radio and discovered that there were hundreds of red Miata's sitting in garages around Denver. The owners of practically every one of them were more than willing to loan them. Frank had insisted that Jes and he do all the driving in the Miata so that they'd be in good practice for the drive up Mount Evans. They had a GPS, and it was easy to follow directions to get to Colorado Springs near the foot of Mount Evans.

There were technical people waiting for them at Colorado Springs with all sorts of small electronics for them to wear—a camera, two-way radios, various sorts of sensors—infrared, microwave. Jes was worried that they would abrogate the agreement. Strangely Frank wasn't. His attitude was that if they didn't explicitly forbid it, then it was OK to take it.

The morning of the meeting, they were up at 5AM. They had breakfast and a lengthy briefing by the techies about how to use all the technology that they were wearing. Most of it needed no attention, other than making sure that they didn't swat it off them, like a horse-fly that some of it resembled. Finally, they were on the road. Frank drove, and Jes watched the GPS. They didn't really need it, but both felt a little more secure with it. As they drove up the mountain, the valley gave way to pine-covered mountain side.

They had been checking in on the radio regularly. Everything was going well when the radio suddenly had more and more interference and finally fell silent. At about the same time the GPS went black. Jes commented, "Well I guess all this fancy electronics is pointless." With that he pulled off the camera and the two way radio.

"Yea. I guess you're right."

Shortly after that they broke through the pine-tree line, they had fleeting glimpses of what they thought was the top. It had become cool, quiet, and spooky above the trees. There began to be traces of snow and ice in the shade as they went up the last mile. When they reached the top, they were surprised to find a tent pitched on the very summit. There was no one in sight, but they walked up toward the tent. As they approached, they discovered that someone was walking out from under the flap. It was the man they'd seen in so many TV images. He held out his hand, apparently to shake. Both Frank and Jes were reluctant to.

"Well, aren't you going to shake? What kind of negotiations are possible between people who don't trust each other on that level?"

Frank held out his hand, and the other grasped it in a brief clasp that was not reluctant though it was short. The man went on, "It's necessary for us to introduce ourselves. I know who you two are, so let me introduce my associate, Minerva McGonagall, and I am James Wendt."

Neither Frank nor Jes could think of something to say, so they simply stared at the faces that they had seen a number of times but without the reality that breathing the same air imparts. Wendt was going on, "Come in. It's rather cool out and is windy at times."

They bent down to enter the tent and found that the inside was much larger than it had any right to be, and that it was even luxurious. It had tapestries and a thick rug for floor. Somehow whatever was under the floor seemed much more smooth and hard than a rock floor could possibly be. There was a large round mahogany table with seats for four around it. There was some sort of candelabra hanging from the ceiling of the tent. It seemed to be powered by gas flames. The result was a soft light that seemed to equally illuminate the entire interior that they could see.

Minerva asked, "Can I bring you something to drink? We have fresh-brewed tea, coffee, cold water, wine if you wish."

Frank said, "I'm not thirsty at the moment. Although later, I might appreciate some tea."

Wendt began, "It's really simple, but we have to work out at least some of the details. How quickly can you leave—absolutely everyone—leave the planet?"

Frank looked at Jes, who began with the bargaining point that they intended to start with, "We are limited by the speed of light. We can only bring the ships in that were originally scheduled to come, as well as recalling some of the more recently departed star-faring ships. We estimate five or six years."

Minerva said, "You must do better than that. We were thinking something more like two months. You surely appreciate the interest we have in being left to restore humanity to the world as quickly as possible."

Jes sputtered, "Two months! Do you have any idea how difficult the logistics of that would be? It's monstrous!"

Minerva said calmly, "Interesting—your use of the word, monstrous. I would think that is precisely what you're best at."

Frank growled softly but said nothing. Then Minerva said, "We could allow you more time—if we received something of value in exchange."

Frank said, "Now, we come to it. Just what is it that you want? The secret of near-light travel? Weapons?"

Wendt laughed, "Oh, you missed your calling in life, Frank. You should have been the Jester that your partner used to be. We've absolutely no interest in those trifles that you mention. No. We want what you've stolen from us."

Both Frank and Jes stared blankly. Jes started, "What are you talking about? We won't take any natural resources. We never have."

Minerva said so softly that what she said was hardly heard, "You've only stolen what is dearest to our hearts—our friends, neighbors, and relatives. Bring back our loved ones when you leave their bodies."

Frank leaned back and shook his head slowly, "You don't know what you ask. We've never studied that art. We've never had to before. No one was ever left to ask for that. I don't know if we can."

Wendt's voice was hard, "I'll bet you've done experiments. I'll bet that you've had to do it on rare occasions. And I'll bet for sure that you'll regret it deeply, if you can't figure out quickly how to do that now."

Frank's eyes took on a lost look, and then he said, "How much time?"

"We'll give you a year, IF you can deliver our people. If you can't, you've got one month—starting now. If I were you, I'd get into that Miata and drive as fast as you can down to where your electronics will work again and get hold of your geniuses and put them on this problem."

Frank and Jes ran to the Miata, jumped in and Frank drove like a madman down the twisting angled curves of the road. As Frank drove, Jes looked up at the sky and shook his head. It seemed an eternity of swerves until the GPS started working again and the radio in his ear hissed to life.

"Frank, can you hear us? What happened up there? We lost all contact with you, once you got into the trees."

Frank said, "No time to talk. No time for anything. We've got to figure out how to revive the hosts after we leave them, and we only have maybe 10 days to do it. Get everyone on the problem. Use information teleportation to find out if anyone on the home worlds knows anything about that."

The voice asked, "But how can they expect us to do that in a mere 10 days?"

"I don't know. I don't care. No time for arguments. Go! Go! Now!"

The only response was, 'Yes, sir."

The foraging party that had left the previous night had just returned. It had been a minor foray—just looking to replace a few items in short supply and top off the rest. It had been decided that Wanda didn't even have to come along. The people at the local Big Box Store had become used to seeing people wearing sunglasses along with Wanda. She wore them most of the time as well. In the late evening shift, the checkout people even recognized Kyle and didn't give him a second glance.

When Kyle and Trevor returned, though, it had been anything but the uneventful unloading of supplies. They left everything in the truck and ran into the cave proper. As they went, they called to everyone they saw, telling them to come to the main meeting cavern. They found Jeb and dragged him along. Even with the newly-released people, the cavern wasn't crowded.

When Jeb was sure that everyone was there, he turned to Kyle, "All right. What is so danged important that it has to have everyone present and right now—even before unloading the truck?" Kyle didn't say anything but seemed hyped up as he'd rarely seen Kyle. He swiveled his field of view to include Trevor. "Well?"

Kyle just raised a newspaper up that he'd been carrying so that Jeb could see the front page but no one else could. "There's a little article here on the front page of the *Chicago Tribune*." He pronounced the first syllable of Chicago like "pie". "It says that there was a big broadcast of a news conference with the Headof the Earth Defense Group."

Jeb turned to Wanda with a puzzled look, "What is that Wanda?"

Wand looked up in as much consternation as Jeb, "I don't know. I've never heard of it. It seems to go against most Soul principles."

Jeb turned back to Kyle, "OK. What did he say in this big news conference?"

Kyle's smile turned so broad that no one would have believed that he wasn't splitting his face. He drew out his answer ever so slowly, "Well, it just says that the Souls have agreed to evacuate the Earth very soon."

Everyone's jaws dropped, and for a moment the silence was so intense that you could have heard a fly buzzing in the next cavern. Then there was a spontaneous cheer that rose from the lips of everyone in the room. The cheer died down and somebody shouted a question, "How can we believe the Souls?"

Kyle turned the paper around so everyone could see the headline in giant typeface, "Souls to Quit Earth!"

Wanda asked incredulously, "How is this possible? I don't believe that the Souls would give up a planet that they'd put so much effort and so many Souls on."

Kyle started to read from the article but was interrupted by Jeb, "Just give us the skinny. I'm sure you two read that article several times on the way back here."

Kyle said, "OK. Here it is. There was a US Navy submarine, the . . . "

Wanda interrupted, "What is a navee submarine?"

Jeb answered, "The Navy is a part of the military of the United States. It operates on the seas.

"A submarine is a boat that can operate underwater for a long time."

Kyle went on, "As I was saying, the USS Ohio, a Trident submarine, . . . "\

Wanda interrupted again and Kyle replied, "I know, I know, what is a Trident submarine? It's a submarine that has rockets that are armed with nuclear bombs." Wanda started to say something, and Kyle went on, "Yes, yes. A nuclear bomb is a weapon that uses atomic nuclear fusion as a source of power. A single nuclear bomb can devastate a city. The rockets can carry a dozen or more bombs and the sub can carry dozens of rockets."

Wanda's mouth fell open and she gasped, "You could kill everyone on a continent with those rockets!"

Jeb spoke up, "Yes, you could. But the US had dozens of those subs; why was there only one that was involved?"

Kyle nodded, "Well, the way I get it from the story, all those subs were ordered home while the Souls were still gaining control. There was no reason for the captains to suspect that there was anything bad going on.

"BUT, this sub was cruising under the Arctic icecap and had not surfaced for a very long time. Apparently, they were doing a study for NASA on men confined in a small space for a very long time—in this case, a year. It was to prepare for a manned mission to Mars.

Wanda stared glassy-eyed, 'You mean that a submarine could stay underwater for more than a year without coming up for air?"

Jeb nodded, "Yes, the only limit on these nuclear subs is the amount of food they can carry."

Kyle went on, "Anyway, the sub had sailed just after the invasion began and had not had contact with bases for more than a year. It had finally surfaced after the invasion was over, and no one was trying to maintain the fiction that the invasion hadn't happened.

"The captain and the Executive Officer had been noted for acting on their own initiative. When they surfaced and got orders to report to their home base for decommissioning, they were very suspicious and started working the Internet. They realized that something was terribly wrong and decided to disobey orders and search for the answer.

"They connected with a resistance group in far northern England and discovered the truth. They formed a plan to force the Souls to leave the Earth."

Wanda asked, "By threatening to destroy billions of Souls? We'd never believe such a hideous threat—even you couldn't be that depraved."

Kyle nodded, "You're right, they didn't believe it at first. So, they gave the Souls a demonstration. They attacked a spaceport outside Paris." Here the admiration for the feat crept into his voice. "The timing was amazing! It happened while a fully loaded ship of Souls was taking off from the spaceport. The ship was vaporized! The ships in the spaceport were destroyed. The Spaceport itself was nearly destroyed. There were tens of thousands of people on the ground in the surrounding suburbs who were killed.

"It happened at night. Everyone in Northern Europe could see the nuclear fireball rising in the sky. It was visible in London."

It was too much for Wanda. Sobbing, she screamed, "You monsters! You killed hundreds of thousands of Souls! How could you do it!"

Jeb looked down at his feet and said softly, "It could have been far worse. If they'd aimed at central Paris, they could have killed ten times, a hundred times, as many. They chose not to."

Ian had drawn her into his arms, and her sobs were buried in his chest as she struck his back with her balled fists. She took in breaths in great gasps, and her sobs subsided. "Yes, that would have done it. Someone who could do that wouldn't stop. They'd carry out their threat."

Jeb turned his head toward Wanda and asked, "Then you believe that it's a true commitment by the Souls to leave the Earth?"

She answered the question, "No Soul would lie—ever." Then, she hesitated and said in a softer voice that was none-the-less loud in the thundering silence, "Except to someone she loved." And she looked over at Melanie with a weak smile.

Then she went on, "In a public speech to the entire world? No Soul could say a lie in those circumstances." It was a simple, flat statement of fact.

Jeb said, "OK. So, it's the truth. What does that mean?"

Wanda slumped against Ian, "Well, for one thing, it means that you don't need me anymore. You can go out and walk anywhere and no Soul will molest you. None would dare. I might as well report for the first ship off-planet."

Ian squeezed her tighter and said, "I still need you."

Jeb looked up, "And even if we don't need you, we love you."

She looked around, and everyone nodded or looked directly at her and said, "Yes, Wanda, we love you."

Wanda shook her head wonderingly, "You are the strangest people. You were rejoicing a minute ago that hundreds of thousands of Souls had died, and now you want one Soul to live with you here."

Jeb chuckled for the first time and said, "What would life be without its little surprises?"

The Senior Genius was standing at the end of the conference table and rehearsing in his mind what he would say. The team filed into the Conference Room and found seats. The SG didn't. Frank came in a couple of minutes late and just said, "Report. Oh, and don't forget that this is day 14."

"We think that we've got it solved. The humans fall into several categories based on how resilient their minds are. The very imaginative are slowest to recover from the shock of being hosts. They seem to be tied up in the experience of being the Soul that they have almost a catatonic response to being separated from the Soul. In general, the less imaginative, the more hardy they are and the more able to recover from the shock of being separated from the Soul that they hosted. In any case, there are a series of shocks of increasing severity that we employ to break the more imaginative hosts from dependence on the Soul. We can gauge something of how easy or hard it will be to revive the host depending on the answers to a brief questionnaire that we administer to Souls before extraction. We've gotten to be pretty effective to judge the level of shock to use."

Jes asked, "Just the bottom line, please. How effective are your methods?"

The SG looked down and seemed to be evading the gaze of Frank when he said, "We're at 90% effectiveness. But we are constantly working to improve that percent."

"I would think so. I don't know how effective we have to be, but it would be really nice to be able to report at our next meeting that you're more than 99% effective. I think we could 'sell' that to the humans."

"But only 5 more days. It's hopeless," he was interrupted by Frank.

"Not hopeless. I've still got hope. Keep working. The percentage is high enough that we could begin using your technique and hold back the failures pending better techniques."

The SG was close to despondent, but he merely nodded his head and said, "We can only try."

The meeting broke up, and Jes and Frank walked slowly back to their wing of the castle. Frank asked, "What do you think?"

"I'd not have thought that they had a chance of better than 75% success. Back in the old days"—they seemed like centuries before— "when we had to extract a Soul to try to get some information from the host that the Soul couldn't seem to extract, we never had better than 50% success."

"Yes, but you weren't working for your lives then."

Minerva and Wendt were preparing for the next meeting with the aliens. Wendt checked his Glock for ammo, action, and arming (safety on). He slipped it back into the old purse that he'd carried for so many years. Minerva, of course, was always ready for action. He nodded to her, and they walked out of the Headmistress's Office and down the hall toward the Quidditch Field where they frequently went to disapparate.

Minerva asked, "So, just how much do we push them. Do we provide them a goal and timetable?" She smiled at the memory, "We don't want them to despair."

"No, we don't want that. I say that we not give them a goal and just say, 'You've made acceptable progress, but you need to do much better.' Then when they whine and complain, we give them another 20 days. How about that?"

"That seems OK." They reached the Quidditch Field where there were the dozen or so others who would be the guards. They would put up the Muggle repelling spell just after the Miata passed their post. Then all the electronics within range would stop working. Everyone nodded around, they came forward and grasped the port key, an old inner tube, and they disappeared.

They were at the summit of Mount Evans. The rest disapparated down the hill to their posts in the pre-dawn light. Minerva set up the tent, and she brought out a couple of camp chairs where they sat and watched the sunrise. They would have a couple of hours alone until the aliens arrived.

Eventually, the Miata rounded the final turn and entered the parking lot. The two aliens got out and came over. Frank asked, "Are we meeting out here?"

"No, I think we'd be more comfortable inside." They walked in but left the camp chairs outside. The same round mahogany table was there. This time the aliens accepted the offer of hot tea. They sat a moment, sipping tea together.

Then Frank said, "OK. We can't make your deadline. We've been doing some selective extractions."

The puzzled look on the humans faces confused Frank, and then he realized that the term was not familiar. "Extractions are what we call it when we remove a Soul from a hos . ." Frank corrected what he was saying to, "human. We've had a lot of success, but there are still a small number of humans left in a catatonic state." Frank paused and decided not to be coy. "Oh, hell. it's about 4%. I'm not happy with that, and we're doing our best to improve to less than 1 %." He saw the expression on the humans' faces, and he quickly added, "Much less than 1 %."

Minerva shook her head slowly, "Now, Mr. Frank. You're really going to have to do better than that if you expect passing marks."

Frank shifted in his chair and turned his head to look toward the entrance to the tent for a moment. He turned back and said, "We're doing our best. We've never faced this problem before. It's a miracle that we've done as well as we have."

Wendt stared into Frank's silver eyes and said, "Not good enough. I begin to wonder if you're really interested in succeeding."

Frank started to rise, anger welling up in him. But he controlled himself and said, "I told you already, I've done everything possible and more. If you're going to kill us all, just go ahead and do it."

Minerva came back with a soft voice, "Oh, no. We've got no intention of killing you. We just want to make sure that you're not trying to get away with slipshod work. I think we can give you another 30 days."

Wendt turned to her quickly and said, "No, twenty."

Minerva smoothly corrected, "That's right. Twenty days. And we want to see some of your 'successes'. We want to be sure that they're being treated humanely and are really returned to their former selves."

Frank was surprised, "You don't believe us?" His race had been so used to being inveterate truth-tellers that the implication that he might not be truthful hurt him more than anything else the humans had said.

"Well, you just don't know humans very well, do you? We just want to make sure that your techniques aren't harming your victims in a subtle way."

Jes winced at the word 'victims'. He had never thought of hosts as victims, although he knew intellectually that a race of hosts might think of themselves that way. He'd always thought of what they did as more like "perfecting". They took imperfect hosts and gave them an opportunity to live truly productive, non-destructive lives.

Jes said, "I'll see that all the ones that we've had success with are available in London at Buckingham Palace two days from today."

Wendt said, "No, you'll bring them here. At the same time three days from now. I think our work is done for now. Don't forget—twenty days."

Jes started to object, but Wendt only said succinctly and forcefully, "Go. Now." Jes could only nod assent. They got up and left the tent, got into the Miata and drove off.

Minerva smiled at Wendt, "You really were pretty hard on them."

"They deserved it—fully." And then he smiled, "And besides, I've really not had much fun lately. That was fun—making the puppet-masters jump."

Two weeks later they were in Azkaban with the Minister of Magic and the Head of the Aurors, the Captain and First Officer of the Ohio and a couple of other government officials.

Pam was reviewing where they stood. "So, the aliens have agreed to vacate the Earth within a year. We are sure that at least upper 90 percentile of all Muggles will be returned pretty intact. What have we got left to do besides wait and watch?"

The Head of the Aurors asked, "How do we know that they'll keep their promises?"

The Auror Longbottom spoke up, "We actually have quite a lot working for us. For one thing, we can and will give everyone the unbreakable oath. Any alien hiding in a human will be flushed out, so to speak."

"But we can't give the oath to 8 billion people!"

Pam looked on at the debate between the Head of the Aurors and one of his staff with some amusement. Longbottom was replying, "Sure we can. We have at least 40,000 wizards and witches qualified to administer it. That's only 200,000 per wizard. That may seem like a lot, but at one every two minutes for 12 hours a day, we could finish in a little over a year. Grueling, but doable."

"OK. But what if they leave caches of those creatures in those thermos bottle thingees, hidden all over the world? How would we deal with them?"

Wendt spoke up for the first time, "I've been thinking about that. I have a suggestion."

Pam raised an eyebrow and looked over at him. "Well, don't hold back. What is it?"

Wendt looked sheepish and said, "Well, it's only an idea off the top of my head, but. . ."

Pam urged, "Come on. What's your idea?"

"Well, what would happen if you used the *accio* spell? You know, '*accio* alien'."

One of the other officials said, laughing, "You mean like calling a dog? Here Rover. Come Rover."

But Pam looked reflective, "Yes. What would happen?"

Longbottom said, "Well, any aliens within range would be dragged toward the one using the spell—dragged hard. And if it were in a person or one of those vacuum bottles or in anything, only the alien would be dragged. It would break through or pull on whatever it was in."

Minerva said, "That would be practically a death spell."

Pam asked, "So how would that work? You know, practically."

"Well, I think that you might get several wizards in an airplane at a couple of miles altitude and fly over the countryside using that spell to extract aliens forcibly from wherever they were. What kind of range does that spell work over?"

Longbottom scratched his chin, "I think I've seen it work across at least a couple of miles. I'll bet it could be extended to several miles."

Pam said, "So, your idea is to cover the whole earth—oceans and all—that way?"

"I guess you'd have to."

"Well, we'll have to get working on preparing these armies of wizards to do those two tasks, don't you think?" Minerva wondered.

Pam said, 'Yes. I think that the Auror Office had better get on it immediately. We'll need some representatives from Muggles too to work closely with the task force." She hesitated as though trying to pull a name out of the air at random. "What about this Muggle, this Brahms. He's bright." Then she added softly, 'I'd have to be on the task force too."

Minerva immediately choked and said, "I think that he's got other important assignments. Right, Wendt?" and she kicked Wendt under the table on his shins.

Wendt gulped, trying to cover the shot of pain he'd just received, and said, "Sure. That is, yes. He's wanted for. . . uh. . . plotting courses for airplanes to follow to apply the *accio* spell most effectively."

Pam asked, "Are there any other holes that we're not filling?" She waited a minute and said, "None? None? Then get to work and keep thinking. We must be forgetting something."

An official that had been sitting back and not commenting on anything spoke up, "What about the economics of having a partial Muggle, partial alien population?"

Pam was dumbfounded, "What do you mean?"

The little man said, "Well, the aliens don't use money. It's a funny sort of system a little like Communism or is it Marxism? You know, 'from those according to their capability and to those according to their need.'"

The Head of the Aurors asked, "No, galleons?"

"Not a single one. How will the Muggles keep the system going until every one of the aliens is gone, and they can go back to pounds or Euros or whatever it is they use?"

Everyone around the room was silent. Finally, Pam said, "There's another little task for the Task Force."

Someone muttered that she was glad that she wasn't on the Task Force.

As they left Wendt asked Minerva, "What's the deal with the Boy Genius? Why didn't you want him on this task force?"

She shook her head at him, "Don't you know that Pam er the Minister has got a 'thing' for Brahms?"

"So what?"

She went on, "And that Sinistra has a 'thing' for him too?"

"Ohhhh. I guess it would be good for me if he were available to absorb Sinistra's attention rather than other people.":

"Yes, like you."

"Like me." Wendt smiled and said, "Good thinking. I hope your idea keeps her attention away from me. It's been a while, but she's altogether too clever to be left to her own devices."

Minerva smiled broadly and said, "Right."

They had reached the row of great hearths, and Wendt stopped and took Minerva by the arm. "By the way, we've been so busy for quite a while, I've not had a chance to ask you a question that I've been carrying around for quite some time."

Minerva answered cautiously, "Oh, what's that?"

"Well, you remember when you turned the Sea of Merlin over to the goblins?"

She answered slowly as though it were a trick question, "Yesssss."

"Do you remember that I wasn't there at the time?"

"Sure."

"Well, people who were there told me that you were the first to look into the Sea."

"Yes, I think I was."

"They also tell me that there were two strange things about what you did after seeing whatever you saw."

"Really?"

"Yes, really. One was that you seemed to be powerfully affected. And the other was that you refused to tell anyone what you saw."

Minerva just stood silent. Finally, Wendt asked, "Well is that true?"

Minerva took a deep breath and said, "It's true, but I want to wait until this alien thing is well in hand to talk about it. Not until the last alien is off the planet, but once we've got a good chunk of the Muggles back and things are running smoothly then I'll talk with you about it. Man, will I talk with you about it."

"And you can't talk now?"

"I really, really want to get this behind us, before I talk with you about it."

"OK. But I absolutely insist on a rain check."

"Why would you want to check on the rain?"

'Don't be funny. Let's go and get this infernal trip through the floo network behind us."

The beginning of the mass extraction of Souls from humans started shakily, but after a couple of weeks, it seemed to be going well. The Auror Longbottom asked Wendt to come see one of the centers. The Aurors were supervising and doing the *Unbreakable Oaths*. Wendt noticed that most of the freed Muggles were leaving without taking the oath. He asked, "What's the heck's going on. I thought we were *Oathing* every one of them?"

"Oh, we will. But the problem of processing them quickly has forced us to come up with an alternative. We use the *accio* charm to determine if any one of the group had aliens. Then we *Oath* as many as we can. The ones that we don't, will turn themselves in later for the *Oath*."

Wendt shook his head. "But how can we guarantee that they'll return."

Longbottom smiled, "We told them that the *Oath* would immunize them from being occupied again. They begged to have us do it then. They've been calling back every day to get 'immunized'." If they ever stop calling, we know that there's a problem. I think it's a very effective program. We can take a little more time *Oathing* everyone— maybe a year or so and get these damn aliens off the planet in 6 months—maybe less."

Just then there was a commotion among the wizards administering *Oaths*. Wendt and Longbottom walked over to the place it was happening. It wasn't what either of them expected. There was a man sobbing and a wizard was trying to calm him down. Longbottom asked the wizard what was going on. Wendt spoke to the Muggle, "What's the problem? Is there anything we can do to help?"

The man just kept sobbing. The Auror answered Longbottom's question, "It's something about his wife sir. I didn't quite get it."

The Muggle calmed a little and said, "He doesn't know where my wife is."

Wendt asked him, "Wasn't she with you when they extracted the alien from you?"

He looked up at Wendt for the first time and said, "No, sir. I don't know where she went."

They were at the Heathrow spaceport. Wendt said to Longbottom, "Let's buy this fellow a cup of tea and see what's going on." So, they accompanied him to a food court and got tea for them all.

Then Wendt asked him, "Please tell us from the beginning what happened."

The man took a deep breath and straightened. "I'm Josiah Ron. My wife and I lived in Chelsea. I drove a lorry. Then those. . ." He gulped hard trying to control his emotions, ". . . things came. They took me first. I don't know how it happened. The last thing I remember was that I was in a pub and . . and . . then that's all until I started having these dreams—nightmares they were really. "

"What were they like?"

"They were like I was watching someone else do things. After a while I realized that the other bloke was using my body." He didn't succeed in holding down a sob that time. "This other bloke was doing things that I didn't understand. He was driving me lorry, but he didn't seem to be very good at it. Have you ever had a dream where you were sure that you were awake, but you just couldn't force your body to move or do anything?"

Longbottom nodded and said, "Sure. It's a really claustrophobic feeling. You think you'll never wake up, and you'll be paralyzed for the rest of your life."

Josiah nodded between sobs.

I said, "Just take your time. There's no hurry."

He went on, "Finally, I almost woke up. This other bloke who was using my, MY BODY was putting something in my wife's tea." He absolutely stopped and held back the emotions for a long time. Then he went on plaintively, "I tried so, so hard to stop him. I think I made him spill the cup once." Then he could not prevent the wail from escaping his throat. "I couldn't stop him the next time. It was brutal. He was talking to her as easy as Bob's your uncle. He was joking, and she laughed." He spit it out as if it were an offense against humanity.

Then he seemed to relax as if he had exerted every ounce of will in trying to stop the inevitable and had given in to the unavoidable. From then on, he simply cried, not trying to hold anything back. "I watched her slowly fall asleep as she drank her tea. It wasn't so fast that she didn't have time to put her teacup down. She laughed a little and said, 'I thought tea was supposed to keep you awake.' She, she," another gap, 'she didn't suspect anything was wrong.

"When she was completely asleep, I opened a little leather kit that I had in the back of a drawer. It had a sealed clear plastic bag with several things. Then I lifted her up and put her on the kitchen table. I broke it open. I pulled some kind of wipe thingee and sponged the back of her neck with it.

"I pulled out the knife, and I. . ." the pain returned to his face and it came out in a rush, ". . . I slit her neck length-wise. Then I opened a little like vacuum bottle by screwing it open. I turned it upside down and it fell onto her neck. I massaged it a little. It was very cold. When it warmed up, it crawled into the slit." He wept and wept at that point.

319

"Then I closed the skin over it and sprayed something onto the cut and then put a bandage on it.

"Finally, I carried her back to our room and laid her on our bed on her stomach. Then I sat down and watched her." At that point Josiah became extremely agitated. He got up and walked back and forth in the food court. Finally, he sat again. "I watched her until she woke up. But it wasn't her. I could tell. She said things differently than my Mary did. She walked differently.

"After that, I seemed to go to sleep for a long time. But dreamed again. We were in the kitchen—the other bloke and the NOT-Mary thing. It was saying something about getting an assignment that would take it far away. I don't know where. I never saw her again.

He looked up at us, turning from Longbottom to me and back again, despair in his eyes, "I'll never see Mary again, will I?"

Longbottom didn't say anything and finally turned away from Josiah. But Wendt said, 'Yes. you will." He said it with a determination and will that made Longbottom look up. Wendt went on, "Your Mary is going to be awakened. Everyone who went to sleep is going to wake up. I don't know where she is, but when she wakes up, she will remember you. She'll remember you, and she'll do everything she can to get back here. And you'll get back to where the two of you used to live. You'll find her, and then no one will make her leave you again." Wendt said it with such strength that Longbottom looked up and smiled and said,

"Wendt's right. He always is. I've never seen him be wrong when he's so sure."

Josiah looked from one to the other and asked, "Do you really think so?"

Longbottom said, "Look. I say so, and Wendt says so. That makes it true. Now, you need to get back to the rest of the people who've just been wakened. There'll be instructions for what you should do."

The man picked up his napkin and blew his nose into it. "Thanks. You know, I almost believe you myself." Both Longbottom and Wendt slapped his back and wished him luck. They walked off through the food court. As soon as they couldn't be seen, Longbottom turned to Wendt.

"Are you sure that his wife will find him?"

Wendt shrugged, "Probably. The probability that she's still alive is upper 90's. The probablility that she'll wake successfully is upper 90's. The chances that she still loves him is 100%. Pretty good chances, but who knows?"

They found a deserted spot, and Wendt held out his hand to Longbottom as if to shake hands. Longbottom clasped his outstretched hand, and the two disappeared.

Jeb had insisted on Wanda's accompanying every foray into the greater world after the announcement of the retreat of the Souls from Earth. He insisted that so close to the end of their ordeal, he wouldn't take any risks whenever they could be avoided. That continued even after the foragers had begun running into crowds of blue-eyed, brown-eyed, hazel-eyed, green-eyed humans on every trip. His people were the only ones who wore the bombardier style sunglasses that were impenetrable to view.

He also insisted that every trip include the collection of one major newspaper. So there were a series of different newspapers that came back—the *Chicago Tribune,* the *Los Angeles Times,* the *New York Times,* the *Cleveland Plain Dealer*, and so on.

One day, there was a newspaper with another massive headline—"Last Day of Souls Announced." It happened that Kyle and Ian and Wanda were on this foray. Kyle had the paper again and collected everyone to the meeting room.

He showed the headline without fanfare. Everyone cheered. Everyone but Jeb. Kyle noticed first and asked, "Jeb, what is it? We can all go now, can't we?" He turned to Wanda, "Your people wouldn't go back on this promise, surely?"

She nodded eagerly, "I can't imagine that they'd break their word! It's over for everyone." She noticed that Jeb hadn't changed his expression at all. "Isn't it Jeb, why wouldn't it be?"

Jeb had been hanging his head, but then he lifted it to look directly at her. "I've been thinking about this ever since that first headline. I've been trying to think a way around the problem ever since, but I'm stuck."

Now Ian had panic in his eyes, "What are you thinking, Jeb?"

Jeb started slowly, thoughtfully, picking his words with care, "You see, the problem, don't you? Think about it. If we ALL go out right now, what will happen to Wanda?"

Ian was the first to get the problem, "The Souls will insist that she has to leave, won't they?" He turned to Wanda, "Would they?"

She discovered she'd been holding her breath. As the truth sunk in, she said, "Yes. They have to. They've just announced a date that ALL Souls have to be off the planet. That would include me."

Ian rapidly intervened, "NO. It wouldn't. Not if you're not around. If WE stay here and nobody is a SNEETCH!" There was a look in his eye that bordered on something like madness. "Then after they're all gone, Wanda, you can come out."

Jeb said, "Not bad. You two could stay here. With only the two of you, there'd be plenty of food and supplies. We could easily re-supply you without any danger. No one will be looking for humans helping a fugitive Soul. . . " Jeb trailed off reflectively.

Ian jumped in, "And a few months after the Souls have left, we could all leave. Wanda would have to be careful—wear sunglasses whenever she was out. We could live in a remote area. . ." Ian too had been trailing off as he thought through what would be necessary.

But Jeb had been shaking his head. "No, it won't do. Do you think that out there in the wild that someone wouldn't find out about Wanda? And when they did, she wouldn't last a day.

"There won't be a single human being who hasn't lost a brother, a sister, a Mother or Father, a lover, or has a close friend who's lost someone.

"Some few could forgive. Most would only hate Wanda, spit in her face when they saw her, scream 'Murderer' at her when they passed on the street. Their kids would throw rocks at her. But I guarantee you that someone would kill her. And it wouldn't be pretty. If she were lucky, they'd lynch her." He hesitated and went on, "They might literally tear her limb from limb."

Wanda's face was covered with tears. "I've got to have 'Doc' keep his promise to me."

Ian held her and just kept saying, "No. No. No. I'll stay here with you forever."

Jeb drawled out, "Well, as old and set in my ways as I am, I'd probably not enjoy it out 'there' anyway, I'll keep you two company."

Then Maggie walked over to Wanda and rubbed her arm gently, "I'll be staying too." One by one, the rest of the people in the cavern walked over and said simply, "Me, too" or "I'm staying" or just hugged her wordlessly as they tried to hold back their own tears.

Eventually, there was a group of people around Wanda and one lone person, standing at a distance, Kyle. His head was bowed, and he seemed deep in thought. Finally, he looked up and said, "Look. I've got friends, relatives out there. They'll be worried about me. The whole world has just opened up to us. I love you Wanda, but I won't stay."

Jeb turned to Kyle, "Well, Kyle, I'm talking to you, but there's lots of time between now and when the Souls are finally done leaving. Anyone can change their minds about staying—there's no shame in that, And no shame in what you've decided, Kyle.

"BUT, and this is for everyone, not just Kyle. If you leave and you give even the slightest hint to anyone about Wanda, I'll come after you, and I'll find you. . . " Again his voice trailed off but there was no doubt about what was left unsaid.

Kyle stood uncertainly, apparently poised on the brink of some cliff. His slack stance stiffened, and he said so softly that no one would have heard were they not all standing in perfect silence deep in the Earth, "Oh, hell. I never could keep a secret."

He then walked over toward the people standing around Wanda. They parted for him. As he approached, he held out his hand to her and said, "Welcome to Earth, Wanda. I guess I'm going to be keeping you all company too."

She shook his hand and then threw herself at him and hugged him, her head only reaching his chest, her tears wetting his shirt. "You're a good Soul, Kyle."

Later, Wendt went to Minerva's office. He told her about the hideous interview that he'd had with Josiah. He was close to sobbing himself. She put her arms around his shoulder and squeezed, "That will never happen to us. And I'll give you some proof of that later." She pulled back and looked at him, "Why don't we go out for dinner? Somewhere special. Do you remember the hotel where that chess tournament was held?"

Wendt's smile betrayed pleasant memories, "Of course. You'd like to have dinner there?"

"Certainly. We can disapparate there."

Wendt scratched his chin, "I wonder if they're still open. Those sorts of establishments didn't always survive the aliens."

She hugged him again and said, "Let's find out."

"OK."

They walked out of the castle to find a place where they could disapparate. Minerva stopped and dragged Wendt to her, "This is far enough." Then they disappeared.

They appeared in an alley which Wendt remembered even though he'd not been there in years and years. They walked to the Trafalgar Hotel, entered, and went up to the rooftop bar. The weather was nice, and they decided to eat there overlooking the city.

The waiter brought them menu's and as they glanced through them, Wendt noticed that there were no prices. "Uh, Minerva, this may be rather pricey. When a menu doesn't have prices, you know that they expect you not to care what the price is."

She leaned back and laughed, "You are the last person in the world who needs to worry about that. The last time you checked, you had increased your vault size to accomodate all the gold that had been accumulating. I was afraid that the goblins would want to vote you the Chairman of the Board of Directors of Gringotts."

"That may be true. And it's true that I have both some galleons and pounds from the old days, but I'm not sure that I even have my credit card. And who knows what currency these people take?"

She patted his hand, "Then we'll just have to wash dishes if they don't take pounds or galleons."

The waiter came over to deliver their drink orders, and Wendt asked The question, "I don't see prices."

The waiter stared at him for a couple of seconds, and then said, "Yes, sir. You're ho. . uh humans, I see. We don't use money."

Wendt noticed then that his eyes were silver and that he was alien. "Even after the humans are coming back?"

"Yes, sir. This hotel works under the principles of the Souls. There is no other payment. We believe that by the time the last Souls are extracted, all human enterprises will continue to function by our principles. No other possibility would work. We really don't know how you'll be able to re-create the monetary system. Perhaps you will."

Minerva nodded and said, "I suppose that's it for the Goblins. I wonder what they'll do?"

Wendt watched the waiter leave. "It's not just Gringotts that's in trouble. All wizards still use money. Do you suppose that we'll continue to?"

Minerva shrugged and they discussed the menu. There were a number of vegetarian delicacies as well as a few tuna dishes. Wendt commented, "I don't remember what the menu was like before, but I've got a feeling that this doesn't bear a lot of resemblance to it."

She agreed and suggested that they try a dish that seemed to have a lot of similarity to vegetarian Indian cuisine. They decided that Wendt should get something as nearly opposite to it as possible. That way one of them would have an edible meal.

The waiter seemed to be pretty efficient. He seemed to realize that they were ready to order even though they'd not signaled him. He took their order and commented that the Tuna dish that Wendt had ordered was new to the menu and that many patrons seemed to like it.

Wendt watched him leave and said, "I'm still kind of creeped out by being served by that alien. I know that he'd be scalped alive by his boss if he tried anything funny, but still . . . "

Minerva didn't say anything, but when their meal arrived, she took a forkful and offered it to Wendt. "Why don't you try this? I'm afraid that I'll hate it."

He shrugged and took the forkful. "It's not bad. As a matter of fact, I wouldn't mind trading dishes with you."

"Really. Go ahead and try yours and see if you still feel that way."

He did. After a minute, he said, "That's good too. Maybe not quite as good as your, but really quite decent. Do you want to try them and decide if you want to swap?"

She smiled and said, "You remember what you said about being a little ambivalent about being served by an alien?"

"Sure. So, what?"

"Well, I think enough time has passed."

Wendt was suspicious, "Enough time for what?"

"Oh, to see if you have some reaction. That's why you're the food taster for me."

Wendt spewed the mouthful he had been chewing out, "You! You!"

"Now, now. You seem to be fine. I'll keep mine."

Just then, the waiter came over, asked if anything was wrong, and cleaned the tablecloth, "Sir, if you didn't like your menu selection, I could provide another."

Wendt just frowned and said, "No, No. It's fine. A little just got down the 'wrong pipe' as we humans say."

The waiter asked if Wendt needed the Heimlich maneuver applied, but Wendt insisted he was fine. "If I can talk then I don't need the Heimlich." Finally satisfied, the waiter left.

Minerva had been enjoying the whole procedure and was on the point of laughing several times. Finally, she spoke:

"But for now," and by the tone of her voice he could tell that she'd turned serious, "I've got to tell you what I saw in the Mirror."

"Go ahead. You were being mighty mysterious about it."

"I looked into the Mirror and I saw my future."

"Are you sure it was your future?"

"What I saw was myself in the mirror. Anyway, I saw myself all in white dress." She hesitated and looked at Wendt expectantly. When nothing happened, she went on. "I was also wearing a white veil and a ring." She raised her left hand and held it out with the third finger raised slightly.

"Yes. What else?"

"What else? What else! It was my wedding."

Wendt looked at her, his mouth agape. He finally said hesitantly, "Whom did you see next to you in that image?"

She said, "No one. Whom did you expect me to see?"

Wendt took a deep gulp and said, "I was afraid to hope it would be me." Wendt's face was downcast. "I see."

Minerva stared at him. "Whatever are you moping about?"

Wendt looked up and said, "Well, I always had this little dream that when you married, it would be me. . ." He trailed off at the end.

Minerva's happy, almost ecstatic face deflated some and she said, "Well, of course, I want it to be you. Do I have to . . . "

Wendt immediately jumped in and said, "Minerva, I asked you so many times that I've lost count. But here it is, one more time for the record."

He practically threw himself down to the floor. He slipped the brown pump off her left foot, kissed the stockinged foot, and said, "My love, I've loved you as long as I have known you—maybe even before that." She chuckled. He went on, "I want for us to be together forever. If it can't be as your husband, I'll take it as your lover; but will you, Minerva L. McGonagall be my wife?"

She reached down, cradled his face in her hands, and started to lift him up when the wine arrived. The embarrassed waiter set the bottle down and back away nervously. Then Minerva drew Wendt toward him and said, "Of course, I'll be your wife." They kissed—not the passionate, fiery kiss of young lovers—but the long confident kiss of those who know it's not going to be the last. "Why you silly goose, whatever in the world made you think it wouldn't be you?"

Wendt asked, "When? Is tomorrow too soon?"

She frowned at that. "You know perfectly well that we can't do a proper wedding before next June."

He seemed to choke and spluttered, "Next June! Why in the world would you wait that long? But if it's a choice between next June and never, I can survive till then."

She smiled again and the joy flooded back into his heart. She said, "Just because we won't be married until then doesn't mean that we can't practice being newlyweds. It's never held you back before."

Raptors at Brighton Beach

The soup at lunch in the Great Hall was especially good. It was a mixed 20 or was it 30 varieties of beans. The tomato basil base was superb. Wendt and Minerva had just allowed their soup to cool enough that it didn't scald their mouths. She was laughing at one of her own jokes when the Boy Genius ran up to their table. "Come on, you've got to get down to the Shrieking Shack right now!"

They got up and ran as fast as they could after Brahms. Minerva commented, "You know, I think he's in the best shape I've ever seen him ."

Wendt just grimaced and said, "Wish he weren't."

Brahms started to explain as they got close to the Shack. He did it in little gasps, "Something awful. Rogue jet fighter planes. Headed for Heathrow.."

Wendt thought, "Shit. What now? I thought we had all this handled."

They arrived at the Shack, were ushered through without the slightest hesitation and up to the Control Room. All the screens were blank except the big one that had a radar display showing Northern Europe. There were blips all over the map, but there were a little constellation of red blips over northern France, apparently headed for England. Brahms got his breath back first but still was speaking in short bursts. "Four Raptors. Stole four air to air missiles. Armed with tactical nuclear warheads. Think they're going to destroy the next shuttle launch. Sort of the way we did."

One of the techs amplified. "It looks like they're going to reach the coast near Brighton."

Wendt said, "Shit. But why can't they shoot them down, scramble friendly fighters?"

One of the techs in the room turned and said, "There's only one air force base left open in Northern Europe—the one they came from. It would take an hour to get another plane in the sky."

"Great! Where's this vaunted alien technology when you need it. Isn't there anything we can do? What about a commercial flight? Maybe they could ram the Raptors."

The tech didn't dignify that suggestion with an answer. Wendt went on. "There's got to be something we can do. He looked around the room from face to face. None held any hope—until he reached Minerva's.

"We could get a broom in the air, over Brighton Beach, but what would it do? We'd need somebody who knew Muggle planes." Suddenly everyone was looking at him.

"Why is everyone looking at me? Everybody here knows Muggle technology."

One of the techs smiled and said, "But only you also know wizard technology. You've flown a broom haven't you?"

"I've ridden on a broom if that's what you mean, but it nearly drove me crazy just staying on-board."

Minerva said, "It looks like it's you and me."

"NO IT DOESN'T. Why you? We just get one of those Quidditch wiz's. They could fly rings around you."

That pesky tech said, "We don't have time. By the time somebody runs up to the castle, finds a good flyer and gets on the way, it'll be all over but the crying."

Wendt objected, "But you don't have your broom, and it's not much for speed, thank God in Heaven."

Minerva just turned to a window, flicked with her wand and the window opened. She then said, "*Accio* Firebolt."

Wendt objected again, "You're going to steal someone's broom."

"This is an emergency. Are you trying to be a pest?" She had begun rolling her R's the way she did when she was getting angry.

"OK. OK. I lose. Great, how are we going to get to Brighton?" He almost immediately answered himself. "Of course, my two favorite things to do all in one adventure—flying on a broom and disapparating."

Minerva slapped his left bun, which was the closer and said, "Don't be a sore loser."

Just then the Firebolt flew into the room, and Minerva caught it in her left hand. She grabbed Wendt's left bun in a vice-like grip, and the two of them disappeared.

Shrieking Shack Spectators

The disappearance of Wendt and McGonagall didn't surprise anyone particularly. They had all been expecting it. What was surprising was that all the electronics in the room went dead at the same time. No one had been there when magic had been performed so close to the equipment. As a matter of fact magic had never been done that close before.

Brahms had everyone reboot all the equipment. Almost immediately everything booted up, and then almost as soon, warning claxons went off. "What the hell is going on! What is that alarm?"

One of the techs in the room got up and looked around for some sign of the problem while Brahms waited for the electronics to boot completely so that they could find out what had happened. He stood up and started to pace. "What did we miss? The magic knocked the electronics down. Then we reboot and something new is going on."

Sinistra stared at him, "What are you talking about?"

He just swung around and snapped, "Are you doing magic?"

She was shocked at his tone of accusation, but she managed to shake her head "no."

He kept pacing but started talking to himself, loud enough and clearly enough for everyone to understand. "OK. Magic knocks down servers and PC's and everything." He paused as if expecting someone to confirm that point. He continued, "We start booting everything up."

He looked around, and no one said anything. "Come on. Someone think besides me. Was that the order of events?"

Then everyone seemed to come to life. Some said, "Right! That was it. Magic. Everything goes flooey. Reboot."

Someone else added, "Yeh. Then the klaxons go off and we aren't even completely booted up yet."

The first hint of a smile creased the Boy Genius' lips. This was more like the team. "So, more magic?"

Sinistra spoke for the first time, and it was definite. "No magic. You can tell when magic is being used, and I don't feel a whiff." She laughed at the mixed metaphor but went on. "Whatever's happening is your equipment not magic."

One of the tech's started to say, "I wonder if . . . magic affects . . ."

But he never finished the sentence because the idea hit Brahms and he didn't have the self-doubt that the tech did. 'It's the generators. Those klaxons are signaling that we're operating on. . . " But at that moment all the power dropped out.

What no one had realized at first was that the fuel cell generators outside had failed as well. The fuel cells had electronics in them to optimize the generators. That electronics had failed, and the battery backups were the only things that were powering everything in the Shrieking Shack.

It was lucky that it was in the afternoon. It would have taken them longer to start up the main generators and the backups and get a little charge into the battery backups. Brahms himself was watching the charge indicator on the UPC, and it wasn't until he was totally satisfied that he gave the signal up the line to reboot for the second time. He ran back up to the Control Room and found everyone staring at the blank main display.

He didn't have to ask. Jeffries, the Watch Commander, reported, "We're up and running but we've not established contact with Northern Europe command. It ought to be up in a minute." Brahms felt the electricity in the room, and it wasn't from the fuel cells. He couldn't remember when he'd felt so helpless before. Even when it had been the aliens versus him alone, he'd felt like he'd had more control. As a matter of fact, that had been the time when he'd felt the most in control. He'd had only himself to depend on, but that was a comfortable feeling, really. Now, he had to depend on all sorts of other people, including, ironically, those jackass aliens in Northern Europe command. He'd used to be happy that they weren't always the super-efficient aliens everyone thought they were. Now, he wished they'd get off their butts and get the connection re-established.

In only a couple of minutes the main screen changed from a screen-saver video of an alien coming out of it's thermos bottle that some joker had put on all the computers to the Northern Europe radar map. Brahms opened his mouth to ask for a close-up of the English coast, but one of the controllers had beat him to it. Then, a close-up of the Southwest of England replaced all of Europe. There were a lot of cryptic symbols that showed the locations of commercial aircraft but there were five red triangles that could only be bogees without transponders. Four of them were in a tight formation approaching the Channel, and the fifth was smaller and seemed to be stationary somewhat inland on the English coast.

Sinistra said uncertainly, "The fifth red triangle is Wendt and McGonagall?"

There was supposed to be a radar interpretation expert in the Control Room at all times. Brahms looked around to see if he recognized him, but the one on duty was unfamiliar. He spoke, "I suppose. That bogee is too small to be a helicopter."

Sinistra nodded, "It's hopeless, isn't it?"

Suddenly, the small red triangle started moving. The radar expert said, "And moving too fast for an ultralight. It looks like they've seen something."

By now the radar showed the quartet of bogees well over the channel. The radar man went on, "it looks like they're on an intercept course."

There was a sigh of released breath as a dozen people suddenly discovered that they'd been holding their breaths for several minutes. The quartet was moving much faster than the lone bogee and would surely cross the coast before it reached them, if it did.

The five red triangles seemed to merge for a second, and then there were only three. There was a gasp and then it was apparent that the one lone bogee had passed the four but that there were now only two of the fast ones. Brahms whooped, "They got two of them." That released the tension, and everyone shouted at once.

Then the small bogee disappeared. The silence was palpable. Brahms broke it, 'OK. We've lost Wendt. Let's keep thinking." The pair of bogees had moved off the screen. "Get us centered on those jets."

He looked at Sinistra and started to mouth a question, "Can you fly?" She nodded. Then he spoke, "Sinistra, get yourself a broom down here and get ready to go after those two."

She was already rising before he finished the question and had her wand out. "*Accio* Firebolt." She stood by the window waiting.

Somehow the electronics held up from that magic, but before the Firebolt appeared, the radar officer shouted, "Look! In the ground clutter! There's another bogee heading toward the others!" This time the shout was thunderous, "Go Wendt!" Everyone's watched the distance between the two shorten.

It was quiet again until Sinistra screamed. Brahms looked around to see that the Firebolt had flown through the window and struck Sinistra on the head. Her attention, like everyone else's, had been locked on the radar screen. A nasty welt was growing on her forehead, but she didn't take her eyes off the screen.

The radar officer was the first to notice it. He said, "The jets are splitting. They're not going to be caught again by Wendt." It was true. There was a moment's hesitation and then the radar screen showed the lone bogee headed for the closer of the jets. It wasn't clear if Wendt and

Minerva would be able to intercept it, but suddenly the two triangles merged for an instant and then there was only one. It was Wendt's.

There would have been another shout, but instead a low groan resulted. The screen showed the one remaining jet split into two bogees. The radar officer's interpretation wasn't needed. The remaining jet had fired a missile. It was far faster than anything on the screen, including the slowly moving alien ship that had been hurried into launch mode.

Brahms made the only comment, "Bloody shit!"

Then something really strange happened. The missile seemed to slow—at first, no one was even sure it was happening—but quickly, it not only slowed but it reversed course. It was flying harmlessly away. Not harmlessly, though. It became apparent that it had locked onto a new target—a small red triangle that was moving nowhere near as fast as it was.

Sinistra gasped, "It's going after Minerva!"

Brahms started to say that he didn't think it could catch up with them, but his words froze in his mouth as he saw the two tiny red triangles merging. Then the screen went blank. "God damn it! What happened this time?" He quickly scanned the monitors around the room. Everything was working.

Jeffries said, "Northern Europe control reports that the missile detonated and the EMP took out the closest radar—the New Heathrow Spaceport one. It should be back on line shortly."

As reported, the radar image returned, and there was lots of ground clutter but no red triangles. Sinistra sobbed quietly, and Brahms just stared at the screen. After a moment, he dropped into his chair and then seemed to realize that there were other people in the room. He got up and went to Sinistra and took her in his arms. She stopped sobbing and nodded to no one in particular. "I'd better go get Professor Slughorn. He'll need to know that he's now the acting Head of Hogwarts." She stood straight and walked out of the room. No one else knew what to do.

▽

Slughorn called a quick staff meeting immediately after dinner in the old Teacher's Lounge. People straggled in. Most didn't know of the events of the afternoon. When everyone arrived, he looked around the room like a first year hoping that someone will show up and take his place in the sorting hat. After no one did, Slughorn said, "It's my bitter duty to inform you all that the Head and Professor Wendt were lost in an action today near London as . . . as . . . " He faltered searching for the right word.

Eventually he found it. "As human terrorists who were determined to blow up an alien ship were intercepted and prevented from carrying out their . . their . . . " He never found a word for that. So, he went on, "I'm acting head. Tomorrow morning, at breakfast, I'll declare a day of mourning for our lost friends.

"I'm sure there will be a formal funeral in time, but I want to give anyone who wants to say something in their memory opportunities at lunch and the evening meal—teacher, staff or student.

"I can't bring myself to occupy the Head's Office until tomorrow's day of mourning is past. So if you need me, I'll be in my old broom closet of an office." At this he broke down into tears for a moment and wandered out of the room.

There was dead silence and then there was a Babel of sounds. Someone asked Sinistra, "You're that Boy Genius' girl friend. What happened?"

Everyone became silent. She found that she was making an announcement, "Well, suddenly there were some Muggles who were trying to shoot down one of the alien ships trying to take aliens off planet.

"Minerva got the idea of trying to stop the airplanes that they were using and suddenly she and Wendt were flying away on a broomstick. We really don't know what happened, but they stopped three of the planes, and the fourth fired a missile."

Somebody in the back called out, "Did you say, 'Fire on the thistle?'"

Her eyes stung with tears, "No. No. They shot at the Head and they hit them. That was the last we saw of them."

Madame Pomfrey asked, "You were there and saw them?"

This was just too much for Sinistra, "No. No." she snapped, "It's complicated. We could tell what was happening. It was over. . . ." She gasped. It *was* over. She faltered, "It was over so quickly. We don't know exactly what happened. Maybe Minerva tried something new and it didn't work."

Another voice said, "But you're boy friend is the Genius. You must know."

"No, I'm not. And no, I don't." She shouted. "I don't know what happened. It was so fast, and it was just over. That's it. Period. Closed door." And she ran out of the Teacher's Lounge, leaving the chaos behind.

The next morning, there was the usual mixture of students, faculty, Muggles, Goblins, and who knew what in the Great Hall for breakfast. At the Headtable, Professor Slughorn stood up and took the podium. No one paid any attention. They all knew that he wasn't the Head. He started to talk, but no one could hear him. He tried again more loudly.

George Weasley who happened to be having breakfast shouted out, "Who died and made you Head?" Even before Slughorn could answer, Angelina, George's wife punched him in the shoulder with a force that would have raised a welt on an elephant. George only weakly replied, "What?"

Slughorn's face took on a determined grimace, and he lifted his wand to his throat and said, "Sonorus."

Then his next words echoed throughout the hall. "I am acting Head because of the loss of Professor McGonagall and her uh uh, Professor Wendt." Those words brought silence as little else could.

Finding that he was booming out over a silent canyon, he took his wand away from his throat and said in a normal tone. "Yesterday afternoon in an air battle over the southern counties, they died defending an alien ship from destruction at the hands of terrorists.

"I declare this a day of mourning at Hogwarts and ask all who live here to keep them in their hearts and minds today. Remind each other of the way you knew them. At lunch and dinner today, I'll offer the podium to anyone who wants to say words of remembrance of them."

The rest of breakfast was subdued. The daily edition of the *Prophet* had a front-page, single column story about their deaths. It was short on detail and long on retrospective of the lives of the victims. Shortly after breakfast, Rita Skeeter showed up and tracked Slughorn down to get an interview. He was in his office, as he'd promised. She walked directly into his office without knocking.

Slughorn looked up, "You're the little Skeeter girl, aren't you?"

Rita stared, and Slughorn went on. "Yes, I remember you. You never made the Slug Club did you?"

Her smile turned hard, "No, but I made the *Prophet*."

Slughorn smiled, "Yes, you did. You always were a little snitch when you were here."

"Yes, and it served me well. What I want to know is what happened to McGonagall and Wendt."

Slughorn laughed, "You ought to read your own paper. They had a front page story on it."

"Oh, that twaddle. They didn't say anything, really but that they died. Where? What? How? Why? None of that was in the story. I'm doing the real story. The inside story. What is it?"

The smile didn't die from Slughorn's face, "Oh, I don't know any of that. I'm just the Head here and *acting* Head at that."

"Who knows then? You must at least know that!"

Slughorn's smile continued, "Try Brahms. He seems to know everything about the defense of the Earth."

Then Rita's smile turned crafty, "I think I'll try Sinistra. She and Brahms are like that." Her middle and index fingers entwined, and she turned and left Slughorn's office.

She had a hard time finding Sinistra. Her office in the Astronomy Tower was empty. She ran into a man in a strange uniform who noticed her staring at him and asked if she needed help.

"Yes, I'm trying to find Professor Sinistra."

The man turned out to be a US Naval officer who suggested, "Oh, these days she spends a lot of time at the Shrieking Shak. But you probably won't . . . " He didn't get to finish his warning because she'd already run off.

She arrived but there was a guard on duty who challenged her, "What's the password."

She sneered, "What is this, a Hogwart's House? Let me pass, I'm here to see Professor Sinistra."

"Sorry, ma'am, I can't let you pass, and even if I did, it wouldn't do you any good. She's not inside."

"Do you know where she is?" She was on the verge of giving up this quest as a bad idea.

"Yes, ma'am. Let me check the duty roster for the day." He flipped through a couple of pages of parchment and said, 'Yes. She's got K.P. duty today."

"Kay P. Who is that and what's she got to do with Sinistra?"

"No. No. Kitchen Patrol. She's in charge of the menus and expected meal count for the day. She's probably down with the house elves."

She slapped her head and thought, "How had an astronomy professor gotten kitchen duty?" Well, it didn't matter. She'd find her, and then they'd see. She headed back to the castle, and by the time she'd arrived, she realized that she didn't know how to get into the kitchens. After asking a half-dozen people at random, she found George Weasley who told her how to get to the kitchens.

"Easy as pie. Just go down the stairs toward the Slytherin's dungeon but stop at the first floor down and turn to the right. That will take you under the Great Hall. It's there."

She turned to leave, but George added one more thing, "Oh, Rita". She turned and he asked, "Who are you slandering today?"

It wasn't the first time, and it certainly wouldn't be the last, but she wasn't here to slander anyone today. She wondered briefly if the Weasley twin who lived was playing one of their famous practical jokes on her, but it didn't matter. She'd find Sinistra sooner or later.

She came to the stairs and started down. Suddenly, she felt something heavy hit the back of her neck followed by a wet feeling that went down the back of her dress—a water balloon. She whirled around and saw the poltergeist, Peaves. She shot a curse at him, but he ducked, and she missed.

Peaves laughed, "Ohhhh, maybe the water balloon is mightier than the Quick Quotes Quill." Then he disappeared up the stairs to wherever the little sneak hid out after a successful attack.

She pointed her wand at the back of her neck and said, "*Secco.*" The spell dried her clothes pretty well. She continued down the stairs and turned right at the bottom of the flight. There was an obscure unmarked door there. She pulled it open and discovered . . .

A bustling kitchen filled with house elves. There were dozens of stainless steel preparation tables. There were huge ovens, and at the other end of the room that looked as large as a Quidditch field were row upon row of ranges. Apparently, lunch was being prepared. In the middle of what seemed like bedlam was a little circle of sanity. Inside it were a couple of elves—one of whom was wearing a fine waistcoat and a chef's hat. Beside him was a witch holding a large parchment that the two were bent over while apparently conferring.

The witch, of course, was Sinistra. Rita walked over to that group dodging flying platters of vegetables. As she approached the group, Sinistra sensed someone approaching and looked around. There was surprise in her eyes for a moment, and then she nodded, "Well, I didn't know that you'd become the food editor for the *Prophet*."

Rita shook her head, "I'd like to interview you about the death of the Headmistress. They tell me that you're likely to know what really happened."

Sinistra glanced at the parchment and thought a moment, "I have to finish with the menu with Kretur. Then I can give you some time." She added, "I suppose that I should introduce you. This is Kretur. He's the Sous chef.

"Kretur, this is a reporter for the *Daily Prophet*, Rita Skeeter."

Rita interrupted, "Just a small correction. I have a column for the paper."

Kretur looked her up and down, his hand clenching, "You're the person who wrote all those articles about Harry Potter and Professor Dumbledore." He seemed to be examining her face to memorize it thoroughly, but he didn't say anything more nor did Rita. He returned to the parchment. Rita backed off, and Sinistra and he discussed the menu for the Goblins.

Then Sinistra walked over to Rita and pointed off to a corner of the room, "Let's go to the Business Pffice. We'll have some privacy there. She led the way and after a moment said over her shoulder to Rita, "Did you know that Kretur was Harry Potter's house elf?"

Rita flicked her eyes to the left and considered, "I guess, come to think of it, that I did, but I didn't remember it until you mentioned it."

"Well, I don't think that I'd hang around the kitchen after we're done if I were you."

By then they'd reached the office. Sinistra used a silent spell to unlock the door and then opened it for Rita. She walked in and took one of the guest chairs in the small office that was packed with file cabinets and a work table. Most of the wall next to the door was a window that looked out on the kitchen. Seated as she was, she couldn't see out the window.

Sinistra took the Office Manager's chair and steepled her fingers as she leaned back in the chair. "Well, what do you want to know?"

Rita opened her bag, and a notepad and Quick Quotes Quill levitated into the air, "You don't mind if I take notes?" It sounded more like a statement of fact than a question.

Sinistra nodded slowly, "If you allow me to edit your notes before you leave the office."

Rita thought about it and said, "I never allow that."

"Then it's been a pleasure talking with you. Please close the door behind you on the way out. And don't forget about Kretur."

A grimace crossed her lips and then resolved into a smile, "OK. I'll allow that as a courtesy to you in your loss." She was silent for a moment, "Provided that you don't remove anything that is a statement of fact."

Sinistra nodded. Rita's forced smile relaxed into a half frown, "Now, tell me what you know about the death of Professor McGonagall."

Sinistra immediately corrected, "Headmistress McGonagall."

Rita nodded, "Of course."

Sinistra began, "First, let me make clear that I may not answer all or even any of your questions.

"Now, as you know, there was a group of recently freed French Air Force officers who were determined to exact revenge on the Souls. They stole four nuclear weapons from a . . . . " Sinistra told the story straight but leaving out details that would reveal any of the workings of the Shrieking Shak. Rita tried to worm those out of her. Unsuccessfully.

They were at it for well over an hour when there was a diffident knock on the door. Sinistra said, "Come in."

The door opened slowly and a timid house elf head entered the room minimally and said, "Excusing me please, miss. It's almost time for lunch." The elf was smiling hopefully.

"Yes, go ahead as we planned. Kretur can help you if any questions come up."

Rita grimaced. Sinistra noticed, "Do you not like house elves?"

"Well, it's not that . . . exactly. It's just that our business is important. Why does it have to interrupt us? Can't it take some initiative?"

Sinistra smiled, "Oh, I can think of a lot of people who think lunch is pretty important."

Rita got back to business, "Now about Wendt. How long have you known him?"

Sinistra took a deep breath and looked down at her feet. A lump formed in her throat, and she glanced up but away from Rita. Rita stared at her and then said slowly, positively, "You had an affair with him."

She looked up fiercely at Rita and said in a cold, low voice, "Get out of here."

Rita's smile was sad, "You might not have been the only one. If you don't want this to show in the paper, you'll talk."

Sinistra's face remained fierce, "This is completely off the record—IF we talk."

Rita nodded slowly, "Only for background. It's a terrible temptation, but I'll not use any of it." Her expression became wistful, "I'll trade you something for it. Something you can hold over me."

Sinistra glanced over at the Quick Quotes Quill and flicked her head in that direction. Rita glanced there, "Oh, yes. No Quick Quill." She flicked her wand and the pad and quill disappeared into her handbag. "Now, why don't we just talk girl to girl, eh?

"Where did you meet him?"

"You first."

Rita shrugged, "OK. It was his first year here. I was covering for the *Prophet*, trying to dig up some dirt—a Squibb teaching at Hogwarts. But Dumbledore had him locked up tighter than a drum. He had his sidekick, Snape, keeping me at broom's length. I couldn't get a thing on him. That fascinated me. I can find something on anyone. But there was nothing on Wendt. I tried all my contacts in the States, but nothing.

"Then a couple of years later our paths crossed the year that Hogwarts hosted the Tri-Wizard tournament. He was old news by then, and nothing new had happened with him. However, I was covering the tournament for the *Prophet,* and I kept seeing him. He seemed to be involved in some way behind the scenes, and I tried a couple of times to find out how. But he wasn't officially involved and no one would admit that he was involved. It was frustrating. Again, he was involved, and I couldn't dig anything up on him. It was beginning to be a bad habit.

"After that, 'You Know Who', became the news story that just kept simmering. I didn't run across Wendt again until the year that Valdemort took over the Ministry. Of course, that year had started out big for me. I'd just published a big expose on Dumbledore. It was juicy and everything just fell into place—especially the contract to write it. The next day after Dumbledore died, the Saturnian press contacted me and wanted me to write just the kind of book that I enjoy sooo much.

"They said that they wanted to be out with the first book on Dumbledore's life, and they wanted a different slant on him. You know, an expose of everyone's hero.

"Well, I didn't suspect it at the time, but they were funded by the Malfoy family. Of course, all the Malfoy family were DeathEaters. They were being pressured by Mr. V. himself to do it. But I didn't know anything about that. Anyway, the sales were spectacular., and then all hell broke loose.

"The publishing business was full of books about the Great Muggle Threat and Public Nuisance #1 or whatever they were calling Potter. It was then that I began to get the idea that there was another reason for all these books to be published besides simple greed. I realized then that I could be part of the Dark Empire or not.

"But it wasn't as easy to just drop out as I thought. The Deatheaters kept track of you, and if you weren't working for them, well then, you were an Undesirable and those Undesirables kept turning up in Azkaban.

"I was seriously thinking of running—going I didn't know where. Then, somebody at the *Prophet* told me about this crazy underground wizarding radio station. I started listening, and I heard an announcement of a chance to go to asylum. I mentally flipped a coin and decided to take it. You had to show up at a specific town at a precise time.

"I was there, and it was horrible."

Sinistra was becoming interested despite herself. Rita went on, "There were Snatchers who showed up, and then suddenly they had dropped their wands and were on the ground. At least one of them was dead." She'd been almost talking to herself, but at that point, she looked up directly into Sinistra's eyes. "He was lying face down, and there was a red spot growing on the shirt on his back. It was then that I knew that it was really about being alive or being dead."

"What happened then?"

"Oh, it was confused. I remember flying in some crazy Muggle machine. But the first clear memory I have is being cold on a little boat going across the Channel. Wendt came up and brought a blanket, and we talked. It was then that I felt—for the first time—that things were going to be OK."

"Is that when you fell for him?"

'It wasn't like that. Later we were on a train. I still don't quite understand how it happened, but we ended up in the same compartment in the train. It was at night. Somehow, we both were in that little fold-out bed." She stopped and gasped. Several tears ran down her cheek, spoiling the perfect makeup. "It was . . . well, complicated."

"It always is."

"No, really. . . . " She seemed to have lost words and finally asked, "You know, you always think there will be time. You think that you have all the time in the world." She looked up again, "And then it's gone, and you can never have it back."

Sinistra wondered at her. Then Rita asked, "And you?"

"Oh, yes. To answer your question, 'No, I never slept with him.'"

"But . . . "

Sinistra shook her head ruefully, "It's complicated. There was one Halloween when I wanted soooo much to sleep with him, and you know, like you, we'd been in bed together, but. . ." She took a deep breath and added, "And then, who knows, it might have been Wendt and I rather than Wendt and Minerva."

It was Rita's turn to wonder at Sinistra, "But you and Brahms are together, right?"

"Sure. Wendt didn't love me. What might have been is in the great land of "Would'a, Should'a, Could'a'. Brahms loves me, and having someone who really loves you, whose face lights up when he sees you makes all the difference in the world."

She seemed to come back to the world of the present and leaned forward in her chair. "Well, I ought to put in at least a token appearance for lunch. Let's go upstairs." She stood, and Rita hesitated, as though leaving that room would destroy the spell of remembrance that had let the two of them share memories safely. They even could travel back in time to someplace where the desire of their hearts was fulfilled for a brief time. She had the certain feeling that after they left that room, they would never be able to return to it or the state of mind there.

Sinistra reached the door, and Rita quickly said, "Wait."

Sinistra's hand was on the doorknob and was poised to turn it, but she waited.

'This is silly, but is there anything else that you would say to me? I think that it's important to say it before you open that door."

Sinistra glanced around as though looking for something. "Just this. If you do anything with what we've said or do anything to malign Minerva's or Wendt's memory. Kretur and I will come for you."

Later Rita reflected that the words might have seemed threatening, but at the time, she didn't feel threatened at all or angry about them. At the time, she just nodded. Sinistra opened the door, and they left. They walked up and went to the Great Hall. As they entered someone was at the podium and was finishing a memory of Minerva. And after a brief delay, a Goblin stood and waddled down to the dais, stepped up and went to the podium. A teacher brought up a chair which he leaped up onto. When he was in position he spoke. "I work at the main Gringott's Branch in Diagon Alley. Professor Wendt invented ways of doing our business that revolutionized banking. These are such things as accessing your gold in any branch."

There was a cheer from the Goblins in the hall. "He invented, the Gringott's credit card account, recognized throughout the world wherever gold is traded." There were more, even stronger cheers. He culminated in a thundering voice. "He treated Goblins everywhere with RESPECT."

The benches with Goblins, which coincidentally happened to be the tables that Slytherins used erupted. They stood on the benches. Then they climbed up on top of the tables and shouted and waved their arms and cheered.

The Goblin speaker raised his hands for silence, and they eventually quieted down. He spoke softly, "It will be a sadder world and one with much less profit for Goblins now that Wendt has left this veil of tears."

With that the Goblins slumped and slowly climbed down off the tables. There was more than one wet eye among them.

Sinistra turned to Rita, "Have you ever seen anything like this?"

"Not since Riddle killed all the Goblins in Gringotts who were there when the sword of Gryffindor was stolen."

Just then, there was a commotion at the back of the Great Hall. They both turned to see what was going on.

Sunbathing at Brighton

They reappeared on a boardwalk on the ocean. Minerva quickly mounted the broom and schootched up to make room for Wendt behind her. He didn't have to be urged but swung a leg over the broom and muttered, "Oh bloody hell." Then they were in the air and accelerating up. Wendt was glad that he hadn't had time for much more than a sip of soup. It was a bright clear day with only wisps of cloud in the sky. They were quickly up to at least 500 meters in altitude.

Wendt gulped and said, "Watch near the horizon. They were coming in low to avoid radar. They'll probably be below us, but we should stay up so we can see a long way."

Minerva said, "Roger."

Wendt couldn't believe his ears, "What did you say?"

"Roger. Isn't that what the co-pilot says to the pilot in aeroplanes?"

"Sometimes. How did you learn about that?"

"I've been watching moovees."

"Right. Er. Roger."

It wasn't too long before Wendt saw something glint with sunlight near the horizon to the left of them. He nudged Minerva and pointed off toward them. She turned the Firebolt to the left and they accelerated. She asked, "What do you suggest we do when we get close?"

"You've got me. What spells do you have for airplanes?"

"None. But what about 'repellum Mugglum'?"

"Sounds as good as any, although I can't see it'll do much good." He quickly added, "Oh, how about a shield charm?"

The glint near the horizon had been getting brighter as they flew along the shore. And it seemed to be coming closer and closer toward them. Wendt shouted over the wind, "You've got to get lower. They're underneath us."

Minerva went into a dive, and Wendt immediately wished he'd not suggested that. They looked like they were probably going to miss the planes, but as they closed, in the last couple of seconds, Wendt could see that there were 4 planes in a tight formation. Minerva raised her wand and said the spell silently Wendt guessed or maybe it was just too loud for him to hear her. The planes missed them by less than 200 meters in altitude and distance. But as they passed, Wendt could see that two of the planes ejected the pilots. Then he noticed the planes fall toward the ground and impact almost instantly.

Minerva slowed and they could talk again. She asked, "What happened to those two planes?"

'I think it was a flame-out. Their jet engines stopped running. They were so low that the only thing the pilots could do was eject. Did you see the parachutes?"

"That's what they were? But what about the other two?"

"Your shield charm worked. If we could catch up with the other two, we could use it again, but they're long gone."

Minerva said, "That's what you think."

"What are you going to do?" Then he realized what she was going to do. "You know, I just discovered something new that beats either disapparation or flying broomsticks. Doing both at the same time."

Minerva pulled her wand again, and they disappeared from Brighton to re-appear in the air over Heathrow. She asked, "Which way is Brighton from here?"

Wendt asked, "Could we just land and ask?"

Her silence was so cutting that he just said, "Turn toward your right until I tell you to stop, and we'll be pointed, more or less, toward Brighton." She slewed the broom around, and Wendt told her, "Now!"

She said, "Now, I'll show you the meaning of speed." With that the Firebolt took off straight ahead. He made the mistake of glancing down. That was a mistake as he'd discovered riding helicopters. After a couple of minutes, Wendt pointed ahead and to the right. There was a glint near the horizon. She turned slightly and—it seemed impossible— but she accelerated. As they approached the glint, it quickly broke into two, and the two planes rapidly split apart.

Wendt said to himself, "Shit." Minerva chose the closer one and tried for an intercept course. She came down, and Wendt thought that they were on a roller-coaster. He lost sight of the other plane, but they were going to come close to the one they wanted to intercept. Minerva raised her wand. This time, when they passed, Wendt turned around and saw the jet engine go dark before it got beyond vision. Again, a pilot ejected, and the plane came down near a small village.

Minerva slowed enough for them to be able to talk, and she did a slow turn, looking for the other plane. Wendt spotted it first. He also saw the shuttle take off, but the fighter fired a missile. Wendt said, "That's it. We'd never catch that jet. It fired the missile anyway. There's nothing we can do but hope. . . "

He stopped and said, "Quick, Minerva, repeat the spell that I'm going to tell you. NOW!"

She started to say, "But."

He immediately said, "*Accio* nuclear weapon."

She repeated, and he said, "Now, show me the meaning of speed."

She turned the broom, and they accelerated away. Wendt was afraid that he was going to fall off, but somehow he didn't. He kept his head turned back to see what was happening with the missile. The engine was still pointing toward the shuttle, but the missile was actually coming toward them. It was accelerating, and it just occurred to Wendt that they probably didn't want to be anywhere near it. He squeezed Minerva and shouted, "Disapparate".

She didn't hear him. He tried to shout louder, "Disapparate!!" But there was no apparent effect. He shouted one more time, but he realized that she wasn't going to hear. He tugged on her shoulder and she shook him off. He did it more insistently, but she didn't pay attention. For a moment he realized that it was the one time in his life he really did want to disapparate and it wasn't going to happen.

Then he had the gut-wrenching feeling that he knew so well, and he thanked God profusely and promised not to miss his prayer time again—ever. Then a second later both he and Minerva were blinded by a flash that caused Minerva to scream. Then she asked, "What was that? Can you see?"

"It was the device going off. Where did you take us? Oh, I hope we'll get our sight back in a minute or so."

"I took us to Brighton. It was the only place that I could think of."

Slowly their vision returned. She maintained altitude until they could see. She slowly lowered the broom to ground on the beach. They were near the town so they walked and found a pub. They entered and found everyone watching the TV with great interest. They walked up to the bar and tried to get the attention of the 'keep. Finally, he came over and took their order.

Minerva said, "I want a fire whiskey."

The barkeep asked, "What?"

Wendt corrected her, "She means a Dewars. I'll have one as well."

"Sorry, we don't serve hard stuff. You should know that." Then his mouth opened and he said, "Oh, you're newly awakened. Sure, we only have beers, ales and wine."

So, Wendt ordered a pint for each of them and asked, "What's on the telly?"

The bartender stared at them. "Where have you been this afternoon? Didn't you see the flash? It was one of those new-clear bombs. Up near London. It's been on the telly for the last half hour." Then he pointed to the set. He took the remote and turned the volume up a bit.

The news announcer said, "We've got a representative of the Air Defense Command on the phone. "Major Bear, what can you tell us about this frightening incident."

The Major hesitated and then said, "Well, it appears that a group of newly-awakened humans decided to try to repeat the attack on the Orly Spaceport. They stole four tactical thermo-nuclear armed air-to-air missiles and jet fighter planes to carry them.

"It's very strange. Two of the planes went down, apparently due to mechanical difficulties near the Channel town of Brighton. One more went down about 15 km from Heathrow. The final one fired its missile at the shuttle that was just taking off. However, the strangest thing of all happened. The missile went far off course and detonated about twenty km away in a lightly populated suburban area."

The announcer continued. "This was very like the attack at Orly, wasn't it."

"Not really. The attack at Orly used a much larger weapon— equivalent to 250 to 300 Kilotons of high explosives. This attack used a tactical weapon that had a power of only a couple of kilotons.

"The Orly attack was successful. This one wasn't. The Orly attack only involved one weapon whereas this involved four. No one knows how the weapon was delivered at Orly, but we know precisely how it was delivered in this case."

The announcer whom Wendt recognized as the same woman who had been reporting when he'd taken over the studio before said, "I have only one last question. Why is it always I who have to report these awful events, and where is the human who always interrupts me?"

Minerva chuckled and whispered, "And what about the woman who accompanies you?"

The woman went on, "There were only a small number of casualties. They were," and she began reading names from a list. When one came up, "Josiah Ron," Wendt snapped to attention. A woman sitting next to him on the opposite side from Minerva asked, "Did you know him?"

Wendt said absently, "Yes, as a matter of fact, I met him just a few weeks ago."

Minerva frowned a question at him and Wendt said *soto voce* to her alone, "He's one of the recent awakees. It's ironic. He was worried that his wife wouldn't find him when she was awakened. I told him not to worry."

The voice droned on, and then another name came up, "Mary Ron." Wendt looked at Minerva and said, "There's a strange thing. Mary was Josiah's wife. I guess they found each other after all."

She looked at him and said, "We almost went with them, didn't we?"

"Yeh. It was close."

"We need to talk. Let's stay the night if we can find a room."

"Sure."

"I need to talk to you about that little proposal you made."

"Oh." Wendt thought a moment and said, "I think that calls for something nicer than here." He called the barman over and asked about the nice restaurants in the area. The barman was offended and protested that his bar had a good grill. Wendt just shook his head. The barman finally said, "Well, if you have to go somewhere else, I need to ask you if you like Indian."

Wendt nodded yes. He and Minerva had frequently (not recently) eaten Indian. The barman suggested a place called "The Chilli Pickle". Then a funny thing happened. Wendt prepared to pull out his wallet that was full of Pounds Sterling, and the barman looked at him, puzzled. Wendt realized that this was one of the restaurants run on the alien principles of economics. They stared at each other for a moment, and then Wendt broke the silence with the words, "I suppose this is it, then?"

The barman nodded, and then Minerva asked if Wendt hadn't forgotten something. Of course, he had, so he inquired if there were a room in the inn for him and Minerva. There was. They went on to the Chilli Pickle and were seated quickly. After ordering, Wendt asked THE question, "So when are we getting married?"

Minerva pursed her lips and said, "Well, I have an idea about that. Let's have a party to announce our engagement."

That evening, after a very long meal in which they ate very little, they returned to the inn and welcomed the bed that they shared. The next day they returned to Hogwarts. Somewhere along the way, they had lost the broom.

▽

They arrived at the end of lunch that day. When they entered the Great Hall, they arrived just in time to see a group of Goblins who had been sitting at the Slytherin tables end some sort of demonstration where they were actually standing on the tables and cheering. There was a Goblin at the podium saying something about the world being a sadder place. The Goblins worked their way tearfully down from the tables.

346

Wendt asked, "I wonder what's been going on. I've never seen Goblins so excited since. . . Well, I can't remember a time when they've been so worked up about anything."

Minerva just shrugged and they started down an aisle toward the dais, hoping to get some lunch before it was all gone. Around them, there seemed to be some sort of commotion going on. Everyone was pointing at something and muttering. It was Minerva who realized that it was they who were being pointed out.

Wendt nodded and said, "You know, I think you're right." They kept walking down the aisle,and eventually got to the podium where the Goblin stared at them with open mouth.

"Hi Gorblatt, what's up?"

Gorblatt asked, "You two don't look like ghosts."

Minerva returned his stare, "And you don't either."

"But you're supposed to be dead."

Wendt walked up on the podium, assisting Minerva to follow him, went to the podium and announced, "The rumors of our deaths are greatly exaggerated."

They didn't announce their engagement, and nobody asked them about it, but somehow everyone knew. They planned the party where they would announce their engagement, and Wendt would give Minerva the ring. It was to be in the Great Hall of Hogwarts and all the staff and half of Hogsmeade were invited. On the day before the party, Brahms took Wendt aside after breakfast and had a lengthy discussion with him.

On the day of the party, there were a million little arrangements to be made. The band, Jabberwocky, was to perform. Wendt had to talk with the leader to arrange the time of the announcement. Minerva spent hours with the house elves of Hogwarts, making sure that the refreshments were both unique and good.

The evening went well. The only thing that seemed odd was that the blessed couple spent hardly any time together. They were always dancing with someone else or talking in large groups. Then at the stroke of midnight, the Boy Genius approached the band and signaled for silence. He took the magically amplified microphone and announced, "Honored guests, the bewitching hour has arrived, and there is a public announcement that Professors Wendt and McGonagall wish to make. Also, as a little added bonus, Professor Sinistra and I also wish to make an announcement.

There was a small gasp from the crowd as the two couples arrived on the stage. Brahms handed the microphone to Wendt and winked at him. Brahms retreated to join Sinistra and said, "I sure hope your timing on the Polyjuice Potion is better than it has been in the past."

She smiled sweetly, and in an exaggerated drawl said, "Oh, I don't know whatever you might be thinking of. And yes, I've got the timing on my Potion brewed to a 'T'."

Brahms said, "Good."

Wendt had taken McGonagall's hand in his and said, "Professor will you." Here he hesitated and Brahms asked Sinistra, "It's time. When are we going to see the transformation?"

She said, "Any minute now."

Wendt went on, "give me your hand in marriage."

No transformation happened, and she said, "Yes, I do." And Wendt slipped the ring onto her finger. Brahms exclaimed loud enough to be heard from the front of the audience, "What's going on here, Sinistra?"

She just said, "Don't you want to propose to me, Brahms?"

"You know perfectly well that I'm not Brahms and that isn't me er Wendt, proposing to Minerva." As he was saying that, the faux Wendt started to change before his eyes and became, as the real Wendt expected, Brahms. He ran over to him and said, "What have you done?" Then he turned to McGonagall and said, "I'm sorry, this wasn't supposed to go that way at all."

And then, McGonagall's hair started to change color to a jet black, and she started to shrink. He looked on in amazement and then quickly turned to see that Sinistra was faux as well. She had started to turn into Professor McGonagall. She walked over to the other three and addressed the real Wendt. "Are you sure you don't want to propose to me?"

"Well, I suppose so!" And he did. She accepted and Wendt signaled the band to start playing again. He turned to Sinistra and said, "I suppose you were all in on this."

But Brahms answered instead, "No, it was just McGonagall and I. Sinistra wanted to engineer this little charade so that you would end up proposing to her—even if not for real."

McGonagall picked up the narrative. "But I thought it would be nice to have the last laugh on Sinistra and put her under the imperious curse and had her take Polyjuice Potion with one of my hairs in it so that it would actually be Brahms proposing to her. Of course, I suppose I should release her now." She did that immediately and continued directly to Sinistra, "Dear, you must excuse me for getting the last laugh on you. Considering all the times that you've played practical jokes on me and Wendt, you really shouldn't object to one being played on you. You know, 'What's sauce for the goose is sauce for the gander.'"

Sinistra frowned and seemed ready to say something sharp, but then a smile broke on her face and said, "I have to admit that you've got the last laugh. OK. Fair is fair."

The rest of the evening was enjoyed by everyone. At one point, Sally pulled Wendt aside, "There's just one thing that I'd like to know."

Wendt shrugged.

"Why is it that all the best guys go for witches?"

Wendt looked carefully at her face to see if she were just joking or really was voicing something deep that it had taken all the public proposals and elf-made wine to bring out. He thought it was the latter, "Well, don't forget that my case was lost long before we met. Who knows what would have happened if I'd met you first?"

He could see that what he'd said was missing the mark. Her lips formed a tight straight line, and she seemed close to tears. He decided to try one more time, "You've got me. I haven't the slightest idea. You know that not even Sinistra is doing anything uh . . magicky to The Boy Genius. I won't say that witches haven't used love potions and even the Imperious Curse to get a husband, but that didn't happen here."

She sobbed and nodded, "Sure. I know you're right, but it's just so disheartening seeing all those other couples happy and getting married—you and Minerva, Brahms and Sinistra, George and Angelina, and . . " Here she completely faltered and broke down.

Wendt could only shake his head. He thought she was probably thinking about Fred, "I know. You could have been one of those cheery couples."

She nodded, the sobs still convulsing her.

He took her shoulder in hand and squeezed, "It's not fair or just and I'd be mad as hell."

She sniffed, pulled a handkerchief from her purse and dabbed at her eyes. "I've got to get into a loo and straighten my face."

"Yeh, I know. No one should know how much you're hurting."

She turned and started to leave, but he interrupted. "Listen, get in touch after this is all over. The one thing that this place doesn't have that it desperately needs is an executive assistant to the Headmistress. She's going to have a lot more duties after the wedding, and I don't want her distracted by mere business. And then, too, you'll probably find it more fun than whatever you were doing before."

She actually chuckled, "Just like all men—always thinking of yourselves."

"You know it."

Toward the end, Sinistra and Brahms came over to Mcgonagall and Wendt who were in a small group of people talking about old times at Hogwarts. Sinistra said, "Nicky had a wonderful idea. He's suggested that the two of us have a double wedding on his day."

349

Minerva asked, "His day?"

"Sure, you know, Saint Nick's day."

Wendt hit his forehead with his hand, "You mean Christmas Day! That's a great idea! What do you say, Minerva?"

She seemed ready to object when a voice spoke up from the back of the group. It was Luna Longbottom. She said, "I think that would be fine, IFFF there's a little unbreakable oath administered."

Wendt asked, "What kind of unbreakable oath."

"Oh, you know. Both ladies swear not to do anything like a practical joke or anything bad on the wedding day."

The two "ladies" agreed, and the oath was administered. Luna administered it. By the end the bands of magic encircling their clasped hands was so tight that both had to rub their hands to renew the circulation. Luna added a final word, "And if either of you two does anything fishy and doesn't get bitten by the oath, I will personally track you down and make you wish it had."

Longbottom added, "And that goes double for me."

Then Luna took Minerva by the arm and led her away and said as she did, "I have a little bone to pick with you. Why did you go and have a double wedding with Sinistra when you could have had one with Teddy and me a year ago?"

Wendt looked over at Longbottom and formed a silent question with his face. Longbottom answered, "I've no idea she wanted a double wedding."

"Well, if you had, maybe I could have talked Minerva into that a year ago."

Just then, Sir Nicholas the nearly headless ghost floated up to the group and said, "Oh, a double wedding at Hogwarts. I don't think there's been one in hundreds of years. You know Nicholas the Balmy was going to have one, but was killed by a troll. Now, who actually had that double wedding?" He tried to pretend to scratch his head and it fell off its perch atop his shoulders.

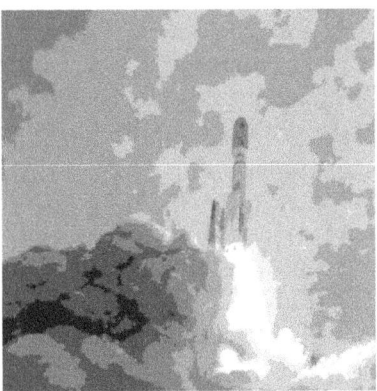

Good King Wenceslaus

The last shuttle off the planet was about to leave. The last Souls were being decanted from their hosts into the vacuum bottles that would be their homes for some time to come. By an odd coincidence, it was Thanksgiving Day in the States. The alien whose nickname was Frank was going to be the last to go, and he had requested that Wendt do the honors. He insisted on talking with Wendt beforehand.

"Why me? There must be a thousand surgeons who would do a surer job?"

"You were my opposite number. You have a tradition, don't you, of the losing commander surrendering his sword to the opposing commander?"

"Well, yes. But, you know, I was not really the commander. We were organized a lot more like you that you realize. People saw things that needed doing, and they did them. Brahms here had no rank of any sort, and he was a big part of the whole effort."

"Perhaps, but just like us, there was someone who had the final decision power for everything. That was you. That was also me."

"I'm not so sure, but I'll not be churlish. I'll grant you that."

"There was another reason."

"What was that?"

"You're getting married next month."

"Yes."

"A double marriage."

"Yes, so?"

"Well, I've never seen a marriage, let alone a double one." He hesitated trying to build up the courage to ask, "I'd like to attend."

Wendt laughed aloud, totally surprised, "And you want to be a wedding guest? That's rich. What interest could you possibly have in weddings—especially mine?"

Frank looked down, "Well, yes. In all my years, in all the planets I've been on, I've never seen a wedding—or anything remotely like it."

Wendt's face creased in a deep frown, "Do you know that I almost killed you a couple of months ago. I was angry about a married couple who'd been separated by you 'Souls' and who had been re-united only to die within days after their re-union. Do you think that I'd let you come to MY wedding after that."

"Your God values forgiveness, doesn't it?"

The words were wrenched from Wendt's throat, "Yes, HE does. But I'm not ready to forgive you or your race. Come back in a hundred years, and maybe I'll be ready."

Frank said, "I never understood tears before. They always seemed wasteful to me. Well, good luck!" He reached out his right hand and held it there until Wendt took it and shook.

Wendt said, "Good luck to you. And it would be good luck for you if you could talk your race into working a way to live in mutual respect with your hosts."

Frank shook his head and then bent it for the scalpel.

The run-up to the wedding went as these things normally do. There was a bachelor party. None of the attendees would talk about what happened— as is proper.

The ladies had a joint wedding shower. It was well-attended but for one prominent invitee. It was noted that Madame Minister had declined the invitation, with thanks, explaining that she had alternate commitments for both the shower and the wedding. Many attendees wondered whether the alternate commitment was washing her hair or reading *Witch Weekly*.

Professor Sinistra said that it was rather bad form not to send gifts in any case. Minerva demurred noting that Pam had given them the best gift that any bride ever receives. "Yes, my dear, after all, she provided us with our husbands." There was general amusement at that comment. But Minerva added that it was rather churlish not to attend the wedding anyway.

Sinistra replied that after all, "One might expect a woman to attend the wedding of a rival who had won her man, but one could hardly expect any woman to attend the double wedding of women who had taken BOTH the men that she had made a play for."

Minerva reluctantly agreed.

Christmas at Hogwarts was always variable, sometimes there was deep snow, and sometimes a vagary of the Gulf Stream brought dry cool weather. That Christmas there were a couple of inches of snow on the ground, and the pine trees, covered with fresh snow gave the world a look of purity that it had not seemed to have in quite a long time.

The bridesmaids were Ginny Potter, Luna Longbottom, Hermione Weasley, Pansey Parkinson, who had surprised everyone by accepting an invitation from Sinistra to be a bridesmaid. The MOH's were Minerva's sister, Marge, who also gave her away and Sinistra's best friend from college, a Muggle physicist at Princeton. Sinistra had rounded out her bridesmaids with a couple of friends who worked somewhere in Diagon Alley.

The best men positions were filled by Colonel Parker from the SAS and Wendt's cousin Paul from the States. Wendt had been surprised by the choice of Parker, but apparently Brahms and he had gone back long before the group that Wendt had worked with. Parker had tried half-heartedly to recruit Wendt to come back as a consultant for the SAS, but he knew that Wendt would never do it, married, as he was, to his teaching position, so to speak.

At the bachelor party, there had almost been a fight between Filch and Haggrid over which would be the best man for Wendt. Wendt assured them that neither was in the running. However, they were both sure that the other had screwed it for him being the best man. If only the other candidate weren't there, then Wendt wouldn't have to avoid playing favorites with people whom he was going to continue to work with. Finally, Wendt assured them both that they were so far back the line of possible candidates that they were both behind the ghost, Sir Nicholas. He also told them that they were ahead of several, "You're way ahead of the Bloody Baron and Peaves."

They objected that a ghost couldn't be a best man because he couldn't carry the ring, but to no avail.

The wedding was indeed one of the most peculiar in the history of that peculiar school, Hogwarts. The guest list included almost all the various orders of magical beings. There were wizards and witches, of course. There were goblins invited, and a few attended, although Wendt thought they were mostly there hoping to detect other examples of goblin art that wizards were holding illegally.

All of the Hogwarts house elves were invited and a good number actually attended. The brides had been quite prepared to bring in a whole crew of outside house elves to prepare the food, but there were enough Hogwarts house elves that actually wanted to participate by preparing and serving the food that it wasn't necessary. Kretur, of course, attended and took great pride in asserting that he was a free elf like Dobey. Although it made everyone who knew Dobey sad, no one had the heart to tell him how hard it was to hear.

There were a few werewolves invited. Only one attended, Lavender Brown.

There were no vampires invited or missed.

There was a general invitation made to the Centaurs but only Forensi attended.

All Hogwarts students had been invited. Among those under 4th year, there were no attendees. There were a number of upper class girls and their boyfriends who had attended. The girls attended because they thought an April-October wedding, as they regarded Wendt and Minerva's, was "romantic". Their boyfriends attended because they had been threatened that they would go dateless for the Yule ball the previous week if they didn't stay for the wedding.

All staff were invited and attended. They attended not because it was compulsory (it wasn't) but because most figured that the Head would be a more sympathetic person after being married and they wanted to see the event. Of course, she wasn't.

There were many Muggles in attendance. There were the relatives, of course. But there were also a number of officers and crew of the USS Ohio and a number of SAS officers and enlisted.

There were two clergy who officiated—a Muggle man and a witch, which was appropriate because there were two witches marrying two Muggles. They were seen only for a short while after the ceremony, and then they mysteriously disappeared—at the same time.

The Durseleys had been invited, including Marjorie, but only Vernon and Petunia had come. Of course, Dudley was there because he was staff at Hogwarts. Vernon had explained that his sister, Marjorie, had refused to come for two reasons. One was that Harry Potter was going to be there, and any wedding that would have an escapee from St. Brutus' School for The Criminally Insane was one that she, for one, was not going to attend. The second was that one of the grooms was James Wendt who had sent her to a German concentration camp when she had come looking for her brother. None of the urging or assurances availed that the German concentration camp was actually a US Air Force base in Germany where she was treated quite civilly as a guest to protect her. Even Petunia's insistence that Wendt's efforts had secured a post for her favorite nephew Dudley cut no mustard with her.

As the Dursleys were going through the reception line, Wendt had decided to have a little fun with Petunia. She seemed to enjoy showing off her fairly decent legs, and this occasion was not an exception. Even though it was mid-winter, she had worn a skirt that was half-way between mini and micro. When she arrived in the reception line, he looked her up and down and leaned toward her and said in a stage whisper, "Petunia! If you had worn that skirt when I first met you, it could have been you up there at the altar with me." He enjoyed seeing her turn a shade of scarlet that reminded him of his Ohio State days on a football Saturday. Minerva kicked him in the shin, but she hadn't been trying seriously, and anyway, it was worth it to see Petunia blush.

All of the Hogwarts ghosts had been invited though Peeves had not been. In a little private conversation with Peeves, Minerva had assured him that she would put a Langloc spell on him that would last a year if he showed up. There were a number of ghosts who had shown up. The ghosts of the Headless Hunt most pointedly were not invited. Sir Nicholas took a prominent seat well toward the front and had occupied it for half a day before the wedding. There were rumors that the Gray Lady and the Bloody Baron had been present at the back of the Great Hall, but no one could affirm or deny the rumor.

Professor Bins was in attendance and declared that the last time there was a double wedding at Hogwarts was in 1375 when Everett Snape had married a Meriope Slytherin. Even Bins didn't know whether Snape was a forebear of the former head-master, Severus. However there was little doubt that Meriope had been a descendant of THE Slytherin. The other couple was Mark Evans and Jane Scofield.

Hermione Weasley had outdone Bins by declaring that never in the history of Hogwarts had there been so many people in Hogwarts on Christmas day.

Most of the guests decided to stay the night—either in the dorms of Hogwarts or at one of the inns of Hogsmeade. The guests had to carry Abeforth Dumbledore back to his inn so that they could get into their rooms. The reception party had been such a success that many of the attendees had continued the party in their rooms afterwards. Whether or not there had ever been so many guests in Hogwarts on Christmas Day as there were that day, it's certain that there had never been so many babies conceived in Hogwarts in one night.

There were a few uninvited guests that had been admitted none-the-less. Among them had been the reporter, Rita Skeeter. Also there, and not unwelcome, was the American Auror, Phil Pearson. Sally Harker was surprised to see him but her surprise turned to pleasure as he insisted on talking with her throughout the reception and dancing most of the dances with her.

In the end, everyone had indeed had a wonderful time.

No one knows where the Wendts and the Brahmses had spent their wedding night. It's certain that they hadn't spent it at Hogwarts.

Rita's column the following week in the *Daily Prophet* was subdued. It included none of the superlatives concerning the wedding guests, their diversity, the unusual nature of the double wedding, or anything else of the sort. It did however, note the unusual choice of white for the wedding dress of a widow.

There was a reference to Rita's interview with the Minister of Magic, Pamela Moertl. It mostly dealt with the propriety of the Headmistress of the foremost magical educational facility in England, perhaps in Europe itself, marrying a Muggle.

The Minister declared that it was not a subject that she was interested in talking over. Rita pointed out, "You are the ex-officio chair of the Board of Hogwarts. Do you really believe it's a subject that you shouldn't speak about?"

Pam stared at her, "Oh, Rita, the only objection that I have to the wedding has nothing to do with education or propriety. I will say no more."

Pam had then continued off the record. "You, I'm sure are aware of the nature of my objection. I suspect that you have a similar objection. If you want to commiserate with me, we could open a bottle of elf-made wine of a rare vintage. I've been saving it up for a big occasion. I suppose that this is about as special an occasion as I'll have."

They had finished off that bottle and opened more than one other over the course of the evening, toasting the various aspects of the perversity of the wedding. Toward the end, Pam had asked, "I shuppose that cradle-robber was glorioushh in her gown?"

Rita had some trouble focusing her eyes on the Minister but she managed and said, "Now that wassh funny. She didn't wear her hair in any shpecial way, it just tumbleed loossh over her shoulders. . . Yes. . . Looshe . . . Looshe. . . No shpecial makeup. You'd think she was jusht a peashant girl getting hooked up with her lover."

There was silence for a moment, and they both sighed.

Postlude

On the two hundred twenty-third day of the Scourging of the Earth of any remaining Souls in the last week of the campaign, the Soul whose human name was Wanda, started to cry out but fell silently to the floor of the cavern where she had been harvesting wheat. Only her husband Ian, who had been working next to her, had heard the beginning of the cry. He saw the silver disappear from her eyes.

She lay in an apparent coma for a week before her body succumb to the harvester who comes for all. She was the last casualty of the War of the Souls. She was survived by her husband and mourned bitterly by the many friends whom she had won in the small community in The Cave.

About the Author

William Wilkin lived in a small Southern Ohio town until he began his college career. He has a Bachelor's degree in Physics from The Ohio State University and a Master's degree in Physics from The University of Chicago.He has a career in corporate Information Technology.and currently lives in Dallas, Texas.

He enjoys music, both "serious" and "classic Rock". He reads classic Detective fiction and Science Fiction & Fantasy as well as trying to stay current in Physics.

He began writing seriously about 2005. He has a blog, in-mid-world, where he writes about Science Fiction & Fantasy and remotely related topics.

www.ingramcontent.com/pod-product-compliance
Lightning Source LLC
Chambersburg PA
CBHW060351260626
47160CB00006B/2274